ON THE ISLE OF DOGS

ON THE ISLE OF DOGS

A Gay MM Historical Romance

JACKIE NORTH

Jackie North

MM Romance Author

This book is dedicated to...

Oliver and Jack
--My Dickensian OTP

To you my paper child

And to all those orphans out there
--You know who you are

"Brass can do better than gold what has stood the fire."
--OLIVER TWIST BY CHARLES DICKENS

CONTENTS

WHEREUPON LETTERS ARE MAILED AND RESPONSES HOPED FOR

J ack ambled up the stairs, leaving the swirl of the taproom behind him. He was done for the day, and it wasn't even late afternoon; he'd bagged two good wallets, nice and fat, and a gold watch besides, along with many silk handkerchiefs, all of which had been handed off to Noah to deal with.

It had been busy in the streets, with the good weather bringing folks out of their houses and making them a bit more casual about their persons than they normally were, which had made the pickings easy. Jack had still worked hard, though, and could feel the sticky sweat on the back of his neck, where his shirt stuck to him in places.

This was not anything he'd have noticed before Nolly, who had a way of showing Jack different habits that at first seemed fussy and unnatural, but that later turned out to be comfortable and fine. Washing up was one of those things, though at the Three Cripples there was no water save what they might haul for themselves from the pump in the alley and, in the days since their arrival, not even a week, there'd not been the time. That meant Nolly must be feeling the effects of going without hot water and soap, something for which Jack wanted to make amends.

With the jingle of coins in his pocket, he thought to surprise Nolly and take him out for a treat. Though Nolly had spoken no complaints and had evidenced all cheeriness and contentment since their arrival at the Three Cripples, it was obvious by his level air and lack of smiles that he did not like living amongst villains and thieves.

But what else could they do? They'd had no time to find someplace else to abide and, besides, the work was steady, and they had plenty of protection while living in the shadow of Noah Claypole. Which, actually, might be part of the problem, as Nolly and Noah were at odds all the day long and far into the evening.

As Jack opened the door to the bedsit at the top of the stairs, a cool breeze rushed through the partially open casement window, fluttering the thin, faded cotton curtain and bringing the smell of faraway rain.

Nolly sat on the bed; the chair had proven too big for the room, so they'd gotten rid of it. He was leaning over the small wooden table beneath the window, looking as studious as a schoolboy, busy with pen and ink and something he was writing.

On his nose was a black smudge, as might have been when Nolly'd been younger, living with old Brownlow, and intent on his lessons. If Jack squinted, he could just make out the shadow of that younger boy, content in his plush little life before Jack had come back to him.

Nolly was not content now, for a bit of wind fluttered his papers and caused the hair on his forehead to whisper across his skin, and he frowned, as if uncertain from whence the breeze had come. Jack wanted nothing more than to go to him that instant and tumble him on the bed. And never mind what would become of the damp nib of the pen, or the open bottle of very black ink. But Jack restrained himself and placed his top hat on the bed to let Nolly know he was there without jostling him overly much.

"Hey?" he asked. "What're you writin', eh?"

"Letters," said Nolly, not in a rude way, but distant, as if his thoughts had been far off, and he was only now returning to where he was, boot heels hooked on the bed frame, a stack of paper at his elbow, and Jack at the door.

Jack closed the door behind him; the breeze, cut off from its path down the stairs, swirled about the room.

"D'you mind?" asked Jack, holding out his hand.

"No," said Nolly. He put down the pen, resting the damp nib on a bit of flannel cloth, and held out a letter. "I don't mind, but I don't want to hear it."

Jack took the folded envelope, which was already addressed and, with wax seal in place, looked to be only missing a stamp to be official. When his eyes caught the address, he shook his head.

"What're you botherin' w'this for?" Jack asked. The letter was addressed to the Dawkins Family on South Church Lane in Hale, and it was on his tongue to say something scathing, but the look on Nolly's face stopped him. "They won't care to read it anyhow," said Jack, more gently than he'd planned.

"Miss Delia might read it," said Nolly. "Or maybe not. It doesn't matter, because I want to write to them."

The firm line of Nolly's mouth as he looked up at Jack, the squareness of his jaw, told Jack that Nolly wasn't to be swayed. This most likely had to do with Nolly's need for connections, and the propriety of when one wrote letters to whom, all of which was beyond Jack's ability, or even his desire, to comprehend. Let Nolly write letters where he would, it was all the same to Jack. Except he could not ignore the faint glower Nolly's brow displayed; it was evident that attending to this very civilized task had left him cross rather than refreshed.

"An' the rest?" asked Jack.

He held out his hand to give back the Dawkins' letter. Nolly took it and handed Jack two more envelopes and a sheaf of paper that had not yet been folded. The two letters were addressed, as expected, given Nolly's mood, to the haberdashery and the parsonage. This represented more attempts to reconcile than

Jack could have imagined. The sheaf of paper, though, as Jack scanned Nolly's beautifully slender handwriting, made no sense.

"You really going to pay that doctor in Lyme back?" asked Jack. "After all this time?"

"He saved your life, Jack," said Nolly. With a snap of his wrist, he took the letters and the piece of paper from Jack's hand. "At the very least, I will know he received the money that he earned, as I'm fairly certain Mrs. Heyland kept whatever money I gave her to console her in her agitated state over the theft of books that were *not* actually stolen."

Nolly's chest rose with a hard, sharp breath, his mouth a downward curl, as if he expected Jack would argue with him about this. Jack changed his mind about the whole matter instantly.

"I'll go with you to the post office, shall I?" asked Jack. "Then I'll treat you to somethin' nice to eat, since I'm flush with cash at the moment."

Jack reached into his pocket to jingle the change there and rustle the five-pound note. He could have had more cash had he simply kept the money and the wallets, but this way, the room was paid for and he didn't have to muck about picking initials out of handkerchiefs.

"We should put some of that money away," said Nolly, which did not surprise Jack, as he'd been expecting such a comment since they'd arrived back in London.

"Where?" asked Jack, raising an eyebrow. "Beneath the floorboards? One of Noah's men'd find that in a heartbeat; it's not a clever hiding place, Nolly." He shook his head, as if to scold, though the truth of it was that thieves who were also friends never truly stole anything of value from each other.

"No," said Nolly, tartly. "The Bank of England."

Nolly stood up and folded the sheaf of paper into an envelope, corked the ink, and wiped the pen nib dry. At the edge of the desk was a small red seal-candle, just a stub really, with both ends charred by the tallow candle in the candleholder.

Where Nolly had gotten the money to pay for all of these things was not beyond Jack to wonder, but he didn't want to invade Nolly's privacy. So instead, he laughed and reached for Nolly's top hat, which hung on the wooden peg on the wall over the foot of the bed, and held it out.

"Never me an' that bank shall ever meet," Jack said. "Now, what d' you reckon? You fancy a pie in the street? Or a roast chicken somewheres where we can sit down?"

"Sitting, definitely," said Nolly.

He began to roll down his shirtsleeves, but his fingers were smudged with ink, so Jack put the hat down, batted Nolly's hands away, and set him to rights, rolling down his shirtsleeves and buttoning his silky gray waistcoat. Jack even straightened the green cravat, as any gentleman friend would, then helped Nolly with his sky-blue jacket. Then finally, with his hands on Nolly's shoulders, he turned Nolly to face him.

"C'n I get a smile?" asked Jack. He wouldn't force one if it wasn't coming, of course, but it seemed of late that Nolly had forgotten how.

"Can I get a kiss?" asked Nolly.

The question came as a bit of a surprise, but Jack obliged him, planting not one but several soft kisses about Nolly's mouth, upon his cheek, beneath his glowering brows.

"There you go," said Jack. "You want more now, or more later?"

"Later," said Nolly. He picked up his hat and put it on his head, patting the top of it to settle it the way he wanted it. He handed Jack his hat, as well, and tugged on Jack's lapel. "If we can get these posted before my courage fails me."

"An' somethin' in your belly," added Jack.

"Then I will be a good deal closer to feeling more content with the world."

"You afraid they won't reply or that they will?" Jack asked with his hand on the door. He wanted to be sure of what Nolly wanted, though there was nothing he could do about the outcome.

"Both," said Nolly. "If they don't reply, I shall be vexed, of course, but if they do reply, then I shall have to apologize even more profusely."

"To your old master an' your aunt."

"Yes, and I am already sore with thinking about it, so can we just go while there is daylight to be had?"

Jack could practically hear Nolly's stomach growl now that it had been alerted to the fact that there was food in its future. That, at least, Jack could take care of, and would, in abundance. He opened the door and gave Nolly a little bow to usher him out.

Nolly tucked the letters and the folded paper in his trouser pocket, curling his fingers close at his side to be sure the papers wouldn't fly away. When Jack closed the door to their room, Nolly reached out and swept his hand down Jack's arm, a long, slow gesture that made Jack want to hustle Nolly right back into the room, and take him on the bed without a second's hesitation. But he was hungry, too, and the walk would do them good; a bit of air freshened with soft rain was just the thing.

Or it would have been had not the rain, as light as it was, set ablaze all the odors of the muck running in the gutter in the middle of the street as they made their way down Field Lane. The familiar stench was sour in Jack's nostrils, reeking of urine and filth, and there looked to be scraps of something red with ribbon-like strands that had jammed up the gutter about halfway down.

Beneath the thin ropes fluttering over the street layered with many handkerchiefs for sale stood two women. With their untidy hair, their hands on their hips, and their laundry-grayed aprons flat against their skirts, they looked at Nolly and Jack. Their expressions were so dour that Jack stepped away from both women, and the foul object that looked like the remains of a dead hog, and tugged on Nolly's sleeve to get him to hustle along.

They should have skipped over a street, but that would have led them straight into Smithfield Market, which, at this time of day, would have smelled even worse than Field Lane. Luckily, they were soon at High Holborn, with its quick traffic and activity and, being occupied by the richer sort of person, both well-heeled pedestrians and the shiny-wheeled gigs and cabs, it had less scent of foul odors than it did of prosperity.

"Is the post office this way?" asked Jack, as he'd never been to or in a post office in his life. "Or that?"

"We go down the hill a ways," said Nolly. He took a moment as they stood on the pavement to adjust his hat, using the fingers of both hands. "Past Newgate and all the way to St. Martin's Le Grand."

"Near St. Paul's," said Jack. He knew the church, but it was also another building he'd never been in, not having had any reason to enter.

"Yes," said Nolly. He pulled on his lapels to smooth them and looked up at Jack. "Thank you for not being cross about the letters. I almost didn't write them, but—"

"Never you mind," said Jack. "You've had your say. Put it on paper, even. If they listen, or they don't, you did what you could. Right?"

"Right," said Nolly.

Jack saw the flicker of a smile around Nolly's mouth, though it seemed to Jack that so few things could manage to bring that smile, not in the days since they'd been back in London. But were Jack to ask, Nolly would insist there was naught amiss, that he was happy to be where Jack wanted to be, and the conversation would be over before it had begun.

In response to these thoughts, Jack wanted to link his arm through Nolly's, as men sometimes did, companions at arms, but knowing how it might draw attention that Nolly would not want, nor himself, for that matter, he didn't. Instead, he bumped his shoulder against Nolly's and started along the pavement, which almost at once began sloping away and down, as though into a ditch. When ice came in the winter, the street was a menace to men and horses alike, but now the way was only slightly slick, and they made it to the bottom near Old Bailey Street without tumbling.

As they neared the corner where the stones of Newgate Prison rose tall and cinder-dark, Jack could smell the raw, sharp resin of new wood. Even before he saw it, he knew that there was a scaffold going up just outside the Debtor's Door.

How many times he and Charlie and the rest of the lads had begged to go to hangings, which Fagin had allowed, but only after delivering a lecture on the importance of watching their backs, on account of the force of law that would be present at such an event. It had always been exciting to watch and see how the men went to their deaths, bravely or not so much.

Jack eyed the scaffold that was now coming into view. It was a double-scaffold; there would be two men hanging in the morning, then, one after the other. The air rang with the sounds of hammers and saws, and shimmered with flakes of wood dust floating in the air that smelled a bit sweet.

As the carpenters continued to erect the scaffold, with its newly hewn wood pale against the dark, sooty walls of Newgate rising behind it, already there were gawkers, rough men and boys of the lower orders, gathering on the shadow-damp cobbled street. They pointed at the scaffold, shouting out encouragement to the men working on it, bending down to grab a curl of pale, shaved wood as a souvenir. Just beyond that crowd were two more well-heeled and well-dressed gentlemen, standing somewhat apart from the spectacle, seemingly drawn to it in spite of themselves.

"Hey?" said Jack, to get Nolly's attention. "What d'you reckon, that they'll hang them both at once? Or will the second fellow piss himself while watchin' the first one go?"

But Nolly was facing away, gazing at the other side of the

street where the taverns and shops crowded around the imposing and more sturdy, stone-built buildings that had to do with the business of law and with justice. Jack could see it in an instant, even as Nolly turned to look at the scaffold, that it had been the wrong thing to say. And, as well, it might be that the polite sort of folk didn't say things like what Jack had just said. But he didn't know for certain, so he would ask.

"D'you not like me talkin' about it, Nolly?" asked Jack. "It happens, you know, men pissin' themselves out of fear when death's starin' them in the face."

"That's true enough," said Nolly. "I'm likely too sensitive about it. At least Mr. Grimwig always said I was."

Jack tipped his head back; his mouth tightened at the thought of anybody, especially some old fart who probably never had a good laugh in his life, saying such things about Nolly. Who, though sensitive in some ways, was rugged and ready in others, and Jack should know.

Besides, for Nolly, the threat of the hangman's noose had been real. That threat still crept about him at odd moments, and nothing Jack had said about it had made any difference. Noah had saved both Nolly and Jack from having to go on the run, but for Nolly the echoes of that dark fate still existed. And, all of a sudden, Jack no longer wanted to linger and gawp.

"Let's walk on, then," said Jack. Now he did link his arm through Nolly's, and for five or so matched steps, they walked thusly together. That is, until Nolly pulled away, but Jack didn't mind, for he understood why.

The road sloped downward until it leveled out, and just as they passed King Edward Street, Jack smelled something roasting and tipped his head toward Nolly.

"That'll be where we'll get supper, don't you think?" asked Jack. "It smells good, anyway."

Nolly shrugged his shoulders and huffed his breath. He looked at Jack as they walked, focusing on him, as if seeing him for the first time since Jack had entered their room. Which meant that, all along, Nolly had been churning in his fears about the reception of the letters, as Nolly was sometimes wont to do.

"Never mind me, Jack," said Nolly. "I'm game to go see the hanging, if you'd like."

"Hell no," said Jack, without hesitation. "They start way too early for me, now that I tarry in the mornin', sleepin' in with a handsome lad in my arms."

He emphasized the statement, as if it were his own creature comforts that concerned him, and not the fact that he was completely aware that a hanging might be too much for Nolly to bear.

With the blush of a sweet pink rose, Nolly smiled and looked away, not as though he were affronted by the bold courtship Jack made him in the street, but rather that he desired to treasure it. Such was the change in Nolly since he and Jack had entwined their lives together, and the knowledge of it alighted in Jack's heart and warmed him throughout.

"Have you ever been to a post office, Jack?" asked Nolly as they turned up the white-scrubbed pavement of St. Martin's Le Grand.

On the whole right side of the street was the post office, a noble and tall edifice decked with fluted columns and topped in the middle by a pointed arch. The surfaces of the columns and the arch were flayed white by the weather, but beneath the eaves were streaks of coal dust so thick they might have been painted on.

Smartly dressed men in dark suits and top hats buzzed about the door, sometimes accompanied by women in somber dresses and bonnets, their gloved hands resting lightly on their men's arms. It was so busy that Jack wondered how they were going to get through the door.

"It's not even near closing time," said Nolly, remarking on the clamor in the street. "I've not yet heard the bells for five o'clock."

But the crowd of people coming and going was of no matter,

as they were only two together. Nolly led them quickly inside to the large, marble-faced room, where there were long, dark lines of people squirming across the floor, determined to get their mail in motion before closing time.

Nolly took himself and Jack to the line furthest from the door, which, as Jack could easily see, was the shortest one. Before too long, they were up at the dark polished wood counter, face-to-face with the white-shirted clerk, his crisp cuffs kept from grit and ink by green armbands that were snugged tight about his elbows.

The clerk took Nolly's envelopes, keeping one eye on his hands and the other on his drawer. It didn't take him but a moment to stamp the three letters, but when he got to the unfolded sheet of paper, he shook it at the two of them.

"Why isn't this folded? Do you think I have time to fold this?" The clerk's starched collar practically dug into his neck as he raged.

"It's a postal order," said Nolly, without batting an eye, so clearly he was used to such rude treatment at the post office. "I want to send seven shillings, and you need to make out the certificate before it can be folded into a letter."

"Yes, yes," said the clerk; he got out a sheet of embossed paper and dipped his sturdy pen in the bottle of ink. "Seven shillings, you say? Hardly worth your while, since the cost to send it is sixpence."

"We've got that," said Jack quickly, wanting to take the irritated force of the clerk's attention away from Nolly.

He pulled out the required number of shillings, and the sixpence as well, and placed them in the brass tray in front of the clerk. It wouldn't do for Nolly to forget that Jack was quite prepared to provide for him, even if it meant paying for a fool's errand.

They both watched while the clerk made out the order; Nolly folded the letter but left it unsealed, and handed it to the clerk. With angry motions, the clerk shoved the certificate in, tipped the dipper stick around in the pot of sealing wax that was warmed by a candle, and sealed the letter with a small slapping sound. Jack could smell the warm wax as it cooled, and watched as the man casually tossed all of the letters in a box that was snatched up by a boy, who had the same green armbands protecting his white shirtsleeves that the clerk wore, and hustled away.

"Will it get there?" asked Jack, looking at the sea of bins behind the counter and the mad tossing of envelopes. His ears rang with the slap of booted feet as clerks and helpers raced about to collect the mail before closing time.

"Of course it will," snapped the clerk. "*Next.*"

"It always has before," said Nolly, smiling. "And if it doesn't, it doesn't, as you are about to say to me."

Jack smiled, even as he tried not to.

"Never *me*," he said, exclaiming, putting his hand to his heart. "But let's get you somethin' to eat," said Jack, pulling on Nolly's arm so they could get out of the marble-clad building that was starting to feel stuffy, even with the high ceilings.

When they reached the street again, Jack looked at Nolly, who was still distracted, it seemed, by the plight of the letters. As if Jack wasn't standing right there, in front of him, ready to fetch and carry at a moment's notice, ready to receive a single indication that there was one thing Nolly would prefer over another.

A group of dark-suited men were trying to enter the post office so, with a jerk of his head, Jack urged Nolly to move off the pavement and into the street. This Nolly did, his shoulders hunched and his mouth scrunched up.

Jack was about to cry foul and make his way to the nearest chop house whether Nolly was with him or no, when Nolly let out a long, slow breath. He shook himself, as if ridding himself of his own foul mood, and began walking up Newgate Street toward the origin of those good roasting smells that Jack had pointed out earlier.

Jack hopped into motion to keep pace with him, and soon they were swallowed up by the sea of respectable and employed men who were, at this time, making their way home.

"I'm sorry, Jack," said Nolly, looking at where his feet were in order not to stumble on the uneven, cobblestone road, along with keeping half an eye out to avoid the steel-rimmed wheels of various carts and cabs whose clatter filled the air. "I'm not sure why you burden yourself with me, when I am poor company, always distracted with my own worries."

"It's not a question of a burden," said Jack, wanting to make it a joke to lighten the dark clouds cloaking over Nolly's shoulders.

Nolly looked at Jack from beneath the brim of his hat. Those blue eyes of his had an intensity that Nolly seemed to reserve for only the most precious of objects, in one case, books, in another case, Jack.

"You're havin' a bad go of it, is all, Nolly," said Jack. He reached out to stroke Nolly's arm. "An' what you wants is feedin', so let me do that."

"Yes," said Nolly. "That would be perfect. And then I can—"

Nolly stopped talking, though luckily he'd not stopped walking because Jack's stomach was turning in on itself. But by the faint pink hue once again on Nolly's cheeks, Jack knew Nolly had to be thinking something that probably felt a little dangerous to be thinking, especially out in the open. As if every passerby had the power to read minds, especially those of a fair-headed young man with such a lovely mouth.

"—give you something in return later. Though we might wash a bit beneath the pump first," said Nolly, finishing.

There had been a point in Jack's life, many points, in fact, when he would have balked had it been pointed out to him that he needed to have a wash before or after any activity. Or that the use of soap and water might precede the sort of activity Nolly was suggesting.

But those days, those pre-Nolly days, were long behind Jack

now. And it wasn't just that being clean made Nolly relaxed and easy, Jack was growing a taste for it as well, but only when it was a full-out bath. Hasty washes just to eat a meal were only denying the fact that while eating, hands would get greasy all over again. But this was nothing Jack needed to tell Nolly at the moment, since they were coming up on Butcher Street, from whence the roasting smells had originated.

2

ENJOYING A MEAL IN A QUIET GARDEN

Butcher Street had an array of little bakeries selling cakes and iced buns, and small cafes with tables along the street where the patrons were eating huge portions of fried fish, and Oliver could not decide which side of the street smelled better.

"Where would you like to eat, Jack?" asked Oliver. Taking a deep breath, he straightened his waistcoat and adjusted his top hat. "Wherever you please, whichever has the best smells of cooking coming from it."

There were many odors on the street, most of them the pleasant smells of baked bread or frying meat. As well, the gutter in the middle of the street had been recently cleaned, so the dearth of filth made the prospect of sharing a meal with Jack that was not at the Three Cripples a more pleasant one.

Along the slope of the street was a blacksmith's shop that Jack wanted to stop at, it was easy to see. Before, Jack had wanted to linger at Newgate to watch the new scaffold go up, and while Jack might have been focused on the less savory aspect of the structure, he'd seemed equally interested in the actions of the carpenters at their intricate tasks. The same seemed to be true now, as Jack, almost in spite of himself, stopped to watch the blacksmith at his anvil.

With the glow of the heat of the fire reflecting on his face, Jack seemed absorbed in the way the man wielded his hammer as he forged a tongue of glowing iron that looked to be a piece for a gate hinge. But when Oliver motioned with his hand that Jack should linger as long as he liked, Jack shook his head and kept walking. The smell of burnt metal and hot coal followed them as they walked, the clang of the hammer bouncing off the cobbled street and joining the general din as handcarts, and men on horseback, and quick-stepping cabs dashed up and down the street, threatening to run them over.

Up ahead, the street wound to the left. That it had a bit of a slant didn't seem to slow the street traffic any. It was even busier the further they went, so when Jack pointed at one of the signs hanging beneath a jagged eave where there were tables along the pavement, Oliver was moved to object.

"Surely the street's too busy, Jack," said Oliver. He shook his head, though he shared Jack's penchant for eating out of doors.

"This one has a sort of shaded bit out back, you see?" asked Jack. He took Oliver by the arm, dragged him right up to the door, and pointed at the dark hunk of slate that was propped up in the windowsill. "Garden open, it says. Shall we give it a try? Get out of the dust for a bit?"

"Certainly," said Oliver, blinking at the sign. "But how do you know this place?"

"Well," said Jack, laying his finger alongside of his nose. "Just between me 'n thee, back in the old days, it used to be a den, one of Fagin's chosen places. Only now it's gone proper. I just hope the beer is as good as it was then."

It was hard to determine whether Jack was telling a fanciful story simply to be amusing, for as they entered the small restaurant, it had all the trappings of a civilized place not at all connected with the dark connivings of a street criminal and his gang of boy thieves. The windows were washed till the glass sparkled, and the wooden floor was swept clean.

The customers at the round tables looked to be good, hard working people, of the type that could afford a bite to eat after a day's labor. There were even some ladies present, obviously married, to go by their somber, dark clothes; the men had taken their hats off, and these all hung on the pegs over the window.

Oliver poked Jack with his elbow and, when Jack turned to look at him, he slowly took off his hat and motioned for Jack to do the same. Together, they gave their hats to the girl when she came over.

"Would you like to be seated, gentlemen?" she asked. Her apron and cap were of common cloth but were starched and pristine, which boded well for the meal they were about to have.

"Yes, an' could you please tell us if we might sit in the garden?" asked Jack with unexpected politeness.

"That's very popular this time of year and on a day so nice," said the girl as she hung their hats on the pegs. "But I will check for you, if you don't mind waiting."

"We don't mind," said Jack.

He reached into his trouser pocket to push a coin into her palm. Then she turned away in a swirl of skirt, walking briskly down a narrow corridor through which Oliver, if he leaned to the right, could see a brick wall thick with ivy and dappled with the faintly purple lace of a wisteria vine.

"You don't mind the wait, d'you, Nolly?" asked Jack.

Waiting with Jack in a pleasant place such as this was hardly a hardship, not to mention the anticipation of a good meal, so Oliver shook his head. Standing next to Jack as he was, he could trace the line of Jack's chin with his eyes, and watch dark eyelashes as they fluttered down, watch Jack as he rubbed his jaw, leaving a bit of a streak, as his hands were somewhat grubby. But what did that matter, as they would have a meal, and then later they could be alone in their room.

Part of the problem with living in London was that, since

they tended to make habits of where they went, they also tended to encounter people Jack knew. Or at least it seemed that way, because at the Three Cripples everybody knew Jack and, since he was one of Noah's favorites, they tended to wave him over, wanted him to linger with them, wanted to hear grand tales of days gone by, and would invite Jack to join them in a game of whist.

Thus, having private time alone together was important. Such as now, when they were on their own in a part of London where they were hardly likely to encounter anybody Jack knew. Except, being where they were made it more likely that they might encounter Mr. McCready or even Mrs. Pierson whilst they were out and about on errands.

It had crossed Oliver's mind to wonder what he might say to his old master and former housekeeper, should they chance to meet. Would they even acknowledge the greeting were Oliver to make it? That it was entirely possible they would not hung heavily deep in his heart.

But there was no sense in dwelling on that, as he knew Jack would tell him were Oliver to bring up the subject. *No sense in borrowing trouble,* Jack might say, so Oliver attempted to relax his shoulders and to concentrate on the moment at hand. On how it felt to have Jack so near in this quiet and civilized restaurant where nobody looked at them askance, or considered whether or not they had the coin to pay for a meal, for it was obvious that they did.

The girl came back down the passage and nodded that they should follow her, which they did, though they had to hustle to keep up with her brisk pace. They were quite soon led out to the garden, a tidy stone area with brick walls traced with green ivy and faint purple wisteria, which made a cool grotto that belied the dusty streets out front. It wouldn't be so pleasant had it kept raining, but for now, with the sun slanting across the rooflines of London, they would have a comfortable time of it among the round tables and within the quiet shelter of the high brick walls.

"Here you are, gentlemen; someone will be with you shortly."

Oliver pointed to the cane-back chair that was flush up against the brick wall and faced toward the door, so that Jack might sit there and comfortably see everything about him. This Jack did, and Oliver, feeling quite companionable, drew the other chair out from beneath the table and placed it so that he might sit closer to Jack. As Oliver sat down, he kept his face still so that nobody would know that their closeness was for any other reason than happenstance. But Jack knew, and he grinned at Oliver and patted his thigh.

"There y'are, my beautiful boy," said Jack, keeping his voice low, as if he knew better than to alert the entire of the small company that they now shared the courtyard with how it was between them.

Sometimes Jack acted as though he did not care to affect those behaviors that reflected the normal mien of civilization, as if, laws and mores be damned, he'd go about his business and hang anybody who would stop him.

That included being flirty and charming to Oliver when they were out and about. This behavior was meant to rile, and it was about to do so when Jack turned his attention to the waiter, who came out of the open doorway and made his way between the occupied tables with customers already eating.

It flickered in the corner of Oliver's mind that all of the customers were men, though surely there existed ladies who would enjoy a meal in such a cool and private garden as this. Instead of saying anything about it, Oliver lifted his attention to the waiter who, in his clean white apron, stood with his hands clasped in front of him.

"We have, gentlemen, a limited menu, either chops, mutton, or roast, with potatoes and greens, so which shall it be?"

"Roast," said Jack, going straight for the beef, as Oliver knew he would; after so many days on the road together, Jack's likes and dislikes were as comfortable and familiar to him as his own. "Is there salt?"

"I'll have the chops," said Oliver. That way, Jack could have a taste of something different, if he wanted it. "And what might you have for after?"

"Oh, we've no pudding left, gentlemen," said the waiter. "It was all taken after dinner today, I'm sorry."

The waiter nodded and went away, leaving them alone before Oliver could ask him for beer or cider to drink while they waited.

"Don't worry, Nolly," said Jack, leaning close to Oliver, as if he were about to tell him a grave secret. "I'll make it up to you."

Oliver did not want to risk a look at Jack's face as he waggled his eyebrows and played at being enticing, for it would make Oliver laugh out loud and, in this quiet place, with the low murmur of conversation, that would draw attention they did not need. Still, Jack would like a response, so Oliver rolled his eyes as though he was peeved, and tried very hard not to smile. And failed. This made Jack snicker, which was all to the better.

Within a short while, the girl came over to them. She carried shiny pint pots of beer, and these she slopped a little on the surface of the table when she put them down, but Jack gave her a penny just the same.

When she was gone, Oliver lifted his pint pot, and Jack lifted his, and together they clinked them, making a toast with their eyes. Then, in the soft light and cool air, surrounded by green ivy and the scent of small, purple flowers, they drank their beers slowly.

When Oliver was halfway done with his beer, he put the pint pot on the table and unrolled his napkin to dab his mouth with. In contrast, Jack used his napkin to scrub at his mouth and, in a mockery of politeness, flipped the napkin out like a sail, making much of placing the napkin in his lap.

"Jack," said Oliver, not chiding but rather acknowledging, as Jack liked him to do whenever Jack would play it up.

"I knows how, Nolly," said Jack. "But that don't mean I always want to."

"And you want to now."

"With you 'n me, here like this, yes, yes I do."

It was a declaration of love, the way Jack said it, and it went a long way to relaxing Oliver's shoulders even further so he could sit back in his chair, in so casual a way that it would alert Jack to the effect he was having.

"It is nice, this," said Oliver, keeping his voice low.

"An' I reckon the meal will taste better than leftovers from the hotel next door."

"It should," said Oliver, with a nod. "But better still is the handsome face of the company I'm currently keeping."

AS THEY LEFT THE RESTAURANT WITH TOP HATS ON THEIR heads and the lovely meal settling in their bellies, Oliver looked down to note the slide of beer stain on his shirt bosom where the drape of his green cravat ended but before his gray waistcoat began.

It was also in the same spot as would show above the top hem of his apron, though at the Three Cripples that would account for nothing, for in spite of the fact that a good deal of his once-fine, once-white shirt had become generally slopped with beer in one way or another, nobody who drank at the tavern would care.

"What's that for, then?" asked Jack, loud in Oliver's ear.

The words startled Oliver away from errant thoughts and into the street, where they were, at the moment, attempting to scale the distance back to the Three Cripples. The pavement had become crowded to a bursting point as the evening's traffic, jammed with folk who were all intent on getting where they were going sooner than anybody else, swirled around them.

"What's what for?" Oliver asked this as he slowed, tugging Jack closer to him along the wall of a building that looked new and wasn't damp. At least not much. The smell of manure-fouled hay rose up in his nostrils; the traffic was too thick for the street sweeper to do anything about it, so Oliver turned his head away and focused on Jack.

"Here." Jack pointed with his thumb at his own brow and shook his head. "After such a fine meal as what we just shared, you're to be singin' my praises right about now. Only you ain't."

Had they been in private, Oliver knew he could do with his hands as he wanted to, such as clasp Jack's face in them and kiss him thoroughly, both in apology for being distracted by his own thoughts, and in praise for the meal that had, indeed, been truly fine.

"I will sing them, Jack," said Oliver, kissing Jack with his eyes, as they were not in private. "And am. It was a grand meal, as fine as the one we had at the Swan."

"Only as good as that? I thought I'd gone one better, frankly." Jack waved Oliver's words away, as though they were beyond belief, but Oliver could tell Jack was pleased by the glint in his green eyes and the tight curve of his cheeks as he attempted to tame a smile and failed.

"I reckon you're frettin' about this." Jack touched Oliver, in spite of any audience, with two fingers gently pressing on the stain that Jack had obviously espied.

"A bit," said Oliver.

It was the stain, along with the press of traffic, and the lack of accommodation by anybody for anybody else besides themselves that troubled Oliver. Two elderly women were attempting to pass by Oliver and Jack on the pavement without mowing them down with the sharp edges of their bell-shaped skirts, though they didn't seem to be trying very hard.

Oliver paused to tip the brim of his hat at the women. Jack merely scowled at them and looked away, as if pretending they weren't even there, but waited until they had passed before speaking again.

"We'll just get you a new shirt, then," said Jack. His eyes

started searching the street, squinting as he read the signs that hung in front of most shops. "Mayhap even two."

Oliver's mouth hung open. He'd thought to begin listing his complaints about the fact that since their return to London, he'd not had a chance for a good, hot bath, let alone the opportunity to rinse out his one and only shirt. But there was no need for his planned tale of small woe, for Jack, with his continual thoughtfulness, had preempted all with a simple solution.

"I think I saw a likely second-hand shop," said Jack. He did not give Oliver a chance to speak, but he was not unaware, it seemed, of what Oliver had been about to say, for he gave Oliver a slow wink and, with a knowing quirk to his smile, pointed down Butcher Street, over the heads of the throng, to the main thoroughfare. "It's one lane over, on Giltspur Street."

Stolen also from Oliver's lips were any words of gratitude, which Jack would not wish to be overly encumbered by, along with any further explanation, which Jack would not need. As Jack would see it, and Oliver knew this for a certainty, if Oliver wanted a new shirt, then a new shirt he would have, and that was the end of it. For this kindness, as Oliver matched his pace with Jack's quick strides, he determined to find a way to thank Jack.

He could barely keep up with Jack who, when on a mission to spend money not his own, was as deterrable as a bullock in its own field. But keep up, Oliver did, almost trodding on Jack's boot heels as Jack turned the corner to head up Newgate Street.

Though the street and the pavement were wide, they presented the same straw-ridden visage where the traffic seemed to surge as one body, a massive moving thing made up of horse carts and wagon wheels, of the shout of drovers, the whistle of cabbies, and the dust of dried, wheel-scattered manure that sifted over the heads and shoulders of everybody, flattering nobody, and equalizing all with a cloud of fine, brown flakes.

"Up along here," said Jack, over his shoulder so as to be heard amongst the din. "This is Giltspur."

Oliver caught up and stayed caught up and now, much closer

to Jack, was able to admire the curve of Jack's jaw, the flash of his sharp teeth as he looked over his dark, wool-clad shoulder and grinned at Oliver's illicit nearness.

With a wave of his hand, Jack led the way in through the open door of a shop whose sign they moved too quickly beneath to read, and they stepped into the cool and quiet stillness of a second-hand clothing shop. At least, it must be such a place, for even Jack would not be as daring as to walk into a gentleman's tailor shop to call for measurements to be taken and order a bespoke suit for himself and his companion. Still, as Oliver looked about him, it seemed that if any of the clothes were used, they were used very gently, indeed.

"And how might I help you—gentlemen?"

A clerk approached them in his tucked white apron. There was not a spot on it anywhere, and his voice carried in the tall-ceilinged shop. And, as such, the slight hesitation in his words as he assessed their statuses rang in Oliver's ears.

He was about to raise his own voice in response and insist to Jack that they leave at once, when Jack placed a hand on Oliver's forearm. This gentle warning was accompanied by a tender look in Jack's eyes. And this from Jack, who normally wouldn't have given a tinker's plug about such niceties as status and manners, or how a mere clerk should address his betters.

"Not as such," said Jack, admitting this with all casualness as he released Oliver's arm. "But we're attemptin' to be upstandin' citizens, just the same. Only there is the matter of stains which cannot be removed."

Oliver did his best not to let his jaw hang open as Jack spoke in the tones of every status-climbing gentleman Oliver had ever heard or encountered, with a gift of mimicry that Oliver would not have, heretofore that very moment, ascribed to Jack.

"Could you supply us with a pair of shirts to reflect the type that my companion is now wearin'? Would that we could purchase half a dozen, but alas, our budget limits us to only two."

"Certainly, sir," said the clerk, without even batting an eye, in spite of the fact that it was obvious, even to Oliver, that Jack was quite flaunting his posh tones, as if wanting to mock the clerk whilst amusing himself and Oliver.

In short order, the clerk brought over two folded shirts and gestured that Oliver and Jack should accompany him to the counter.

"Would the gentleman require the shirts altered, or would at least try them on to see if they suit and if they fit?"

Oliver could see that in a place such as this, a bit more upscale than the typical used-clothing shop, and the quality of the shirts being held out to them was evidence of this, that such a service would be on offer, but would make the shirts cost extra. Not that the cost, be it dear or cheap, was of any matter, since money came and went so freely from Jack's hands. But while normally the fuss would have been pleasant, with Oliver being measured like a gentleman and Jack watching with avid eyes, Oliver only wanted to get home and be alone with Jack.

"They'll fit very well, I'm sure," said Oliver.

He nodded to the clerk and then looked at Jack. If the shirts didn't fit, they could be altered another day, for currently his need to be near Jack, to be *alone* with Jack, was being hampered by the fact that they were away from the Three Cripples and had been for some time.

"We should be going," said Oliver now.

"Would the gentleman care to try on a jacket to go with the new shirts?" The clerk, persistent in his craft, had placed the folded shirts on the counter and was drawing up a jacket that hung on the wooden rack at the end of the counter. "Such a fine, thin wool for spring, wouldn't you think?"

The jacket the clerk held out was indeed a quality article: a deep, dark blue, as fine and as still as a starless night. The clerk drew a finger along the lapel, where could be seen slender piping of an even richer blue.

"It would suit the darker of you two very well," said the clerk.

He held out the jacket, as if he expected Jack to try it on that very moment.

"No," said Jack. "That's too fine for the likes of me."

Oliver did not agree, for the jacket would look very well curved around Jack's shoulders, and would nip in at his waist, which would make the tail of the jacket flare out a little. But he could not and would not make Jack try on the garment. So he shook his head at the clerk.

"Sadly, we must be going," said Oliver. "But if you could write up the bill for the shirts?"

"Certainly, sir," said the clerk. "I'll only be a moment."

Off the clerk went to the back room, in the manner of such posh shops, to write up the bill and total the amounts out of sight, as if the discussion of money were far too delicate to be discussed out in the open.

Oliver watched Jack watching the clerk go off. Then Jack shook his head, in bemusement perhaps, or in mockery of the tender details that made up a rich man's life.

"Will two shirts do, or might you need aught else?" asked Jack, turning his attention to Oliver.

"I want for naught," said Oliver, not bothering to hide his smile. "Only to go home to be with you."

"In our lush and roomy bood hour," said Jack, doing that silent, open-mouthed laugh of his.

"In our *what?*" Now thoroughly distracted from what the clerk was doing and what was taking him so long, Oliver turned his attention fully to Jack, who was looking at him quite seriously, though his smile was turning to a frown.

"Did I say it wrongly?" asked Jack. "'Twas a word I read in one of Noah's newspapers, about some royal caught in the bood hour of his wife's best friend, only it was spelled b-o-u-d—"

"Oh, you mean *boudoir*," said Oliver, giving the word his best French pronunciation, not to mock Jack, but merely to demonstrate how the word might be said. Nor did he want to correct Jack about the fact that a boudoir was a lady's chambers and not a gentleman's. Still, it need not make any difference between the two of them, for he knew what Jack meant. "But yes, you and me in our bood hour, that's where I'd like to be right now."

The clerk came back at that moment, carrying a thin sheet of paper with the cost of both shirts written out in ink, no less, and the total amount due written at the bottom. He began to hand the bill to Oliver, who nodded in Jack's direction: as Jack earned the money, it was his right to spend it.

Jack handed the appropriate amount of coin over generously, then took the change from the clerk's hand in return. Taking the bill that was handed to him, he folded it and placed in his trouser pocket, though Oliver knew full and well that Jack did not care about keeping his accounts in order, for they were like a river that flowed broad or waned where it might, with no heed to the banks that bound it.

"Shall we go home now, Jack?" asked Oliver, as the clerk turned to wait upon another gentleman who had just entered the shop.

Oliver was gratified to see Jack nod at him in a slow, pleased way. Their errand had been run and their supper had, and the early evening air, as they stepped out into the street to follow the pavement back home, was warm and balmy, with no promise of additional rain.

"Those shirts will look well on you," said Jack, walking at Oliver's side.

"And I thank you for them, Jack," said Oliver. "'Twas very thoughtful of you."

Though normally Jack did not like to be gushed over for small favors, he ducked his head to slip ahead on the pavement, and Oliver caught a silvery glimpse of Jack's smile, and was well pleased.

ॐ 3 ॐ

TOGETHER IN THEIR PRIVATE
BOOD HOUR

Oliver smiled as they walked home, for it was pleasant in the fine evening weather to saunter along with his new shirts rolled beneath his arm, and to be shoulder to shoulder with Jack. The street along which they were walking grew quiet. There were still carriages bustling past, and dray horses pulling wagons, and apprentices on errands, to be sure. But this did not affect them; they were headed home to the Three Cripples.

Which, as they neared it, had the usual crush at the door, with men trying to get in as other men, having already drunk their pennies away, tried to get out. The whole of the doorway was one mad tangle of boots and legs and arms.

Oliver and Jack had to wait a moment before a gap appeared. Then, tugging Oliver behind him, Jack plowed through, laughing as his hat fell off. He caught it before it was stomped on and yanked Oliver's arm hard enough to get him all the way through without mishap.

"Beer?" asked Jack.

He seemed quite ready to march up to the bar and demand one for each of them. But as Jack looked back at him, Oliver half-closed his eyes and shook his head.

"Hey?" asked Jack. He trudged back to Oliver and stood there at his side, reaching out to touch Oliver on the arm, as if this might tell him what was amiss.

"Mayhap we might get a drink later," said Oliver. He placed his hand over Jack's to keep it there. "But I've a mind to go upstairs, if you'd care to go with me."

"Oh, I *say*," said Jack, his smile bright enough to draw attention. But this he did not suffer himself to hide because he never did, and Oliver did not want to make him. Not when Jack's eyes looked so green, the faint trail of freckles across his nose somehow more endearing in that moment than they had been all day. "Well, then, up we go."

Jack turned to plow his way through the taproom and up the stairs, his boot heels thumping loudly, for effect, of course, and Oliver followed close behind. At the top of the stairs, Jack flung open the door and dragged Oliver in behind him to close the door and push Oliver up against it.

The rough movement caused Oliver to drop his shirts, but Jack caught them with as much grace as he'd caught his own hat, and tossed the rolled bundle on the table.

"Let me open that window an' we'll have at it—or have at each other, right? See what I said there, *have* each other?"

Normally, Jack would have winked, but he was too busy with the window, though Oliver knew he was laughing to himself. And indeed, it was easy to be amused at Jack's antics, so irascible and hoping for praise, as though he knew he was well loved and wanted that praise, but only from Oliver.

"I do love you, Jack," said Oliver as he stepped close to clasp Jack's shoulders in his hands. He leaned forward and planted a kiss along the back of Jack's neck, and watched Jack arch so Oliver might kiss where he would. So over and over, Oliver did, till Jack's eyes half-closed, one hand coming up to clasp Oliver's.

"We should do this slowly," said Oliver. The words came without specific thought, though they felt warm with the idea that Jack should be languorously sprawled on the sheets, head thrown back, dark hair like traces of ink on the pillowslip while Oliver did things to him that might make him speak in whispers, and say the things from his heart.

"As slow as you like, sweetheart," said Jack. He licked his lower lip, unconsciously, it seemed, making it glisten, and nodded, as if to indicate how compliant he would be.

Jack let Oliver undress him, which he did, but slowly. He started at the bottom with Jack's boots and stockings and then moved up the length of Jack's body. With each item that Oliver removed from Jack, he removed from himself, and folded the garments and piled them beneath the table, till at last they were standing naked, wearing only their top hats, the dark, sleek felt in high contrast to their warm, flushed skins.

"My, my," said Jack, as he tipped his hat at Oliver and then took it off. "You're such a one for being in the altogether, though nobody'd think it to look at you."

This was not meant as criticism, as Oliver well knew, but was merely an observation that Oliver was so different about his modesty in private than he was in public.

"Only with you, Jack," said Oliver.

He took off his hat as well and gave it to Jack so he might hang both hats on the pegs on the wall. Then Jack returned to him, a sweet glimmer in his eyes, and his hands reached out to Oliver's waist, fingers clasping gently at Oliver's hips to pull Oliver to him. Now their hips touched, and their chests were close, and Jack's private hair scratched at Oliver's skin in those places that were soft and sensitive to it.

"On the bed, if you please," said Oliver. He stepped forward, which caused Jack to step backwards, and bit by bit they went, for the room was not very wide, until the backs of Jack's knees hit the mattress.

"You should be on the sheets, such that—" said Oliver. Then he stopped.

Finding it impossible to explain the picture in his head, Oliver pulled the blue-striped muslin coverlet back. With a small sigh of dismay, he brushed at bed lice, the small flecks of brown and pale tan that had gathered together where the bed was against the wall.

He didn't say anything about it to Jack. Instead, he pushed Jack until he was forced to sit down, and urged Jack with his hands to rest his head on the pillow. And sighed again because, at some point, somebody had come into the room and taken two of the pillows, and now there was only one, the thinnest one. At least Jack's soft skin encountered the cotton bedsheets and nothing else.

Oliver slipped into the bed alongside Jack and made Jack lie back. He petted Jack's chest, and kissed his shoulder, and waited until Jack's skin seemed soothed beneath his hands before he rose up to kneel at Jack's side.

"What are you on about, Nolly?" asked Jack. His eyebrows drew together for a fraction of a moment, because what Oliver was doing was not how they usually went about this.

It was just that Oliver wanted to touch every part of Jack, to luxuriate in the nearness of Jack, with the sunlight still on the roofs and gables across the alley, and in the pleasantly warm air that streamed in through the open casement window. So he did what he wanted, starting with Jack's feet and legs, which he had to scoot down to get to, with Jack trying to hide a smile that was meant to be sly but that seemed more tender, and kept petting. Stroking, long and slow, stopping to plant a kiss, light as a feather, here and there, wherever Jack's body seemed to want it.

By the time he'd made it up Jack's thighs, Jack was trembling, his chest rising and falling with quick, little breaths, and he seemed to want to grab for Oliver, either to encourage him or stop him. So Oliver took Jack's hand and placed it on his thigh as he crouched, bent over Jack, and planted kisses along Jack's hip and up along his waist.

"You mustn't skip anywhere, Nolly," said Jack, his voice a tad desperate. "You're kissin' an' pettin' everywhere else, so why not *there*, for pity's sake?"

"I won't skip, my bright bird," said Oliver. "Never fear."

Then, with his hands on Jack, Oliver shifted one leg so it was on the other side of Jack's hips, and leaned down to kiss Jack's belly, just at that place where the thin line of dark hair pointed the way to Jack's cock. That line was not quite like an arrow, for Jack's cock was already hard, curving against his skin.

Oliver kissed along the length of it, hands still on Jack's hip, gripping lightly, oh, so lightly, while he feathered kisses and absorbed the heat of Jack's body into his own. And all the while, Jack shifted beneath him, his eyes fluttering closed, lashes like tender, dark wings on his cheeks, and his hair as Oliver had wanted it, sprawling across the pillowslip.

Oliver straddled Jack, full on, though his own weight was balanced on his knees, for he didn't want to startle Jack to the point where he would throw Oliver off him. No, he wanted it to be a slow, drowsy thing when Jack became aware of it to help Jack with this fear that had come from darker times.

Quietly, he sucked his fingers into his mouth to wet them, then reached down to trace between Jack's legs, pushing gently in with one finger as he bent to suck on Jack's cock.

Jack tasted like salt and musk, the dust of the day that was in the air. Oliver went slowly, and was gratified at the low, low sounds coming from Jack's mouth, the way he tossed his head on the pillow, how his hands reached out to touch Oliver, how he placed his hands on Oliver's knees.

Bestilled, Oliver watched as Jack opened his eyes, slowly, as though he were awakening from a deep sleep. Jack's fingers clenched Oliver's knees, and Oliver looked down to see the white outlines his fingers left there.

"I see," said Jack. "I see."

Jack's thighs trembled beneath Oliver, then surged up as if he indeed wanted to throw Oliver off him. Oliver was quite prepared to remove his weight, only Jack sank his head back onto the pillow, and his tight fingers loosened to become draped along Oliver's thighs. Oliver watched as Jack's breathing slowed down.

"As you were, sweetheart," said Jack, almost whispering. "As you were."

Thus given permission, Oliver continued, slowly, slowly, every touch of his fingers an act of love, every sweep of his mouth on Jack's skin a declaration of how he felt for his bright bird. Every breath a willing prayer that they would be this way, together, always.

He kept on until Jack's belly tightened, and his body tightened around Oliver's fingers, so he pulled them out and concentrated on Jack's cock, petting and kissing and sucking until Jack's body jerked, a low grunt coming from Jack's chest as he spent himself, sending white streaks across his own belly.

It was then that Oliver moved off Jack to lie down beside Jack and pet him while he sighed, and kiss his shoulder again, until Jack turned his head to look at Oliver, his eyes opening like two green jewels.

Jack reached up and, with his thumb, wiped Oliver's lower lip, and then sucked it into his own mouth.

"Wherever do you learn these things?" asked Jack, half shaking his head. "I didn't teach you that, an' that's a fact."

"Well, you did, in a way," said Oliver. He kept his voice soft as he tucked himself into the hollow of Jack's shoulder and traced the lines of Jack's ribs with enough firmness not to be ticklish. "I just took what you taught me and turned it about in my mind a bit, then settled on how I wanted it to go."

"Which was how?" asked Jack.

A bit of sweat trickled down his neck as he pulled Oliver to him. Oliver was close enough to whisper in his ear, as if they might be overheard by some passerby.

"With you like this," said Oliver. He kissed Jack's temple. "All pleasured and relaxed and not thinking of anything but this moment."

"In our bood hour," said Jack, with a little laugh.

He turned toward Oliver, and pulled him in his arms, and kissed him on the forehead, on his nose, on his mouth, laughing a bit the whole while, the shine of his teeth glinting, the feel of them sharp on Oliver's lips when he kissed him.

This was how it should be, always, between him and Jack. This way, this peaceful way, in the slow part of the afternoon with nowhere else to be and nothing to keep them from this, this quiet moment.

❧ 4 ❧

JACK'S BIRTHDAY MORNING

Though Jack woke sleepily when Nolly was getting dressed, he fell back asleep as soon as the door was gently closed. Only to awaken again when it opened and the sun came streaming in through the dust-spotted casement window. It was so bright that the end of the room by the door was a box of shadow, though he knew it was Nolly standing there, poised between the darkness and the squares of bright yellow that stretched across the brown floor.

"Are you awake, Jack?"

Nolly's voice came to Jack eager and bright, and he could hear the sound of Nolly's boots on the floorboards as he strode up to the bed. Then Jack sensed that Nolly was near, and opened his eyes fully to see Nolly sitting on the bed as he doffed his top hat. Nolly laid some bundles on the striped counterpane in the space between Jack's legs beneath the bedclothes and Nolly's above.

Nolly was quite dapper in his light blue jacket. The collar of his new shirt stood up white and starched, the green cravat crisp at the bow and softer where the shiny silk tumbled down his breast. Jack thought all over again how sweet Nolly was to look at. Especially with the way the sweat on his forehead made small gold curls of his hair and brightened his cheeks to pink.

"Where've you been, my lovely one?" asked Jack, his voice morning rough.

He sat up in bed and scooted back, snagging an errant bed bug that had made its way from beneath the bed-linen, and squished it between his fingers before he flicked it on the floor. Then he tugged his shirt down to cover the fact that he did not have on his underdrawers and leaned against the low iron bed frame and held out his hand.

"Come to me now and give us a kiss."

Nolly was eager as he bent close, his lips warm, bestirring the soft feeling in Jack's belly to something more quick and urgent. But Nolly pulled away, petting his lips with the backs of his fingers, and touched the parcels on the bed with his other hand.

"What's this, then?" asked Jack, his attention drawn to where Nolly wanted it to be. Which was no hardship, not with Nolly so near, and the curiosity of the reason for the parcels bringing Jack fully awake. "What is it?"

Looking at Jack, his eyes so very blue and shining with plea-sure, Nolly ducked his chin a little and looked up at Jack through his eyelashes.

"Happy birthday, Jack," said Nolly.

"Happy *birthday*?" asked Jack. It was nonsense to imagine it was so, but yet there Nolly was, still and intent on Jack's dubious reaction. Jack could give him a better response, if he could make sense of the idea of it. "It's my *birthday*?"

"Don't you remember?" asked Nolly. He lifted up the smallest of the parcels and gave it to Jack. It was wrapped in brown paper, as though for mailing a long distance, but instead of being tied with ordinary string, it was tied with a bit of purple silk. "Delia, your sister Delia. She told us when we were looking at your portrait that your birthday was May fifth, which, incidentally, is today."

For a moment, all Jack could do was to sit back and say nothing, his mouth open and his eyes on Nolly, whose pleasure seemed to be dimming away with each heartbeat that Jack did not act pleased.

Not ever, not even once, had the fifth of May been remarked upon as having been more important, more extraordinary, than any other day; nobody had ever wished him a happy birthday, let alone brought him presents. Jack knew about birthdays, of course he did, but never one for him. He'd never even thought about it until now.

Nolly sat, a little expectant, his brow furrowing together as though he were concluding, as he must be, that Jack did not want his birthday celebrated. This Jack knew he needed to fix, and directly, too.

"Nolly," said Jack.

His brain raced all about to discover what he might say to repair the damage, even as he felt it, right below his breastbone, in his heart, the flutter of pleasure and gratitude. Simmering below that, however, was the pang of loss and discovery, all at once, at never before having known a moment such as this. His indrawn breath was shaky, and he had to blink rather quickly and close his mouth over words his tongue had no idea how to form.

"Are you pleased?" asked Nolly, still worried. "I didn't have time to order a cake, which is all the rage now, I'm told, with candles in it, one for each year, that you blow out and make a wish upon."

Jack sat there, absolutely still. He held the small parcel in his hands as he ran his finger along the slender purple silk ribbon.

"Nothin' to wish for," said Jack, swallowing, pretending that he sounded gruff, rather than that his voice reflected all the tender feelings rattling about inside of him. "Gots you, don't I."

This was not a question as much as it was an affirmation that only needed Nolly's agreement to seal it.

"So you are pleased," said Nolly, nodding a bit, almost to himself.

In response, Jack took the parcel and held it to his forehead, partly to hide his eyes, which felt rather hot, but also to give himself a moment. Just one, where he could take a breath and let it out slowly. Then he shook the package and looked at it, then shook it again and held it to one ear.

"It don't sound much like one-penny nails," said Jack. He swallowed to clear his throat. "Nor does it sound like the jewels from the Queen's crown." Jack shook his head, as if to show how disappointed he was in this.

"Just open it," said Nolly with a small laugh as he sat back, the wrinkle disappearing between his eyebrows, his eyes glittering and happy once more.

Jack did as he was told and slipped the soft purple ribbon off without tearing it. Let loose from its restraints, the brown paper bounced up to reveal the gift within, which turned out to be a tin box. It was square and flat and a bit bigger than the size of his palm with a slide-on lid. On the surface were engraved three Scottish thistles and a round rose, with the words *De La Rue & Co, London*. Jack knew at once what it was that he held.

"Playin' cards, Nolly, *brand-new*, never-been-besmirched playin' cards." Jack tipped the tin box into his hand. The cards slid out of a piece, all silky and slightly shiny and slick in his hand, and he let out a sigh of delight.

"Only the best for you, my bright bird," said Nolly, very softly.

Jack looked up into Nolly's eyes.

"How did you know?" asked Jack.

He tucked the cards in his hands and gazed at the bright black and red suits, at the colorful images of queens and kings. He lifted and cut them, as if preparing them for their virginal voyage.

"Well, you'd mentioned on more than one occasion that Noah's cards were certainly cut and marked to his advantage. Otherwise, how could you be losing so much when playing with him? I saw these in one of the shops when we came back yesterday and went to fetch them before they were sold."

This simple, straightforward explanation didn't describe half of the delight in Nolly's face, the upward curve of his smile, the bright rose of his cheeks, the affection in his eyes. Surely, to buy a pack of playing cards was nothing but to pick out such a fine set, and then to *wrap* it—

"Thank you," said Jack, for he could demonstrate a gentleman's manners when the occasion warranted it. Such as it did now.

"And now this one," said Nolly. He picked up a fairly large box, bigger than Jack's lap. The present was also wrapped in brown paper for mailing, but was soft at the edges this time, and bound with blue felt that was tied in a bow.

Jack tucked the cards at his hip, the tin of the case cool on his bare skin. This time he didn't hesitate to take the box when offered, to tear through the felt and open the brown paper. This present was a bundle of blue cloth that, when Jack unfolded it, proved to be the midnight-blue jacket the clerk had shown them the day before. Tucked inside of the jacket was a pure white shirt, the crisp collar standing up sharply enough to cut through wire. Jack recognized it at once as one of the shirts that he'd purchased for Nolly.

"What's this, then?" asked Jack, laying the garments on his lap, tracing the dark blue piping. "I bought the shirt for you."

"I have two shirts, Jack, one to wash and one to wear, while you—at any rate, now we both have two shirts."

The question arose again in Jack's mind as to where Nolly had gotten the money. But to bring up the matter now would place Nolly in a state where he imagined he'd done wrongly, not to mention it would ruin the jolly time Nolly must have had picking the items out. And, as well, the jacket was very fine, except—

"My jacket's good enough," said Jack, petting the placket of the one in his lap. "Why do I need two of 'em?"

"Open this last present," said Nolly. He handed Jack a slim

parcel that was also wrapped in brown paper, but this time it was tied up with plain string. "And then I'll explain."

The parcel Nolly handed Jack was light in his hand, and he sensed that the brown paper wrapped another box within it, indicating that the present was something fine indeed. Therefore, Jack opened it with great care, fully untying the string rather than slipping it off, and unfolded the brown paper until the box, cream-colored and clean, lay in the nest of brown paper.

There was no lettering on the lid to indicate from whence the box had come. Jack lifted the lid, whereupon was revealed a bright red cravat that looked strangely familiar.

"'Tis your cravat, Jack," said Nolly. "I took it to the shop when I bought the jacket, and the clerk was quite willing to launder and press it for me. It was looking so wrinkled and spotted that I couldn't bear to see you wear it, only now, well, now you shall look quite fine."

"Why you want me lookin' so posh, then, Nolly?" Normally, it was easier than this to determine what Nolly was thinking. But now, with the new clothes piled in Jack's lap, Nolly had ducked his chin and was playing with the crisply tucked edge of the midnight-blue cuff. "Nolly, don't hide from me so, just tell me true."

It took a moment, but Nolly took a deep breath and looked up at Jack, quite serious and still, as if he were about to impart knowledge that was deep and grave.

"You always look like a pickpocket," said Nolly so bluntly that Jack felt his eyebrows rise up. "Well, you *do*. You look like a pickpocket and, well, if you didn't look like one, even if you are picking pockets or whatever, nobody would suspect you, and it'll be less likely that you get arrested.

"Nolly—" began Jack, completely astonished.

"I cannot stop you from doing what you like, nor would I want to, but I can help keep you safe, and dressing you as a gentleman is one way of doing that." Nolly snapped his mouth closed, and Jack saw him swallow. "You don't have to wear—you don't have to dress that way if you don't want to," Nolly said, speaking quickly.

Nolly, who had a will as mighty as a pair of draft horses, could have gotten Jack to stop being a pickpocket if he'd wanted to. Jack would have resisted, of course and, between the two of them, they would have torn themselves asunder. But this—Jack felt a swelling beneath his breastbone, the feelings rising up again, tender and soft.

Had Nolly, in that moment, asked Jack to give up picking pockets forever, he believed that he would have done it. But Nolly had not, and it seemed he would not. Instead, he would put his own touch upon it, that if Jack were to do this dangerous thing he insisted on doing, then he would do it with style, and be dressed as a gentleman, and walk the streets in the manner to which Nolly would like him to become accustomed.

"I suppose you'll be wantin' me to wash my face an' hands regular now, put Macassar oil in my hair, an' trim my nails, an' use a handkerchief an' all. Except you didn't buy me one o' them."

"We'll get one when we go out for cake or something sweet," said Nolly, which they would do since they had been denied it after supper the night before. His voice was obviously meant to be serious and stern, but Jack saw the pleasure in Nolly's eyes, because Nolly knew, as well as Jack did, that he was going to go along with this. And not only because Nolly wished it, but because it made sense. *Perfect* sense.

"I'll be a cut above, I will," said Jack. "An' nobody will ever suspect what I'm doing."

"You will indeed," said Nolly. "You'll go to posh places as though you belonged, and I've seen you do it, Jack. Talking to people as if you had a right to be there. Only now you'll *look* like you belong as well."

"So says you," said Jack, trying to keep the mirth out of his voice. "But I can't wear these clothes, I just can't."

There was only a brief flicker of distress in Nolly's eyes, before Nolly caught on that Jack was joking.

"Can't or won't?" asked Nolly, going along with it.

"Both," said Jack. "I wouldn't want to soil these fine Sunday clothes afore I've had a bath. That is, if anybody I know is interested in goin' along with me to have one."

"Such a gift," said Nolly, teasing. "And it's not even my birthday."

"Which is when?"

"January the twenty-ninth."

As Nolly finished saying the date, Jack thought of that time of year, when the wind would be so cold, with snow on the ground and heaps of frozen mud, and all the lanes slippery, where nothing was warm or safe or dry. And how Nolly's mam, the bright young thing she must have been when she fell in love with the man in the long blue coat, bedding him without a promise for the morrow, had crawled to the closest workhouse to give birth to Nolly and then to die.

Whether or not Nolly was thinking of this now, of his image of her and how she had been, or whether he was concerned that, indeed, he'd purchased no handkerchief or any other fine articles for Jack's impending daily toilet, his face was once again showing his distress. Jack hastened to fix this.

"Shall we gather together an' go?" asked Jack. "I've a mind for a bath, an' you've promised me a new handkerchief, though I could just as easily pick a pocket for one, as you know."

"Birthday presents should not be of the stolen variety," said Nolly, arching his neck to look down at Jack. "It wouldn't be right. Just as you purchased that book you gave me, I would purchase your handkerchief for you."

"Then how did you get the money for all this?" Jack could not stop himself from asking this even as he pushed the blue jacket and white shirt off his lap, and scrabbled with his fingers to collect the playing cards to tap them straight and put them back in their tin box.

"I received an advance on my wages," said Nolly. "But what does that matter? I'll make it back. Now you—here, let me take the cravat and the clothes. You can dress in your old clothes and put the new ones on after you bathe."

"An' you'll bathe, too, right?" It could not be borne if Nolly were to stand aside while Jack performed his ablutions, seeing as how Nolly would then appear to be his manservant, and this could not be tolerated. Not between them, not after everything that they'd been through together.

"Of course, Jack," said Nolly. He petted Jack's leg where it was stretched beneath the coverlet, seeming contended to let them sit there together for a time before making the day start, in that way that only Nolly could do. "I know a lovely, posh place, just right for you on your birthday."

Jack ambled himself out from under the covers just the same, and pushed aside the new jacket, but carefully so it wouldn't fall on the floor. As well, he placed the tin of playing cards in the drawer of the small table beneath the window, where was stored Nolly's pen and paper and ink and sealing wax, as well as Jack's pipe and tobacco and, finally, got out of bed.

"Old clothes?" he asked, stretching, watching Nolly watching him as he pulled his shirt into place and reached for his under-drawers and trousers, which were in a humped pile on the floor.

"Old clothes," said Nolly.

He took the new shirt and jacket and carefully rolled them to tuck beneath his arm. The freshly pressed red cravat, he tucked into his trouser pocket and, lastly, he put his top hat back upon his head. That Nolly was so attentive to Jack, watching him as he dressed, was a sign that he wanted Jack's birthday to go well, and that his plan to keep Jack safe was dear to his heart.

Jack did not want any of that to go wrong. So he dressed as quickly as he might, stockings and boots and waistcoat and all, though, as he put on his own top hat, his neck felt bare to the skin without the cravat to tie the collar closed. Still, nobody would be noticing him when he walked down the street, for all eyes would be on Nolly, as they should be.

"Shall we?" asked Jack, finally ready. "You mean to carry all of that? I could carry somethin'."

"That's all right, Jack. It's your birthday, so let me do this for you."

Nolly followed these words with another kiss that was meant to be brief, but that lingered on Jack's skin as they opened the door and began their path to the bathhouse that Nolly had picked out.

THE BATHHOUSE OLIVER HAD PICKED OUT WAS ON NEWGATE Street, just past the Old Bailey where, once again, a scaffold was being built. Jack looked as though he wanted to linger, to dwell in the smell of newly cut wood and the excitement of the crowd that had gathered.

Of course he might do exactly that, seeing as it was his birthday, but even as they paused at the corner to watch the crowds gather, Jack seemed to realize that Oliver did not want to stop, so he shook himself and kept walking at Oliver's side.

Jack bumped a friendly elbow when Oliver got too near to him on the pavement, but moved even closer when Oliver pulled away. There was a lively smirk on his mouth at the pleasure in this play, and he reached out from time to time to pet the smooth wool of the new jacket that was rolled up and tucked in the curve of Oliver's elbow.

"I could carry that a ways, y'know," said Jack, reaching for the bundle beneath Oliver's arm.

"I know," said Oliver, keeping the bundle close. "But we're arrived now, so there's nothing for you to carry."

Oliver stopped on the pavement in front of a modest two-story bathhouse that had nothing in common with the rag-tangle canvas and found-wood structure of the bathhouse just north of Smithfield Market. He had determined that the Smith-field bathhouse was not fine enough for Jack's birthday, and on the way back from the post office the day before had noted the location of this one.

The creamy hill stone of the building was cut into swags above the doorway, which was flanked on either side by modest carved columns. Above the door was the simple sign that said *Faulkner's Bath House* in dark green letters that were gilt in gold against a paler green background.

A gentleman was going into the bathhouse, taking off his hat as he crossed the threshold. As Oliver and Jack entered behind the gentleman, the foyer, which was covered in smooth, green-and-white checkerboard tiles, was quiet and cool and a welcome break from the busy street.

To each side of the foyer were sitting rooms, where several gentlemen tarried, reading newspapers or talking amongst themselves. Ahead, through a wide arched doorway, was a counter where two clerks were waiting on the gentleman who had entered ahead of them.

One of the clerks, noting Oliver and Jack's presence, beckoned for them to approach, and left his fellow to deal with the other customer. So, in spite of his hasty planning the day before, Oliver felt well pleased at the place he had picked out.

"Have you come for a bath, gentlemen?" asked the clerk. He seemed young and had a pretty face, though his clothing was plain, of dark wool, covered by a neck-to-floor apron. "One shilling hot or cold, with a plunge available for ninepence. Or we have our Turkish bath, if you'd rather, which is two and sixpence before five o'clock."

"An entire shilling for just a bath?" Jack asked, perhaps shocked that such a genteel activity would come so dear.

Jack dipped his head to look at Oliver while all about them swirled the scents of clean, hot water and flowery scented soap. Jack's voice was low and was obviously meant only for Oliver, but the clerk heard him just the same.

"We supply clean, hot water, sir, with fine Castile soap rather than lye. We also have thick, white towels of Egyptian cotton, and flannel washcloths, cleaned and heated in front of a fire, laundered after each use rather than being reused, as some bath-houses will do."

In such a place as this, the service would be quick and clever, and nobody would remark on the filth of the water after they'd gotten out of it. Or rather, after Jack had gotten out of it, since the amount Oliver had procured in advance of his next three weeks worth of salary was quickly dwindling down to nil.

He had only enough for Jack's bath and thruppence tip for the clerk, if he would take it. But this was not for Jack to know. Perhaps Oliver could distract Jack from the conversation that would surely come when Jack observed that Oliver was not also taking a bath.

"Very well," said Oliver, quite calmly, as if this had been his plan all along. "We'll have one bath, please. Hot water."

"Just the one, sir?" asked the clerk.

Oliver felt Jack looking at him askance, a sidelong glance with green eyes narrowed as Oliver handed over his last shilling and the three pennies.

"I ain't takin' one if you ain't," said Jack stoutly as the clerk began to write up the order. "But then—"

Jack sputtered to a stop, and Oliver could see him adding up the cost of the presents in his head. But perhaps Jack didn't seem to care that the bath was paid for with his own, stolen money, because he simply looked down and reached into his pocket to pull out another coin.

"Here. Here's another shillin'. We'll have two baths, if you please." The shilling made a clink as Jack placed it on the counter. "Ain't them baths side by side, in a place like this?"

"If you like, sir," said the clerk. He took Jack's shilling and placed it and Oliver's shilling in a drawer beneath the counter, and updated the order on a slip of paper, which he handed to Oliver. "Generally, the baths are all in one room, in keeping with Roman times, you see. But for two baths in one room, that's sixpence extra."

Oliver frowned. He didn't mean to show his distress, but his grand plan, paying for everything so Jack wouldn't have to, seemed ruined as Jack handed over a shiny sixpence. And now, as they were led down the side hallway to a room at the end, which the clerk opened for them as he bowed, Jack's mouth was in a tight line, as though he were still troubled by the high cost of the baths, which was not like him.

But neither of them spoke as the clerk pointed out the chairs for their garments, the hooks on the wall for their hats. Two servants, dressed much as the clerk, carried in eight-gallon buckets of steaming hot water and poured them into the two white porcelain tubs with claw feet that stood side by side on the green-and-white tile floor. The poshness of the place began to seem overwhelming, even though Oliver found the whole of it elegant and fine.

"We'll have more hot water brought in and, when the tubs are filled, there will be two buckets of cold for after." The clerk went to a side cupboard and brought out a tray of soaps for them to choose from. "Now, if the gentlemen care to pick their soaps?"

With some dignity, Jack picked up a bar of soap, sniffing at it as though he'd been doing this for years. Shaking his head, he handed the soap to Oliver, who had to move aside to let the servants pass by him, though he managed to take the soap without dropping it, and sniffed at it. It smelled a little flowery for his taste, and the clerk smiled.

"Perhaps the young gentleman would like to try the sandal-wood, as it's far from overpowering and very popular." The clerk held the tray in one hand and pointed at the slightly yellow bar of soap in the corner of the tray. "Very popular," the clerk said again.

Oliver put the bar of soap he was holding back on the tray, his arm quivering a bit in an effort not to drop the bundle of Jack's clothes, and watched as Jack sniffed at the sandalwood soap and nodded.

"Yes, this one," said Jack in posh tones meant to mock,

though the clerk didn't seem to notice this at all, as though a gentleman who could afford a shilling for a bath at a moment's notice was allowed to speak in whatever tones he liked. "Here, Nolly, try this one."

Oliver took the bar that Jack was offering. It smelled like flowers and something else that reminded him of a grassy field in summertime.

"That's clove soap, sir," said the clerk. "A very discriminating scent, if I do say so."

Oliver nodded and watched as the clerk placed each bar of soap in the metal tray over each tub.

Water was still being carried in and poured into the tubs by the quick-footed servants, with towels being laid over the backs of wooden chairs. Finally, two buckets of cold water were placed by each tub by a thin serving lad.

As the servants and the clerk left for the last time, Jack moved quickly to lock the door behind them and turned around with his back to the door.

"We're flyin' a bit high, eh?" Jack said this statement plainly, pausing as he hung his jacket on a hook on the wall. Then he moved quickly, taking the bundle from Oliver's arms and placed it on the chair beneath the hook. Close now, he put his hands on Oliver's face. Jack's eyes were green and, the sparks having dimmed, he seemed almost sleepy-eyed as he kissed Oliver on the mouth. "You did all this for me."

"Yes, Jack," said Oliver, somewhat breathless, thinking that perhaps Jack's birthday wouldn't be ruined if Oliver could get over the fact that Jack had to pay for part of it. "I wanted it all to be a surprise, you see."

"And you did, dear heart. Come now, take off your things, an' let us bathe like posh gentlemen do."

Jack took off Oliver's hat, and petted his hair smooth, and tugged at Oliver's jacket until Oliver realized that Jack was not overwhelmed by where they were, but only wanted to enjoy what Oliver's plan had wrought. Quickly, they undressed in the warm, sweet-smelling room, with Oliver taking command of folding or hanging their garments while Jack stood with his arms crossed over his chest, watching, his hip cocked in an insouciant manner.

Finally, Oliver was done with his arrangements and turned to see Jack standing thus, in a state of nature, his skin pale where his garments hid it from the sun. His muscles sleek beneath that skin, tufts of dark hair beneath his arms, his private hair bundled thickly around his sweetly relaxed pink cock.

Jack smiled, a slow, lascivious grin that had a hint of sweetness about it, which made Oliver go to him, almost without thought, to place his hands on Jack's hands and draw them away from his body so he could admire Jack while Jack admired him in return.

There they stood, naked together, their hips almost touching, and Oliver felt a rush of pleasure in his groin. Jack smiled even broader now, and Oliver smiled in return at the sight of them in the altogether in a bathhouse on Newgate Street in the middle of a spring day, with nobody to frown at them, or to cast judgment.

"In we get," said Jack. "Which fancy tub's mine, oh, the one with the white soap; yours has got the cream-colored one."

Sliding into a white, claw-footed tub in a brightly lit room with the warm water steaming all round him was its own sort of bliss. That Jack was close at hand only added to that, while Jack's sputters as he pretended to be annoyed at the heat and texture of the water made Oliver laugh, and he felt a sense of contentment return to him.

He allowed himself to sink low in the tub till his chin was underwater, and only the round, pink moons of his knees broke the surface. It might be nice to fall asleep like this, to soak and soak until he vanished forever into the warmth. But of course he must look over at Jack, at the damp spikes of Jack's dark hair that stuck up on his head, the flush on Jack's cheeks from the hot water, the green glint of his eyes, the pleasure in them.

Oliver refrained from making a jest of it, that Jack's aversion to bathing might forever be laid to rest, and wasn't Oliver right about this? Because now, in this moment between them, the world of London—the stirring streets, and the fast-dashing cabs, the clonk of horse hooves, and the smell of the gutters, of the river itself—all of that floated far, far away.

Contented, Oliver scooted forward in the tub and picked up the flannel washing cloth and the clove-scented soap and began to bathe in earnest. After a moment, Jack followed suit. The only sounds that could be heard were the lapping of the water and the damp movements of bathing, while overhead the reflection of the moving water bounced white and silver against the walls. Once in a while there came a shuddery sigh from Jack, as though he were becoming acclimated to the pleasure of it.

After a time, after Oliver had washed his hair and all the rest of him, he submerged himself and rinsed his hair. Then he broke through the surface of the water to relax his back against the curve of the tub.

He soaked as he took in the very fine surroundings, the clean white walls, the sweet smell of soap, and the high ceiling that showed not a single spot of dampness or rot. He propped his arms along the edge of the tub and, with some ease, turned his eyes toward Jack, whose body echoed Oliver's in the pose of relaxation, though he noted that Jack had not yet washed his hair.

Getting out of the tub without a single regret, Oliver took a towel and buffed himself dry, quite pleased to be in this state with his skin clean all over. Feeling a bit frisky, he wrapped the towel around his middle and folded a knot to keep it secure.

Drawing a short green-painted stool over to the head of Jack's tub, Oliver ignored Jack's look of puzzlement. Instead, he reached for the white bar of soap, taking it from the broad grid that went across the tub at the far end, near Jack's mostly submerged toes.

"What're you about, Nolly?" asked Jack, his voice somewhat clogged from the damp.

"I'm going to wash your hair, I should think," said Oliver, leaning forward to kiss Jack's temple. The towel felt rough against his naked groin and made him shiver a bit. "Unless you object."

"I should say not," said Jack, and he ducked his chin so Oliver could get at him.

Which Oliver did. He soaped up Jack's hair and ran his fingers through the dark, slippery locks, but gently. He used the pads of his fingers to get the suds everywhere, after which he used a small dish to ladle warm bathwater over Jack's head.

"Stand up, and I'll rinse you off properly," said Oliver.

Nodding, Jack stood up. As Oliver lifted the bucket and poured, the warm bathwater rushed off Jack's body in slow, thick ribbons, following the jut of his hip, tracing the line of his back, the broad muscles in his thighs.

For a moment, Oliver paused with the bucket in his hands and gazed with contentment at Jack's wet skin, sighing a small sigh that he would have thought so quiet that Jack could not have noticed. But notice Jack did, and his eyes turned Oliver's way.

"Like what you see, eh?" asked Jack with a wink and a smile.

"Yes," said Oliver. It barely came out a whisper, so he swallowed and tried again, this time in a more businesslike manner. Otherwise, their ablutions would take much longer than the time the room had been rented for.

"It'll take a dash of cold to get all the soap out," said Oliver. "Then you can rinse my hair afterwards."

"G'on an' pour. I'll stand as still as a mountain."

Jack tipped his head down again. Oliver lifted the bucket over Jack's head and slowly poured the cold water, focusing on Jack's hair, not wanting to torment Jack more than he needed with the cold-water rinse. Jack shivered, but he didn't try to move away, though his chin tightened, as though he didn't want to squeal at the cold.

When the last of the soap was gone from Jack's skin, and the bucket was empty, Oliver put the one bucket aside and picked up the other one.

"Will you rinse me now, Jack?" Oliver asked.

"Take off that towel an' get in with me, an' I will."

The question moved across Oliver's skin as though warm hands were embracing him, a shimmy of pleasure bestirring his belly, quickening the flesh between his legs. Unfolding the knot on the white towel about his waist, Oliver let it drop to the floor. Then, naked once more, he handed Jack the bucket, and got into the tub with Jack.

They were both knee deep in lukewarm water. Oliver stood close and lifted his chin for a kiss, which Jack gave him, slow and soft and wet, his fingers tracing the line of Oliver's jaw.

"It'll be cold," said Jack, low, keeping his voice between their bodies.

"I know it," said Oliver. "Just pour."

Jack lifted the bucket over Oliver's head and poured the cold water, which rushed over Oliver like the icy slant of a winter's rain, shocking his whole skin into awareness as it traced every part of him. But he couldn't shriek or complain, for Jack had not, so he wouldn't.

Finally, when Jack bent to put the bucket on the floor, Oliver clasped Jack about the waist and pulled him upright, held him close. They stood there in the fast-cooling water, chest to chest, hip to hip, the scratch of Jack's private hair creating a warm pulse within Oliver, making his blood run fast and hot beneath his skin.

For a moment, the closeness, the damp, the warmth of Jack's skin against the coolness of his own, rippled the pleasure inside of him, and he kissed Jack again, petting his back with long, slow pets.

"Bathin' ain't so bad," said Jack, cupping the curve of Oliver's bottom with both hands. "Long as you're with me."

"We'll do it this way always," said Oliver. "Even if it does cost dear."

"Dear it is, an' posh, as well, though don't it occur to you to wonder why there's a general room of tubs, an' then one like this with only two?"

"For the gentlemen who like to converse while bathing?" Oliver shrugged. It hadn't occurred to him, but more, what did it matter?

"Could be," said Jack.

The water was becoming too cold to enjoy, and Oliver could see Jack's skin prickling into goosebumps, so Oliver got out and pulled Jack after him. Lifting up a clean, warm towel from the rack, Oliver gently rubbed Jack's hair, which dried to silky, dark strands.

With even more care, he dried Jack's body, moving slowly over damp lengths of skin, staying no longer in one place than another, but drawing out the whole of it. Taking it slow, making it last, thinking of how it had been in the beginning, when he could barely think of taking his clothes off when Jack was near, and how it was now between them, when he could barely stand to put them back on.

"Hey?"

Oliver looked up from where he was kneeling at Jack's feet and patted Jack's ankles.

"You look mighty fine from any angle," said Jack, smiling, his eyes soft. "But I'd rather you were up here w'me, than down there."

As Jack reached out his hands, Oliver took them and let the towel fall where it might. Then Jack pulled him close, and the warmth of their bodies joined, keeping away the cold. Oliver buried his face in Jack's neck, kissing the curve of it, inhaling the scent of Jack's skin, clean from the soap and warm from his heartbeat.

"Goin' to stop now," said Jack. "Rather than take you on the floor of a gentleman's bathhouse, I think."

Oliver laughed against Jack's skin and kissed his neck one last time before pulling back.

"We should get dressed," said Oliver

"In my new togs," said Jack in reply, his smile broad. "M'birthday suit," he said now, laughing outright. "Get it? My *birthday* suit?"

"Yes, Jack, very amusing." Oliver attempted to be gruff, but the pun was a good one, and he could not help but smile as he tugged Jack over to the pile of clothes and began to help him dress.

5

JACK'S BIRTHDAY AFTERNOON

It was not precisely that Jack felt as though he were Nolly's favorite doll being dressed and tended to, but the truth of it was that he was. He would have felt more the fool had Nolly not been so intent on getting Jack dressed precisely so.

Nolly was standing in his underdrawers with a serious expression that darkened his brow. A dapple of sweat had curled his forelock dark gold on his forehead, for the bathing room was quite warm and damp, with the bathwater in the two claw-footed tubs only barely cooled down and the crown glass window only partially opened.

"Could we get a window goin' a bit more, Nolly?" Jack asked as he stood there in his underdrawers and stockings, with Nolly holding out his trousers for him to step into.

"Yes, yes," said Nolly. He hastened over to the window, turned the white iron latch, and pushed the window open wider. "There's a bit of a breeze, will that do?"

"Better," said Jack.

Truth be told, although he was sweaty beneath his arms and along the backs of his knees, the pleasure in Nolly's face as he helped Jack into his trousers, and drew up the crisp white shirt, and pulled it onto Jack's arms, was a treat all on its own. As was the intensity of Nolly's study of him when the silky blue waist-coat went on, and the buttons were done with Nolly's nimble fingers. And the kiss he got as Nolly drew the red cravat around Jack's neck, tying it briskly and not making it overly tight, as someone else might have done.

The dark blue jacket was the last touch, and though Jack was truly warm with it on, he spread his arms out so Nolly might better admire him.

"Eh?" asked Jack.

"You *are* fine, Jack," said Nolly, smiling slow. "And handsome, as well. I'm half a mind not to let anybody else have a look at you, the way you are now. Such a treat for my eyes."

"Can't keep me in a box, Nolly," replied Jack, teasing.

"And I shouldn't want to," said Nolly, solemnly. "But I am loath to return to the Three Cripples, with you looking so dashing—"

But Nolly stopped there, though Jack knew what he was thinking, that with Jack dressed so fine, those at the tavern would only make fun of him or draw him into a game of cards, causing him to doff his hat and jacket and pull his cravat loose. And while this was not unheard of as a sensible course of action, and might do very well later, it was too early for that. Besides, today was his birthday, and he meant to share it with Nolly and Nolly alone.

"We'll walk a bit, shall we?" asked Jack. He'd thought to suggest going down by the river, but this time of year, whether at high tide or low, the stench would be thick in the air and would make any activity unpleasant. "Why don't we take a cab up to Regent's Park?"

"But Jack—"

"Ain't we posh enough?" asked Jack. "Once we get you dressed, the both of us will shine so brightly they'll let us in, sure enough."

"I've not any coin for that."

"Never you mind, Nolly-me-lad," said Jack. He reached into

the pocket of his trousers and jingled the coin there. "What's mine is yours an' back again, d'you see? An' besides, I ain't never did get you nothin' for your birthday."

"You weren't even in England then."

Nolly had a scowl on his face, and whether he was thinking of their first quarrel, or the cold weather that had brought about old Brownlow's unhappy demise, Jack could not entirely be sure. Only that the situation must be rectified and at such a brisk pace that Nolly would have no time to argue with him. For never was there a lad more likely to want to turn a day sour, even when it was fine.

"I'll have you know that since today's my birthday, as was happily announced by you, I shall do whatever I please, an' that is to fetch us a cab an' take you w'me to Regent's Park."

There was nothing Nolly could do but agree to this, and Jack sealed the deal with several sweet kisses, almost pressing Nolly against the cool, white walls before remembering how very close and warm it was. He let Nolly alone to get dressed while he put on his boots and hat, and waited while Nolly fussed with his cravat until, finally, he pushed Nolly's hands away to do up the green silk himself.

Jack watched while Nolly rolled up Jack's older shirt inside the more careworn blue jacket. He tucked the bundle beneath one arm, where he obviously meant to carry it, in spite of the fact that Jack could acquire anything he might want at a moment's notice.

"Just leave it, Nolly," said Jack.

"What? What do you mean, just leave this here?"

"Yes," said Jack. He tugged the bundle from Nolly's arms and placed it on the chair. "They can sell these or trade them or mayhap some young gentleman will be in need of it after a bath. But there's no need for you to trundle it about all day, not on my birthday, anyhow."

"Well, if you're quite sure—"

Jack silenced him with a kiss, petting Nolly's arms to keep

him from picking up the bundle again. With the outing they were about to partake of, he did not want Nolly being burdened with anything.

"I'm sure," said Jack, and waited until Nolly gave him a nod.

When Jack opened the door to the hallway, there was a lovely breeze coming in from somewhere that he could not see. They nodded to the attendants as they went up the hall and out into Newgate Street, where Jack hailed a cab using the gesture he'd seen many a fine gentleman use. And, since they were both clean from the bath and dressed in their best outfits, the cab was soon in coming.

As they pulled themselves inside, the cab started off with the crack of the driver's whip and a jerk of the harness. Jack had a terrible moment where he thought he might be quickly sick all over his new jacket and Nolly, too. But the cab smoothed out into a slow trot, and the streets of London, while bumpy, uneven, and dusty, weren't gone at with the pace of six horses pulling a country coach being driven to beat time itself.

The pace of the cab was brisk but gentle and, with a sigh, Jack settled back against the stiff, black-leather seat. He watched Newgate Prison go by on one side and the lane that led to Saffron Hill on the other, before turning to watch Nolly. Who, being the sturdy lad he was, had no trouble with the movement of the cab, and who was watching Jack in return, a rare, broad smile on his face.

"You have the best ideas, you know," said Nolly. "I thought you were mad to suggest it, but it's quite fine, quite fine to take a little journey like this."

"Sit back a little," said Jack.

The coach turned up the wide avenue of Grey's Inn Lane, where the shops were done up with rich, dark drapes and bright flower bins of decoration. As well, the townhouses were of the expensive variety, with their polished and gleaming white and gray marble steps and thin, elegant pane glass windows, and everything looked quite civilized.

Jack took his top hat off and held it in front of the open window of the cab on Nolly's side. Then he leaned forward slowly, giving Nolly all the time in the world to refuse him a kiss.

But Nolly did not refuse, and though they were in plain sight, in the middle of London, amidst all the well-to-do folk who would surely tear them apart at the slightest indication that they were two lads who loved each other and not anybody else, Jack half-closed his eyes and kissed Nolly.

Their mouths met feathery soft together, making Jack shiver with the pleasure of it, the sheer wickedness of it. And all of this with Nolly responding in kind, his eyes fully closed, trusting Jack implicitly to keep watch. Nolly's long lashes fanned his cheeks, and there was a faint, indrawn breath as Nolly pushed into the kiss, his mouth against Jack's, tender and enticing.

Then Jack felt Nolly's tongue on his lips, and all at once the blood rushed to Jack's cock. He had to sit back and traced Nolly's cheek with his hand to let him know there was nothing in the drawing back other than what it was.

"You do me in, you do," said Jack as he put his hat back on.

He watched Nolly smile with a twinkle in his eyes that told Jack what he needed to know. That Nolly knew how much Jack loved him and wasn't afraid to show it back. Then, to take it a little bit further, Nolly ran his hand up Jack's thigh, cupping between Jack's legs to give Jack's cock a quick pet just to mess with Jack, to make it amusing, because he could, because they were together in the heart of London with a bright, shiny day all around them as the cab clicked its way along to Regent's Park.

When the cab stopped, Nolly and Jack alighted onto the smooth pavement along the edge of the park. After Jack paid an extra shilling as a tip, the cab picked up a lone gentleman heading the other direction and clopped away at the same steady pace.

As they turned to face the park, the avenue of dark, green and leafy trees and long strips of sun-bright flowers of every hue were spread out before them. Between the trees and on either side of the middle strip of trimmed grass were two walkways lined with fine gravel.

Those avenues, which stretched up ahead for what seemed a great distance, were so staid and dignified, with quiet couples walking arm in arm, or the single soldier walking slowly with his cane, that suddenly Jack couldn't see the pleasure in this at all, and determined that he'd made a dreadful mistake.

But, beside him, Nolly stood riveted, his face soft, his eyes wide.

"Oh, Jack, this is *splendid*."

Jack had allowed himself to forget, which was understandable, what with one thing and another, how Nolly liked the country. Liked trees and green things growing, the gentle civility of a long bed of bright flowers, none of which were forget-me-nots, blue or otherwise, or anything Jack could recognize.

He looked at the park and, in that moment, saw it through Nolly's eyes, saw the polite, gentle forest that they might stroll through, just walking, not having to keep a sharp eye out, not working to pick pockets, not in a hurry to get anywhere, merely walking.

Green-leafed trees of every type reached tall and lush into a crystal blue sky. The air, while warm and still, had a freshness about it, sweet with the scent of sun-warmed petals and lively with the dense, green undercurrent of fir trees filling the breeze. The bite of coal dust and ash from fires, the sludge of the river, the open ditches and sewers that were everywhere on Saffron Hill—all of those were far away.

Nolly was close and looked at Jack, eyes bright, his smile broad and fond all at once. Taking off his top hat and blinking rather quickly, Nolly carded through his hair with his fingers, then put the hat back on.

"This is the finest birthday present, Jack, thank you."

"Ain't nothin' but a garden," said Jack, feeling his cheeks grow hot with the praise, so open and unguarded as it was.

"You know that's not true," said Nolly, moving close. He

brought his hand up to stroke Jack's lapel, an action that might be taken as very ordinary, if it weren't for the tender affection with which the action was done. Then Nolly, taking a quick look about them, linked his arm through Jack's, as Jack had sometimes wanted to do and, tipping his head to one side, nodded at Jack. "Let us walk together, like this."

Jack felt his eyebrows rise high in his forehead. Sodomites got hung, pure and simple, so he planted his feet and tried to pull away.

"I've seen it done," said Nolly with some firmness, his hand hooking through Jack's elbow so he could not escape. "I've seen pairs of soldiers walking arm in arm, or two ladies, and they are only taken as friends. In such a place, it is quite done in this way."

"Are you quite, *quite* sure?"

Jack scanned the row of trees and the wide grassy area to the left, and looked onward to the bit of a hill upon which more trees grew, green and lush, rising up as if to hide their own secrets. There wasn't much of anybody about, so perhaps Nolly was right that nobody would care.

So, with a little nod, Jack re-linked their arms and made himself settle at Nolly's side as they began strolling, as gentlemen did, up the gravel path. It only took a few slow strides for Jack to relax, and Nolly as well, from his former tenseness, which told Jack that he'd not been as assured as he'd seemed.

It turned out well that they'd settled together about walking arm-in-arm in spite of their fears, for coming towards them were two ladies, brightly dressed for the warm spring day. The yellow and pink ribbons that tied their straw bonnets were turning slowly in the breeze, and their pale, flower-sprigged skirts ballooned out before them as they walked. Their arms were also linked, their pale-gloved hands trailing over each other's arms, their bonnets turned toward each other as they shared a confidence and giggled, as small girls might.

One of the women noticed Nolly and Jack walking together,

and though each pair was unknown to the other, the lady nodded at Nolly. Her bonnet brim hid her eyes and shaded her face, but the nod seemed kind.

Nolly tipped his hat in return, and the two women walked on by Nolly and Jack, and nothing was said. No shout was given, no constables called for.

Coming along behind the pair of women was a group of four gentlemen in sensible frock coats, their dark top hats shading them from the sun as they walked two-by-two. They strolled in and out of the shadows of the row of trees, making no comment while they passed Nolly and Jack on the left. Thusly, Nolly and Jack walked onward, arm-in-arm, with Jack very contented to be so as the gentlemen's strides carried them onward out of the park.

At a point, a faint footpath cut off to the left. Nolly tugged and Jack followed, ducking between the dark trees to the open, grassy area where, as it was more in the open than the row of trees, Nolly dropped Jack's arm.

"I believe there is a smaller garden over that hillock there," said Nolly, pointing. "And beyond that is a curved lake where the birds gather to feed. I don't know much of anything about birds, but it's always pleasant to watch them settle on the water."

Jack nodded, and so they crossed the grass on the faint path. In the warmth of the bare sun, Jack wanted to pull at his cravat and collar, but didn't, not wanting to disturb Nolly's arrangement of him.

Though later, with the mood Nolly was building between them, Jack knew he might un-arrange himself and Nolly both when at last they returned to the tavern. But for now, Jack followed Nolly through a gap in the shrubbery until they were on a circular avenue, again of fine gravel and bordered by lush green trees.

In the center of the curve of the gravel was a large, square garden of newly turned earth. The young green plants were being tended to by well-dressed gardeners, their sleeves held back by bands about their forearms, their canvas aprons tied tidily about their waists.

They bent over long, low boxes of flowers, or small, thin trees, raking the dark earth, pulling out weeds, almost whispering as they bent over the tiny, budding growing things that were speckled with color and shades of pale green.

This was pleasant enough, but Nolly kept going, leading Jack around the curved path until the watery shore of the lake came into view. It was easy to see why this was where Nolly had been headed, for there, along the smooth blue surface, a small flock of birds was winging in to land, scattering the water with their broad, fluttery wings, filling the air with their bird cries.

"Those are herons," said Nolly, moving forward to watch.

"Thought you didn't know birds," said Jack, joining him, pulling Nolly back from the damp, waterlogged shore along the reed-bed when he was about to fall in. There was a pleasant full smell of mud and still, green-flecked water beneath their boots.

"Those are herons, sure enough," said Nolly, his eyes fixing on them.

From along the bank, a young couple stood arm-in-arm, and they were also watching the birds with some pleasure.

"Yes," said the young man as he tipped his hat at them. "Yes, indeed. Gray herons; you can tell by the color of their wings."

The young lady didn't say anything, but smiled at her lad, her arm twined with his, and they looked very happy together, standing in the sunshine.

Jack envied the couple for their casual boldness. Though he shouldn't be too jealous, for while he and Nolly might not kiss, not out in the open, nor could they stand arm-in-arm, they could stand as they were, close together, without having to hide the friendship between them.

He heard Nolly sigh, and turned to look at Nolly's happy face, his absorption in the birds, his pleasure in the blue of the water beneath the shining sun. The fresh air twirled the hair on

Nolly's forehead, where it curled out beneath the brim of his top hat.

When Nolly looked at Jack, his smile brightened. Jack vowed to nevermore forget that such an outing, with fresh air and abundant green-growth all around, was what brought good color to Nolly's cheeks, what relaxed the slope of his shoulders, and what made it seem as though Nolly wanted to reach out for Jack with each breath. How on earth could he forget something as wonderful as this?

Just then, sloping low over their heads, another heron came to land to be with its own kind. The bird's white face and dark eyes were sharp against the blue sky, and its beak could be seen up close, glowing orange and hollow in the sunlight.

The spread of its wings, like a soft cloak of new gray velvet, fluttered so near that Jack could almost reach out and touch them. Could feel the whisper-trail that the heron's wings left in the air.

Nolly took off his top hat and followed the bird with his eyes, mouth open, transfixed.

"Did you see how close it came as it flew by, Jack? Did you see?"

Nolly's attention returned to Jack once more, and Jack felt the flush of it. Had there been a bower or a bood hour nearby, he would have attended to Nolly in a moment. But he stayed himself from saying or doing anything, here in this public place with the kind couple nearby and who-knew-who-else coming through the shrubbery or up the path.

But Nolly, who sometimes surprised Jack by being more observant of his surroundings rather than less, at least of late, stepped closer to Jack. And, seemingly by accident, he bumped into Jack's arm, then ran his hand up and down Jack's jacket sleeve, as if to soothe his jostled friend. But the look in his eyes said something different; there was a quiet acceptance of the desire Jack felt, which was met and matched Nolly's desire.

"Shall we walk around the lake, Jack?" asked Nolly, with pleasure in his eyes.

"'Tis quite far going on that side of the lake," said the young man. "But there's a path that goes on this side of the water, do you see?"

Jack turned his head to look where the young man was gesturing. A slender path skirted the reed-bed and wended along beneath the shadow of broad-limbed trees.

"Goes past the villa, that does," said the young man with a nod.

"Shall we?" asked Nolly.

Nolly looked as though he wanted to hold out his elbow for Jack to take so they might walk along, arm-in-arm as they had before. But they had an audience yet present, and Jack didn't feel so readily able to pretend the gesture was something else other than what it was. He gave his head a slight shake and then nodded, as if only now he was answering Nolly's question.

"Thank you," said Nolly to the young gentleman and his ladyfriend, and tipped his hat to both of them.

Jack did the same and then tugged on Nolly's shirt cuff to get his attention. He wanted Nolly to come along so they might walk beside the water and beneath the shade-trees, by themselves for a moment, so that, at the very least, they might exchange a kiss or two and share silent promises for later.

But as they began to walk, a stern-looking governess came toward them, pushing a wide-wheeled pram and dragging two charges behind her.

There wasn't enough room for everybody on the narrow path, so Jack's hopes were dashed. And Nolly's as well; he had begun to scowl again, at the governess in particular, and the children in general, though being well-dressed and tended to, they could hardly be at fault. Jack blamed the governess, who should have known better than to take a pram on what was merely a track in the grass.

Nolly and Jack went wide toward the shoreline. They hustled

past the little group and, by the time they got to the other side, were well out of the shade, and arrived at the edge of a glade, next to a white-columned house that Jack surmised was the villa the young man had spoken of earlier.

The villa was tall and narrow, with fluted marble columns holding up the tall gables in the front. Scattered across the villa's broad, sloping lawn were young ladies with their wide, pale dresses tied back with smocks, all standing with paint brushes in their hands in front of thinly wrought stands. Having not known that ladies could paint at all, let alone that such well-to-do ones were allowed, made Jack slow down, Nolly at his heels, to take a better look.

The paintings in front of each of the young ladies were all done in pale colors, and were washed with more pale colors, till hardly anything could be seen but an ink outline of the villa. In fact, almost the exact same image was reflected on each canvas, as if, led by their instructor, the young ladies could see nothing else.

Even Nolly shook his head, and Jack surmised he was comparing this bit of art with anything he might have seen in a museum, for it was a done-for conclusion that Nolly had been in one, though Jack never had.

Maybe they should one day. If such an outing as today, so simple and so spur to the moment, did Nolly this much good, then maybe another outing, one with more planning behind it, would do him even better. And Jack as well, for why should he work with his nose to the grindstone every day? Why should anybody?

As they walked back along the path, they cut across the grass and went through more shrubbery to get on the curved path that Jack could see would take them out of the park. Along the way was a little stone footbridge that took them across the narrow end of the lake. It was there Nolly stopped and turned around.

Jack stopped as well to see what Nolly was looking at, which turned out to be the view back along the lake, which was narrow at this end and flanked by green trees, some of which trailed their branches in the water in a way pleasant to the eye.

From this far away, the canvases of the young lady painters looked like pale winter leaves. And, as well, there was the villa, white against the green lawn, with the sun-speckled trees coming up behind it like a verdant and golden frame.

"That's lovely, that is," said Jack, waiting a moment to see what Nolly might want to add to this observation.

Nolly turned from where he was propped up with his hands on the stone sides of the bridge and leaned back against it. He looked straight at Jack, his blue eyes steady, a lovely pink flush to his cheeks, as if a silent kiss waited for Jack when the moment presented itself.

"*You* are what is lovely, Jack," said Nolly, not low at all, but instead, because there was nobody about, in a bright, clear voice. "You are what is loveliest of this day."

It was hardly anything to be taken aback by, as it was a sentiment truly spoken, but so rare, so out loud as it was, without being hindered by anybody that might be near, sent a sweet freshet of wind through Jack's heart.

From somewhere long ago, an inauspicious beginning, as Nolly might have put it, they had come to here, to this moment. Where Nolly had planned a day for Jack's birthday and, with only a slight grumble, had let Jack take the reins to direct them both here, and then to announce his pleasure in it, well.

It did overwhelm Jack a little; he did not know what to say. But never mind that, not when his dearest lad, his Nolly, had moved a bit closer and stole a kiss from Jack, right there in the open.

"I shall take you to a country-like place whenever you ask it, Nolly," said Jack, breathless.

Smiling, Nolly tweaked Jack's cravat and tipped his head in the direction of the path to indicate that they should keep walking. This they did, following the path to the main gravel avenue that led them out of the park. They paused just outside the gate and looked at the street traffic and the carts and the carriages passing by.

"Should we get a bite to eat, or take a cab straight back to the tavern?" asked Nolly.

"A bite, I should think, as there might be plenty of places nearby, even if we have to stand in the street and eat," said Jack.

"Yes, Jack," said Nolly, his lips curling in a smile. "All of this has given me an appetite."

"Now that's the Nolly I know," said Jack. "There's a place. There along that street, across the way, with the bit of a sign that you can just see behind the trees."

Nolly nodded and, with their shoulders close, their hands bumping together from time to time, they crossed the street to the little restaurant. Jack jingled the coins in his pocket, but he had plenty of cash, and if it turned out that he did not, well, he could easily pick up more. Anything for Nolly, anything at all.

WITH THEIR BELLIES FULL, JACK HAILED A CAB AND DIRECTED the driver to High Holborn, which was as close as a reputable cab would take them to home. Their return to the Three Cripples came unannounced, as no one but Nolly knew it had been his birthday, but Jack preferred it that way. For none of Noah's lads, let alone Noah himself, would have wanted to be seen to be so gentle as to greet Jack kindly on such a day, a day that had always come and gone every year without even the slightest indication as to what it meant.

Besides, such a celebration as the one he and Nolly had shared would have been seen as being soft and far too foolish for men such as them. But though it was soft, and felt that way to Jack, even as he followed Nolly along the bar where they might get a few pints of beer to soothe their dry throats, he liked it, and was liking it, just the same.

That part of Nolly, the soft, tender part, was only for Jack. As

Nolly showed it to nobody else, Jack was loath to put his dear boy up for any sort of ridicule whatsoever. To do that would be to close Nolly off, and Jack found he wanted more of that softness, of the gentleness that could be had between them, which anybody in the tavern might scoff at and mock Nolly for. Thus, never from Jack's lips would he remark upon it.

"It's been Jack's birthday today," said Nolly, brightly and directly to Len, who stood behind the bar, and to the girls who, in a slatternly way with their hair done up untidily behind, were lollygagging and leaning on their elbows where they might, seeing as how Noah was nowhere about. "He's got a new deck of cards that are clean and unmarked, and would like to get a game, so who's in?"

"*Nolly!*" Jack's jaw dropped at this, astounded, for he thought the day had been a private thing between them. "What'd you have to go an' say that for?"

"Because it's true," said Nolly, pert and unconcerned at this sudden divulgence.

"I should watch the bar," said Len, looking at Jack. "But clean cards so the boss can't cheat? I've got coin to bet with."

"Go and fetch them, Jack," said Nolly, somewhat bossily. "Go and get your cards, and I shall take Len's shift. As it's grown so hot and still, it's likely to be not very busy, anyway. Go on, now, Jack, and I'll keep you plied with beer."

And this rather than any slyness about it, for in Nolly's mind, Jack wanted a game of cards with his new deck, and Nolly had made it happen. Which might not be a bad thing, for Jack could play and win a few hands and show off a bit for Nolly. He might even be able to convince Nolly to sit beside him a moment or two, for it was his birthday, and that was what Jack wanted.

"Can do," said Len. "I'll fetch Nick and the boys. Are we up for whist or what?"

"Depends on how many," said Jack. He watched as Nolly doffed his hat and his jacket, and took Len's apron and tied it about his middle. The apron string was white against the taut line of his gray waistcoat and was quite distracting. "Are you sure, Nolly? Don't seem as though it'd be very amusin' for you."

"I'll get to watch you having a good time, beating the smalls off of Noah," said Nolly, ducking his chin to hide his smile. "He won't see it coming, so run and fetch your new cards, and Len, tell the boys not to say anything to Noah."

"You are a wicked lad, Nolly," Jack said over his shoulder as he raced up the stairs to their room.

It was baking hot at the end of the day, so he propped open the casement window, grabbed his cards from the drawer, and raced down the stairs again. Len and Nick had already called two other lads, and they and Noah were assembled at the round table beneath the window, so that would make six.

"We should play five-card loo," said Jack as he came over to them. He pulled the cards out of their tin case and hid the case in his trouser pocket, lest Noah find out how new the cards were. "We've enough for tricks an' trumps, ain't we? An' if we play with pennies, it'll be more for amusement, lest someone lose all out."

Jack said this as if it were he himself who might lose, rather than Noah. But the lads' grins were sly, and Len leaned down to where Noah was already scooting in his chair to whisper something into the boss's ear.

"Ah, so it's your birthday, is it, Jack?" asked Noah a little too brightly. "Finally let go of your mother's tit, have you?"

This was not amusing, but lest a fight break out between Nolly and Noah, Jack gave a short bark of laughter and started shifting the cards in one hand. Then, as he sat down, he spread the cards on the table and did a bit of cutting and shuffling.

Nolly came by, unannounced, and took Jack's hat off his head, and motioned that Jack should hand over his jacket. Jack did this, and still Nolly waited, while all around the table the snickers started, but with good humor, for nobody besides Noah knew how it truly was between them.

"And the cravat, Jack," said Nolly. "You'll get beer on it, else."

Untying the cravat with one hand, Jack pulled the length of red silk from around his neck, then unbuttoned the collar, and rolled up his sleeves while he was at it. As he handed the cravat to Nolly, Nolly gave him a kiss with his eyes and strolled off, as a waiter might who has just had a tip from an advantageous table.

Noah stuck out his leg so Nolly might trip over it, but Nolly merely moved nimbly aside it and kept going to the bar. There, he took up serving customers and wiping down beer slops, pursing his lips as though he were whistling under his breath, almost unaware of it.

With a last, fond smile at Nolly, Jack turned his attention back to the table and dealt the cards.

"I'm dealin' out, lads, so put your pennies in the pool."

"Pennies?" asked Noah, astounded even before the game had fully begun.

"What, can't afford it?" asked Jack with some humor.

Around the table, Noah's men laughed, but Jack could see it in their eyes that they were ready for the huge joke to be played on Noah. For the cards, new and crisp, could have come from anybody's hand, as Noah had no idea who they belonged to. Yet.

"I can, of that you can be sure," Noah sputtered, and shook his head to examine the cards as he gathered them up from the tabletop.

"Be ready, gents," said Jack, cutting through the cards once more to place them in a pile at his side. "Be ready, an' I'm stakin' sixpence to the pool. Ante up or you can't play. Len, you're up. Abandon or play?"

The game started in earnest, and Jack smiled. As he examined his cards, he thought about his pipe and how nice a smoke would be. He pretended to be quite concerned about his hand, but he had the Pam card, so the game was nearly in the pocket, that is, if he could string Noah along and pretend he didn't have it.

"Come on, Len, it's not got to take you that bloody long, eh?"

Jack jabbed Len with his elbow and then looked up to where

Nolly was carrying a tray of pint pots, pale yellow foam slopping over as he steadied the tray on the edge of the table.

Silently and briskly, Nolly handed out the pots. The lads grunted, but never said thank you. Jack did, but with his eyes only, and it was a smile that felt as though it came from within.

Money couldn't buy the kind of affection that was there in Nolly's face, in his actions, the arch of his neck, proud that he could give Jack this. As Nolly walked away in the direction of the bar, Jack admired Nolly's backside and vowed to make it up to him until he had Nolly moaning into his pillow. But later, after the game.

6

WATCHING JACK PLAY AT CARDS

The heat of the day did not cool by very much, but instead kept up an oppressive weight that could have made the evening unpleasant to be indoors. Oliver propped open the door from the kitchen into the back alley, and was able to chive open one or two of the front windows, though paint and time had soldered most of them shut. Still and all, there was a current moving the air and stirring the sounds of coins clinking on the round table beneath the windows, with customers coming and going, smiling a bit at the frivolity of the game, of such tough men playing for pennies.

Added to that was Noah's evident dismay that he was not winning, for he made loud cries and had the most astonished, hard-done-by looks that Oliver found it very difficult not to laugh. So he let himself laugh, though he did it behind Noah's back, where Noah couldn't see. Oliver exchanged broad smiles with Noah's men, however, and especially with Jack, who pretended he was completely taken aback that Noah wasn't doing so well this time out.

Stripped of his cravat, jacket, and top hat, his apron re-tied so it was only at his waist, Oliver brought pint pots of beer to the table and smiled with the memory of his and Jack's outing in

Regent's Park, and how well Jack's birthday had gone. Then he brought more pint pots of beer and even dashed out into the shops on High Holborn to bring back pickled onions and street pies of beef with who-knows-what inside of them, and all of these were gratefully taken and eaten.

Lest anyone remark as to how Oliver was waiting on them hand and foot, and thought to demean him for it, he brought pipes and tobacco from Noah's office for all of the men, and made a special run to their room to bring Jack's own pipe and his special brand of tobacco. And matches. And more beer.

The card players were too satisfied and contented to say anything ill of anybody, and thus peace was kept, for Oliver knew he would have come in swinging had anybody thought to ruin the tail end of Jack's birthday. Still, there were some comments, which Oliver heard when he came over to the table to check on them, wiping his hands on his apron.

"How old're you now, then, Jack?" asked Nick as he shuffled and dealt the cards around the table.

"Nineteen," said Jack. "At least I think so. Could be twenty, for all I know."

"Why don't y'know?" asked Noah, though it was a common thing for anybody not to know, for if you were a child of the streets, of the lower orders, nobody cared to remark upon your entry into the world.

"Told Fagin I was four when he took me in," said Jack, conversationally. He spread his cards before him and examined them closely, as though they might take him to golden treasure. Then he looked up and, over Noah's head, smiled at Oliver. "Was only little at the time, but I've recently found that I'd had my portrait done by very lovin' parents when I was four, an' that was the last they saw of me, after that."

This was not quite the whole story, but it was enough to be going on with, as nobody seemed much interested to hear the full truth behind Jack's tale. But it was interesting to see how Jack told it, how he'd skipped over whole chunks of it, rather than regale the company with what they would consider trivial details of a wee lad who, after his mother had neglected to remember that she'd left him sitting on the edge of a fountain, had been taken far from home by a band of gypsies. How, years later, his own sister, Delia Dawkins, had been the one to show him the portrait, done in miniature and kept on the mantelpiece at home, treasured, though only by her.

Oliver considered Delia now, how she might have been saddened by their sudden departure from the village of Hale. She'd truly seemed to care for Jack, as a person, as her brother, while the mother and father, such as they were, had only seemed concerned with each other.

Which was how parents might be; Oliver had no experience with that himself, though he did know what it felt like to be looked after and loved. As he was looking after Jack this day, expressing his love in a way that he hoped Jack could see.

And it seemed that Jack did see, for he looked up at Oliver, took a swift draw on his pipe, and let the smoke go in a stream from his nostrils as he put the pipe back in the small clay bowl that Oliver had brought to him. Jack's smile was for Oliver and Oliver alone, so who cared about the rest of the company? Not Oliver, not he, not when Jack looked so very happy, contented and sweet, dashing in his shirtsleeves, handsome with that confident look on his face.

It might have been only months ago that Jack, as he was now, would have seemed quite dangerous to Oliver. Dangerous and casual at the same time, half-undressed, his sleeves rolled up and his cravat gone, collar undone, the buttons sprung free halfway down his chest in deference to the warmth in the room.

Sweat gleamed on the dip above Jack's collarbones, and speckles of it were on his forehead, making his hair stick to his skin, making his green eyes drowsy and pleased, his smile only a slight show of teeth. All of this, it was clear, was making it rather difficult for Oliver to concentrate on anything other than Jack.

Luck would have it that Oliver's predictions were true, that because it was so warm there were few customers to be found indoors, content to nurse one or two beers with their elbows on the counter, as though they were great men of leisure.

Thusly, Oliver could stare, contented and sure nobody could see that he was staring, could let his eyes take in and enjoy what would have before quite dismayed him. Leaning on his elbows on the surface of the counter, he found he was now only dismayed by the physical distance between himself and Jack.

"Nolly," called Jack, not looking up from his cards. "Could y'bring more beer?"

"Yes, Jack," said Oliver.

He hustled to do as he was asked, and never mind the tab, for he'd not been keeping any. That could be Noah's contribution to the birthday celebration, which had gone so well that Oliver felt the glad stirrings in his mind of what he might do for the next year, and the year after. And smiled as he hefted the tray full of pint pots and brought it over to the table.

He placed the edge of the tray on the table's edge, as the whole of the table was awash in cards and pennies, each pile of copper coin fairly bleeding into the next, for nobody thought how much he might actually have won, not when more pennies could be had just by taking a walk down the street. Amidst the copper were flashes of silver, which Oliver took to be shillings somebody had slipped into the game, but never mind that.

He placed pint pots near the pile of coins in the middle of the table and hastened to clear away the empty pots, and did not miss the sweet smile Jack gave him by way of thanks. Nor how much warmer the room actually became now that he was standing right next to Jack, holding the tray in front of him.

The closeness, the smell of Jack's pipe smoke, the view of Jack's open shirt, the warm skin of the backs of his hands—all of this was making Oliver somewhat unsteady. He longed to bend down for all to see and kiss the tender curve of Jack's neck and press more kisses along Jack's jaw until Jack was well unsettled, and would determine that, for him, the game was complete.

To his surprise, Jack looked right up at Oliver.

"Have you had enough, waitin' on us?" asked Jack, arching his neck.

"Why no, Jack," Oliver said quickly. "Not if you're content to go on playing. I shall be here as you need me." He nodded to assure Jack of the truth of this, for Jack, on his birthday, should play at cards as long as he wished.

To this statement, Noah gave a gruff cough, though he did not comment upon it further than that. Which was good, for if he had, Oliver would not have hesitated in chuffing him across the back of his head, at the very least.

Oliver refrained from touching Jack at all, not even to put his hand on Jack's shoulder, for Jack might take that as indication that Oliver wanted him—which he *did*, and so felt the heat in his face and tried looking away. He didn't get further from looking from Jack's face to his hands when Jack's fingers picked up a few round pennies and let them fall back to the table like copper water.

"Well, I say you 'ave had enough," said Jack. Somewhat unexpectedly, he put his cards on the table, face up, fanning them out. He pushed his pile of pennies to the center of the table, knocking some pint pots aside as he did so. "Gentlemen, I'm all in, an' as it's my birthday, I can do as I please."

Standing up, Jack motioned to the tray in Oliver's hands and, half-ignoring the pint pots raised around the table in his honor, helped Oliver clear away the empty pint pots. As Jack scraped back his chair, another of Noah's men sat down in his place, took up the just-released hand of cards, and shook his head.

"You're shite at cards, Jack," said the man. "But at least these ain't marked."

Around the table, Noah's men groaned and, as Noah took a look at the backs of the cards in his hand, Jack just laughed.

"That'll teach you to cheat with your own men," Jack said. "I'll let you keep playin' with 'em, but be sure to return 'em to me in the mornin', *without* any marks."

With that, Jack picked up the tray and carried it with his own hands to the counter, where he slammed the tray down and turned around to face Oliver.

"Done with cards, now," said Jack, leaning back, his elbows on the bar.

"You were meant to play as long as you pleased," said Oliver in return, feeling breathless, unable to stop staring at Jack, his eyes wide.

"An' so I did," said Jack. "I mean to go upstairs, now, but hopefully not alone."

"I should think not," said Oliver, though the words did not convey the tumble of his head and the pleasant tightness of his belly. For this was the way a birthday should go, a pleasant outing, a good evening at cards, and then the two of them alone until morning. "I could not bear to let you do that. Not on your birthday."

"No, indeed," said Jack. He levered himself up from the bar and tugged on Oliver's sleeve as he went past him, going up the stairs to open the door to their room.

Oliver grabbed Jack's things, along with his own, from the back of a chair where he'd placed them, but was quick on Jack's heels, racing up the stairs to shut the door behind them both. He tossed the clothes on the floor and, leaning against the door, drew Jack to him.

Jack came easily to him, leaning on Oliver so they were hip to hip and belly to belly. Then slowly, almost lazily, he kissed Oliver's mouth and brushed his thumb along Oliver's jawline.

"Was beginnin' to think," said Jack, with half-lidded eyes. "That you only had desire for me when I was dressed up, like I was today. By your hand, at your design."

"Like a prince, you looked," said Oliver. He leaned his face into Jack's palm without any dismay at Jack's small observation, for he knew the truth of it and would share it with Jack. "A stunning young prince, a feast for my eyes, and all of London's, which is as it should be. But—"

He put his fingers to Jack's mouth to stay the comment that seemed to be forming, that Jack might refute Oliver for thinking Jack looked as handsome as a prince. Because while that was true, there was more beneath it for Jack to know.

"This—" Oliver petted Jack's face with a long stroke, letting his palm cup the curve of Jack's neck, leaning in to kiss that curve as he had wanted to in the taproom. "How you are—how you are in this state, warm from playing cards and drinking beer —this is what I have been longing for."

It might be that Jack would tease Oliver that Oliver had called Jack a prince, but for now, Jack let Oliver kiss him tenderly up and down the length of his neck until Jack was arching with pleasure. Jack held the back of Oliver's neck to keep him there, as if Jack was absorbing what Oliver was doing to him. Wanted more of it. And this Oliver intended to do, to give Jack what Jack liked best.

"Can I remove the remainder of your princely garb?" asked Oliver, his hands coming up to grip the edges of Jack's collar, thinking he could rip the shirt off of Jack if he wanted, but that it would be more pleasurable to tender the buttons undone, one by one.

"As it pleases you, Nolly," said Jack, his lips barely moving. His eyes were half closed, his dark hair witch-weed wild over his forehead.

"It does please me," said Oliver, his fingers on the buttons of Jack's shirt, his mouth on Jack's, covering any words Jack might say, taking Jack's breath into his own. "It pleases me very much indeed."

Oliver removed Jack's waistcoat, undoing the buttons before returning to the shirt, and peeled it from Jack's shoulders, as though revealing a sculpture of living skin and bone. He kissed all of Jack's chest with small presses of his mouth, urging Jack backward to the bed while he kissed him.

He undid the tabs and buttons on Jack's trousers, doing it blind, and made Jack sit down so he could kneel and remove

Jack's boots and stockings. Then, he left Jack in a state of half-undress as Oliver bent down to undo his own boots and take off his stockings. All the while, he felt Jack's eyes upon him, and while he was warm with the attention, he was not shy as he once might have been, no, not any longer.

As Oliver straightened up, he saw Jack leaning back on the bed, resting his weight on his elbows as he had on the counter in the taproom. And now that Jack's chest was bare and his trousers were partly undone and opened, all at once, Oliver felt taken aback at the state of them both.

He'd maneuvered Jack into that very position, and now Jack was just waiting for him, waiting for whatever it was that Oliver indicated he might like. Which, since it was Jack's birthday, should be what *Jack* wanted, and this without Oliver hesitating or drawing back.

"Jack," said Oliver. He came closer until his knee was side-by-side with Jack's knee, though Oliver remained standing. "Do tell me what you'd like, anything you want. 'Tis your birthday, after all."

"Anythin'?" Jack asked with a sense of laziness that belied the fact that Jack was bestirred. His chest rose and fell a little more quickly than it had before, so Oliver knew his offer of *anything* was the right gift to give.

"Anything you'd like, Jack." Oliver let his hand trail at his side, with just his fingertips brushing the top of Jack's bent knee. "Except for the crown jewels, as I don't have access to those."

"For lack of effort only, I'm sure," said Jack.

Oliver let Jack think a moment longer, then undid the cuffs on his shirt and pulled the cravat from around his neck. He slid the green silk down along his front, as though he were disrobing for Jack's pleasure, doing it slowly, just waiting for Jack to decide.

"All right, then," said Jack, sitting up a bit, though he was still resting on his elbows. He gestured with one finger between his legs. "On your knees."

"Dressed as I am?" asked Oliver, wanting to be sure.

He wasn't hesitating, only remembering. The last time he'd done what Jack was asking him to do, Oliver had been naked to the skin, and Jack had been standing. Though maybe Oliver had been wearing his shirt when he'd knelt before Jack in their room at the Swan and taken Jack in his mouth.

Afterwards, Jack had pulled Oliver to him and held him about the waist, quite tightly, and then Jack had told Oliver that he loved him, loved him more each day. Oliver's heart had almost stopped, from the words themselves, from the rough tremor in Jack's voice; the heat of that simple declaration had spread through him until he was so overtaken that his throat had closed.

Then, swimming in that lovely moment, he had hugged Jack back. And remembered, also, how moved Jack had been with Oliver on his knees before him. If he could do it that well again, it would be a fine present for Jack.

Going to his knees, Oliver didn't bother to undress any further, though his shirt buttons were undone, and he looked up at Jack to see Jack's eyes widen. There was enough daylight through the window to cast the angles of Jack's face in light tinted with rose, the blush of Jack's mouth dark and sleek as he licked his lips and took a quick breath.

Jack didn't say anything, only watched with care and utter stillness as Oliver undid the buttons on Jack's trousers the rest of the way and tugged the trousers past Jack's hips. Oliver used tender fingers on the tabs and strings of Jack's undergarment, warm from Jack's skin, and leaned in to inhale the salt of Jack, tasting the warmth of Jack's belly with his mouth.

He tugged and tugged again to get Jack out of his clothes, pushing the trousers and undergarment all the way to Jack's ankles, leaving Jack bare from neck to shin, his cock hard against his belly.

"C'n I keep my eyes open the whole way this time?" asked Jack, his belly hollow with his quick breaths.

The question came out rather small and meek, as if Jack were sure Oliver would refuse him. Back at the Swan, when Oliver had done this before, he'd felt so shy and unsure of himself that he'd asked Jack to close his eyes. Jack had obliged him, though he had, at least at one point, opened his eyes to watch.

"Yes, indeed," said Oliver. He went up on his knees between Jack's bare thighs, running his hands along the inside of them, a long slow sweep of skin-to-skin. "For it is your birthday, and you have full sway."

"Well, between you an' me," said Jack, as though he were aspiring to casualness, except that his voice broke midway through. "I'd like to see that beautiful mouth upon me, if you don't mind."

With a little laugh, for Jack was always at ease saying exactly what he thought, Oliver leaned forward and kissed Jack's skin directly beside where the rosy length of his cock curved upon his belly. This caused Jack to jump a little beneath him, so Oliver broadened the touch so that Jack wouldn't seem so ticklish. Then, with his lips closed, he ran his mouth along Jack's cock, from base to tip and then back again, feeling the warmth of Jack on his skin, inhaling the scent of Jack, dark and salt together, and then opened his mouth to blow cool air.

"Where'd you learn that, then?" asked Jack, his voice rumbling up from his chest.

"I don't know, exactly," said Oliver, low, not taking his attention away from his task. "Only that you inspire me to be brave."

"Well, onward then, my brave prince," said Jack, as if he were trying to be jolly, and again failed.

To reward Jack and also to assure Jack that he needn't be doing anything other than what he was doing, Oliver splayed his hands on Jack's bare hips. He traced the hard curve of bone with the tips of his fingers and bent close, so very close, to where he could lick the long side of Jack's cock with his tongue. He tasted the heat of it on his lips, the soft skin over the hard pulse, and sighed.

Before lifting up on his knees, he circled the base of Jack's cock with one hand and cupped between Jack's legs the soft skin of his bollocks, playing there while he swirled the top of Jack's cock with his tongue. He felt the shallow rise and fall of Jack's belly, and heard the words that tumbled from Jack's lips, as though he was in a dream from which he did not want to awaken.

When Oliver peeked just to be sure of Jack, Jack's head was tipped back till the long column of his throat was exposed, as though he were swamped with pleasure when Oliver had hardly done anything yet. But this was how it had gone last time, starting off slow because Oliver never half knew what he was doing, what he was supposed to do. But he did know that if he floated along on the dreamy sea between them, at some point the conscious part of him would become distant, and the other part of him, the one that waited, dark and still for moments like these, would hold sway, and it would be wonderful. Could be, if Oliver could only find that other part.

So he closed his eyes and suckled Jack with his mouth, leaving behind traces of moisture that he blew on, stopping from time to time to plant wide-mouth kisses on Jack's warm skin. And all the while he moved his hand slowly up and down on the base of Jack's cock, till at last the spark in his mind flew, and Oliver opened his jaw and sucked Jack's cock fully into his mouth, mindless, following a rhythm of pleasure that knew no master save what would please Jack.

Warmth grew beneath Oliver's hand, and slick eased the slide, the movement, that had Jack's belly quivering. Then Jack's elbows broke beneath his weight and he was flat on his back on the bed, his dark hair a sprawl on the coverlet, his fists gripping sheet and pillow as he whispered a low, moaning sound as Oliver stroked and licked him, and did sweet things to him, everywhere that Jack was soft, everywhere that he was hard.

Pausing, Oliver swallowed the moisture in his throat, giving Jack a chance to breathe. While not terribly sure how he was able to have such an effect in only moments, Oliver smiled into

Jack's thigh and kissed him there before returning his attention to between Jack's legs, where the stiffness of his cock was in shadowed twilight that was dark and hard and soft all at once.

"Are you ready, Jack?" asked Oliver, thinking only too late that it might be cruel to make Jack talk at this very moment. So he stood up, balancing on his toes and, planting a hand on either side of Jack's shoulders, leaned in to kiss him, to quiet him. "Shhh, shhh, never mind, you don't have to answer."

But Jack did answer, in a way. With his hair sticking to his forehead in dark, wild locks, he opened his eyes, glazed and so very green, and tried to answer. He did his very best, so Oliver kissed him again, and gentled him by pressing his forehead to Jack's. Then he scooted down Jack's body, peppering kisses along Jack's breastbone, his navel, his belly, as he went.

Oliver knelt on the floor once more to finish what he started, glowing deep inside at the noises Jack made, at the sweep and pull between them. How his hands knew what to do, his mouth, and how, when he closed his eyes when hearing Jack cry out, he felt the pulse of semen, hot and salty, on his tongue.

Oliver leaned into this and very gently held Jack in his mouth as Jack came, and swallowed. Then he sweetly kissed the top of Jack's cock before laying it down with careful hands on Jack's belly, for after such attention, as he knew, the skin became very tender indeed.

Laying his hand on the inside of Jack's thigh, Oliver petted with slow pets while he waited, and sat on his heels and wiped his mouth with the back of his other hand, swallowing the remainder of Jack's spend with some difficulty, but doing it just the same.

"Jack?" asked Oliver. "Was that all right?"

Jack only grunted.

"I shall take that as a yes," said Oliver, smiling to himself.

He pulled Jack's trousers all of the way off and stood to move Jack's bare legs on the bed. Jack let him, though he reached up at the last and pulled Oliver to lie down beside him.

Both of their heads now rested on the pillow, their legs tangled together, and Jack breathed long, slow breaths. Oliver snugged his head in the crook of Jack's shoulder, with Jack's hand, his fingers, trailing down like a soft vine to play with the ends of Oliver's hair.

"Are all birthdays like this?" Jack asked, sighing.

Sudden memories flung themselves into Oliver's head, of him at nine being taken on his birthday across a cold January field from Mrs. Manning's baby farm to the Hardingstone Workhouse. Of the birthdays with Uncle Brownlow, which had always seemed more like a celebration for the grown-ups around him than for himself. And of Jack, who had had his portrait painted for his fourth birthday, only to lose his family shortly afterwards.

The urge came upon Oliver to start talking about those times, those events, and normally he would have done so. That is, before. Before Chertsey, before Hale, before Axminster— before everything. Before Jack.

But he didn't want to trouble Jack with any of this, so he only stroked his hand up and down Jack's chest, firmly enough so as not to tickle, and pretended he'd only been considering what he might say before speaking.

"Some are and some aren't," Oliver said now, lightly. "It depends, you see. But the important thing is your birthday today. I'm already planning for next year."

Oliver looked up just in time to see Jack's smile broaden, the unconscious joy in his eyes, as if at the thought of it.

"I'll look forward to it, then, though it would be hard to beat this one, my first." Jack looked down at Oliver, his long, dark lashes sweeping low. "An' I'll be plannin' for yours as well, eh?"

It was on the tip of Oliver's tongue to demur, to say it wasn't necessary, that Jack needn't bother. But then, again, he stopped himself. Half of the pleasure was in the planning. At least it had been for him, though he would do better with the planning for Jack's next birthday, especially as to how much cash outlay it would take. Then again, next year they might be flush with cash or strapped for it. Either way, he would do his best for Jack.

"I'm sure whatever you come up with will be splendid, Jack," said Oliver, instead of giving voice to any of the other, more practical thoughts spinning in his mind. "I shall look forward to it."

With this, Jack sighed again and closed his eyes. Oliver ducked his chin and curled up against the length of Jack's body, enjoying the warmth between them as the room grew dark and Jack's breaths evened out.

It was almost overly warm, but Oliver felt with the palm of his hand the sweat on Jack's chest as his skin became cool. Oliver pulled up a bit of sheet to cover Jack's feet, at least, though Jack, at once, kicked the sheet off.

"Don't need it," said Jack as he rolled toward Oliver and half covered him with his body. "You're m'blanket."

"Very well," said Oliver. He smiled to himself as the darkness grew and settled and the room became quiet.

Below them, the sounds of the card game were going strong, coming up through the floorboards with thumps and shouts. Oliver felt Jack's breath slow, as did his own, as contented they lay together, their heads bowed toward one another, though Oliver was getting a crick in his neck from it still being cradled in Jack's elbow. He shifted Jack's arm, and Jack, sleepy, let him. And then Oliver let himself drift into a doze, in the warmth of the room, with Jack there, with Jack close.

7

PICKING POCKETS AT ST. PAUL'S
AND WHAT HAPPENED AFTER

The noise level at the Three Cripples rose and fell about Oliver's ears like ribbons attached to a lady's bonnet on a windy day, but without as much grace. And, being singularly rough in nature, din was intermingled with swearing and spitting, the hasty shout, and stomping feet on the wooden floorboards.

This collection of sounds, quite jarring on the ear, was not as easy to get used to as the more distant pitch and din on the street outside the crown glass windows. Which, at present, wanted vinegar, elbow grease, and a good sturdy cloth to get them clean.

Not that that would ever happen, not completely. But as the sun was shining presently, though not for long, the effect would have been definitively good and would have settled the current clientele and enjoined them that they were in a classier place than they'd hitherto thought. At least a little classier, though not much.

However, Oliver could not attend to the windows, for he was finding it more difficult than he imagined getting Noah to see his way as they stood at the end of the bar and stared at each other

"A brass foot rail, you say?" asked Noah. He put his hands on his hips, and his red and white checkered pants, which were strapped tight at the foot beneath the sole of his boots, made him look rather a foolish yokel attempting to imitate his more fashion-savvy, citified friends. "Won't it just get in the way, get busted?"

"*No*," said Oliver.

The skin along his neck felt shivery and cool. Noah was standing too close for comfort, but they were at the end of the bar, and the rush of customers, as they slopped beer and swallowed tots of gin, was a sad crush. This Oliver could bear; it was that type of place, in a certain part of town, after all, but it could be made better.

"Men like to prop their feet when they drink," said Oliver. "I've seen it myself, and think of it this way. If you make these improvements, such as the sweeping I described, and rinsing the glasses and pots in warm soapy water, you'll have a good business on your hands, rather than just a byway tavern whose name nobody can or would care to remember."

"You've got a mouth on you," said Noah, scowling, as though Oliver had slapped him. "So damn superior. Can't you see that every man in here is as loyal as a dog to the Three Cripples?"

"You're borrowing on a glamor from years ago, Noah," said Oliver, keeping his voice firm. "It won't cost you extra to get the girls to sweep and scrub the floor and wash the windows, and if you *let* me—"

"Didn't hire them to clean," said Noah. He spat on the floor and rubbed it into the floorboards with the toe of his boot. "I hired 'em to show their bosoms an' sashay about whilst serving up beer. Besides, they'll squawk if I were to ask 'em. An' the brass rail'll cost a pretty penny, I'll be bound. Nobody will see it anyhow in this crush; it won't be worth it."

"What's it to you how much it costs?" asked Oliver.

He wanted to go on in that vein, to point out that any money Noah might or might not spend would not come out of the profits from the tavern. As all the money being earned was, essentially, free money, gathered by picked pockets, and snatched handkerchiefs, and rolled drunks, or whatever nefarious activities took place in the cellar, none of any expense would come out of Noah's pocket.

But while he didn't say it, Noah's expression, his beetled brows and the furious downturn of his mouth, told Oliver that Noah had heard the criticism loudly and clearly.

"'Tis a waste, I tells you, like throwin' money away, that is. An' all for what? So a fellow can pretend for a quarter of an hour that he's a gentleman in a posh place ? Bollocks to that, I say. *Bollocks.*"

Noah's response left a taste in Oliver's mouth that made him realize he had been biting his tongue, the tip of it, between his front teeth. Thus it had ever been between him and Noah, arguing like shrill fishwives, and always with the potential of coming to blows.

"I only hired you to make Jack 'appy, Work'us, an' not to bring any pleasure to *you*, so mind me now, an' no more of this stupid shite."

"You'd bring in more money with this foot rail," said Oliver, insisting, but in a low voice, though it took effort to keep his hands at his sides and not ball them up into fists. "And you'd look respectable, which is the thing, isn't it? Respectable enough to throw off any suspicion, though why I'm telling you any of this is beyond me. So you can *rot*, for all I care. Let the whole place *rot* until it falls about your ears."

Nose to nose they were now, with Oliver's breath rising hard in his chest, knowing that if Noah so much as raised a hand to him, he would find himself with such a fight, and never mind that Noah was in charge of the Three Cripples.

"Say, say, say," said Jack, his voice greeting them as he came between them, a merry smile on his mouth as his hands pushed Oliver and Noah apart. "Now, tell your beloved Jack what's wrong, eh? You two ain't about to come to blows, are you?"

They were, but Oliver could see in Noah's eyes the moment he determined that they wouldn't, and Oliver could only go along with it. Their beloved Jack didn't deserve to have them at each other like this, though it probably wouldn't have come to much, not in such a crowd. Besides, having Jack near to him suddenly righted the world all around Oliver, for foot rails and shiny, clean crown glass windows never could compare with the wave of contentment that swept through him, not with the glance of Jack's green eyes that was meant only for him.

"What is it, then, Nolly, m'love?"

Oliver flickered a glance Jack's way, a small warning and acknowledgement all at once. Most would take Jack's endearment for what it seemed to be, sarcastic and jolly and nothing near the truth.

"He means me to buy a brass foot rail," said Noah, breath huffing out his nose, as though Oliver had enjoined him to drag a dead horse carcass into the place. "Costin' me money before the day's gotten old. Just this week I hired him, an' he's already at it! Wants me to get the girls scrubbin' and cleanin' like they was housemaids." He stabbed a finger in Oliver's face without actually touching him. "I hired them for their comely faces and large bosoms, for saucy smiles an' a willingness to not cheat me overly much. Not to scrub *floors*." This last came out a roar, turning several heads in the place in their direction.

"Sounds posh to me," said Jack, as though he were unaware of the derisive tone in which Noah had said the same word only moments ago. "You'd be a step ahead if you listen to Nolly, here. He's got trainin'. Worked in a tidy, upscale shop, he did, as their best an' brightest."

Jack jerked his chin in Oliver's direction, a little smile on his mouth. Of course Jack was on his side, standing right beside him in all things, in a way that made Oliver's breath catch in his throat.

To have such a friend who could soothe the very air between Oliver and the man he most despised in the world, well, that was something. Something to cherish and hold close, and Oliver resolved that if Noah still resisted, he'd drop the idea about the foot rail and go about the cleaning on his own, for Jack didn't deserve to be caught between them every moment of every day.

"Foot rail," said Noah. He rubbed his chin, as if considering this anew, and of course he might, simply because Jack had given it the nod. "I'll get one of my boys on it. Brass, you say?"

"Yes," said Oliver, with absolutely no tone of gloat in his voice. "It doesn't have to be new. I'd be willing to polish it up, if it could be installed. But what about the girls?"

Noah shook his head on this one. "You go on," he said. "Clean all you like. If it does make a mark, an' there's more coin in the coffers at the end of the day, then I'll think about it."

"Think about what?" asked Oliver, narrowing his eyes, as it was always better to be suspicious about Noah than to not.

"Think about makin' 'em do that sort of thing, that's what. Put you in charge of 'em, an' all, but I'm to see it before I pay into it, see that it works, or by God—"

"Yes, indeed," said Jack, as if the modifications in the way the Three Cripples was run had all been his idea. "You'll see, soon enough, how right Nolly is about this. Why, there was a time when he'd suggest anythin' to do with soap, an' I just wouldn't want to know, but within moments of tryin' it out, I was a changed man, a changed man, I tells you."

Noah merely scowled at this and waved away the air between the three of them, as though it suddenly smelled foul. Then he turned on his heel and stalked off, going along the bar toward his office, the crowd of men parting before him as he went.

"Hey," said Jack, up close now, his eyes half-lidded, a smirky smile tugging at his mouth. "You must like causin' trouble, goin' on the way you do. Tell me true, now, an' don't hold back."

"If it's trouble to Noah, I do," said Oliver, doing his very best to sound belligerent about it, but with Jack looking at him as he was, tender and proud at the same time, it was very difficult to pretend to be cross, let alone to actually *be* cross. "But I am right about this, you know I am, Jack. It's not that the Three Cripples needs to become Buckingham Palace or anything, but with a bit of a sweep more often than once a year, and the windows clean, and a sense of industry about the place—"

"It'll be crawlin' with customers, I know, I know." But again, Jack wasn't mocking Oliver, nor did he seem to doubt the success of Oliver's plan. It was only that there was a certain slant to his eyebrows as he looked at Oliver and seemed to consider the rush of customers up to the bar, the roughness that stamped each and every one of them.

"What is it, then, Jack?" asked Oliver.

"Don't like the idea of you doin' all this on your own, so I mean to aid you in this mad plan of yours," said Jack. "Help you with the scrubbin' an' sweepin' an' all that."

Oliver stopped himself from reaching up to brush a stray dark hair from Jack's forehead. Jack tipped his head, as if he sensed Oliver's desire to touch him, and wanted to help him in this. So, in spite of who might be watching, Oliver did it anyway, tracing the curve of Jack's forehead, quickly pulling his hand away almost as soon as he'd touched Jack.

"I can't let you do that, Jack, because of your hands, don't you see? I can't have you ruining them and leaving you unable to work."

To Oliver, this sounded the veriest sense. Jack's hands were his livelihood and had only just begun to return to their pre-workhouse state, skin soft and unsullied, fingers nimble and quick. But Oliver felt somewhat bewildered when Jack blinked very fast and looked at Oliver, his mouth dropping open.

Before Oliver could ask, however, Jack shook his head and looked away, and Oliver had to bend close to hear when Jack began to speak.

"It's like you to be this way," Jack said with another little shake of his head, taking his fingers to trace the unpolished curve of the bar, streaking the long-aged soot stains. "You don't care for it, what I do, but you'd make it so that I can, don't you."

"But, of course, Jack," said Oliver, a sense rushing through him that he was astounded that Jack didn't already know this. "Besides, you're all dressed and ready to go out."

Oliver reached to tighten the knot on Jack's red cravat, tweaking the slant of the silk folds. Then he allowed his hands to move downward, to straighten the tuck and fall of Jack's blue waistcoat, which now seemed a little careworn against the trim, dark midnight-blue of the new jacket, the sleek, silky trim along the lapel.

The dark trousers Jack wore could have used a good brushing, and his boots a good polishing, but that might have led to more fussing than Jack could have withstood, so Oliver left it as it was, seeking only to remind himself that they'd never gone shopping for a handkerchief for Jack.

"You look fine, Jack," Oliver said, giving the lapel of Jack's jacket one long, final slow stroke. "Quite fine, in fact. Almost too fine to let out of my sight."

This bold remark, said low for only Jack's ears, brought Oliver the reward of a smile, one that glinted Jack's eyes. A wave of love, low and deep, swept all through Oliver's body. It was as if the connection between them since their return to London had become more solid and pure and, now, reflected there on Jack's face, felt to Oliver like a promise.

Some of this, it could be realized, had to do with the fact that Jack had been so delighted with the idea of Oliver dressing him to do something so low and illegal. Obviously, Jack knew Oliver didn't approve of picking pockets, but that because Jack wanted it, Oliver would not merely stand to one side. Instead, he would assist Jack in some way. In this way. In the buying of a jacket, and giving Jack one of his new shirts that now pressed, crisply white, against the soft skin along Jack's neck.

"You will have a care, won't you, Jack? I will expect you back here, safe and sound, for I have no wish to visit you in Newgate. So promise me."

"Promise," said Jack. He bent close and gave Oliver the

gentlest of kisses on the corner of his mouth, slight and quick, for they were still amidst the crowd hustling up to the bar for pints of beer and tots of gin. "Like I always promise."

Putting on his top hat, Jack winked at Oliver and tipped the hat at him before sauntering through the crowd and out the front door, head held high, a jaunty air to the line of his shoulders.

Oliver wondered at the pride he felt about Jack's skills, when he knew full well and good that Jack was headed out to relieve unsuspecting persons of their most prized possessions and even the most trivial of items that they might be carrying in their pockets. He watched until Jack was out the door and headed down the lane toward High Holborn before he made himself take a look about the taproom to imagine what other changes might be made.

IN THE BEFORE TIMES, BEFORE NOLLY, JACK WOULD NEVER have dared to work the lanes around St. Paul's, given that the area was home to those fine folk who could afford to wear clothes decent enough to go inside. Who could afford to have a personal carriage and four horses and a coach driver who dropped them right out in front of the marble steps so they didn't have to scuff their fine leather shoes. Who were greeted at the door by white and scarlet-robed servants of a God who had long ago forgotten Jack even existed.

Which was how Jack preferred it. Even after the beautiful morning he and Nolly had spent listening to Mister Harry preach in St. Peter's Church in Chertsey, Jack couldn't imagine a regular Sunday spent indoors when the weather was so fine.

Silky cloud puffs of white lazed over the pale, buff-colored dome of St. Paul's, seeming barely in a hurry to move along. They strung themselves over the blue sky, which was not exactly a clear blue, but rather was dusted with smoke from various chimneys and factories.

Every now and then, Jack caught the scent of the Thames, which was now at high tide and moved out to sea, taking the dregs of pipes, the filth from chamber pots and cesspits, and the leavings of the tanners across the river.

All of this, Jack pulled into his lungs. They would become more prominent, these smells, once summer was fully underway, but for now they eased out a dusky, thick perfume that told Jack once again, and there were never too many times for this, that he was safe at home.

A strolling pair of ladies made their way past Jack, who stood in the walk along Paternoster Row, which, at this time on a weekday, wasn't as busy as it might be on a Sunday. He tipped his hat at the ladies, and they both nodded their somberly bonneted heads at him in response, as though they might have already made his acquaintance.

At the very least, he himself did not stand out as much as he might have done, for Nolly and he had taken baths only a day ago, as part of his birthday treat. As well as giving Jack one of his own new shirts, white and crisp at collar and wrist, Nolly had gotten Jack a new jacket. The jacket was dark blue as before, but the wool was thin and fine and cut just so at Jack's waist.

He felt quite the dandy in it, especially since Nolly had taken special care to adjust Jack's red cravat about his neck. Thus, dressed as he was, nobody was paying him any particular mind. Not the strolling ladies, not the pair of coppers coming up the path toward him, not the lad with his boot-black kit holding his hand out for a job. Not even the well-dressed couple moving past him as they went toward the stairs of the church. He fit in so well, it was as if he belonged.

This run was a test, to see if wearing proper gear, as a gentleman might, would move Jack to new hunting grounds, which, being not so dicey in nature, would set those about him at their ease, and allow Jack easy pickings. Or it might be that the crowd of polite folk was a bit thin, and Jack's actions would make him stand out.

There was no way to determine this but to try, though it would be different than his more recent forays into the streets of London, where he'd plied his craft much as he'd always done, both before his transportation to Port Jackson and after his return.

Though, at present, Jack found he missed seeing Nolly out of the corner of his eyes, Nolly who had watched Jack work his way into a man's pockets to withdraw his wallet without him knowing, as if Jack were performing a conjuring trick. Or even if he was not picking pockets but was only smoking his pipe and watching the evening draw dark, Nolly looked at Jack as though he were a thing of precious wonder, if the intensity of Nolly's gaze was anything to go by.

This new attentiveness had been happening since their departure from Axminster workhouse, though precisely what had changed Jack did not know, as he was the same as he'd always been. Perhaps it was what they had gone through together that had roused Nolly from mere acceptance to full-out adoration, which bothered Jack not at all. Only the thought of it was distracting him from his work, which was, on this fine afternoon in May, to pick some pockets, and perhaps later talk Nolly into going to a cobbler to get his boots repaired, or better yet, to purchase him a new pair. Well, nearly new, as brand-new boots would get stolen the moment Nolly's back was turned; the streets were full of thieves, after all.

Jack began to saunter, approximating his stride and speed to match those of the gentlemen around him. He strolled up and down the walk and looked at the stalls to the north of the church, which offered Bibles, small crosses, white handkerchiefs, and bottles of holy oil—all for sale at a price that was far more dear when compared to anywhere else, as if the Lord had determined that anything being sold on church grounds deserved a higher tariff.

It was ridiculous, as any of those things could be had for a lot less, if the high-minded folk would just go over a street or two. But then, there wouldn't be easy pickings for Jack now, so he did not roll his eyes, nor snort with disbelief, but merely shifted up behind a certain gentleman and assayed his chosen mark.

The gentleman was of the sort that Nolly preferred Jack to thieve from: well fed, well tended, and one who would not miss his wallet overly much. As well, the man's cologne, being pricy and thus not watered down, smelled as thick as if it had been poured on with a bucket. Moreover, Nolly would want Jack to come back with a fine description of how Jack had only taken from those who could afford it, and this gentleman was such a one.

Moving up alongside, Jack could see the gentleman's watering eyes, red-flecked with the drink, his collar and cravat tight against his sweating throat, the shoulders of his jacket straining with his bulk. Very well fed, then, and not the sort who could chase after Jack, let alone, with such unfocused eyes, be able to point him out in a crowd.

Leaning slightly toward the gentleman, as though reaching across him to pick up an object on the far side of the table, Jack pretended to stumble. As he stepped back, he reached in and plucked the wallet from the inner pocket of the man's jacket.

"Oh, I'm terribly sorry, sir," said Jack in his most polite voice. "I didn't see the break in the pavin' stone beneath my feet, but are you all right?"

"Fine, fine," said the man, his throat thick with phlegm. He took out a handkerchief and spat into it, then put it, folded, back into his trouser pocket. "No harm done, eh?"

"No," said Jack, laughing a bit to demonstrate what a clumsy but remorseful fool he was. "Well," he said now, tipping his hat as he slid the man's wallet into the inner pocket of his own jacket. "Good day to you, sir."

He strolled slowly away, and went toward the next stall that sold, of all things, fine leather wallets, all shiny and new with unfrayed edges and smooth surfaces. He wanted to reach out and touch them, but then later, if questions were asked, he did not want to be identified as the young man with a large interest in wallets. So he kept strolling until he came to the next stall, which sold stationery much like the stuff that Nolly had been using the day he'd written all those letters. Making Jack wonder if Nolly had come all this way just to buy paper and pen. Then he realized that no, even Nolly would have found more of a bargain closer to home.

Just there, leaning over the table of stacked collections of pale paper, was a young woman, dressed in light skirts and a fussy, beribboned jacket. Even Jack, with his lack of fashion sense, could see that if she actually stepped into the street, the whole of her hem would be chuffed black within moments, and her bonnet flayed with coal dust.

The pale colors she wore were more appropriate for the seaside, or somewhere fresh-aired in the country, not the gritty, smoky streets of London. Though perhaps that was the signal for Jack that the young lady could afford a personal laundress and didn't have to care how dirty her clothes might get, nor how they were cleaned.

At that moment, the curve of her bonnet was turned Jack's way. He could see her prissy mouth and her wide eyes beneath her blond fringe as she complained to the plainly dressed woman next to her, a governess, perhaps, or a paid companion.

The complaints were high-pitched, having to do with her not wanting to be where she was, and not wanting to go visit her doddering old aunt afterwards. As Jack considered the young lady for his next mark, he determined that the old aunt would probably prefer that the brightly flounced brat stay away as far as possible.

Better yet, the young lady was holding onto her blue silk reticule by two gilded strings at her side; the reticule was beaded with jet and trimmed with braid, and heavy. As the reticule gaped open, Jack could see the curve of a clasped change purse of dull red leather. Which, as he recalled, almost matched the change purse he'd taken off Nolly some time ago.

Given Nolly's generosity to him, it might be kind of Jack to finally make good on his promise he'd made that day that he would return the change purse. This time full of solid coins, rather than empty.

Taking a quick breath, Jack pretended to fuss with the buttons on his waistcoat, walking forward as he did so, very definitely not looking where he was going. As he brushed the back of her skirts, she turned to him, scowling, but he winked at her and tipped his hat at her.

Turning away, affronted, she made as though he wasn't there at all, which was the perfect point for Jack to bend toward her gaped-open reticule and tweak the change purse out with his fingers.

He popped the change purse directly into his trouser pocket, shoved his fist in after, and walked along that way, as though while strolling he was only looking for a bit of shade. This he found near the low gate that led to the back warrens beyond Paternoster Row.

He sat on a marble bench. The wallet from the florid gentleman and change purse from the fussy young lady were heavy, and pulled down his jacket and trousers, respectively.

In a moment, sitting beneath the bow of an overgrown yew tree, Jack saw the gentleman stumble off, not even aware, as his footmen and carriage met him at the curb, that he'd been fleeced. As for the young woman, she fluttered in front of the stalls, and when she discovered her reticule open, looked about the paving stones beneath her feet, as though she thought her change purse had merely fallen out.

Her companion helped her look, both of their skirts fluttering as they twisted about. The change purse might be directly beneath their feet, after all, and the voluminous skirts did not aid their search.

Finally, as the young lady's face began to grow quite pink and heated, she turned to the busker behind the stall selling writing paper, and raised her voice to him. Soon, his voice was raised in return, and the two coppers calmly came over to sort out the matter.

At which point Jack determined that she might remember him bumping into her, or the stall owner might, and that it was time for him to leave.

So with both of his fists in his pockets, he slowly walked off the way he came, up Ludgate Hill, taking a right along Old Bailey to go past Newgate Prison, which rose up with dark shoulders all along one side of the street. He looked at where there might still be signs in the cobblestones that would tell him whether or not either of the men who were hung that morning had pissed themselves.

Up ahead, just as he was coming close to the Debtor's Door, where the scaffold was only now being dismantled, there were several boys, younger than himself, shouting at each other in a game of chase. From time to time they would disperse into a small circle as the boys shouted at the carpenters, that or they would hunker to the ground as though searching for something they had lost.

Jack suspected it was loose iron nails that the boys were after. As mementoes of a hanging, they were supposedly worth a ha'penny each, which was ridiculous, since there was no way the article could be verified as having come from a hanging scaffold.

This Jack and the rest of Fagin's lads had discovered quite early on, that the best that could be garnered from iron nails was a trip to the ironmonger's shop, where they might have traded a fistful of iron nails for a penny, or not, as the mood suited the blacksmith. Jack had always taken the money and spent it on food, and usually one of the lads would squall to Fagin, who would shout that any earnings always be turned over to him, though he never seemed to enforce this particular edict.

Thus immersed in fancies from the past, Jack boldly went up to the remains of the scaffold to touch the wood, so recently hewn it still smelled of resin and wood dust. Why the magistrate didn't simply leave the scaffold in place was beyond Jack to understand, though, if there was a profit in it to put it up and take it down each time there was a hanging, as a demonstration of the might of the law, perhaps that was reason enough.

Jack looked down at his feet and scuffed the cobbles with the toe of his boot. There was a running puddle, oozing between the stones, but as it had sawdust in it, it meant it had been there since before the scaffold had gone up and was probably just the remains of a chamber pot tossed in the street. That or some onlooker, much jostled by the excited crowd at the hanging, had spilled his beer.

It was a shame, really, that he'd not taken Nolly up on his offer to see the hanging that morning, though it might have been that Nolly had been saying it only for form's sake. Or perhaps he'd meant it. Either way, if the offer came up again, Jack would say yes, and never mind that he'd have to get up at such an early hour.

Though disappointed in the lack of piss in the street that would signify a mighty event had occurred that day, Jack pursed his lips in an aimless whistle and made his way up the street to the steepness of Holborn Hill. Then he went up Field Lane, which dipped until it rose up again. He paused amidst the familiar swags of handkerchiefs that, hanging in the breeze in front of pretty much every shop, seemed to wave a greeting to him, as they did each time.

Two women, careworn with work, wearing time-grayed aprons over their nondescript skirts, their arms akimbo, came out to stare at him with some distrust, as if they had already determined he meant to rob them. But even this, and especially after the sojourn that Jack had shared with Nolly, the sight of it, of the gritty dale of Field Lane, relaxed his shoulders and calmed him inside, all over again. And would do, until it didn't, until he didn't need it to anymore.

The doorway to the Three Cripples was swinging open and

shut, as it tended to do in the late afternoons, with men coming and going, slipping in and out of the tavern, either thirsty, hands in their pockets scrupling for tuppence, or sated, wiping their mouths free of beer foam.

Jack tipped his hat at those who greeted him and slipped inside the cool shade of the taproom, where instantly the smell of beer, gone slightly warm, filled his nose, along with that of pipe smoke, all dusty with ash, and the musky scent of straw soaked with beer by being set in bowls beneath the taps when they leaked.

Making his way up to the bar, Jack took off his hat and planted a booted foot on the brass rail that must have been installed whilst he'd been out working. And found that though it was a contrivance Noah had agreed to to give the place elegance, and in spite of the fact that the brass was faded dull and in need of a good polish, it did allow Jack to relax, his hip jutted out, his shoulders slouched. Besides, the view was good, for there across the bar and standing in front of the stack of barrels with his back to Jack was Nolly.

He was pulling a beer from a tap for a customer. Three pint pots stood at the waiting, and Jack watched as Nolly tilted the pot and allowed the beer to run from the tap in a gentle line, rather than in a hard rush that would froth the beer and ruin the head.

There were dark sweat-circles beneath Nolly's arms, and the back of his neck glistened, traced by the dark-gold of his hair where it stuck to his skin. Which made Jack feel a tad strange at the fact that Nolly looked work-worn and grubby, while Jack himself looked as fresh as though he'd only taken a stroll along the river.

Nolly turned around with the pint pot in his hands, now filled. He didn't quite see Jack, but instead put all four pints on the tray the serving girl was holding onto while she waited patiently for her order to be filled.

It struck Jack, as Nolly concentrated on his task and gave the girl a nod that she might carry on, how still Nolly's expression was. Perhaps it was the business at hand that made him so serious, his eyes not smiling, nor his mouth, which might put anybody off wanting to break through to him. Which was certainly how the serving girl felt, as she picked up her tray and dashed off, heedless that her haste made the beer slop out of the pots and onto the tray.

But the second Nolly saw Jack standing there, his eyebrows flew up. Jack was greeted with that sunburst smile, and a quiet blush of pleasure in Nolly's cheeks that Jack always found a bit flirty, though Nolly probably wasn't doing it on purpose.

"Jack," said Nolly, his smile reaching his eyes. "Are you back already?"

"Pockets full," said Jack, with a little sideways grin. "Can't you hear 'em jingle?" He shook his trouser pocket for effect. "An' I got somethin' for you, for later, when you're done here."

"Soon," said Nolly. He picked up a flannel cloth and wiped his hands on it. "Noah is currying your favor, I think, as he's told me not to worry about working to midnight every night, just on the rush nights, like Friday and Saturday."

"That's Christian of him," said Jack.

Nolly was right. Noah had Nolly working no harder than anybody else, nor had he given him the worst tasks, and all of this was all for Jack's favor. Though cleaning out the drain pots at the end of the day was a nasty bit of work, and Nolly'd done his share of that and had complained to Jack loud and long.

"We could go to supper in an hour, I think," said Nolly now. "But Noah had a message for you and wanted to know if you knew anything about cutting coin."

"*Shite*, Nolly," said Jack, jumping forward with his hands up. "Don't say that so loud or everybody will hear."

Nolly ducked his head, finished wiping his hands, and put the cloth behind the counter. When he looked up at Jack, his mouth was in a thin line and, for a moment, Jack thought Nolly might have reached his limit with being unconcerned about how Jack made his living, how the people all around them made their livings.

It was on the tip of Jack's tongue to say something to Nolly that would give him the impression that it wasn't a bad thing necessarily, but at the same time, as Nolly eyed him and took a deep breath, Jack realized Nolly would see the lie for what it was.

"Noah didn't say exactly what he meant," said Nolly. "Only that—I'm sorry, Jack. It didn't appear as though it was one of *those* things, you know?"

"Yes, I know, an' never mind it now," said Jack, wishing he had a private moment to soothe the distress from Nolly's brow. "I'll go see him directly. He's in the cellar, is he?"

"That's where he said he was heading," said Nolly, his shoulders relaxing from their tense line. "When you're done, there's a place one of the girls told me about, where they fry fish and potatoes in fresh lard."

Someone stumbled into Jack with pointed elbows, thrusting up to the counter as if Jack wasn't even there.

"I want a beer, you," said the man, growling as though Nolly had delayed him his request for hours. "Make sharp and get it."

"Yes, right away," said Nolly.

He turned to his task, but not, Jack was pleased to see, in a way that made him look meek or scared, which was how it would have been when they'd first met during the winter. Nolly had only been working behind the bar for less than a week, but his experience as an apprentice clerk had served him well, and Jack doubted the rude stranger would get better service anywhere else.

"Back in a bit," Jack said, raising his voice to be heard over the man's shoulders. He saw Nolly nodding, as if to himself, but the message was for Jack, that Nolly would be ready when he was.

Jack turned and made his way through the after-work crowd, shoving with his elbows and stamping on booted feet as need be. When he finally arrived at the stairs, he took a right and opened the door to the stairway that went down to the cellar. He followed its zigzag pattern as it turned back on itself in the blacked-brick passage to the depths below the Three Cripples.

There, carved out of rock, were caverns and grottos of stone, with pillars in-between and sometimes tiled with brick, all soot-ceilinged and dusty-floored and thick with damp. In some places, niter crawled in the corners and, in others, streams of yellow wax sculpted small rivers beneath flickering candles.

Noah stood in the round doorway to one of the small alcoves, his hands on his hips as he watched over what one of his men was doing. Jack went to him, pleased to be asked to join in the scheme. Though he'd never learned to cut coin back in the day, he was sure he could learn, for didn't he have the most nimble of fingers in the whole of London?

"Jack," said Noah, by way of greeting. "What d'you know about cuttin' coin?"

"I know what it is, sure enough," said Jack. "But I ain't never done it. D'you want me to learn?"

"Nick here says he's an expert an' can teach anybody. If we cut coin, we make a third more on every penny, you see, which has to be a laudable goal."

Jack peered over Noah's shoulder, where Nick, implacable and silent, leather-aproned with his sleeves rolled up his strong forearms, was taking a fine-ridged file to a shilling. With very small strokes, he took bits off the edge with the file. The curls of silver landed on a bit of paper placed in a wooden bowl, the curls so delicate and light that the landing of each made no sound at all. After a few strokes, Nick pressed the coin with his thumb, as if to soothe it, then rotated the shilling a bit more and began filing again.

"Are we going to counterfeit?" asked Jack. He looked beyond the table to the small brazier, beneath which was a coal fire, smoking blue and hot, and traced the bite of acrid smoke in the air that rose to the mottled ceiling and circled around with nowhere to go. "That's not—"

He wanted to bring up the fact that making counterfeit money was treason and a risk he was not personally willing to take, but Noah stopped him.

"No, no," said Noah, with both hands up in the air, waving as though trying to draw Jack's attention. "We melt it and sell it, completely innocent of what they will do with it. I know a man of particular notions who wants to buy whatever I can produce. I need someone with a steady hand, an' thought you might be wantin' to make extra on the side."

"How much?" asked Jack. His eyebrows went up at the thought of having more brass to treat Nolly to nice things.

"A guinea for every block as big as a potato might fit in your hand, an' what do you think of that?"

Noah lifted a block from the other side of the table and put it in Jack's hands. It was almost cooled, but Jack could feel the warmth beneath the surface, as if the silver was alive and trying to push through to Jack's skin.

"I reckon I could manage," said Jack with some hesitation, for although he could already think ahead to Nolly's birthday next January, counterfeiting, and dealing with those who cut coin was never an easy burden, and could soon land him in the dock. If he was in the dock, he'd be separated from his beloved Nolly, so maybe being part of Noah's scheme wasn't the best idea, after all. Still, he'd have to play it close to the chest or risk Noah's ire.

"It wouldn't be required of you, not every day," said Noah, as if to reassure Jack. He put the block back down on the table, nodding as Nick pushed it to the side where it could continue to cool. "But Nick'll teach you an' give you the nod when he needs some help; he's particular about who he works with, ain't you, Nick."

The dour and silent Nick nodded, not taking his eyes or his attention from his work.

"What you got for me today, Jack, then? You come back swimmin' after a stroll around St. Paul's?"

"I'd say," said Jack. He pulled out the wallet from his inside jacket pocket and slapped it into Noah's hand. "From the feel of that, there's both paper an' coin. Three big guineas, I think. An' this." Jack pulled out the change purse and dumped the contents, all shiny, not a single copper piece among them, on the table next to Nick's elbow. "I'm keepin' the change purse, an' I'll have whatever you reckon my share of the take is, now, if you please." He tucked the change purse back in his pocket and held up the flat of his hand.

Amiably, Noah made Jack wait while he thumbed through the wallet, nodding as his eyes took in the thick pad of bills, which would be far easier for Noah to get rid of than it would have been for Jack, as there were so many. Then Noah's eyes widened at the three gold guineas that fell into his hand. They were so new that there was not a speck of wear on them.

He gave Jack one of these, and a fistful of the shiny silver coins from the table. Which left Jack still holding a pretty big handful of change, and he didn't have to worry about getting rid of the bills. *And* Noah had let him keep the change purse.

"That's about fifty percent, I reckon," said Noah. "An' tell Work'us he still owes me, for he ain't earned but six shillin's, an' not quite that, as it's still not the end of the day. "

"*What?*" asked Jack, surprised not only at the sudden turn in the conversation, but at the amount of Nolly's debt.

"Lent him money, didn't I," said Noah, looking at Jack as if quite surprised Jack didn't already know this. "One an' five an' thruppence for your birthday, an' what's left that he still owes me for the ten shillin's he needed for paper an' ink an' whatnot."

Jack did the math in his head, quite briskly. Whilst on the road, the money had flowed easily both into and out of Jack's hands. Nolly had never seemed to count the cost, yet, at the same time, Nolly had borrowed almost two pounds from Noah, without ever coming to Jack for it.

But why hadn't he? Jack had ever been there for Nolly, hands out, the coins flowing—Jack stopped his spark of irritation and thought that putting the red change purse in a drawer that both Nolly and he could take money from would be a good solution.

"I see," said Jack. He did not add anything to that, for he did not want Noah to know that he and Nolly had not yet talked about how the money between them should be handled. "Well, I'll be off, then."

"Will you go back to St. Paul's tomorrow?"

"Might," said Jack. "It was easy pickin's, but the crowd was thin, an' so it might not do to go every day."

"Try one of the bridges. They're good in fine weather," said Noah, sounding knowledgeable. "Waterloo, I should think."

Jack nodded and, feeling pleased with himself, went back up the dark, rickety stairway to the taproom that was even more busy than before. One of the serving girls was going around and lighting the candles in their sconces before the crowd got too thick.

As Jack looked about him, he saw that there was an empty space at the end of the counter. This was at the far end from where Nolly was working, to be sure, but Jack could watch him from a distance and rest his mind while he took in the movements of the men drinking.

There were one or two whores who had managed to make their way inside the taproom, on the lookout for likely customers. Jack didn't know whether Noah was aware, or whether or not he would object, but while it could go either way, and who knew with Noah, Jack wanted to be known as the fellow who was on the lookout for his boss's concerns.

So he determined to tell Noah, if he remembered it. Then he leaned one elbow on the wooden counter where it began to curve toward the back of the room, set one booted foot on the newly installed brass railing, and looked over at Nolly.

Nolly was busy bending beneath the counter to rinse pint pots in warm water and, with a twist of his wrists, he had six of them upside-down on the wooden grill, dripping dry. They would never dry properly, the Three Cripples was too busy a place for that, but Nolly had objected to reusing pots without at least rinsing them off.

In a likewise manner, the short glasses for draughts of gin and sherry and whatnot, those Nolly rinsed off and dried very quickly with a flannel cloth, as he had insisted upon.

Noah had complained about the extra fuss, as usual, but Nolly was more stubborn and had gotten his way. Jack knew it wouldn't be long before the profits would rise from such a small thing. Then Nolly could get the serving girls and whoever worked behind the bar to do it his way.

Nolly was now making the serving girl wait on him while he tended to a customer, who was saying something and roaring with laughter. Jack watched as the customer, happy with the service, slipped Nolly a penny, which Nolly put directly in his trouser pocket. The serving girl got her various drinks and pints of beer and staggered away with her tray.

Jack thought it might be nice to let Nolly know he was there, so he stood up with both feet on the rail and pounded on the counter.

"You there," said Jack, as loud as he might in the din. "I've been a-waitin' for hours. Where's my beer?"

Startled, Nolly looked over at him, grinning when he saw it was Jack. Which was followed by a hasty wave at the bar to let the customers know he was occupied. Then, just about rushing, Nolly pulled some beer into a pint pot and hurried over to give it to Jack.

"On the house," said Nolly. "With my pleasure."

"Oh, I'll give you my pleasure," said Jack, winking. "Except there's a bit of froth on this here beer, an' don't you know it can ruin the taste?"

"Just drink it, Jack, a little foam won't hurt you." Wiping his hands down the front of his apron, Nolly seemed pleased with himself, with his work, with just about everything. "But drink it slow, and by the time you're done, I'll be done. All right?"

"Yes," said Jack, contented to have had a bit of Nolly's attention as he had, and the beer as well. All that was missing was a deck of cards to flip through while he waited, but they were stored in the drawer in their room, and he didn't feel up to fetching them. "I'll be here."

But by the time Jack was halfway done with his beer, the crowd had grown so thick that he could not see Nolly at the far end of the counter. The serving girls swelled to three in their ranks, and even Len came behind the bar to help out.

He stood near to Jack and frankly got in the way of Jack seeing anything but Len's shoulders and broad back. So he swallowed the rest of the beer and reached out to tug on Len's sleeve.

"What?" asked Len, not looking up from what he was doing.

"Tell himself that I've gone upstairs for a smoke, will you?" Jack had to shout this, and when Len looked at him as if confused, Jack pointed hard at the far end of the bar, where he could just see the top of Nolly's golden head. "Tell him—I'm *upstairs*. You got it? *Upstairs.*"

Jack pointed at the ceiling for good measure and, when satisfied Len understood, pushed the empty pint pot to the middle of the bar. He struggled through the throng to the stairs and raced halfway up, pausing to see Len saying something to Nolly, and Nolly's head nodding while he rinsed and wiped behind the counter.

Satisfied, Jack took off his hat and went the rest of the way up, opening the door to their room and shutting it behind him. He opened the casement window and propped it with a little sliver of wood that they kept for the purpose.

Pulling the red change purse from his trouser pocket, he tucked it in the drawer next to his playing cards and the rest of what they'd accumulated: Nolly's paper, pen, and ink, Jack's smoking supplies, and whatnot. The red change purse would be safe in the drawer if they didn't blab about it, and could be the source for anything that Nolly or he might need. And this rather than Nolly borrowing any more money from Noah.

Closing the drawer, Jack peeled off his jacket, sat on the bed, and brushed his hands through his hair. For the moment, he merely looked out the window, where the warm air was rushing in and smelled like soot and the dregs of the river at low tide and, faintly, like soap, as if someone had tipped their washbasin into the gutter.

He thought about lighting up his pipe, now tucked in the drawer courtesy of Nolly, but then thought again that it might be nice to smoke it later, after they'd eaten, and share it with Nolly that way, when the skies over the City grew dark with night.

As Jack sat on the bed and leaned against the wall with his boot-shod feet on the table, the wait for Nolly to come through the door was anything but unpleasant. He was relaxed down to his bones with the way he and Nolly had settled together, into their routines, into the hum and movement of the City, into deciding who slept on the outside and who slept on the inside.

There'd never been any need to determine their positions in bed as, from the very first, Nolly had been using Jack as his bulwark against whatever dangerous and scary thing the night might bring. And Jack had been using Nolly as his pillow. They only needed to talk a bit about the money.

Quite soon, even before Jack expected it, the knob on the door turned, and Nolly stepped into the room. He'd taken off his apron and had undone his shirt collar buttons and peeled off his cravat. After closing the door behind him, he stood, sweaty and looking a bit tired as he unbuttoned his waistcoat. But, warmed by the work behind the bar, his color was ruddy and almost golden, and Jack could smell the beer on his skin.

"Noah won't be pleased I left so early," said Nolly with a small smile that spoke of what must be his private joy at the prospect of it. "But I've not seen you all day, and it seems like it lasted forever without you."

"Such pretty words," said Jack with tones of seriousness that belied his pleasure in them. "Should they pass for an apology, d'you think?"

"Why, yes, of course," said Nolly, brows drawn together in his confusion. "That is—"

But as Jack stood and came up to Nolly in two quick strides and placed his hands on Nolly's face, Nolly stopped speaking, his mouth in a round circle of some surprise. But only a little, as he looked at Jack and saw what he was doing.

"I'm all over sweat, Jack," said Nolly.

This wasn't any protestation that Jack wanted to regard so, instead, he moved forward until Nolly was pressed against the closed door. Then, with his hands clasped on Nolly's face, he traced his thumbs across Nolly's cheekbones.

"You are," said Jack, low, whispering against Nolly's mouth. "You're all sweat an' beer spray, which is all to the better."

"Better?" asked Nolly.

Jack covered whatever else Nolly might have wanted to say with kisses, slow, sweet kisses as he drew Nolly away from his labors of the day and toward where they were now, alone together in their room with the whole night ahead of them.

"Better," said Jack, nodding as he pulled away and began to lead Nolly backward toward the bed. When his own knees hit the edge of it, he sat down and, with a quick tug, yanked Nolly with him as he lay down, boots and all, tumbling them both upon the bedclothes, making the bed ropes creak with displeasure against the thin iron bed frame. "An' better still."

Without waiting for explicit permission, as by this time the give and take was agreed upon between them, Jack pressed Nolly into the pillows and ran his mouth up the lines of Nolly's neck, where the day's sweat had gathered and made Nolly's skin warm. Then Jack kissed Nolly and kissed him again, using his hands to card through Nolly's hair, using his weight to hold Nolly in place.

Though Nolly squirmed a bit, he did not try to get away, only moved closer, it seemed, to pull Jack fully on top of him, and wrapped his arms about Jack's waist to hold him there. Jack felt the hardness of Nolly's cock pressing against his trouser leg, a warm brand to match his own, making the pleasure ripple up his spine.

"Steady now," said Jack.

He took one of his hands and, as he rolled half-off Nolly, he slipped his hand down Nolly's trousers and beneath his undergarments, cradling Nolly's very warm, hard cock in his palm. Beneath him, Nolly shifted, and Jack could just about hear his protests of wanting it fair, wanting Jack to have his share, too.

Only sometimes, such as now, Jack wanted so badly to give Nolly pleasure, pure and simple, just as he was, wanted to force it upon Nolly to take it like that, which he seemed to enjoy just the same, in spite of any words of protestation that he might speak. Theirs was sometimes a rough-and-tumble game; Jack had to catch Nolly off guard, as he had done now, and hold him tight with gritted teeth and hard pressure, and make him take it, because that's what he loved, though he could hardly say it out loud.

Which Jack did, almost growling beneath his breath. Pressing down upon Nolly, he stripped his cock with three hard shakes of his wrist, all the while watching Nolly's mouth open in a soundless howl as his eyelashes fluttered on his cheeks, and his neck arched, and his back arched, and he shot himself off in Jack's hand.

The hot spunk made a mess in his undergarments that Jack would tease him about later. Only now, as Nolly's body relaxed on the bed in Jack's arms, there was a hard-red color in his cheeks beneath the mess the pillowslip had made of his flaxen hair, and his blue eyes glittered with the aftershocks of pleasure.

"There you are, my lovely," said Jack softly as he released his tight hold and traced a line across Nolly's damp forehead with the tips of his fingers. "Better now?"

"Yes," said Nolly, the word coming almost soundless from his lips.

With a sigh, he reached up and circled his arm around Jack's neck to pull him close and breathe his pleasure against Jack's skin, to brush his soft mouth against Jack's. And when the words came, Jack was ready for them.

"What about you?" asked Nolly, his eyes opening wide in the half-gloom that had grown in the room.

"Later," said Jack. "After we've had a bit of a rest, an' maybe a bit of somethin' to eat, we'll come back an' have a smoke an' you can pleasure me nice 'n slow, like I like it, an' in the dark, like you like it."

"Do we have enough balm for that?" asked Nolly, ever practical.

"We might do," said Jack. "But we can always get more an' be prepared for when the notion takes us."

THERE WASN'T MUCH LIGHT TO SEE BY NOW THAT OLIVER HAD blown out the candle, but the silence between them was like a gentle pact as they lay in the bed together, back to front. Oliver nuzzled the length of Jack's neck, and his own body settled into stillness.

"Felt like cock o' the-walk today, struttin' around in my new suit jacket."

The words came softly from Jack's lips, and Oliver could feel through his chest the slight breath that Jack took.

"I'm glad of it," said Oliver, equally soft. "And you looked a treat, as well."

Which was true, and though it might be that clothes made a man, it was Jack's frame that had filled out the sharp lines of the jacket, nipped in his waist, and gave his gait a graceful air. Thusly was proven the value of fine tailoring, however dear the cost.

"They moved aside when I stepped in the tavern, both yesterday an' today," said Jack. He seemed to tuck his chin down, as if examining where his hands covered Oliver's, whose arms were wrapped around Jack's waist. "Ain't never had that happen afore, not to mention that we pulled the wool over Noah's eyes with my new cards yesterday."

"Noah can't cheat any more, can he," said Oliver, pleased with himself beyond measure about this. He gave Jack's waist a small squeeze and smiled into Jack's hair, planting a light kiss there.

Jack's hands tightened on his, and Oliver pressed close, enjoying the moment where their bodies touched and their chests rose and fell together, and all seemed right and perfect in the world.

"But how long till you pay Noah back?" asked Jack, startling Oliver. "Till when do you owe him your wages?"

Oliver had known the question would come, eventually, though Jack had done him a courtesy by not asking it until the birthday was well and truly over and their lives had gone back to their regular ways. Oliver coughed deep in his throat and calculated the amount in his mind.

"Three weeks out," he said, saying it quietly in the hopes it would not vex Jack terribly much. "Or thereabouts."

"Fuckin' *Christ*, Nolly," said Jack. His body became tense within Oliver's arms, and then Jack spun, slipping around to face Oliver, to circle Oliver's shoulders and pull him close until they were almost nose-to-nose in the near darkness, with Oliver's head on the pillow. "Why-ever didn't you come to me for the coin?"

"For the stationery? Why, I couldn't have, Jack," said Oliver, quite certain on this point. "You didn't even know I was writing letters, so why should you have to pay for them?"

"*Bollocks* to that," said Jack. He gripped Oliver's shoulders tightly and gave him a little shake. "I'd've paid for all that, an' given you money for the new jacket besides. You know I would have, an' gladly."

"Not for your birthday," said Oliver. He felt himself curling forward within Jack's arms, as if to tuck himself beneath Jack's chin and beg for forgiveness that way. "I wanted it to be all on me, not you doling it out to pay for something I wanted to get you."

"You've a strange set of what's proper an' what ain't," said Jack, his voice gruff while he lifted his hand and spread his fingers through Oliver's hair.

"I wanted it to be a surprise," said Oliver. He buried his face against Jack's chest, unable to explain the sudden urge to make much of Jack's birthday without Jack knowing about it beforehand. "I couldn't do that if I asked you for the sum."

"I ain't cross, Nolly," said Jack. He accompanied this statement with more kisses, alighting them on Oliver's forehead, his lips stirring Oliver's hair. "On no account, I ain't cross, only we'll figure out a different way, you an' me."

"I don't need all that much, Jack," said Oliver. "Besides, I want to be able to make my own way."

"You should live like a prince, Nolly," said Jack. "As you were meant to do."

In the way Jack said it, that Oliver should live like a prince, made all the difference in the world, for when Jack said it, he meant it with affection. Even if he might tease Oliver about it now and again, Jack would begrudge Oliver nothing, to the point of handing all of his takings over, if Oliver asked it.

Which he would not, for it seemed, in Jack's mind at least, that was not the way it should go. Instead, a percentage would be handed over to the head man, the fence, who would dispose of coin and wallet alike, and sell off the handkerchiefs and other fine goods, making a hefty profit along the way.

"Look," said Jack now "I'll keep more back from Noah an' hand it over to you so you might spend as much as you please. We'll keep the money in the red change purse I picked up for you today. It's there in the drawer, d'you want to see?"

"Yes," said Oliver, a little surprised at the present.

He sat up, naked except for his shirt, and lit the candle blindly. Then he pulled open the drawer and, searching in the shadowed depths, pulled out the change purse. In the candle's light, it was a dark blood red and was soft in his hands. Coins jingled in the bottom, so Oliver shook the change purse for effect, and opened and closed the clasp to hear it click.

"It's lovely, Jack," said Oliver, half turning to where Jack had curled about his hips. "So very neatly and nicely made, and so well lined, too."

This last was added as a joke, for it was what Fagin had said to Jack upon those occasions when he'd returned from picking pockets in the streets and had brought Fagin several nice, fat wallets. For a moment, Jack looked puzzled, then buried his face against Oliver's hip, almost giggling. Oliver waited, smiling to himself at the success of making Jack laugh.

When Jack collected himself, he sat up and leaned against Oliver, petting his arm while Oliver put the red change purse back safely in the drawer.

"I know it is dull to talk about accounts," began Oliver.

"Oh, here we go." But Jack laughed as he said it and pulled back, shifting low on the pillow, ready, it seemed, to listen.

"It's one thing to not keep our money in a real bank, but why do you hand over all your money to Noah? What does he give you for it?"

"Well, this room for one."

"Which is a shilling a week and no more," said Oliver, interrupting him. "Maybe when you were with Fagin—"

"*Say* now—"

"He protected you and taught you, but Noah? He only takes, and of what percentage? Sixty percent? Seventy?"

"Fifty," said Jack. "Or thereabouts."

"He doesn't give you much for your efforts."

"Listen to you," said Jack, laughing out loud. "Tottin' up the averages to determine that the pickpocket he shares his bed with ain't takin' home enough of his fair share. But heed me now—" Jack paused to pull Oliver close so he could kiss his face and his mouth and whisper half a kiss across his forehead. "Take the cash from the change purse when you need it, an' don't borrow any more money from Noah, right?"

"Yes, Jack," said Oliver, his heart warming with Jack's kisses as well as his words. He lifted himself up to blow out the candle and inhaled the scent of burnt wax. "Now, I think we should be concentrating on having another go, don't you?"

"Another go?"

Jack pretended to be astonished, his mouth quite open, eyes wide with mock surprise, but he peppered Oliver with more kisses.

Oliver, pretending ire he simply did not feel, clamped his mouth shut from Jack's kisses, all for the pleasure of having Jack try harder, resulting in Jack's kisses becoming softer, but there being more of them. Laughter bubbled from Oliver's chest as he gave in with a sigh, contented and easy in Jack's arms.

❧ 8 ❧

AT THE THREE CRIPPLES OR THE
FUTILITY OF INDUSTRY

B y the time Jack turned homeward to return to the Three
Cripples, having garnered another wallet along the way,
the rain had let up. The clouds above the steeple of St.
Paul's were fluffy and pale, promising a warm day on the morrow
with plenty of sunshine, should he care to go out on a Saturday
morning.

The streets were alive with folk at the end of their workday,
bumping along with bare handbarrows or whipping up the
horses with empty hay wagons headed away from Smithfield
Market.

This was fine enough, though Jack had to jump several times
to huddle in the lee of a building when someone would toss a
bucket of water in the street, or a street sweeper was too violent
with his little broom. But this was London, alive with clattering
wheels and the shouts of coach drivers as they urged people to
get out of the street or get run over, and Jack wouldn't have it
any other way.

The dip in Field Lane was quiet for once. The hanging handkerchiefs, arrayed in all colors, fluttered a silent greeting on the
spring-freshened wind, though the two women from before were
not at their post to glower at him. Up Jack went from the dell of

Field Lane, scrambling along the rain-slick pavement, for always in the shadows the small distance of Field Lane never seemed to truly stray from dampness, even in the hottest weather.

Jack strolled into the Three Cripples, slamming the door behind him and smiling at all in general. He got a wave from Len behind the bar because, as was usual on a Friday, the taproom was swamped with men, drinking their week's wages in several hastily quaffed pints of beer and ale while they propped their boots on the brass foot rail, as the more well-to-do gentlemen did.

Casting his eye around for Nolly and not finding him, Jack went up to the bar and was just about to ask when Len jerked his thumb over his shoulder, in the direction of the kitchen.

Jack had to plow back out into the taproom to be able to make it around the corner and, halfway down the passage to Noah's office, struggled to open the door to the kitchen, as it had thickened on its hinges in the recent rain and didn't want to open. Finally it did with a stern twist of his wrist on the handle.

Jack went in, boots clonking on the stone floor, to see Nolly on his hands and knees by the door at the far end of the kitchen, scrubbing away. He was almost finished with the task, by the clean smell of the room and the fact that the rest of the stone floor had just about dried to a dull sheen.

But it was the sight of Nolly doing this common task that brought Jack up quick, his jaw jerking in surprise.

"Nolly, whatever are you doin' down there?" Jack hadn't meant to snap, but the words came out sharp and unpleasant, as though Nolly were actually doing something wrong. Which, in a way, he was. "That's for the charwoman to do, or one of the girls."

For a moment, Nolly continued to scrub, getting the last of the floor in the corner behind the closed door to the back alley. Then, finishing with a flourish, Nolly let the scrub brush drop in the wooden bucket with a clonk and a splash.

He stood up, brushing his hands together, wiping his forehead with the length of his forearm. His knees were damp in large soap-edged circles, and his shirtfront was spattered with dark gray flecks.

"I'm only scrubbing, Jack," said Nolly. The wrinkle was there between his eyebrows, its appearance of no surprise to Jack.

"One of the girls should do this. It's woman's work," said Jack, insisting on this point as he walked across the floor, leaving ghosts of boot tracks where the stone was still slightly wet. "Not you, not you."

Right up to Nolly he went, to take Nolly's hands in his own and examine the evidence with his own eyes. Nolly's hands were red, and the washing soda had bitten into the creases of his knuckles, as though he'd been scrubbing for a while. A good charwoman could be tested by the shape of her hands: the more rubbed raw, the better a char she was. As for Nolly—

"Look," said Jack. "Look at the state of your hands. A gentleman's hands never look like that."

"I'm not a gentleman," said Nolly. He tried to jerk his hands out of Jack's, but Jack held him fast. "Not any longer."

"Yes, you *are.*"

"You're a thief, Jack," said Nolly. Now he did take his hands away and scowled at Jack as he rubbed the knuckles of one hand in the palm of the other. "And as I abide with thieves, I can assure you I'm not a gentleman, so scrubbing a floor is not beneath me."

"An' I tell you it *is.*" Jack felt mulish behind the truth of this. "I can't imagine why you're in here anyhow."

He stopped and tried again to look at what was before him, the true reason behind Nolly's expression. Which, at this point, as Jack had been scolding him, had dipped below the point of defiance, and an honest defiance at that, to stubborn resistance. Nolly never did well when Jack pushed, so now he would coax and expect better results.

"Typically," said Jack, more softly and with a quick touch to the soap-sopped edge of Nolly's sleeve. "Typically, you're in behind the counter this time of day, and it's quite busy out there, so why, why are you in here now?"

Looking at the floor, Nolly's gaze seemed to take in a sight that was far away, a middle distance somewhere only he could see. But then he lifted his eyes to look at Jack, and rubbed the back of his neck, grimacing, as if at the rough feel of his hand against his neck, which was unsullied by washing soda.

"The postman came," said Nolly. "He carried letters for Noah, and a note for one of the girls from her fancy man."

"And none for you."

Now the reason for Nolly's unhappiness became clear, but as Jack reached out again, Nolly sighed and shook his head. He looked at Jack as if he expected Jack to mock him for being brought so low by an event that, if it hadn't happened already, would never happen. But Jack didn't have the heart, nor the desire, to do such a thing.

"You don't deserve to be slighted by those you wrote to, who, by *God*, don't deserve even a moment of your attention if they're goin' to treat you so cruelly." Jack declared this with all of his heart, unable to understand how such an utterly earnest attempt at reconciliation could be met with such indifference.

"You are sweet to say so, Jack," said Nolly, as some of his disappointment over the lack of letters seemed to be easing away. He moved close so he could look at Jack and brush his arm, and inhaled a long, slow breath, as if only now, with Jack near him, he could bear it.

"I must go back to work, dear Jack," said Nolly. "For working keeps my hands busy."

"And your frettin' at bay," said Jack, knowing that this was true.

With a quick kiss, Nolly slid his hand along Jack's trouser leg. It was not anything Nolly would have done some months ago, being daring and forward and all. But Jack didn't mind it, for he liked the look in Nolly's eyes when he did it, that half-lidded sleepy gleam, and the slow, languid way Nolly released Jack from his touch.

"Will you be going out again?" asked Nolly. He took an almost-clean apron down from the hook by the door, slipped it over his neck, and tied it around his waist. "Or staying in?"

"In," said Jack, deciding at that very moment that the last place he wanted to be on such a lovely evening was miles away from anywhere that Nolly was. "Cards and whatnot."

"I'll open a tab for you, then," said Nolly, which was a joke, as all of Jack's drinks were on the house.

Nolly opened the door to the passage and stepped out of the kitchen, going toward the counter in the taproom. Jack followed, idly looking about to see if any of Noah's men were loitering in the taproom or nearby so they could start up a game of piquet or something else, if there were more players present.

As Jack watched Nolly slide behind the counter to pat Len on the back, Jack dashed upstairs to leave his hat and jacket behind on the bed to grab his pipe and tobacco and cards, and hurried back down to snag the table by the window that Noah liked.

Just then, Nick came in the front door and spotted Jack and gave him a jerk of his chin by way of hello. Two more of Noah's men, whom Jack did not know, came over to the table, and they all determined on a game of whist. This would be lively but not so engaging that Jack couldn't smoke his pipe and keep an eye on Nolly as the crowd grew thicker and more rowdy, it being pay day for many.

Contented, Jack passed on being the dealer and, while the cards were being dealt, he tucked some tobacco into the bowl of his pipe. Pressing it down with his thumb, he tipped it sideways to light it with a candle that was on the windowsill. Sucking in with small puffs, he drew the pipe until the tobacco began to smoke in low, gray tendrils.

"Get that wax out of here," said Nick. "You'll spatter the cards, you fool. Are you tryin' to mark them to get back at me?"

Jack just smiled, for Nick wasn't really complaining, only making noise, as he sometimes did.

Nick dealt out the cards, and they played for a bit, then Nick sent one of the girls up to the counter to fetch them some beer to drink. When she came back, and Jack saw Nick hadn't given her any money as a tip, he tossed a shilling at her.

Jack had plenty of money on him, so what of it? Such a small expense to make the girl smile. She'd be back to tend to them and see if they needed more drink; Nick was a fool if he didn't understand how it worked.

Not too long into the game it became apparent that one of the other men in the game was able to get drunk on very little, and was soon wasting tricks and losing track of which hand was in play. He and Nick got into an argument over this, and the third man threw down his cards and walked away.

At this point, Jack determined the game was over for himself as well, but rather than stomp off, he placed his cards down, leaving them and the rest of the deck to be returned to him later. He shoved back in his chair casually, as if it were of no importance to him that Nick and his friend might come to blows. Nick would win, as he was taller and not so drunk, but Jack eased himself out of the line of fire just the same.

As was his wont, Jack walked up to the bar and stopped at the spot where, on the other side of the bar, Nolly was hard at work. Jack slumped over the edge of the bar with one foot on the new brass foot rail, his elbow and fist holding up his head, and slowly smoked his pipe.

From behind him, he felt a tug on his sleeve. Turning around, he saw it was Noah who, again, had a peculiar look on his face, his mouth screwed up, eyes narrowed.

"Y'can't just stand here lookin' at him all night long, y'know."

"I can if it pleases me to do so," said Jack. He shrugged and did not add that, while he might work for Noah, Noah was not the boss of him. "Just keepin' an eye out, is all."

"Well, there are plenty of eyes to see you havin' eyes, ain't you aware of that?" Noah had to shout to be heard over the rising din, as the taproom fairly swarmed with men intent on getting drunk. "You got no sense if you ain't."

"I've plenty of sense—"

Jack took a breath to go on in this vein, determined to make a game of repeating back to Noah everything he might say. But a crash along the crowded counter brought both of their attention to bear upon the fact that a male customer, heavy about the face and thick about the shoulders, had smashed his pint pot on the counter and was grabbing Nolly by his shirtfront to pull him over. The look in the man's eyes, his dark scowl, his mouth slick with spittle and drink, boded nothing good.

In an instant, Noah took off along the bar to grab the man and pull him back, and Jack was up on the surface of the bar. He used his boots to kick away elbows and hands so he could move fast enough to get between the man and Nolly, before the man punched Nolly, or before Nolly took a bottle to smash it in half to do real damage with it. Either way, there would be blood on the floor, which Jack didn't reckon would clean easily, given the number of witnesses they'd have to convince that nothing untoward had happened.

With his pipe clenched in his teeth, Jack shoved his booted foot at the man's wrists, flinging a hard kick just as Noah and Nick, who had been spoiling for a fight anyway, pulled the man backwards and shoved him to the floor. Jack turned away as they began giving him a good thumping and focused his attention on Nolly.

"You can get off the counter, Jack, everybody is staring at you."

Nolly's cheeks were that dark red they got when he was really worked up, and his eyes flashed, any bit of a smile long gone. When Jack obliged him by jumping down behind the counter to stand next to Nolly, Nolly's breath was fast in his throat and his fists were clenched at his sides.

"What happened?" asked Jack, giving Nolly a once-over to

see if there was any damage. There was none, unless he wanted to count the wrinkles in Nolly's apron.

"He wouldn't pay," said Nolly. His nostrils flared. "Two pints of beer and he wouldn't pay. He demanded a third, and I wouldn't give it to him."

That didn't sound quite right to Jack, though it didn't surprise him that only Nolly would consider, in a tavern full of thieves, that the theft of a beer would be wrong. Still, as the man was dragged across the room and thrown out the door into the street, Noah would appreciate the gesture made on his behalf.

"Why not just call on one of Noah's bully men, 'stead of takin' on a brute like that yourself?"

The question made perfect sense to Jack, and the answer was obvious, as well, but Nolly shrugged off Jack's hand and turned to the bar as he wiped his hands on his apron.

"Who's next?" he shouted to nobody in particular.

Nolly began pulling pint pots of beer from the tap in one of the barrels, continuing on as though Jack wasn't there, his mouth down-turned, sweat speckled along his hairline. Noah came up to the bar, his task of taking care of troublemakers neatly in hand, and waved to get Nolly's attention.

"Work'us—Jack, tell him I want him—*Work'us!*"

"What?" asked Nolly, his voice rising. "What do you want?" He turned with his hands out, as though Noah had been shouting at him for hours.

"What was he doin' that you looked as though you wanted to kill him?"

Nolly took a deep breath, his jaw clenched, though the color in his face began to fade.

"He wouldn't pay," Nolly said with a level voice; Jack could see him trying to keep calm about it. "So I wouldn't serve him."

Noah's eyebrows went up to his hairline. He scoffed in his throat and jerked his thumb at Nolly while he turned around to Nick.

"D'you hear that, Nick?" Noah said. "Now, that's 'ow to do business, I'm tellin' you. Good business. Keep on it, Work'us."

Noah slung his arm around Nick's neck and the two of them shoved through the milling crowd. They made their way to Noah's office, where, no doubt, they would sing each other's praises for putting such a brute down the way they had.

Of course, Nolly would be unaffected by Noah's outright praise, for he only rolled his eyes and turned back to his tasks, going hard at it until Jack tapped him on the shoulder.

"Leave me be, Jack."

For a moment, Jack felt a dip in his belly, bereft at the thought that Nolly was cross with him when all he'd done was break up a fight that Nolly had no place being in. But before he could speak and argue his side, Nolly turned around. His chin was lowered and, handing several pint pots across the bar to one of the girls, he looked at Jack.

"I lied to you just now," said Nolly.

"You what?" Jack moved closer, ignoring the customers who had come up to the bar expecting to be served. "What d'you mean?"

"I wanted to punch him, Jack, for shoving his way up and demanding to be served before anybody else."

"That's rude," said Jack, not really sure where Nolly was leading him.

"Yes, rude, Jack," said Nolly, with his hands up, as if waiting to take a package from Jack. "It is rude, but so is every man in here. It's the Three Cripples; I should be used to it by now, or, at the very least, should not expect anything else. But this time—"

Jack knew he couldn't agree that Nolly'd get used to it, as he might have before, as he didn't think Nolly would ever get used to it. And it wasn't fair to force him to try, to keep putting him in a situation where he'd have to accept and come face to face with everything he abhorred. But Jack was at a loss as to how to help him.

"What c'n I do, Nolly?" Jack asked. "What d'you want me to do about it?"

"It isn't only that, Jack," said Nolly, his shoulders slumping. "It was what he said to me. He told me that he'd pay me to—he said that I had the mouth for it, and that he'd pay me to service him. If it was one thing and not the other—but it isn't, it's everything. I didn't want Noah to know, or his lads, so I lied. But I couldn't lie to you, even if you might tease me about it."

"Nolly," said Jack, drawing in a breath. He looked about the taproom, crowded with rough men and shrill women, all clamoring for gin or beer and practically throwing their pennies at Len, who had stepped in to take off the slack.

"He's lucky he's gone," said Jack now, looking at Nolly. He wanted to reach out and comfort him, to wrap his arms about Nolly's shoulders, and tell Noah that Nolly was done for the night.

"He *is* lucky," said Nolly, clenching his hands into fists.

This made Jack smile in a way. For no other lad would be as fierce as this and, had the rude gentleman still been about, Nolly would have given him what for, and then some. Shaking off his fright and ready as anything for a fight, if it offered itself.

"I'll look out for you," said Jack stoutly. "Keep you in eyeshot the whole of the evenin'. Then, come midnight, I'll tell Noah you ain't workin' the rest of the night, an' he c'n hang himself if he don't like it. All right? We'll get it sorted, you 'n me."

Jack wanted to touch Nolly's face and get him to smile, but there were customers behind the bar and a general roar that demanded beer and gin and anything else as might be brought to them that would soothe them into a nothingness that would allow them to turn a blind eye to their lackluster lives.

"I'll be over there smokin' my pipe; just whistle if you need me."

"Thank you, though I don't think he'll come back," said Nolly. He was doing his best to appear sturdy, and perhaps wanted to be left alone about this. "I should get back to work, I think."

Jack scooted out from behind the bar, letting one of the girls skirt past him in her hurry to serve up more beers, and wandered back to the table beneath the window. As expected, his place at the game of whist had been taken, and the hand had already been dealt and was underway. He could have objected and forced the issue, but he didn't feel like playing at the moment.

Someone, some *man*, had demanded of Nolly what he'd so freely given to Jack on his birthday and other occasions, and now Jack knew a bit of the way Nolly must have felt upon hearing that Jack had been forced into a more intimate acquaintance against his will. Jack was swamped with a drowning, sinking feeling of helplessness, because that mouth, while beautiful, was not for sale, was not for the taking—

Jack grew angry, and almost wished Nolly had told Noah the truth, because then Noah might be stirred up about it enough to let his lads have a go at said gentleman the next time he was in the tavern. But it was a secret, as Nolly didn't want to be teased by Noah, which was fine by Jack, because the less friction made available between Nolly and Noah, the better.

Standing on his toes for a moment, Jack lifted his chin to look at Nolly behind the bar. Nolly was scowling as he served, not looking up, most likely fuming himself into quite the sweat. So maybe Jack oughtn't to get angry himself but, instead, he should find a way to distract Nolly, to get his mind on other things. Which normally would involve a kiss and a cuddle, though the opportunity for either wouldn't come for ages.

Jack needed to do something now, though, to mend the situation, so he rolled up his sleeves and pushed through the crowd to slip once more behind the bar. He grabbed an apron from the small stack beneath the bar and tied it about his waist, folding it over so as to leave his chest uncovered by it and thus remain more cool. Then, giving Len a wink, Jack sidled up to Nolly and bumped shoulders with him and, without giving Nolly a chance to speak, turned to the crowd in the taproom.

"Come on, then, who's next? Who's next?" Jack stepped up and eyed a pair of slatternly ladies who looked as though they barely had a coin between them. "Don't be shy, what'll you have?"

"Two brandies, love," said one of the women. Her bonnet strings dangled in puddles of beer as she pushed over a tuppence with a thin, gnarled hand.

"Ain't got it. There's gin an' there's beer, so what'll it be?"

"Gin," said her equally unkempt friend, whose mouth was missing half of its teeth. "That'll get us a gin, right?"

"Tonight it will get you two," said Jack with a smile.

Noah was all the way across the room and would never know of Jack's generosity. Besides which, the staff drank a lot of the profits anyway, so Jack was not likely to be singled out.

He poured two tots of gin all the way to the brim instead of three-quarters. He pushed the short glasses towards the ladies while scooping up the tuppence and slapped it in Nolly's waiting hand. And looked into Nolly's eyes, which were sparkling with startlement, his lovely mouth moving into a small smile.

"You here to protect me, Jack?" asked Nolly with a whisper that was loud enough to be heard over the din.

Jack nodded, glad he could take care of his beautiful boy.

"You are my sweet prince, and I shan't forget it," said Nolly, looking as though he wanted to kiss Jack just then.

From behind them, Len loomed.

"Get workin', Jack, or get out!" Len jerked his thumb toward the end of the bar, but Jack just made a rude gesture and turned toward the customers, who moved forward like a pack of dogs coming in for the kill.

"Gin or beer, what'll you have, sir?" Jack asked this of a gentleman who was wearing the remains of a felted top hat that had seen better days and a coat that was more hole than cloth.

"Beer," said the man, showing that he did have enough teeth to chew with, but that only barely.

"Tuppence," said Jack, taking the coin that the man slapped on the bar. Then he filled a pint pot all the way to the brim, and slid it slowly and carefully toward the man so the beer could be sucked from the brim to ease the level before being picked up and drunk halfway down in one gulp.

"Another?" asked Jack.

"Ain't got tuppence," said the man, looking a little confused.

"Too bad," said Jack, shouting. "Here's another'n, so drink up." He shoved a pint pot of beer that Nolly had just filled toward the old man and laughed at Nolly's indignation.

"Jack, you can't do that!" Now Nolly was shouting, too, even as he served up three pint pots clutched in one hand to a trio of gentlemen who looked as though they had been drinking themselves solidly through every tavern and pub in the City.

"I don't work for Noah in this tavern," said Jack. "So I can do precisely an' exactly as I please."

"I'm goin' to tell the boss you're given' away the goods." This came from Len as he passed by with two full bottles of gin that he handed to each of the girls.

"Tell him," said Jack. "See if I care, especially when the rumor spreads that drink is available for free at the Three Cripples, an' in come the swarms of customers, just dyin' for a taste."

"Word of mouth is very good for a shop's profits," said Nolly, also shouting, looking up at Len as if a very great joke was being played, and Len was a fool if he wasn't going to go along with it.

Len only shook his head, held up his hands, and went to the far end of the bar to serve customers there. Which was very good, of course, because it meant Jack could do as he liked and make Nolly laugh at Jack's antics, and create a great deal of good will throughout the taproom. Which would go a very long way of erasing the look on Nolly's face, and the tightness in Jack's gut that made him feel as though he should have done something more about that horrible pervert coming at Nolly like he had, and done it sooner. But he could only work with what he had now, so he waved the next customer in.

"Yes, you sir, penny for a gin, penny for a pint o' beer, what'll you have?"

"Two gins, an' two beers," said the man, as he pushed over four large copper pennies. "That all right? You served them ladies, an' I was watchin', so it's a tuppence for two gins, and a tuppence for two beers."

Jack held the power of the gin bottle, one of which he grabbed from one of the girls. He poured gin liberally in the glass of everybody that asked, and sometimes forgot he'd already served them and taken their money, but instead, after they'd drunk the first glass, insisted on filling their glass all the way to the top a second time, as though to apologize for how foolish he had been to not have already completed the transaction between them. Then he urged Nolly to go get him more bottles of gin.

"Noah's going to be quite cross," said Nolly, as he came up with three bottles of gin, cradled in his arms like slender, damp babies.

"I don't give a fuck if he does," said Jack, taking the opportunity to pour a tot of gin for Nolly, for himself and, of course for Len, who scowled at them but did not refuse the offering. They all drank, then Jack poured a second drink for himself and Nolly and, sweating through his shirt, wiped the glass with his apron and placed it on the counter.

"Who's next? Two tots of gin for only a penny!"

The crowd surged forward like a massive wave, all reaching for their glasses, all holding up their pennies as though they were tokens that might get them into heaven. So Jack poured and poured some more, leaving the pint pots of beer for Nolly to draw.

At one point, Jack lined up ten gin glasses, glittering like diamonds on the bar, and poured gin into them, one after the other, in one long pour, until the glasses were almost overflowing. As for Jack, well, he forgot to collect the pennies.

"You're quite mad," said Nolly, breathless and laughing in Jack's ear.

But he was smiling. Jack could even *feel* Nolly smiling before he turned to check on his sweetheart, who had a wide grin, though he was sweating beneath his arms, and his golden hair was burnished dark against his head. But, by God, Jack's ploy had worked and now, once again, the tavern was a good place to be, at least for this while.

❧ 9 ❧

DETAILS OF THE GREENWICH
FISH FRY

From the wind that had kicked up the night before, Jack was not surprised to wake up Saturday morning to the sound of rain hitting the windowpanes. Nor to waking up alone. Church bells told him it was ten o'clock in the morning, and far too late for Nolly to be abed.

Jack let his head stay on the pillow and idly squished the bedbugs brave enough to crawl upon the bed-linen. He could lollygag to his heart's content, but his belly rumbled. Besides, the idea of catching Nolly hard at work was a fine one, as nothing was more relaxing to Jack than to watch Nolly putter about, serene and content with his tasks. That is, if they were tasks he approved of.

Jack determined to get up, so he did, and got dressed, tucking in his shirt and tying up his boots before thumping downstairs. The taproom was mostly empty this time of day, except for the girls working behind the counter and a handful of old men who were sitting as close to the fireplace as they could manage. The room echoed with the sounds of rain on the roof and on the windows; the air was thick with damp and a slight chill, such as could be found on any rainy morning in the City, year 'round.

Over at the far end of the bar, Jack espied Nolly in front of it. He was on his hands and knees, polishing the brass railing. The small bit that he had already done shone as bright as a new penny, which left most of the rail to be tended to. Though why Nolly should bother was beyond Jack; the rail was meant for feet, which would soon muddy it up and leave it dull again.

"Hey," said Jack. He walked over, his footsteps clonking on the floorboards. "You're bound an' determined to make this place over, ain't you."

"Not so as you'd notice," said Nolly, giving the rail a hard swipe as he sat back on his heels to look up at Jack.

But Jack did notice, for as content as Nolly should be, given that he was playing the part of a clerk in a smart shop whose master would be proud of his extra efforts, there was no smile lighting Nolly's features.

"Got blisters already?" asked Jack, making a joke out of it, wanting to raise Nolly's spirits, for there was nothing like a good, solid session of complaining to make a man feel better about his life.

"There have been no replies to my letters," said Nolly. With the polishing cloth clenched between his hands, he was hunkered down as if prepared to weather a rebuke, though this Jack did not have the heart to deliver.

"Told you yesterday it's too soon to be thinkin' that, eh?" asked Jack.

The situation had obviously not been fixed, so Jack hunkered down to sit on his heels as well. That way, they could be face to face and close enough to have a private conversation. The old men were too far away to hear them, and the girls behind the counter were banging about so loudly they probably couldn't even hear themselves think.

"The post office is very fast, Jack," said Nolly with some venom, though a moment later, he reached out to pat Jack's knee, and let his hand stay in place for as long as it might before slipping off again. "A day is all it would take for the ones addressed in London to arrive, and two days for the others, though the London letters were the ones I was expecting—that is, I *wanted* a reply to. My aunt and uncle, if they were going to respond, *would* have, and the same goes for—well, the same goes for the haberdashery. I raised up my hopes for nothing."

"Mayhap you have," said Jack, but only that.

There was no denying Nolly's hopes had been sky high, nor that the post office was quite fast. Jack did not, however, know a way to easily explain that just because there'd been no replies did not mean there would never be any. Some folks had a way of changing their minds, sometimes for no apparent reason at all, but it would take a mightier man than Jack to show Nolly how to reason this out, not when he was so glum about the mouth.

"Will you be going out, Jack?" asked Nolly, and Jack could tell he was trying to think about anything, anything atall, other than his own worries.

"Indeed, I will," said Jack, for the rain might let up, and never mind if it didn't, for London's odors were always sharpened by a bit of rain.

"Would you bring me—" Here Nolly stopped to rub his nose with the back of his hand, leaving a bit of a polish smear behind on his lovely, flushed face. "Bring me a book, and I'll read it out to you later. Could you do that for me, Jack?"

That Nolly was actually asking Jack for something couldn't bear questioning, for it almost never—had *never*—happened. But perhaps this was a reflection that their conversation about money had borne fruit, for Nolly was, at last, coming to Jack for what he wanted. It was good to have the issue settled between them, so Jack only nodded solemnly, given the circumstances, and took the cleaning cloth and used a corner of it to wipe Nolly's upper lip.

"You want one of the ones we already started or—?"

"Anything, Jack," said Nolly, shaking his head. "Anything. I don't care if it's the Bible, or a book of children's verses. Just something."

"Sweetheart—"

"A book, Jack," said Nolly, waving away Jack's attempt at commiseration. "I'll carry on here till you get back, and it will be all right if the replies don't come."

"No, it won't."

"It'll have to be," said Nolly. "Life has been generous with me, so I can't expect more than I already have."

"D'you mean me?" Jack jerked his thumb at his own chest, feeling the smile broaden his face.

For a moment, Nolly scowled, as if he meant to belie what he'd just said, but then he shook his head and, with a slight pat on Jack's bent arm, smiled at the cloth in his hands.

"Of course I mean you," said Nolly, flirting up at Jack through his eyelashes. "Now, get going before Noah accuses you of lollygagging when there's work to be done."

"He's not the boss of me," said Jack, nodding his head sharply to make the declaration clear. "I am my own boss, d'you hear?"

"Yes, I hear."

Jack could now see the laugh in Nolly's eyes, and considered it a job well done. Casting a look about the room, just to make sure, Jack turned back around and gave Nolly a quick kiss on the forehead. He saw Nolly's eyes close halfway, as if he might want another kiss straight away, and this in spite of the fact they were at the end of the counter nearest the door, and anybody could be coming through it and would see them.

"Right," said Jack. He stood up. "Book for you. Anythin' else?"

"Just you back safely," said Nolly.

As Nolly turned back to tend to his polishing, he seemed unconscious of how that simple statement went straight to Jack's heart and nestled there like a small bird safely returned to its nest by a spring wind.

But Jack could not give voice to this, did not even know the words to describe it, so he headed back up the stairs to assemble to rest of his attire, clomping loudly to be as amusing as possible, and considered where he might go that day to find the appropriate fellow to steal from, and in what bookshop he might find what Nolly had asked for.

~

As Jack got closer to the river, a brisk wind raced up from the pilings. A smatter of rain came down on the brim of his hat, sounding like tacks hitting the cobbled street, as he looked about him to reconnoiter. He was just at the Queen Anne stairs, having wandered a bit further than he'd thought while musing the contents of his pockets.

Noah would be pleased at the silver watch-fob and chain, though the watch itself was broken. The hands lay limp at the bottom of the face, sadly jittering about the middle of the dial whenever Jack shook the watch. Which was often, as he'd been pretending he was the owner of the article in the hopes someone would stop him and recommend a good watchmaker who could repair it for him. At which point, he'd be close enough to the do-gooder to skin him clean of money.

But no such offer came and so Jack now found himself looking down the steep, moss-edged stairway.

The stone steps had been in place so long that each was curved low in their middles, as though they'd been scooped out by a dipper. The river at the bottom of the stairs coursed swiftly past with secret turns and pulls beneath the water, and lapped against the bank, dark brown and pale brown, reminding Jack of a turn of tobacco held in the hand before being placed in the bowl of a pipe.

Instead of going down, for the river was always too sad to contemplate at low tide, Jack turned to walk along the footpath that, in a jutting back-and-forth line, followed the river just above the piers and pilings and floating wharfs.

At various points, Lower Thames Street poked out to meet the path, and it was at these points that Jack had to jump and move quickly along or get trampled by the crowds rushing to catch the ferry steamers, or drays of oxen carrying loads to be ported to the sea.

Eventually he came to London Bridge, which, neat and tidy with its stone arches, looked nothing like a picture Jack had once seen of the old London Bridge. Back in the day, the bridge had houses and shops built upon it and was where everything imaginable happened. Fagin had often said that the old London Bridge had the best pickings, albeit a slim escape route; he'd had many of his richest takings there and had drunk himself sick when the bridge had been replaced.

Now, though, there was not much to steal on the plain London Bridge, so Jack walked to the down-river side of the bridge and looked out at the boats with their sails and at the mudlarks on the shore beneath brightening skies, although the rain continued to patter down like a spoiled child.

Just below him was the London Bridge pier, a wharf floating low in the river, bobbing up and down as the tide came in. A steamer ferry was pushing away from the wharf, loaded to the brim with passengers. Black smoke billowed from the coal-smoke stained gray boiler pipe, and near the top of the vessel, in a wood-sheltered area, the captain pulled the steam whistle, which shrieked a goodbye to the wharf and welcomed itself into the river, pushing arrow-shaped foam before it.

Left behind was a man in a tiny stall at the wharf's edge. He looked like he was doing a rousing business selling tickets for the next ferry trip, and Jack nodded to himself. Folks disembarking to wherever they might be headed were less likely to attend to their surroundings, being set on their destination, so picking pockets would be good.

He ambled down the stairs, which were wooden though they were still moss-edged and slippery, until he got to the wharf where the stall was. A small group of people, all young men, were coming away from the stall, holding slips of paper in their hands and talking amongst themselves.

Jack let them go without reaching into their pockets, for young men who would revel in a slip of paper bought at a wharf along the river were not likely to be the types who would not miss it when Jack took it. Instead, he walked up to the stall and saw the man inside turning around, as if to take care of clerking business. On the front of the stall was a sign in large letters that stated: *Steamer Ferry and Fish Fry: One Price! Greenwich Fish Fry!*

"How much?" asked Jack before he could stop himself. Nolly was always up for eating, and Jack was as well, and a trip aboard a steamer ferry was just the thing to take Nolly's mind off his current woes. "D'you have something for tomorrow?"

"That I do," said the man as he flared out a handful of brightly colored tickets on thick stock, as a man might deal a deck of valuable cards. "How many you want? Three? Five? Only two shillings each."

Two shillings was dear, and just as Jack was about to say so, the man tapped the tickets together and fanned them out again.

"Two shillings includes fare both ways and fried fish and beer in Greenwich, a lovely spot for lovers and friends alike. Are you buyin', boy, 'cause I gots customers waitin'."

There were no customers waiting, not behind Jack, at any rate, but only several men in top hats on the other side of the wharf, urgent on whatever business they needed to catch the next passenger ferry for. But Jack nodded and reached into his pocket to pull out four shillings, which he clunked brightly on the counter in front of the man.

"Two," Jack said. He watched as the man peeled away two bright blue tickets and slapped them into Jack's palm.

"Open seating," said the man. "Ferry leaves at 10:30, meal at noon, returns at 2 o'clock in the afternoon."

"Thanks ever so," said Jack. He put the tickets in his pocket and held his hand there to keep the flap closed, thinking the gift was sure to make Nolly smile upon his return to the Three Cripples.

He took a shortcut up a back lane until he reached the broad avenue of King William Street, which was busy but orderly with a stream of thin-wheeled gigs and high-stepping horses. The street itself was lined with high-quality shops such as a lady's tea room and an establishment that sold only top hats for gentlemen.

The shops were of such a variety that Jack considered he might, on another day, use it as a hunting ground to give the area around St. Paul's a rest, as it wouldn't be too clever of him, after all, if his became a known face there.

With this object in mind, Jack walked with the other posh folk, knowing that he could, on account of his outfit. To complete the picture, he did not whistle or amble along with his hands in his pockets, but instead walked with purpose, with his fingers lightly curled about the waist of his jacket, as he saw the other fellows doing.

By-and-bye, when the Bank of England could be seen just ahead, and the wide avenue Jack was heading up would turn left onto Cheapside or right onto Cornell, Jack espied a stationer's shop. Normally, he would not have given even the barest attention to such an establishment. Only this time around, the memory of Nolly's face, eyes downcast and a small pout curving his mouth, was almost right in front of him.

Nolly deserved to be happy, but wasn't because there were no letters in his life. True, one from Jack would hardly be akin to getting a reply to those Nolly had sent out, but perhaps it would be a start. So Jack scanned the street, skipped his eyes over the bookshop, and walked along the pavement toward the stationer's shop.

A sign, cut in a curved line on the top and the bottom to represent a piece of paper, hung over the open doorway, propped thusly, no doubt, to help catch a breeze. A pair of ladies, properly bonneted and gloved, came out of the shop just then, which indicated that it should be a rather elegant place, and it gave Jack a moment of amusement to imagine how he might be received there.

He paused on the newly swept pavement in front of it. In the window, he could see sheets of legal papers, printed and pinned up with mock seal-tags and cloth ribbons, angled so any passersby might see how thin the parchment was, how finely made.

As he stepped inside, he noted one of the walls was lined with wooden pigeon holes, each stacked with a certain type of paper for sale. Along the other wall were three writing tables, one of which was occupied by a young man writing something with a metal pen nib and black ink. The whole of the shop had a studious air, as Jack imagined a schoolroom might.

"Can I help you, sir?" asked a voice from behind Jack.

Jack turned to see a middle-aged man wearing the full apron of a shop clerk, complete with green leather sleeve garters about his forearms. Just coming up behind him was a young girl, also wearing an apron and the same sleeve garters. Their nicely shod feet poked out from beneath their matching aprons while they both looked at him as though he might be quite lost and in the wrong shop. Which was amusing, and Jack would have made much of their trepidation, except that today he had a small errand that he needed their help with.

"I mean to write a letter to my friend, an' I be wantin' to deliver it by hand. Like a gift, you see."

Jack stood there a moment and watched as their faces altered, only by a hair's breadth, but he could see it. He might be wearing a jacket and hat fine enough to dine with the Queen, but he'd given himself away merely by opening his mouth. As to whether they would shoo him out the door or call the nearest constable, he wasn't quite sure, for, after a moment went by, they were still looking at him, almost as if he'd not even spoken.

"I wish to write a letter," said Jack now, more slowly, taking care to pronounce each word as Nolly might, with those crisp edges around each word that always sounded so delightful when Nolly said them. "A little note to go with some tickets I bought, an' I mean to make a gift of it to my friend."

"Oh, yes, yes, certainly," said the man, finally. He nodded at Jack and folded his hands in front of him, resting them on his apron, as a clerk might while waiting on a proper gentleman. "A letter for a friend, you say? And you would deliver this yourself?"

That hand-delivering a letter was considered an uncertain decision by the clerk was clear. Also clear was that the clerk and the young lady, without even a glance exchanged between them, had determined Jack was either simple or that he had newly come into funds, by inheritance, say, as that would explain his fine clothes but rough voice and manners, as well as his lack of knowledge as to how stationery shops functioned.

Still and all, the clerk nodded and guided Jack to one of the tables along the wall, the one furthest away from the open door, as if in fear that Jack might frighten any prospective patrons. Jack sat down and placed both hands on the table.

Satisfied with Jack's behavior, it seemed, the clerk gestured to the young lady, who brought over several pieces of fine linen paper, a pen with a slender metal nib, and a bottle of black ink. This last, she opened for him and arranged the items on a dark brown blotter on the table.

The clerk's expectations seemed rather high, for though Jack knew how to write, most of his experience was with a lead pencil stub on leftover scraps of paper, such as had been given to him by the farmer in Port Jackson. He could sign his name in cursive, after a fashion, but with a pencil, rather than a pen. And, in addition, he'd never written a letter before, but had not considered that until this very moment.

"Does the young gentleman require a guide?" asked the clerk. He bent forward from his waist, still clasping his hands, but Jack had to place credit where it was due, as the clerk was doing his very best.

"Yes," said Jack, even though he had no proper idea what the guide might be. "I would indeed, could you be so kind."

Again, the young lady provided the necessary item, which she handed without a word to the clerk. The clerk then placed the guide on the blotter next to the blank sheets of paper. The instructions on the guide were written in cursive letters, which were not terribly fancy, but Jack still had to squint to make everything out.

"Do you see, sir?" said the clerk. "These are the parts of a letter. Here, the date, here, the address, here, your opening salutation, followed by the letter itself, and then your closing salutation, such as Very Best Regards, and so on." As he announced each part of the guide, the clerk pointed with the whole of his hand, palm flat, as though he expected that Jack, once reminded, would quickly pick up on the finer details and be able to proceed.

"Does it have to have all these bits?" asked Jack. The idea of it, so recently precious and fresh, now felt a tad overwhelming. Not that he'd admit that to the clerk, of course.

"No, I suppose not, if indeed this is a missive for a friend you will be delivering personally. So, in that case, you would only need an opening salutation, the body of the letter, and then—" The clerk paused and smiled, almost to himself, as if with the whimsy of the idea of it, of ignoring the letter-writing rules in favor of a more personal touch. "—and then the closing salutation. When you're done, perhaps I might fold it for you. We have wax up at the counter to seal it afterwards."

"How much, then?" asked Jack. He picked up the pen and tested the sharpness of the metal nib with his forefinger.

"Oh, don't press that way, sir, you'll puncture yourself." The clerk's hands fluttered close to Jack's hands but didn't actually touch him. "The whole should cost about a shilling, more if you need additional sheets, you see."

"Thank you kindly," said Jack. He reached into his pocket and pulled out a shilling and placed it on the table next to the blotter, where it made a dull clinking sound on the wooden surface. "I'll give it a go, shall I?"

"Very good, sir," said the clerk. He backed away with a small bow, his clasped hands once more in place in front of him. "But do let us know if there is aught you need."

Jack nodded, then turned to the papers before him. He took a good long read of the order of events in the guide, skipping the bits where the cursive was too curly. The language he could read was somewhat flowery and fancy, but it was what was wanted.

Then, taking a small breath and doffing his hat to rest on the table at the far edge, furthest from the bottle of ink, Jack picked up the pen. He dipped the pen nib in the bottle, tapped it along the edge of the bottle of ink to remove any extra and, with determination, carefully balanced the heel of his palm on the edge of the white linen paper, and began to write.

WITH THE RAIN ON THE VERGE OF LETTING UP, JACK TROTTED out the door of the tavern. He had been in high spirits, as was indicated by the angle of his top hat, and now Oliver was left alone in the swamp of the taproom. It was slowly filling with folk with not enough to do on such a muggy day and so who were crowding into the Three Cripples in the hopes of being amused, diverted, and so brined in beer and gin that they could blot out the whole of their respective existences.

At least that's what it seemed like to Oliver, who was pulled in behind the bar to slide an apron over his neck to help the girls, as Len and the rest of Noah's men were nowhere to be found. Even Noah had vacated the premises, perhaps for cooler, less sticky parts of London, though if those were to be found, Oliver would like to know of them. He would take Jack there, and enjoy a bit of a fresh breeze and watch Jack as he looked at birds taking flight, or the spill of water-foam over a low weir while they took a stroll down a country lane somewhere—

"Nolly," said one of the girls.

Oliver had to hold back the snapping comment that only Jack called him by that pet name. But as the girls at the Three

Cripples would not ever be intimate acquaintances, it was either that or they'd pick up on Noah's name for him, which would be deplorable.

"Yes, what do you need?" he asked, as politely as he might.

"Re-tap this keg for me, eh? The spout ain't all the way in an' the beer's seepin'."

It took Oliver an odd moment to realize that she was asking *him* because he was the only male figure on the premises, besides those worthies on the other side of the bar, who were only waiting to be doused with beer. As such, it was his responsibility to take care of these things because girls weren't strong enough to tap a keg, though evidently they were perfectly able to carry large, round trays ladened with many pint pots of sloshing beer.

"Very well," he said.

He bent to pick up the old buggy wheel hammer that Noah kept around for the odd repair, and walked over to the keg in its cradle that she was pointing to. Indeed, beer had leaked out around the tap like a puddle of piss and, warming on the slick stone, was beginning to brew itself into something quite different than what it was meant to be. As Oliver applied several quick flicks of the hammer, the tap clicked into place and the dribbling stopped.

"Can you get something to clean this up with?" He motioned with the hammer at the floor.

The girl stared at him for a long moment, as a cat might eye a bird upon which it was preparing to pounce. Oliver wasn't asking her to do anything he wouldn't do, except that, with such an audience, which had now quieted down to watch and listen, it was impossible. Unless it was for his own benefit or for Jack's, where Oliver was completely willing to tidy up and fetch and carry, it was a woman's place to clean.

"Could you *please* get something to clean this up with?" asked Oliver. "I'm sure we'll all appreciate not slipping in it later."

"Fine," she said with a proud attitude she'd acquired from somewhere. She lifted her skirts high enough to flash the round curve of her calf and announce to one and all that she was wearing a sky-blue petticoat. This caused the majority of the customers to whistle and clap, and actually emboldened her to do a little sashay, as though she were a dancer on display and wouldn't mind having coins thrown at her.

No coins were thrown, not that Oliver could have stopped any of it, but he stepped up to the bar to serve the now enlivened customers. He took their pennies and put them in the open box right below the counter, and served beer from the now properly tapped keg, and spilled gin whilst pouring it into small, short glasses, and sweated through his shirt for the next hour.

The girl had done as he'd asked and he thanked her quite nicely, he thought, though she didn't seem to know what to make of that, and didn't respond in kind afterwards. But if he was left in charge, then he needed to *be* in charge and to direct their work as he saw fit. This he did, doing it the way he remembered Mr. McCready doing it, and the afternoon wore on quite a bit more smoothly than he had anticipated.

The girls, both of them, began to turn to him to fetch bottles of gin, to stay a rough customer who insisted that one of them should sit in his lap when she'd gone out to deliver a tray of drinks. They also responded when he sent each of them in turn out to catch a breath of fresh air, such as it was, and it was he who reminded them that they might take some beer if in need of refreshment.

By the time a bit of wind picked up, enough to take away the damp so Oliver could take a deep breath, there were long circles drawn on his shirt, beneath his arms, the center of his back, and right in the center of his chest, where the apron couldn't hide it. Even worse, he'd been able to get a girl out only the one time to give the front step a sweep in the hope of engendering interest of more prosperous customers, who would recognize the sign of a respectable tavern, or at least one where they wouldn't get robbed so immediately after entry.

But since there'd been only the one sweep out front, and too many customers to ever give the taproom a good going-over, dust and detritus had built underfoot, beer spill went untended, and the flannel cloths used to wipe out the gin glasses reeked of old gin gone sour. There didn't seem to be anything Oliver could do about it, for he only had two hands, and was busy waiting on the customers himself, rather than making the Three Cripples presentable.

Such was the problem each time he was behind the bar. Chores that might make a meaningful difference went undone, and the Three Cripples remained as it ever had been, a down-at-the-heels sort of tavern in an insalubrious part of the City, a place where a man might drink without being asked too many of the wrong sort of questions.

So the dirt dragged in by the men's boots lay where it lay, and the smell of uncleared ash in the fireplace lingered at the end of the room, the ash now soaked from the rain that had dripped down the chimney earlier, smelling like something had been badly burnt. But nobody cared. Nobody but Oliver, and were he to stand on the counter and vent his frustration at the top of his voice, still nobody would care, and that was the most infuriating part about it.

But the constant flow of customers kept Oliver too busy to perform such a foolish and unrewarding act, and presently Noah came in with a few of his men, one of whom, Len, stepped behind the counter and began helping the girls. With only a grunt in Oliver's direction, and barely that, Len took over, and Oliver let the mantle of responsibility fall from his shoulders.

Len didn't put on an apron and so could have been anybody, but the customers knew him, recognized what he was doing, and kept ordering just the same. It gave Oliver leave, however, to peel off his own apron and carry it back to the kitchen.

There were two other aprons on a hook, both of them soiled, and Oliver stared at them, contemplating how much it might cost to take them and his extra shirt, also sweaty and currently unwearable, to a laundress. And not a local one, a proper laundress, who knew the power of soap and hot water and a stiff scrubbing board.

"What you doin' back here, then, eh?"

Oliver whirled around, putting the apron on the hook with the others, and felt the warm, slow sense of contentment running all through him, now that Jack was back. The low sun over the rooflines through the open doorway of the kitchen suddenly seemed more placid and golden, the air not so surly and foul smelling.

"Jack," said Oliver.

There was nobody near and, when he took a quick look, he saw there was nobody behind Jack in the passageway, so Oliver gave Jack a kiss and then another, and slid a fond hand around the back of Jack's neck. Jack was warm in his jacket from his walk from wherever he'd been that day, and when Jack slid off his top hat to give Oliver a kiss of his own, the dark ink of his hair was plastered to his forehead with sweat.

"I could rinse your head beneath the pump," said Oliver. "And then you could rinse mine."

"That'd be good," said Jack. He pulled his arms back as though he were about to peel off his jacket and cravat and waistcoat for this very act, but then stopped and smiled. "I gots somethin' for you."

Oliver looked at him. There was no book on Jack's person, unless it was that Jack had procured one of those small-scale books that looked intriguing but which only contained the poorest of poetry. But if that were the case, then Oliver would be grateful, for Jack had been kind to have asked if Oliver wanted anything, to have thought of Oliver while out and about in his beloved London. And if not, then perhaps they might later saunter out into the streets and find a bookshop and pick something out together.

"What is it?" asked Oliver. He was a bit dismayed at himself that he was not expecting much. But why should he need anything when he had Jack in front of him, looking slightly disheveled and contented to be so, with that saucy look in his eye and all of his attention on Oliver? He did not need anything, then, not when he had Jack, and anything Jack brought to him was extra. Oliver held out his hand. "Show me."

"I've got just the thing to cheer you up," said Jack. He reached into his jacket, then held out something on the flat of his palm.

It was immediately clear what the object was: a letter folded into its own envelope and sealed at the back with a round blob of red wax.

"Is this for me?" asked Oliver, reaching for it.

Just as his fingers curled around the edges of the paper, and before he could examine the address and confirm from whom it had come, whether that be the haberdashery, as was his first hope, his aunt and uncle, which was a sky-high impossibility, or from the Dawkins family, which was such a distant prospect as to be laughable, Jack lifted the letter up and turned it over.

"'Tis a letter," said Jack with a smile. "From me."

For a moment, Oliver remained still, but his heart, rather than slowing down with dashed hopes, from the lack of response to his earlier missives, sped up. His chest filled and filled until he was swimming in a vast sea of the most tender of emotions, that Jack would think to do *this*, that Jack would take the time. For there, on the front of the envelope, was the simple address of *Oliver Twist, The Three Cripples, Saffron Hill, London*.

This was written in what must be Jack's own hand, for the writing, while in cursive, was spatted with several pinpoints of ink that indicated the creator of such letters was ill-acquainted with how to shape the upward stroke using what had surely been one of those new-fangled metal pen nibs. As well, there was a long splotch in the lower right corner that looked very much like an ink-print of the edge of Jack's thumb.

"Don't you like it?" asked Jack.

Oliver found that he could not speak. Could not utter a single sound, though his mouth opened and he took a breath to at least try. With Jack's eyes fixed upon him, Oliver cradled the letter in his hands, curving his fingers around the edges with as much care as if he'd caught a small, cream-colored dove.

"Oh, Jack," said Oliver, his voice faint, which he knew did not convey the depth of his gratitude, his joy, his complete love for this boy from the streets who would do such a thing, such a delicate, *intricate* thing—

"Jack," said Oliver, quite breathless, looking up at Jack. "You wrote me a letter."

"An' so I did," said Jack. "So you should open it."

Though Jack's words might have been intended to be casual, Jack's smile told Oliver that Jack knew differently, that even if Oliver hadn't said as much, Jack's letter meant everything to him, meant the world. And thus proffered, made by Jack's own *hands,* his beautiful, clever hands.

"C'mon, Nolly," said Jack, stepping near to circle his arms about Oliver's waist and bring them close together. "You needed cheerin' up, so here you are, but you must open it. Ain't you goin' to open it? I'll hold you for as long as it takes you to read it."

"Then I shall take forever, Jack," said Oliver. He looked up to smile at Jack through his eyelashes in a flirty way that he imagined Jack rather quite liked. He stroked the back of the letter, turning it to the other side to run his fingers over the red wax stamp.

"'Tis only a bit of grubby paper with some writin' scratched upon it," said Jack. He stepped back a bit to give Oliver room, but still held onto Oliver's waist, his hands warm through Oliver's shirt. "An' I don't know what the stamp is on the wax, a tree or somethin'. 'Twas what the shop had."

Thus directed, Oliver cracked open the seal and, with great care, unfolded the letter.

Directly, two pale blue tickets fell into his palm, and he caught them before they fluttered to the floor. Their purpose was instantly known to him because while he'd never been, he'd certainly heard of the fish fry in Greenwich.

It had been deemed too wild and boisterous for any of Mr. McCready's boys, and way beneath the dignity of even being noticed whilst he'd lived with Uncle Brownlow. But for him and Jack, it would be a delightful outing, a ride in a river steamer to a place he'd never been, where they might practice a complete lack of dignity whilst eating and drinking with a large, noisy group of strangers beneath the boiling-hot sun. Unless it rained, of course.

Oliver felt Jack's fingers in his palm as he took the tickets for safekeeping and turned his attention to the letter. As with the outside of the envelope, the cursive handwriting had proven to be more difficult than Jack had probably anticipated, as splotches and pinpricks of black ink had been left where there oughtn't to be any.

In spite of this, Oliver held the edges of the letter as he might a fine sheet of beautiful colored glass, and scanned it. There, at the bottom, was Jack's lumpy signature. Whereupon Oliver's throat closed up, and though he had to blink rather fast, he read the entire of the letter without further delay.

From somewhere, Jack had divined the order of events in such a missive. This he had replicated to the best of his ability, for there, along with the sprawling handwriting and ink blotches, the whole of the letter was comprised of a single, streaming sentence.

Oliver took a breath and, holding the letter in one slightly shaky hand while he scrubbed at his eyes with the back of the other, he read the entire of it again, this time aloud, and was hardly able to keep his voice from trembling.

My Dearest Nolly,

In hoping this letter finds you well, I invite you to accompany me to the fish fry in Greenwich, please see the enclosed tickets for the journey and the dinner, with beer included.

Yours truly and forever,

Jack

"This is the finest letter I've ever received," said Oliver, swallowing the thickness in his throat. He gestured with the letter at Jack. "And your handwriting—I've never seen it before now."

"That's me, all right, an' nothin' to compare to your lovely hand, I'll wager, so it don't need sayin' now."

"I wasn't going to," said Oliver, with as much earnestness as he might. Then he bowed his head and read the letter again, each word, just for himself, seeing the care with which it had been wrought, the thoughtfulness of it, this, Jack's creation for him.

Jack's fingers curled beneath Oliver's chin and he looked up, raising his eyes to Jack's, and Jack smiled at him.

"There's that spark in those blue eyes I been missin'," said Jack. "I aim to do whatever it takes, every day, to keep them bright stars in your eyes what shine so brightly now."

Oliver swallowed and searched for the words, any words, to convey the sense he had of being loved, of being cared for. But, as ever, only the most practical matters revealed themselves.

"I've not been sullen, have I?" asked Oliver, truly wondering, for if he had, and it had given Jack any trouble, any trouble at all, then Oliver must rectify it at once, and take care not to let it be so again.

"No," said Jack, shaking his head. "You quite like havin' a go at this place, draggin' it into a respectable state, all unwillin'. But when you think I ain't lookin', I know you're poutin' about them letters, an' all. So I thought I'd fix it. An' who knows, maybe they'll come tomorrow."

"There's no mail on Sundays, Jack," said Oliver, but it was said without any heat, for how could Jack possibly know the timetables of the Royal Mail? "But the tickets, let me see them again. They're for tomorrow, right?"

Jack held out the two blue tickets between his finger and thumb; the ink was cheap enough that it had rubbed off on Jack's slightly damp skin. Oliver took the tickets for a moment to verify, then handed them back to Jack, but only after rubbing away the smudge on Jack's fingers with his own.

"We'll have to get up early," said Jack. "Or, more rightly, you'll have to get me up early." He laughed at himself, as if at his own laziness, to acknowledge it and perhaps to get Oliver to laugh a bit with him. "Are you game for the task?"

"Yes," said Oliver, feeling buoyed up by the thought of it, the instant pleasure of the outing that would happen the very next day without having to wait, and felt the smile on his face echo all throughout him. And, as Jack cupped Oliver's face with his hand and kissed him solidly, he fell in love with Jack all over again. "If the steamer—what's it called, the *Teal?*—departs at 10:30, and it's a quarter of an hour walk to London Bridge—"

"So let me sleep in till half-past," said Jack, to finish the thought for him.

"I will," said Oliver with a nod. "Will you hold onto the tickets? I fear I might lose them."

"Sweetheart," said Jack. "For you, the world."

Oliver took the tickets from Jack's hand and slid them into his left trouser pocket, slowly letting his hand slide along Jack's thigh before pulling his hand out and patting the front of the pocket. Jack's face softened, a small sigh on his lips.

He leaned forward to kiss Jack, but from beyond the closed door to the kitchen came a shout. Oliver distinctly recognized the proud tone of Noah, who could now bellow and have his orders followed to the letter, though either Jack or himself could have told him that Cromwell once ruled the place with only a few nods and a gesture or two. Oh, and yes, with some blows to the head, when needs called for it, but Oliver didn't imagine Noah would have listened, anyway.

Bursting through the door, Noah caught them mid-kiss and waved his hand in front of his face with a snarl, as if he wanted to erase the image from his memory.

"Fuckin' *shite*, Jack, I could have been anybody! Will you do that somewheres else where I can't see you? And you, Work'us, you have to be headin' up front, as Len might have to go out." Then Noah stormed out, slamming the kitchen door behind him.

Oliver laughed, right out loud and brushed off the sting that Noah's words were meant to incur. And, turning to Jack, kissed him boldly, folded up the letter, and held it to his chest.

"I should put this someplace safe," said Oliver, realizing only too late that what he meant to say was that because he was going to treasure the letter forever, it deserved to be put in a location safe from prying eyes and destroying hands. But Jack seemed to understand just the same what Oliver had wanted to say, for he nodded and flipped the tickets between his fingers.

"We can tuck all this away upstairs, an' then you an' I can skive off for a bit an' get somethin' to eat. An' then mayhap forget to return for a good long while? The breeze is freshenin' up, down by the river in particular, an' if we stand upwind of it—"

"Yes, Jack," said Oliver, almost immediately.

Never mind that with such weather, bold and changeable, the taproom would be quite busy. Len and the girls could handle it, and if Len had to go out, and the girls couldn't handle it, well, then it would prove to Noah that they needed additional girls, rather than fewer. Girls who could be hired with the under-standing that sweeping the floor and wiping down the counter were a basic portion of their duties, and that they should mind Oliver when he told them what they should be doing.

"We could go down to Blackfriars Bridge," said Jack, smiling. "An' stand in the middle, where the breeze should be strongest."

"I should like to change," said Oliver before he could stop himself.

"You've got two shirts," said Jack. "You c'n wear the other one."

"The older one, not the new one," said Oliver, eying the crispness of Jack's collar to ensure he was indeed wearing the new shirt Oliver had given him for his birthday.

"Pump," said Jack abruptly. "You go out to the pump, an' I'll put this away an' fetch you your clean shirt, an' the rest of your kit, for you look as though you could do with more than one rinsin'."

"It was sweltering, Jack," said Oliver, but without any argument.

He kissed Jack on the nose and handed him the envelope; such a sacred thing he would have entrusted to nobody else. Jack took the letter and smiled at Oliver again, and if he was terribly pleased with himself, well, he should be, for nobody had ever done anything so kind for Oliver. Not ever.

"Off you get," said Jack. "I won't be a moment, so go."

Jack shooed Oliver toward the door that led to the alley and the pump, and hurried off to do Oliver yet another kindness, in fetching a clean shirt, in not teasing him about it, for the thoughtfulness was always there, and Oliver knew he did not want to forget it.

10

THE DARKEST HOUR

"Will you stand still, Jack?" Oliver reached again for the tails of the red cravat and used them to pull Jack closer to him. "It will only take a moment, if you would just stand *still*."

"You're pullin' too tight, Nolly," said Jack.

"Your fingers are in the way," said Oliver in response.

The room was warm, the sun was up, and somewhere church bells were tolling half-past nine. At which point, when the bells stopped ringing, they needed to leave to get to London Bridge on time to catch the ferry to Greenwich.

Oliver used a quick moment to finish tying Jack's cravat, and to tweak the bow so it was a straight line below Jack's clean white collar. Handing Jack his top hat, Oliver took a step back, pleased with the view, the lines of Jack's shoulders beneath dark blue wool, the spin of the jacket's hem across Jack's thighs. For a moment, he considered that the fish fry could wait, even in the face of losing the cost of the tickets, so that he might disrobe Jack all over again and tumble him to the bed.

"I know what you're thinkin'," said Jack, putting on the leer that had the power to irritate.

Oliver didn't let it. Because, of course Jack was right, Jack could read Oliver's mind sometimes, but not today. The sky was a bright blue out of the dust-spotted window, and the warmth of the air coming in beneath the door spoke of a brilliant day, the perfect day, to take a steamer ferry ride and eat fish and drink beer out of doors.

"Yes, I am thinking it," said Oliver, giving Jack's nose a kiss. "But will you come along now and leave that for later? We don't want to miss the boat."

"There's a shortcut I know of," said Jack. He pulled on Oliver's jacket lapels a tug. "We'll be first in line, just you wait an' see."

They went out of the room, shut the door behind them, and clattered down the wooden steps, as if unaware of the spectacle they were making. Though certainly Noah remarked upon it by rolling his eyes and turning away, as if it were of no matter to him that he'd not been invited.

Outside of the Three Cripples, the sun was indeed bright. The air was a swamp of damp warmth beneath the rooflines of the houses that leaned over the sides of Saffron Hill as Oliver and Jack made their way down Field Lane to High Holborn. There, the traffic rambled at a fast pace, as it always did, making them quick-step it to avoid getting run over or trod upon. Along Holborn they went, and Oliver was very glad that it was not raining, for the slant of the hill would have been slippery, not to mention it would have mucked up their trouser hems and splattered Jack's new jacket.

As they hustled, Jack tugged on Oliver's sleeve and pulled him across the street to the pavement on the other side.

"We can save a full minute," said Jack, still walking fast, "if we go down Queen's Lane and cut across Pancras to Cannon Street. It's only a handful of moments from there to London Bridge."

Nodding without speaking, Oliver motioned with his hand that Jack should lead the way, for even if the path was less than salubrious in Oliver's mind, Jack knew the streets of London better than he. And, if it would allow them not to miss the ferry, then Oliver could bear anything, even the narrow rookeries that grew thick as they neared the banks of the Thames, with the effluvia of cesspits and privies, and the sweet dankness of an overflowing churchyard dug deep with too many bodies in not enough soil.

Jack turned into a lane that went between two buildings. The lane was so narrow that it might have been an alley, save for the open doors and racks of dried goods of such a low quality, dirty and grimy in the breeze on either side that Oliver couldn't imagine anybody wanting to buy them, let alone who would take the trouble to put them out to sell.

Then, just as the lane opened up and went in three direc-tions, Jack paused, as if determining the best way. Up ahead seemed the right direction to go, as Oliver could see. The space between two buildings must surely lead to stairs that went down to the river, for he could see the glint of the sunlight on the moving water.

If they stood there, even if only for a moment, they could find their bearings. But the clocks of the City were already striking 10 o'clock and, obviously hastened by this, Jack turned to his left, and grabbed Oliver's arm to pull him into what looked to be a dead end. There was a breeze floating about their heads, and the smell was dank and sour, as though someone had slaugh-tered an animal and forgot to collect the offal, but instead had left it to stink.

"This is not the way, Jack," said Oliver. He could not help but lift his jacket sleeve to his face to bury his nose in the smell of the lanolin of the wool, rather than rotting guts and blood.

"You're right, I think," said Jack. He looked as though he wanted to shrink from the smell, but, by force of will, was not going to.

As they stood in the shadow of the overhanging rooflines of the sagging buildings that lined the alley, there came the sound of a two-wheeled cart rumbling at a quick pace. This was not so odd, in and of itself, for the lane was too narrow for a regular, horse-drawn conveyance. What did trouble Oliver was the high pitch of the clatter, which indicated that the cart was going at speed, as fast as it might.

When the cart turned the corner and appeared before them, Oliver grabbed Jack's elbow to pull him against the damp and crumbling brick wall, in case the cart, in such haste, was thrown out of its owner's control and came crashing toward them. But instead of this happening, the cart came to a quick halt directly in front of them.

In the slanted shadows of the close alleyway, it was difficult to see whether the wheel had come off or that the cart needed to be turned around, or whether the owner meant to ask them for directions. But instead of any of those things happening, the man quickly put the handles of the cart down and came toward them, tall and broad shouldered.

Oliver had only a glimpse of the edge of a dark-brimmed hat before Jack backed up and bumped into Oliver, pressing him against the wall. The figure swung at Oliver and hit him in the head with something hard and solid. The blow tumbled Oliver to the ground, where his face slapped on the edge of the gutter that ran thick with muck, the smell of it filling his nostrils.

As Oliver looked up, he saw who the man was.

"Chalenheim," said Oliver, though his voice came out in a whisper and the ringing in his head made it hard to move, to call out to Jack, to warn him.

In the haze his vision had become, he saw Chalenheim clamp a broad hand over Jack's mouth, covering it with a brown cloth, the faint, acrid smell slicing through the stench of the filth and gutter rot. Oliver tried to get up, to raise his hand, to call out to Jack, but could only watch through vague, fogged eyes as Jack was tumbled into the cart, and sacking was pulled over him.

Then Chalenheim came at Oliver with the same motion he had used on Jack. A hand swept down over Oliver's mouth. The square of brown cloth had been soaked with something that smelled bitter, though his lungs could not resist drawing a breath, nor could his body resist as Chalenheim pulled him up and jerked the sacking back long enough to drop Oliver next to Jack.

Blackness covered Oliver as the sacking was tossed over him; there was the sound of creaking rope as the sacking was tied down. The cart titled when the handles were lifted up, and the wheels creaked as the cart began to move, bouncing over the cobbled road, the iron-clad wood striking the edges of stones.

The cart rocked gently as it was pushed along, at a normal pace now. Chalenheim's casual whistle belied his earlier haste, it seemed, though as Oliver sank down into blackness, barely able to feel Jack's still form beside him, he knew not where they were bound, only that he was unable to fight, to save himself and, worse, that he was unable to save Jack.

THE ARCH OF WOOD OVER OLIVER'S HEAD CREAKED WHEN HE put his weight on it, though it was only with part of his mind that he could comprehend this, for any thoughts he had, focused or no, seemed to wither away as soon as they formed. Right behind his eyes was a throbbing, sick feeling, like a fever that was just building and which would not soon abate. His arms ached, strung taut over his head, and his feet hung leaden and cold as the water splashed up around his knees.

Across a small divide of not much more distance than his own height was a bale of what could have been paper or cotton, which was soaked through halfway up its side. Over it was bent Jack, his hands bound behind him. Chalenheim stood close by, his hand on Jack's hip, a possessive curl.

Before this moment, before Axminster, Oliver would not have known what Chalenheim meant to do, nor what any man might want another man in that way, with Jack bent over, tied down, and unable to resist. Oliver did know now; he knew what

Chalenheim wanted, how Jack, immobile and spattered with mud, his trousers damp from the water that was at least ankle deep everywhere, was *exactly* what Chalenheim wanted.

Oliver tugged on the ropes that bound his hands and kicked at the water as best as he was able. He gritted his teeth, feeling the low rage that swamped through him as it cut back the haggard din, the remnants of the queer scent of the brown cloth clamped over his mouth, the coal-tar smell of the water—all of this flashed away, as if from a hard breeze.

"No," he said. He took a breath and said it louder. "No, let him go, untie him and let him *go*."

With these words, Chalenheim's attention became directed at Oliver. Instead of seeming cross, however, Chalenheim smiled his crooked-lipped smile, nodding his head as if in greeting as he sloshed through brackish brown water and came over to Oliver. Quietly, almost pleasantly, as if they were long-met companions at a small, friendly gathering.

"You won't have him, you won't *have* him." The words felt ground out as though Oliver were pushing apart heavy stones, but he took another breath and shouted, the words ripping through him. "With my bare hands, workmaster, do you hear? If you lay one hand on him, I'll tear you apart, with my bare hands —come closer now, you coward, untie me and I'll *show* you."

Chalenheim did come closer, tipping his head to one side, as if amused by Oliver's proclamations rather than concerned by them.

"You'll show me, will you? When I untie you? And why on earth would I do that?" The words were spoken with some derision, as though Chalenheim had put on this whole tableau merely to laugh at Oliver, to laugh at Jack, and then to assault him—

"You want *me*," said Oliver, taking a deep breath; his lips were numb, but he did his best to make sure the words were as clear as he could make them while his body shivered as the ice cold water soaked into him. "You don't want him."

"Oh, don't I? Why-ever would you think that?"

Chalenheim was so close to Oliver now, so close that had Oliver enough moisture in his mouth he could have spat in the workmaster's face. But it was more important to convince the workmaster that his desire to—that to take Jack was not his true desire. That his passion ran deeper, ran elsewhere, should be focused on someone other than Jack.

"Because," said Oliver. He licked his lips and tugged on the rope, but his mouth remained perfectly dry and the rope stayed sound. "You don't want him, you know you don't—what you really want is me—"

"You think I should want you because you're beautiful?" asked Chalenheim, serious, his amusement gone. "When it's your very beauty that repulses me? All the perfection of your class—so tame, so ordinary. Why would I want you when I could have the liveliness that is Jack?"

It wasn't going to work; Oliver strangled the cry in his throat and jerked on the ropes once more. They bit into his wrists, and when Chalenheim punched him in the stomach, the ropes had no leeway, and Oliver could not even curl to ease his gut, nor take a breath before the workmaster had his fist in Oliver's hair, pulling Oliver to stillness, the workmaster's quiet rage only inches away from his face.

"I should be grateful to you, you know," said Chalenheim, his voice a ragged whisper in Oliver's ear.

Oliver's only response was a gasp, but barely that as he struggled to breathe, to count the pulses of blood before his belly eased and he could open his eyes again.

"Yes, very grateful to you, but not enough to use you in Jack's place," said Chalenheim.

"What?" With his eyes madly watering, Oliver tried to focus, unable to understand what Chalenheim was saying.

"It was your letter to the kindly doctor what looks after the whores at the workhouses, the whores and their bastard brats. You paid him and he, very puzzled, came to the master, wanting to know why the return address was here in London, and why you weren't still being held for the June assizes."

For a moment, the blood thudded in Oliver's temple, as a raw, unbridled horror ripped through his chest.

"Yes," said Chalenheim, almost close enough that Oliver could feel the movement of the workmaster's mouth against his face as he spoke. "That's how I found you. Foolish boy, sending postal orders to pay a doctor who wouldn't even have missed the wages. Doing the right thing, weren't you. The proper thing. The *honorable* thing. Well, now you see where honor has gotten you, where it has gotten your friend."

To this, Oliver could say nothing, for there was no lie in any of the workmaster's words. Oliver *had* been proud of doing right by Dr. McMurtry, had wanted to show Jack how it was done, how a gentleman did things. Only to bring ruin down on Jack.

"Now, you watch, watch me take Jack good and hard, as he's been asking for from the day he stepped foot in that workhouse. And if you take your eyes away, then I'll know and I'll ravage Jack, and then I'll find a good sharp stick and fuck him with that, d'you hear? He'll bleed to death before the tide comes in."

Chalenheim took his hand away and patted Oliver on the cheek with sharp slaps. The sound of the slaps echoed in the damp air over the water that glittered brown and bronze from points of light that sliced through the wooden structure as it curved around them. Then Chalenheim moved away from Oliver and toward Jack.

Chalenheim stripped Jack of his trousers, undid his own trousers, shifted Jack's legs, and moved between them.

With eyes so dry he could barely blink, Oliver watched as he'd been told to do. He didn't wince or turn away, or even cry out when Chalenheim used Jack so roughly that Jack began to whimper, small, shiny tears dappling his face, Jack who never cried nor complained. *Jack—*

∾

THE SMELL OF OLD PLUMS, SOUR WITH THE ROTTING STINK OF sitting in the sun too long, filled Jack's nostrils. He could not breathe in without tasting that smell, but his lungs screamed with the need for breathing, and so he did, hearing the ragged sounds of it, as though they came from far away. His arms were tied behind his back, and he was bent over something that was soft around the edges, but which had gone rigid with time and the absence of activity.

Face down, he tried to blink away the sense of sinking below the surface into a black space, quite still and distant, like the depths of an ocean. An ocean he knew in his mind, rolling beneath the creaking wooden hull of a ship tendering crew and convicts far, far from home.

There was that familiar smell, too, of damp rope and tar that had been sprung loose by splashes of salt water; nothing could resist the effects of salt and water, Jack knew this. Just as he knew that the side of his face was sore, and the back of his head thumped with each pulse of his blood. And that he couldn't move.

All around him, he heard the creak of wood as water moved against it, though he was certain he was not at sea, no matter how much part of him felt that rocking movement, the slow sway of a ship's deck as it cut through the water. He was in London. The stink of coal tar told him this, as did the foment of the Thames stirring the filth and refuse that floated the particular and familiar scent that would always remind him of home.

Blinking, he tried to lift his head and even as his neck screamed at him to stop, a broad hand pushed his head back down, scraping his cheek against the once-soft surface.

"Ho there, Jack," said a voice that Jack strained to remember. "You'll not want to move, not when I put you just as you are for a reason."

Jack's top hat was floating in front of his eyes, bobbing like a black buoy on the muck-flecked water, but where was his jacket? It was gone. He shuddered with cold, though the day had promised to be warm and sunny, and he and Nolly had plans and tickets for the fish fry—

A man picked his way among the puddles, moving between Jack and his floating hat. Jack arched his neck, wincing, blinking, trying to see—and then saw. The man was Workmaster Chalenheim, and he was dressed in a dark suit for the City rather than the brown clothes of the workhouse.

Jack did not feel surprise, but only the dull recognition that, of course, it would come to this. He should have been on his guard, more aware of his surroundings. He should have known, should have *known*—

Where the workmaster walked was mostly dry, though his steps seemed to squish as he went to where Nolly was, tied up to a post, his arms over his head, which made him reach high and left him unsteady. Jack could see Nolly keeping his eyes on Chalenheim; he must not know Jack was awake now, or those blue eyes would be on him, and Jack did not know which was worse. That Nolly was ignoring him, or the reason for it.

Chalenheim stopped just in front of Nolly and, though it was hard to focus, it seemed that Nolly was shin-deep in brown, still water, and that the water just lapped at Chalenheim's boot tops, as though the water didn't dare touch him. All around, the curve of water-darkened wood arched like the ceiling in a church, but there must have been a gap somewhere behind Jack's head, for the light rushed in like the flames of angelic fury, though there were no angels to be found. Only Nolly, who was shouting something in words Jack could not discern, so fierce in his tone that had Nolly been untied, Jack would have feared for Chalenheim's safety.

Untroubled by Nolly's fury, Chalenheim was speaking to him, his tone low. But then, just as Jack screwed his eyes open and squinted, as if that would help him hear beyond the booming fog in his head, Chalenheim drew back and sent his fist into Nolly's stomach. Nolly lurched, though he wasn't able to curl forward to ease the whole-body collapse that would follow a blow such as that.

Jack winced for him, licked his lips, and tried to talk, but it was no use. The smell of rotten plums rose up in his nostrils each time he moved even slightly. But as though a picture were being drawn in front of his eyes in slow motion, Jack saw Chalenheim grab Nolly by the hair and yank him upright.

Chalenheim was saying something; Jack could see that mouth, the way it moved, harsh and stiff, as if Nolly had stepped out of line, and Chalenheim needed to remind him of his manners or he'd be back in the refractory room before he took another breath. Finally, Chalenheim let go of Nolly's hair with a shove, patted his cheek soundly, almost as if he were slapping him, then he turned away from Nolly. Toward Jack.

Jack's whole body jerked, though not a hand had yet been laid upon him. The ache in his head reared up, and he closed his eyes and tensed against it. When he opened his eyes again, the world still smelled like rotten plums and was colored a vivid white-gold, speckled with reflections of the brown water as it lapped against the wooden walls.

For a moment, he thought to concentrate on all of this, on his surroundings that looked like the lower decks of a ship, except tilted sideways, with the bottom hull sinking low about them, and the walls sagging, as though pushed down by an unbearable weight.

But these thoughts, as they climbed toward the edge of knowing where he was and inside of what type of structure, were vanquished by the feel of Chalenheim's broad, strong hand on the back of his neck.

"Are you ready for me, Jack?" asked Chalenheim, in a voice that slipped over the surface of Jack's skin like used ship oil. "I can see that you're not, so let me assist you."

Jack tried to move, but his arms were bound behind him, flat against his back, and pulled at his shoulders. He was sprawled face down with his legs trailing over the edge of the side of whatever he was on that was, inexplicably, as soft as a flannel cloth. If he scooted down and got his feet solidly beneath him, he might be able to get away, but this thought was yanked from him as Chalenheim's hands, with hot-surfaced palms, pulled him down over the edge until he was bent at the waist, with just the toes of his boots scuffing wooden boards.

Chalenheim's hands were at Jack's waist, and reached around him in a mockery of an embrace to undo the buttons on his trousers, the tabs on his undergarment, and yanked the strings loose. With a sharp tug, Chalenheim took Jack's trousers and undergarments down to his knees, where they sagged limply and shook themselves about his ankles.

"You won't need those for a bit, eh, Jack?" asked Chalenheim.

He moved behind Jack and grasped him by both hips, his long fingers digging in as they pulled Jack closer. The motion stirred up stringy wisps of powder that Jack inhaled with his breath of shock; it tasted like old paper, which, left too long on the shelf, had untangled itself from a firm, silky press and left only dust behind.

But the surface was not soft. The edges were hard, and the surface brittle, scraping at Jack's bare thighs, catching at the private hair between his legs. It scuffed his belly as Chalenheim, his fingers still locked around the bones of Jack's hips, pushed him down, as though he were trying to flatten him.

There was movement behind Jack that he could not discern, but then he felt his trousers and undergarment yanked all the way off his legs, which, bared to the damp air, twitched, and the shiver rushed up his back as Chalenheim placed the flat of his hand just at Jack's naked waist.

As he squinted, he saw Nolly watching, looking right at Jack with wide, unblinking eyes. It was strange why Nolly would be doing such a thing instead of raging against what was happening, to gnaw at the ropes that bound his wrists, to break free— though his wrists were red-raw, and his face tinged with gray from the blow to his stomach. If Nolly could have gotten free, he would have, so that meant he couldn't. Couldn't save himself. Couldn't save Jack.

Jack thought to garner enough moisture in his mouth to say something to Nolly, to calm him, but he felt the blade of Chalenheim's fingers pushing up to separate Jack's buttocks, as though to cleave him in two. Then the fingers were withdrawn.

Jack heard Chalenheim spit, and before Jack could breathe or tense his muscles, two fingers, side by side, jabbed into Jack's anus, scraping delicate inner skin, blunt as an unsharpened knife. Jack's whole body tightened around it, but Chalenheim smacked Jack along the length of his bare thigh, which stung and made Jack curl away.

In less than a heartbeat, Chalenheim withdrew his fingers, and his weight was upon Jack, the scratch of his woolen waistcoat on Jack's spine. He grabbed Jack's jaw in his fist as he wrenched Jack's head sideways.

"You will not resist me," said Chalenheim, and his words seemed simple, though there was a hissing, scraped sound beneath them. "Do not make me use other means to enforce your compliance, or you will regret it."

Jack could not make sense of the threat, beyond that it was a threat, for the hard length of Chalenheim's body pressed down on Jack so the edge of whatever he was lying on bit into the bones of his hips. Just beyond that feeling, merely an inch or two down, the layered softness sprang up to caress the front of Jack's thighs.

With another jerk of Jack's head, Chalenheim moved back, taking his weight off of Jack. The fast-cooling spit on Chalenheim's fingertips swirled around Jack's anus just before being thrust in again, scraping inside of him, the shove jerking him forward, making him gasp aloud.

"That pleases you, Jack?" asked Chalenheim, his breath coming thick in his throat. When Jack didn't answer, Chalenheim withdrew his fingers and patted Jack's buttock, his fingers curving against Jack's skin to squeeze. "Well, it pleases me."

Jack heard the rustle of cloth being moved, felt the shift of weight behind him as Chalenheim moved between Jack's legs, his hands upon Jack, his fingers biting into the tender skin along the inside of Jack's thighs, spreading him wide. When Jack's legs couldn't accommodate that, Chalenheim pushed up on Jack's left leg, hefting it high enough to bend and rest on the rough surface.

Jack felt the damp air move between his legs, and tightened his throat against crying out, for Nolly still watched Jack. And though Nolly could have turned away or stared at something else, he did nothing. Nothing but watch.

Jack closed his eyes.

Chalenheim's cock, hard and blunt, entered Jack, pushing its way into his body. The round nub of its head scraped into him, rendering him quite still. He remembered it would hurt if he jerked about, that it might cut him if he resisted. He fought the cry in his throat, the hot tears in his eyes that would stay nothing, would appease no man, nor alter his purpose.

Jack had tried resisting the lieutenant in Australia, but only the once, and now Jack knew resistance would not work. He swallowed everything, the cry, the tears, and the feeling in his heart. Just for now, he would become nothing, while Chalenheim shoved his cock all the way in, his bollocks warm for brief touches against him as Chalenheim sawed in and out.

The workmaster's spit had dried away to nothing; Jack felt his insides being scraped out of him and then shoved back in. The horribleness of it seemed faint, almost distant, until Chalenheim leaned in. He pressed his scratchy wool-suited front to Jack's back, which squeezed Jack's bound hands between their bodies. His hands clamped on Jack's shoulders, almost damp with their pressure as he stilled, his mouth on Jack's ear.

"There, Jack, there," Chalenheim said, his words almost as tender as a lover's kiss. "Do you see, do you see how easy it is to come to me as I have wanted it?"

Jack's stomach surged about, as though he'd been all day on a coach being pulled by six horses with nothing to steady him, with Nolly miles away while Jack was being rocked to his own death. It wasn't enough for Chalenheim to abuse him, to fuck Jack raw as he was doing; Chalenheim wanted the reward of Jack's approval.

Chalenheim kissed Jack, his mouth open on the back of Jack's neck, as though he was giving Jack something sweet, something Jack wanted. Chalenheim wanted Jack to like it, as he must have wanted it from all the wee boys in his care as he took them, one after the other.

He'd confused those boys with kisses and sweet words, all the while plundering bodies too small to accommodate him, too new to the world to understand the meaning of it. Those boys, some of them at least, must have whispered *yes, yes* in the dark to stave off the nightmare that had come to life, an act so monstrous it would make all the scant meals and miserable drudge-work seem tame by comparison.

Jack opened his mouth, bile rising in his throat. Chalenheim, as if sensing Jack's resistance to his courtship, curled his hands around Jack's shoulders and pulled back just as he thrust his hips forward, sinking his cock so deep into Jack that Jack yelped out loud. He felt the sting of something tearing, deep, felt the welt of it, as if nerves had came to life at that very moment, dormant until cut apart.

Now the tears did come, pelting down Jack's face, his cheeks numb, his mouth tasting salt. Chalenheim must have determined that the depth of his cock was the exact right one, for he repeated his thrust, over and over, until Jack's throat closed up around his scream.

Chalenheim stiffened and pushed in once more, leaving behind shudders that echoed into Jack's bones, and the spray of his spunk scattered behind Jack's eyes. Then Chalenheim pulled out, and Jack was left cold, his breath sharp and ragged.

Warmth dripped out of him, oozing slowly between his legs to where his own sex hid in his private hair. If he could have curled up around himself, he would have, but Chalenheim remained between Jack's sprawled legs and patted him.

"I'll leave you boys here," said Chalenheim. Jack could hear sounds of trousers being pulled up and waistcoat being smoothed to rights. "This old hulk, well, she's not as seaworthy as she used to be, what with all her beams waterlogged as they are. As she's scheduled for scuttling, it's of no consequence to anybody that she goes below the waterline when the tide comes in, as it is now."

Bending close, Chalenheim took Jack's head in his hands and tilted Jack's chin to the side. He kissed Jack on the mouth, moist and wet, with tender lips and a stab of his tongue. Chalenheim's hands clenched Jack's jaw to make him open his mouth, and Jack struggled to pull away, but the kiss deepened, slick with pressure, against which Jack had no resistance.

Jack could taste his own tears, and the beer on Chalenheim's breath, and the sour tang of Chalenheim's spit. It choked him. His throat closed up, and just as Jack was about to jerk his head away, Chalenheim withdrew, patted Jack's cheek, and kissed him on the forehead.

"Good boy, Jack," Chalenheim said, with warm fondness in his voice. "You've been a good boy."

Jack closed his eyes and listened to the steady tread of the workmaster as he walked away. He heard the faint splash as the workmaster's boots skirted a puddle, and heard the faraway clang of a bell, the hooting hiss of a steamer passing on the river, just out of reach, out of eyeshot.

He sensed that his body shook, that his belly ached, that between his legs the flesh thumped as blood pounded from his heart, that his anus leaked something warm that cooled as it dribbled along, and he thought of the stains. What would Nanny make of the stains? She would surely tell Missus Rose, who would tell Mister Harry, and then what would happen? Nolly would be cross—

Nolly.

Something tightened around Jack's spine and streaked across his back as he tried to move. White spots shot in front of his eyes, making his head reel sideways, as if the whole space around him tilted in a circle. But there was nothing to cling to, nothing to grab onto.

As the water rose, he felt it around his ankles and heard the splash of it against the wooden hull. The reek of sewage and the smell of water-soaked wood filled the air about him, and he clamped his mouth shut. Waited while the whispers of someone calling his name echoed against the water lapping against the hull. There was a low, dull thud of a rocking boat hitting the waves the wrong way and being tumbled down below the surface of the water.

He held his breath as long as he could or the water would take him, and the smell of rotten plums would come back, and he wouldn't make it home, home to where Nolly was.

But in that space, that black space between one thought and the next, an eternity between them, he heard a thud and splashing, and felt damp hands on his arms. He jerked away, thinking Chalenheim had come back for another go at him.

"Jack."

From far away, a voice said his name. Up close, Jack felt the pressure on his arms, but his shoulders felt screwed on backwards, and he wanted to howl at whoever it was to get them to stop touching him. But the voice said his name again, and somebody leaned close, smelling like river water, yes, but also like beer and sweat from simple labor, and it made Jack want to go toward the sound.

"*Jack.*"

Jack tried to open his eyes, but blinking brought on a rush of dizziness, making the world swirl around and around like a leaf in a spin-storm.

"Jack!"

The voice was shouting now. It meant business and wasn't going away simply because Jack was ignoring it.

"Jack, wake up, *please*, wake up—"

There was a flurry of action as someone untied the ropes that bound Jack's arms behind his back. Then warm hands pulled his arms to his sides, gently, slowly, as if the utmost care were the very least Jack deserved. There were more splashing sounds and the smack of something wet as it landed on the surface of the water near his head.

"Please, Jack, please—I'll help you get dressed, but we need to go. He said he would leave us, but it might be a trick, and he might mean to come back and do the deed himself before the tide can take us."

As much as Jack wanted to follow this lengthy statement, it being said with such earnestness, he only could focus on the bit where the voice said that it would help him get dressed. There was only one person who would do that for him in the state that he was in—

"Nolly?"

"Yes, Jack, yes," said Nolly, coming in quite clear, quite close, making Jack wince as the sound echoed in his head. "Will you get up? Can you get up?"

Jack opened his eyes. Nolly was bent down, looking at Jack, and he was drenched from head to toe. His wrists were rubbed raw, his face white, hair dripping water down the sides of his face.

"Dressed," said Jack.

He meant that as an agreement, but before he got dressed, he needed to be sure he could walk. Reaching back behind him, he drew his fingers along the cleft between his buttocks. The touch stung like a rusty saw blade, but as he brought his hand up, he opened his eyes as well as he could to examine what he'd drawn forth: Chalenheim's spunk, drying thick white, with only the faintest, palest sliver of pink.

"If it ain't bleedin', it ain't bad," Jack said, holding his hand up so Nolly could see, so the truth of it could be made plain, so

Nolly would scrub away the worried squelch of his brows, and swallow the hasty gasp that he did not hide.

Nolly took Jack's hand and rubbed it against the dampness of his own trousers, spreading a film of drying white, a stain that would never come out. But this did not seem to matter to Nolly who, with a steadiness about him that did not quite seem real, shook out Jack's trousers and laid them down, then helped Jack to ease himself up.

With his shirt hanging to his bare knees, Jack finally saw what it was that he'd been bent over. It was a bale of cotton rag paper, slick-surfaced but soft along the edges. Having been left behind, the bale had soaked up river water and dried, and soaked and dried, over and over, till the surface was stiff and the edges had split like feathers.

The rising tide was bringing the water up to their knees, and only Nolly's quick thinking saved Jack's hat from floating away. As Jack reached down and tried to pull his trousers up from where they now dangled in the water, Nolly helped him. His hands were sure and strong, so Jack only had to stand as still as he could, though the worried look was etched on Nolly's face.

"How did you get out of—" Jack pointed to the beam where Nolly had been tied, his shoulders snapped in pain as he did so.

"The—" Nolly swallowed and pushed wet hair out of his eyes. "The water was coming in, and you wouldn't wake up. I kept shouting—but there was this wooden beam, so I stepped on it and climbed up. The beam he tied me to didn't go all the way up. Or sideways, I'm not sure. Only—we need to go, Jack."

Jack got down from the bale of rag paper, his feet splashing, the water up to his knees, and shoved his hat on his head. It felt foolish to be wearing the hat with no waistcoat and no jacket and no—

"Where's my cravat?" Jack asked, his hands at his throat. But then he saw that Nolly only had his shirt and trousers as well, so it might be that Chalenheim had taken the garments to sell to pay for his ticket back to Axminster. "Don't matter," he said now. "Where are we?"

Above them, as the tide came in and the water splashed higher, the hull of the derelict ship moved, groaning with the effort of staying afloat, faithful to the last, even without a captain to man her.

"We must get outside," said Nolly, grabbing Jack's arm and pulling, as if it were Jack's hesitation that was delaying them. "When we get outside, out of the water, then we can figure out where we are. Where he took us."

Nolly snapped his mouth shut and began walking toward the narrow end of the hulk, away from where the sun was shining in like stabs of gold, lighting up the brown water as it slapped against the hull.

Jack wanted to point out that they should go to where the sun was coming in, as that would lead them to a way out. However, Nolly seemed insistent and went the other direction, which left Jack with nothing to do but follow.

Which he did, limping, his middle aching, his arms wrapped about himself in a way that made it hard to keep his balance. But Nolly's hand was on Jack's elbow, holding him up, leading him through the narrowest gap in the layered planks of wood.

Just when Jack was sure they'd have to turn back, they came out in the open air. They were up to their ankles in mud, water sloshing about their feet on the slanted bank of the River Thames as the tide came in.

Ahead of them, along the north bank of the river, was a series of piers, docks, and brick warehouses, some of which were quite burned from the inside. Between two of the buildings was a set of steep stairs that must have been used to load and unload cargo, allowing men access to ships, whether or not the tide was in.

Nolly pulled them across the muddy bank, then clambered up the stone steps, dragging Jack behind him. Jack gasped aloud as Nolly jerked him to the top of the landing, turned them both about, and then pointed to the horizon. There, to the right and above the rooflines of the houses and structures of London, was the mushroom-colored dome of St. Paul's Cathedral.

"We're south of the City," said Nolly.

"We're on the Isle of Dogs," said Jack.

"Halfway to Greenwich."

"Didn't make it to the fish fry," said Jack, trying for levity. "D'you think they'll give us a refund?"

Turning to look at him, Nolly opened his mouth as if to speak, but the words must have scattered before he could grab them, for he only drew in the slightest breath, not enough to make even the smallest sound.

"Don't look at me that way, Nolly," said Jack. "I've been through it before, y'know. I told you about that time an' this is no different."

Nolly stood there, both hands clasped to his forehead, looking for all the world as if he were alone and contemplating the direction he might take to get back to the Three Cripples. It almost seemed that Nolly didn't believe a word of anything Jack had just said, neither the joke about the refund nor the reassurance.

Jack didn't say again what he'd said at the Three Cripples when the snow had still been on the ground, that boys got buggered every day, for surely Nolly knew the truth of it, now that he'd seen it with his own eyes. But maybe that was the problem, the reason Nolly's mouth trembled as he looked at Jack, the reason for his wide eyes, and the way he shook his head as his arms dropped to his sides.

"I'm all right, Nolly, I've been through worse. C'mon, now." Jack moved forward, his hands out. His trousers slapped against his thighs and raked his skin, grabbing at every scrape and bruise till Jack could hardly stand it. "Just take me home an' get me some dry clothes. I'll be right as rain, I promise. You need dry clothes too, don't you? And somethin' for them wrists?"

"My *wrists*?" The words broke as they came out of Nolly's

mouth, which was drawn in a thin, stiff line, rather than being sweet and rosy, as Jack wanted them to be. "You're worried about my *wrists*, after what he did to *you*?"

"Nothin' Allingham hadn't done," said Jack. "But with more force, I reckon."

"You *reckon*."

Nolly blinked hard, his face white with fury, and seemed on the verge of tears.

It would be better for him if he did cry, and better for Jack, as well, because then Jack could comfort Nolly and assure him that everything would be fine, once they were into dry clothes and had a laugh about it over pints of beer. Or rather, gin and sugar for Nolly, he who'd been sticking to beer since their arrival at the Three Cripples. No wonder he was wearing that wounded look on his face, seeing as how he'd been betrayed by the lack of gin.

11

A RESCUE MADE TOO LATE

The bank of the Thames was thick with damp, sucking mud, which made their trousers slap against their legs with each step. And though it occurred to Oliver to wonder how the workmaster had gotten two inert bodies all the way from above London Bridge, down the stone steps, across the bank, and into the hulk of the derelict ship, he did not stop to think about it. For he had Jack's arm slung around his shoulders, and though Jack was able to walk, at least mostly, he stumbled through the slog of mud, his feet almost dragging.

Jack was heavy in Oliver's arms with a weight that seemed made up of more than of his own body, as though it had been added to by the abuse that now hobbled his spirit and was dragging it under.

"There, Jack, the stairs. We'll go up those, and once we get out of the mud, it'll be easier. Just hang on to me, and I'll get you out of here."

Almost tripping over the heaviness of the mud and the scarred rocks that jutted above the surface, Oliver turned and tried to bring Jack with him to move them toward the stairs. Not that Oliver could think much beyond the stairs and the road home. For as Jack struggled in the mud beside him, he seemed to be heading off in his own direction, straight up the bank to the wooden posts that kept the water from flooding the cellars of the warehouses in high tide, and this rather than heading across toward the stairs.

"This way, Jack," said Oliver, as he tugged on Jack, keeping his grip firm.

His voice was clogged with damp, his breath strangled by effort. Beneath that, his heart raced, his entire strength of will spliced through with deep cuts that kept him from putting his whole effort into it. For if Jack didn't want to return to the Three Cripples, then Oliver could not make him, though surely that was the only place they could go.

"Leave me be," said Jack, tugging himself away, pulling out of Oliver's arms. "I'm all right, I tells you, 'm all *right*."

This was certainly not so, for just then Jack's knees buckled beneath him, and it was only by a hair's breadth that Oliver was able to tighten his grasp to keep Jack from tumbling into the mud. But he couldn't scold Jack, nor point out that Jack was wrong, for Jack could be stubborn in his own way, and certainly now he seemed to be denying that anything out of the ordinary had happened to him at all.

By the single factor of not saying anything, Oliver managed to guide Jack to the stairs. Bit by bit, they stumbled up them, with Oliver staggering beneath Jack's weight as they rose above the incoming tide, where the brown water of the Thames was easily swallowing the muddy banks and the brown ribs of the ship that listed in the water.

At the top of the steps, Oliver turned, Jack's arm over his shoulder, and saw along the bow of the ship, in curling, broad blue letters that were dappled into shadows by time and weather and the water of the river, the name of the vessel: *HMS Scylla*.

Oliver turned away and made Jack go with him along the narrow passage between two sagging warehouses, their frames touched by fire, the smell of soot and burned coal tar strong in Oliver's nostrils. Jack made no comment, not even when they got to a main street of pounded dirt, and Oliver stopped and stared about him.

The street, Westferry Street, as the sign indicated, was not known to him, but he did know there was a great deal of distance between them and the Three Cripples, at least four miles, if not more. He could not carry Jack all that way, nor continue to urge Jack to walk if he did not want to.

Jack's head hung on his shoulders, which caused the top hat to tumble to the dirt. Oliver considered the hat. It was soaked with foul river water, making the felt stand up into wretched spikes; the smell of it alone would have turned heads even in the grottiest, more sinister parts of London. So Oliver didn't remark upon it as he tugged Jack along the street, going uphill a bit and toward London, and left the hat where it was.

"D'you have any coin on you, Jack?" Oliver asked.

"Spent all of it on you an' the tickets," said Jack, amusement in his voice.

Oliver felt his heart twist, for if Jack was going to make a joke of the whole of it, then Oliver would be left alone to struggle beneath the weight of what had happened to them both. Well, truth be told, what had happened had happened to Jack, and Oliver, while affronted by Jack's casual air, could not judge, for he'd not been through what Jack had.

But he did not know if he could ever scrub the images of what he'd seen. Of Chalenheim using force to enter Jack's body, to touch Jack as Oliver had done many a time, but without the gentleness, the sweetness, that Jack liked, that he *deserved*. Oliver felt his throat closing up and swallowed the tension away. Gave his head a small shake and tried again.

"Not even a small coin, like a sixpence?" asked Oliver.

With even that small amount, they might, *might*, be able to catch an omnibus. But, besides being too far out to catch one that went near the Three Cripples, the way they smelled, the way they were dressed, the mud and river-water stains driven through their clothes, not to mention Jack's hollow-eyed expression, there was no way any omnibus would even stop for them, let alone admit them on board.

With a sigh, Jack stopped and shook off Oliver's arm. Standing alone in the dirt street, mostly steady, Jack reached into his pocket with a perfectly blank expression on his face.

As if his trousers weren't drenched.

As if he weren't standing there half naked.

As if this were an ordinary moment where Oliver had asked Jack for some money, and Jack, because he loved Oliver, would reach into his pocket and hand over whatever amount he had. Which he did this time, as well, presenting to Oliver an entire, somewhat oddly shiny shilling, and this he pressed into Oliver's hand, curling Oliver's fingers around it.

"You c'n buy whatever pleases you, Nolly," said Jack, not looking Oliver in the eyes. "Though I've not any idea what you might want to buy all the way out 'ere that couldn't be 'ad fresher, for cheaper, in London."

These words indicated that Jack knew where they were, even if he didn't seem to want to acknowledge *why* they were so far from home. It was as if his mind had become cut off from the rest of himself, detached in the way a body might be just upon waking, when the sense of one's surroundings were not quite the same as the dreamland from whence one had come.

A frightful slice of shock spread throughout Oliver's chest and, with his mouth slightly open, brow furrowed, he looked at Jack, trying to understand it all, why Jack was acting the way that he was.

"We need to get home, Jack," said Oliver now. "You and I, we need to get home. We'll walk a bit and see if we can't find some form of transportation."

But Jack wasn't really listening to Oliver, as his eyes were staring at a middle distance, focused on nothing as the water dried in streaks on his face, and his arms hung listless at his sides. It would be up to Oliver, then, to find a likely delivery wagon that would be carrying goods rough enough so the driver would not care how they looked, or how they smelled, and wouldn't mind earning an entire shilling for carting them close enough to the Three Cripples so they could slink inside without attracting overly much notice.

Ignoring the stares of anybody that they passed on the dirt road, Oliver kept Jack close, his arm about Jack's waist to keep him steady, to keep him walking. Jack kept his head down, breathing through his mouth as though wracked with a long-standing chest ailment, which spiraled Oliver's worry up into jagged peaks that no amount of steady thought could abate.

But Oliver could not let himself care what anybody might think upon seeing them as they were, filthy and half-undressed and hatless, their clothes drying into sharp folds about them, ruined beyond all repair, boots squeaking water at each step, leaving small puddles as they went. His forehead was coated with sweat, the dust from the road settling on his skin everywhere, the panic he felt making him hot and then cold in turns, and still he needed to keep them walking in the direction they must go.

If they'd had a fat wallet of money, between them they could have managed to find a good hotel, somewhere close and local. But with the lack of that, the Three Cripples was the only place they could go, the only place that would admit them without question.

This thought, the irony of it, churned in Oliver's mind, scattering most other thoughts elsewhere. Until, that is, he heard the clatter of horse hooves and the hard rattle of large, iron-clad wagon wheels coming up the road behind them.

Oliver pulled Jack to the side of the road, holding him close, his eyes on the wagon that was now in front of them. The wagon held dirt and smelled of manure, as if destined for a fine garden somewhere in town that needed the refreshment of dark, country earth.

"Sir," said Oliver. "Sir, could you spare us a ride into town? How far are you going?"

"Take you into town, you say?" asked the driver from the

bench of his slow moving wagon. He tipped back his flat country hat of straw and spat a long, dark streak of tobacco on the road. "What, and ruin my fine load?"

The question was a joke, of course, since the wagon was only hauling dirt. But this, along with the fact that the horses were going slowly, gave Oliver some hope.

"I could pay you a shilling," said Oliver. He let go of Jack and, leaping into the wagon's way, held up the coin. "My friend and I only need to get home. We've had a rough night."

"I'll say you have," said the man. In spite of his straw hat, he was not a common farmer, but was dressed like a proper gardener with tall boots and dark knee patches on his thick trousers. His hands were seamed with dirt.

"Hand it over and get on," said the man, as he pulled on the reins to slow the two horses. "There'll be no refreshment, mind."

This, again, was obviously meant to be amusing, but Oliver couldn't laugh, not now. As the wagon slowed, he pulled Jack into the road, and waited till the wagon stopped.

Oliver got Jack to use one of the wheel spokes as a step, made him put his booted foot upon it, and half-lifted Jack up until there was nothing else Jack could do but to go where Oliver pushed him. Oliver quickly followed suit, taking his foot off the wheel just as the driver clicked the horses into motion.

"How far are you going?" asked Oliver over the clatter of the wheels as he handed the driver the shilling. With the smell of the rich dirt beneath him, he settled on his backside, and drew Jack to sit next to him, near the center of the load so they would not fall out.

"Just this side of Smithfield," said the driver, not turning his head to look at them. "For the gardens at Charterhouse Square."

Oliver knew where that was. It was only a few moments' walk from the Three Cripples. The narrow alleys between the gardens and the tavern would provide a path for them that would draw the fewest remarks so Oliver could keep their state a secret, and could hustle Jack inside, where Oliver could care for him.

"That would be fine," said Oliver. "Thank you."

"Ain't no trouble to me," said the driver.

The wheels clattered as the wagon was driven from the dirt road onto a cobbled street that was flanked by newly built warehouses. The tallness of the buildings cut off Oliver's view of St. Paul's, but he knew they were headed in the right direction. As well, not having to walk all the way home would save Jack's strength, which was good, because sitting with his legs crumpled beneath him, Jack seemed to sway with the motion of the wagon, his eyes unfocused, shoulders slumped.

Oliver did not think Jack's mindless posture was based on his trust in Oliver to manage things, but more that Jack was asleep, lost in his mind somewhere, in some dream state that kept him from attending to his surroundings. But at least he wasn't resisting Oliver now. At least there was that, though the freedom from this one worry whipped all of Oliver's other concerns into a spin-storm.

AT CHARTERHOUSE SQUARE, THEY ALIGHTED FROM THE gardener's delivery wagon and slipped off without saying good-bye. The dust of the street coated them. This, added to the clumps of earth from the wagon that had sifted into every fold of cloth, made them more conspicuous than Oliver would have liked. Though they had kept to the back alleys as they went from Charterhouse Square to the Three Cripples, and had used the most insalubrious passageways, they had been noticed, for an old woman had pointed at them, and two men had tried to stop them.

In spite of that, nobody had called the constables, and here they were, home at last. But while the front door didn't seem the way to go in, to go around to the back alley meant staying in the streets longer than necessary.

Oliver took a deep breath and opened the front door, dragging Jack behind him, his hand on Jack's arm, not letting go as they entered the cool darkness of the tavern. The irony of the Three Cripples being a safe haven for Jack as well for himself was not lost on him.

A mid-afternoon crowd was in attendance, as was usual on a Sunday. The taproom was packed with men whose pay packets were still full enough to allow them to gear up early for their pre-Monday carousing, as well as those hangers on, who had no labor on offer, but who were hoping for a taste of free beer from a more generous companion. Most of the crowd of men were pushing at the bar, where only Nick and one of the girls was in attendance, overwhelmed already.

Normally, Oliver would have grabbed an apron and jumped into the fray, eager to show them how a place like this could be run, how not to give in when a man begged for a dram of gin, how to keep the counter clean from slopped-over beer. But this time, no. He had Jack at his side, Jack whose head was still down, the stench of the river on them both a strong reek in Oliver's nostrils in this closed space.

Rising over the heads of the men at the bar was Noah, dressed in his Sunday usual, his trousers too brightly patterned, his top hat in place, ready to greet anybody who would say hello to him. He was holding a newspaper in his hand, but was frowning at Oliver and Jack, as if they'd disappointed him somehow.

Now there would be no way to get past Noah and up the stairs, to hide Jack in the room where Oliver could tend to him to the point where nobody would be the wiser. Still, he kept guiding Jack across the floor, weaving his way through tables and customers alike, not letting himself be distracted by the sudden glances, the rising curiosity. But Noah intercepted them at the foot of the stairs, just the same.

"Say now," said Noah. "Where you lads been? An' what you been up to? Surely a fish fry don't end with you lookin' like you been drug through a bush backwards, eh?"

Noah's tone was full of jocularity. And, in normal circumstances, Noah would have been on the very verge of reminding Oliver of his scheduled time behind the bar, would point to the growing crowd of demanding clientele. Then, of course, he would slyly remind Oliver of his debt to Noah, three weeks' worth of wages and then some, chiding Oliver into guilt. But Oliver couldn't leave Jack alone, not in the state that he was, half-asleep and unaware of anything going on about him.

"Why're you 'oldin' on to him so tight for, Work'us?"

Oliver made himself look up, not letting go of Jack. His entire body tightened for action, whether it be to sprint up the stairs, dragging Jack behind him, or to dash out the door and find shelter elsewhere, though as to where, Oliver had no idea.

Noah was staring hard at Jack, his brows drawing together, which made him seem serious for once. The comic effect of this novel expression on Noah's face was erased by the fact that Noah looked unlike his usual self and more like someone concerned with something outside of his own existence.

"What happened to 'im? Did somethin' happen? Work'us, why does he look like that?"

"Please, just let us go upstairs, Noah. This is nothing that need concern you." Oliver's tone carried the weight of their history behind it, at least in Oliver's own ears, a tone he hoped Noah would understand everything without him having to explain it out loud.

But Noah wouldn't be swayed. Instead, he reached out to Jack, who averted his head, his gaze, and struggled as though to get free from Oliver's grasp. Oliver took that moment to slip past Noah and push Jack up the stairs ahead of them, as quietly as he might, without fuss, though Jack seemed to be trying to say something over his shoulder to Oliver.

"Why's he walkin' so strangely, Work'us, did someone 'ave a go at him?"

Whatever Noah meant by *a go at him*, Oliver did not want to stop and discuss, but only kept climbing the stairs, taking a deep breath when they arrived at the landing just at their door. Oliver turned the knob and opened the door, urging Jack to go in.

Noah was right there, following them, and pushed them before him, and shut the door behind him, trapping the three of them together. There, in the small, stuffy room, their river-stained state was obvious, the low odor of river mud and muck more blatant in the closed space. Oliver reached to open the casement window, just as Jack sat down on the bed, slumped forward, his hands on his knees.

"It don't matter, Nolly," said Jack, very low, so low that Noah took a step closer to hear him.

Oliver could not trust that Noah's attention wasn't out of bald curiosity, or what his reaction might be if he found out what had happened but, short of forcing Noah out of the room, there was almost nothing Oliver could do.

"Don't matter," said Jack again. "Don't matter if Noah knows. I been fucked against my will, an' what of it? Happens every day, as I've told you more 'n once."

To Oliver's surprise, Noah was looking at *him* now.

"You let this happen?" asked Noah, his brow rising to his hairline.

"*Let?*" asked Oliver, the word coming out a hiss. "You think that I *allowed* this to happen? Are you mad?"

Oliver clenched his hands into fists, his whole body tightening, fiercely glad to have such a simple foe presented to him, for as he'd beaten Noah to a standstill once, he could do it again. Right now, here in this room.

"Fuckin' shites both of you," said Jack, all at once and completely unexpectedly. "Noah, fetch me some cool beer. Nolly, help me with these damn boots, for I mean to lie down."

Both Oliver and Noah turned to look at Jack, their heads

pivoting in an echoing motion. Jack sat on the bed, and though the ghost of detachment flitted behind his eyes, he seemed to know where he was and what had happened to him. True to Jack's nature, the simplest, most practical of solutions had presented themselves to him, and now he was making his wants known.

Noah, even in his exalted state as the owner of the Three Cripples and its attached empire, was ever in Jack's thrall. And so, without another word, he opened the door and dashed down the stairs to do Jack's bidding.

Which left Oliver alone and trembling from the sudden change in Jack's behavior. Moving close to kneel at Jack's feet, he began to undo the river-soaked laces.

He looked up at Jack, his fingers going through the actions blindly. He wanted Jack to look at him, though he did not know what he wanted from that point forward. For Jack to react in some way, as he had at Axminster? For Jack to cry, as he had when Chalenheim had been at him? But Jack only sat there, his dark hair stuck to his pale face, his lips ashen gray, his green eyes blank and still.

Jack's hands tightened and then loosened on his knees, but he made no other movements as Oliver undid the final turn on the laces and then pulled both off both of Jack's boots. They were quite ruined, the tips already curling up as they dried, the tongue leather mangled beyond repair. But while boots could be replaced, and easily so, the ruin the day had left behind were of far more import. As was Jack's state; surely he was uncomfortable, sitting there on the bed.

"Stockin's," said Jack, in a flat voice, ghosts in his eyes.

He looked directly at Oliver as he said it, as if daring Oliver to object to the request. Oliver obediently pulled off Jack's stockings, but these were ruined as well, so he tossed them on top of the wretched boots.

"Jack, are you in pain? Shall I fetch a doctor?" Oliver asked as he held Jack's cold bare feet in his hands.

"A doctor?" Jack almost laughed at this, though the sound that came out was more derisive than Oliver had imagined it might be. "Whatever for? To have him poke an' prod an' turn his nose up at an ill-used street lad?"

"But he'll have medicines for you, something to take away—"

"Take away the pain? Dear Nolly, it'll fade on its own. Besides, I have enough to be dealin' with now, what with you lookin' at me like you are, like you're fixin' to dig inside me an' see the damage for yourself."

This was exactly what Oliver wanted to do. He wanted to strip Jack to the skin so he could examine each bruise, each hurt, to tend to them with kisses and salve, to wash Jack clean of what had happened to him. To cover Jack's body with his own and shield him forever from the rest of the world.

Oliver paused, still kneeling at Jack's feet. Jack's crotch was just at eye level, and Oliver realized his eyes were resting there, looking for stains, looking for evidence as to whether Jack was bleeding—because while Jack had shown Oliver he wasn't bleeding, at least not very much, that had been at the *Scylla*. Now it was later, and Jack had walked and climbed stairs, and been lifted into a wagon and pulled out of it again. Pushed up the steep stairs at the Three Cripples.

"Are you bleeding, Jack?" Oliver swallowed as he placed Jack's now-bare feet gently on the floorboards and stood up. He didn't mean to loom over Jack, but it was necessary to make his point perfectly clear. "Because if you are, I'm going to fetch a doctor, whether you want it or no."

Darkness flickered in Jack's eyes, reminiscent of the time, back in the winter of the year, when Jack had demanded that Oliver tell him what had happened to Fagin's gang, and the anger that had shone in those eyes when Oliver had denied knowing anything. For it seemed Jack had known better than to believe Oliver then, and now, now he seemed only a heartbeat away from being truly angry, for he pointed a finger up at Oliver, his mouth curved as though he were on the verge of snarling. His eyes were so dark they were almost black.

"You so much as walk in the direction of a doctor, Nolly, an' so help me God, I will lay you low."

Jack did not make threats, nor had Oliver ever heard him speak in such a tone, and never to Oliver. With his mouth open, his eyes blinking as the shock of it trembled through him, Oliver took a step back.

"But Jack—"

"You mind me, y'hear? I mean it, Nolly, no doctor, won't have 'em near me, stickin' their instruments in, stirrin' me about, no, I won't *have* it."

Oliver tried to think of it the way Jack was thinking of it, of doctors who fumbled and caused pain rather than healing, who administered treatment, only to have the patient die, anyway. But there were good doctors as well, ones like Dr. McMurtry, who were sensible and kind—

Oliver put the back of his hand to his mouth to keep his thoughts from tumbling out. Jack was in such a state that any refusal from Oliver, any rebuke at all to indicate Jack was not in his right mind and therefore not able to make these sorts of decisions, would most certainly be met with the most unpredictable of reactions from Jack. Jack, who was always easygoing and mild, but who now looked at Oliver as though Oliver might betray him at any moment.

Oliver was saved by his own confusion when the door opened, and Noah walked in with a pint pot, which Oliver fervently hoped was filled to the brim with beer, as that was as good as any tonic a doctor might bring.

Without asking, Noah pushed Oliver to one side and handed the pint pot to Jack. Jack took it, his fingers curling around the sides rather than holding it by the handle, and drank half the contents in one go. With a panting breath, he lowered the pint pot; his eyes flicked back and forth as he looked at Oliver and then at Noah.

"No doctors, Noah, y'hear? You keep *this* one from goin' behind my back, as well you can."

Even Noah seemed taken aback by Jack's terse gesture at Oliver, who knew that, given the single opportunity, he *would* go behind Jack's back. But to Noah's credit, he did not crow about this, as he normally would have done.

"Get us clothes, somethin' clean an' dry, an' I'll pay you for it later." Jack lifted the pint pot to his mouth, his sentence drowned out by the interior of the pot as he drank the last half of its contents.

"That I can do, Jack," said Noah with a voice that, for once, lacked any tone to indicate he would gloat later that Jack had turned to him for help, rather than to Oliver. "I'll have one of the lads fetch them at once. Boots as well?"

"The lot," said Jack. He handed the pint pot back to Noah and, for a moment it was as if Oliver wasn't even in the room. "Now out. I mean to lie down."

Noah, the pint pot clutched in both hands, gave Jack a small nod and did as he was told. He left the door ajar, as he might do if he assumed Oliver was going to completely obey Jack in this and would also leave.

"You, as well," said Jack. "I don't need nobody watchin' over me whilst I sleep."

Oliver tightened his jaw. He pushed the door shut with one hand, and stood there, his palm resting on the panels of the door.

"I mean to stay with you," said Oliver as firmly as he could. "You don't want a doctor, that's up to you, but I won't leave you when you've just been—assaulted as you were. I shall lie down with you."

"Not on the bed w'me," said Jack. His eyes narrowed to slits as he looked at Oliver.

Oliver nodded and took his hand away from the door, glad that Jack was letting him stay, for what if Jack were to be taken by a seizure, or called out for assistance and nobody was there?

"The floor, then," said Oliver. "Give me the blanket, at least, and I'll sleep on the floor. To be nearby, in case you need me."

For a moment in the dusty room, with the breeze coming in warm through the open window, taking the smell of river water out and bringing in more dank smells from outside, there was silence. Then Jack shifted and tugged the blanket from the bed and tossed it on the floor. He kept the pillow for himself and, turning in the bed, lay down, facing the wall, curled on the mattress, covered only in the sheet, pulled the pillow beneath his head, and was still.

Oliver longed to go to him, to curl behind Jack in the bed, to soothe Jack and be himself soothed by Jack's nearness. But the tense line of Jack's back, the silence that grew awkward without the ease that was usually between them, kept Oliver from doing this. So even though it was only in the afternoon, and well before the shadows of twilight stretched across the rooftops of London, he spread the blanket over the floorboards and lay down upon it.

The floor was hard, and the blanket was scratchy. Each bump and bruise in his body, whereas before they had been miserly and alone in their complaints, now joined in a chorus, remarking on each discomfort. The jagged feel of his wrists, the soreness of his belly, the ache Chalenheim's fist had left behind—all sang loudly to him, and all he could do was close his eyes and focus on the sound of Jack's breathing.

They had gotten out of the *Scylla* before the tide had come in, and they were both alive. And, for the moment, they were safe in the Three Cripples. Though, if Chalenheim had been able to find them before, he surely could again, if he wanted to, if and ever he found out they'd made it out of the hulk alive.

Exhaustion welled up and circled through Oliver's body, numbing his brain to the point where he could no longer make sense of his own thoughts, his memories of the day, let alone concentrate on how he and Jack might see each other through to tomorrow.

12

JACK LIGHTS OUT

It wasn't noise that had awoken Jack, but the silence. The stillness. He opened his eyes, felt them widen, and took stock of the room with the pre-dawn haze coming through the window. It was early. He was alone in the bed, though he could hear Nolly breathing. Uncurling his body, Jack peered over the edge of the bed.

Nolly was asleep on the floor with no pillow beneath his head, and only the one blanket to shield him from the hardness and grit of the floor. Nolly slept with his back to the wall and his face toward the bed, as if he'd meant to keep an eye on Jack throughout the night but had dozed off, unable to stay awake.

Though Jack shifted on the bed, pushed on his elbows to sit up, Nolly did not stir. He only slept on, his face gentled in sleep, his mud-streaked fair hair mussed about his head, his mouth soft and slightly open. As the room grew a little brighter, Jack could see Nolly's closed eyes were purpled, as if he'd been in a battle, and there were streaks of river mud on his jaw, his shirtfront, the knees of his trousers.

There was a sour smell building in the room, thick with undulating ripeness that threatened to blossom into something even more unwholesome. That is, if boots weren't cleaned, and clothes not given a good scrubbing, not to mention their bodies and their faces.

But Jack couldn't bear the thought of stripping to the skin in front of Nolly, which was why, even with Noah's willingness to get them a fresh change of clothes, Jack had not wanted to change or wash up the night before. Instead, other than taking off their stockings and boots, he and Nolly had slept as they were, and now the room had the odor of murky water, of unhindered sewage that floated down the Thames night and day.

When Nolly woke up, as he was no doubt soon to do, given his natural inclination to be an early riser, he would tend to Jack, as if it were not only his duty, but his *right*. Nolly would want to feed Jack and find some soft balm for his bruises and scrapes. He would be tender. He would be kind. He would be relentless in all of this, until Jack knew he would break, frayed at the edges by an unquenchable love, the kind Jack had all along encouraged, but would now only find unbearable.

And, worst of all, Nolly would urge Jack to allow himself to be led to the nearest bathhouse, where Nolly would order the freshest hot water, the sweetest soap. Then Nolly, stripping Jack to the skin, would be able to see the marks left by Chalenheim's hands, the punishing bruises, the scrapes on Jack's belly and the front of his thighs.

Far better would it have been for Jack to have been alone with Chalenheim in the hulk, the HMS *Scylla*. Far better that Chalenheim had raped Jack twice more than to have had Nolly as a witness. It had been bad enough to have Nolly there in the workhouse when Chalenheim had been pawing at him, and then to have been forced to tell the story of the situation in Port Jackson. And situation was all that it had been, an agreement between two parties who each stood to gain by it.

Mutual affection there might not have been between Lt. Allingham and Jack, but benefit there most certainly had been. Allingham had acquired a house boy, a boot boy, and a bed boy, all rolled into one, with the status of it being so. For his part, Jack had been able to avoid rougher treatment, and never mind that he'd not always been in the mood when Allingham had gestured to the bed. Jack had survived, and that was all that mattered.

Jack had survived Chalenheim's full onslaught in the *Scylla*, as well, and both he and Nolly had come out of it with their whole skins. Only from Nolly's expression at the time, that had not been enough. For to look at Nolly, at the hard shine in his blue eyes as he'd untied Jack, was to know that while Nolly had kept a level head about him, leading the way out of the hulk, all of that had not taken as much toll as being in the same place when such unholy things were happening.

Worse still was being there when Nolly woke up. For though Nolly most assuredly was exhausted from the day before, drenched with river water, overcome by exposure to cruelty, when the sun came up, he would be right *there*. Looking up from his spot on the floor. At Jack, with those eyes of his. And, knowing Jack as he now did, after spending so much time together, Nolly would be able to see where the chinks were. Where the cracks in Jack were that let the darkness slip out and slip in.

That could not be allowed, because Nolly should not be exposed any more than he already had been by what had happened to Jack. Nolly mustn't see or be near or touch or anything. He could not be tainted by *any* of this.

Jack needed to hole up, just as he'd holed up when Kayema had been chopped up for dog food. It would only take a little while, a few days, and then all the cracks would be stoppered up, and Nolly would not have to experience any of it. Jack would be well, and then they could go on as they had been.

Except perhaps a bit more gingerly. As Jack stood up, the back of his legs stiffened in protest, his head wobbled on his shoulders, and he had to put his hand out and hold on to the table or topple over, right onto Nolly. Who was still sleeping and, God willing, would continue to do so until Jack was well away.

Jack took the red leather change purse from the drawer of the table beneath the window and grabbed his stockings and boots from beneath the bed. As he moved sideways between the bed frame and where Nolly slept on the floor, Nolly stirred, took a breath, and fell still once more.

All the while, Jack held his breath. Nolly would not want Jack to go anywhere, let alone on his own, but Jack knew he needed to. With quiet intention and the slowest, most careful hand, he turned the doorknob and slipped out of the room, closing the door behind him.

The air in the stairway, as he went down, was much fresher than that in the room, which was a miracle and a relief on his overly hot and sticky skin. He knew he smelled. Like the river. Like the dust of a rag-paper bale. Like Chalenheim's spit, the musk of his cock. And all over, it seemed, Jack itched from long-dried spunk.

He should have washed last night, but again, the length of his skin, his whole body, would have been open to Nolly's eyes, to his hands. Jack could not have borne the look on Nolly's face. Not that Nolly would despise him, no. But he would pity him, and that Jack could not stand.

At the bottom of the stairs, Jack was met with the empty taproom, which was still and quiet, as it would be early on a Monday morning, with a ghostly sheen of ash and dust from the night before, the faint smell of beer and sweat. An echo of shouting and laughing, of cursing. And there, at the end of the counter, on a high stool, sat Noah, pouring coffee out of a small pot into a white china mug.

"Hey?" said Noah. "You're up early? An' where's himself? Still abed, the lazy fuck?"

Jack did not correct Noah, nor chide him, for he was intent on what he needed to do, on what needed to happen before Nolly got up. He remembered this feeling from that time after

Kayema had died. Of needing to find some place still and quiet, of feeling there were horse blinkers on his head, that he could only see straight forward and everywhere else was a white shroud, coming down upon his senses like fog.

"I'm goin' out," Jack said. "Need to hole up. Will you tell Nolly?"

"Dressed like that? You're all river muck. Some copper's bound to notice." Noah jerked his thumb in the direction of the kitchen. "Got your clothes last night; you can grab 'em on your way out. An' never fear, I'll share the word w' Work'us."

Noah's calm response to the announcement of Jack's plan eased the tight line of Jack's shoulders that he'd been holding without even knowing it. This was the right thing to do. To go off and get well and come back to Nolly in one piece.

"Thanks for the clothes. Look after 'im for me."

That this was not something he would normally ask of Noah. That Nolly would not be pleased Jack had left was only a faint trace of worry along the edge of the shroud about Jack's head, for he could only focus on what was in front of him. On that and the strain along the backs of his thighs, between his legs, the dull thump of blood beneath his skin. That it ached to draw breath as he hurried through the kitchen, grabbing the closest pile of clothes and a pair of dry boots as he raced out the back door of the kitchen to the alley.

At the pump, he laid down the bundle of clothes and shed his shirt and trousers, still damp and smelling like rat piss. Then, naked in the alley, he pumped water over his head and sluiced it down his body, not looking at the black circles and handprints on his hips, nor at the black and green welts along the front of his thighs, the crust of spunk in his private hair.

Shivering and scrubbing at his skin with his nails, he would have murdered for some soap, but to stop and get some was to risk Nolly coming awake to find Jack gone. At that point, Nolly would try to find Jack. Jack planned to be long gone by then. But he'd not much time; the sun was already sending yellow streaks over the rooftops; the smell of something frying in grease came along the alleyway.

Jack shook the water from his hair and pulled on the new stockings, rough but blissfully dry, the thin cotton undergarments and the dark workman's canvas trousers, the faded muslin shirt. A dark cloth cap for his head. A thin blue waistcoat. There was even a sun-faded belcher handkerchief to tie about his neck, and a thick belt for his waist.

He put these things on, knowing that he looked like a common laborer and, with luck, resembled one who had never stolen a thing in his whole life. He drew the red leather change purse from the pocket of his old trousers and shoved it in the pocket of his new ones.

Walking up the alley, he left his old clothes in a pile; they'd be snatched up within the half hour. Then he headed uphill and ambled along, he, a working man, not in any hurry to get to wherever his supposed labor would start. With his hands in his pockets, he attempted a whistle, but his mouth was too dry and he hadn't the heart for it, so he stopped that and just kept walking, which was all he could manage.

WHEN IT WAS MORNING, OLIVER WOKE UP INSTANTLY, sitting up on the blanket, his hands beside his thighs. He looked at his booted feet and wondered why he'd not thought to take his boots and stockings off before he'd gone to bed the night before. And wondered some more, for a brief moment, why he was sleeping on the floor.

He looked up at the open casement window, at the thin cotton curtain fluttering in the breeze. At the empty bed. And then remembered. But there was no Jack, sleeping the morning in, as he liked to do, as surely he would continue to like to do, in spite of what had happened. For if what Chalenheim had done to Jack changed him irrevocably and forever, then Oliver would—

Would what? Well, hunt Chalenheim down, for one. And take Jack away from London, to the seaside—but no. Oliver had heard the words Jack had spoken about missing London, had heard the echo of those words in Jack's heart, how he wanted to be in the City. Oliver had returned with Jack to London on purpose, for Jack, so he could not now drag Jack away from his beloved City, even for his health. That is, unless Jack wanted it so.

As to where Jack was now, the main taproom was likely the answer, even at so early an hour. So Oliver stood up and brushed himself off, watching the flakes of dried mud and dust sift in the air before falling to the floor, only to be picked up again by the breeze coming in from the open window. But there was nothing to be done about the disaster the room had become; Jack was more important than anything.

As Oliver walked down the stairs, he realized it was quite early on a Monday, which would explain the dearth of customers, of noise, of activity. Over by the fireplace on the far side of the room was a small group of men who looked to be coal-whippers, if their soot-stained aprons were anything to go by, having a quick drink and intense conversation amongst themselves.

At the near end of the bar, as was his habit, was Noah with his nose in a newspaper, his shoulders hunched down so that almost nothing of him could be seen.

"Noah," said Oliver, walking up to jerk the paper down out of Noah's hands. "Where's Jack? He's not upstairs. When did he come down?"

"Oh, an hour ago, I'm thinkin'." Noah tugged the paper out of Oliver's hands and laid it out flat on the counter, and attempted to smooth it with his hands. "He said to tell you he'd gone to hole up, an' that I was to look after you." This last bit made Noah smirk, in that way he always did when he felt he'd gotten the upper hand, and meant to squash Oliver further by gloating.

"And you let him go?" Oliver's voice rose high enough and hard enough to attract the attention of the coal-whippers by the fire, but he didn't care. "In the state that he's in, you *let* him go? What if he's hurt? What if he bleeds to death?"

All of a sudden, the calmness and restraint that had, up to that moment and on Jack's behalf, restrained Oliver, left him in a hard rush, and all of the anger, the pulsing frustration, the worry over Jack, burst forth. Oliver grabbed Noah by one of his lapels and punched him with a curled fist. Then he drew back and punched him again.

Noah went tumbling from his stool, hands pinwheeling in a wild way that Oliver might have laughed at, but now only made him bend down and draw Noah up again to strike him once more.

But Noah, once on his feet, was not about to be caught unawares and drew up both fists to protect himself, and to jab out a blow. Oliver dodged as he shoved Noah against the counter and held him down, punching him, teeth bared, so angry and so very glad to have something to take all of it out on, and no one was more deserving of being a punching bag than Noah Claypole.

"He was all *right*," said Noah with a shriek, raising his hands to shield his face, blood curling about his mouth in a lurid, red circle. "He looked steady on his feet with his wits about him."

"You shouldn't have done it, Noah, letting him go." Oliver snarled the words, then, using the flat of his hand against Noah's face, slammed it onto the surface of the bar. "Should *not* have done it."

From behind Oliver came a thunder of feet, and suddenly somebody was pulling him away from Noah who, with his hands crumpled against his neck, looked at Oliver with hot, hard eyes.

"Shall we take him out back, boss?" asked one of the men,

Nick, by the sounds of it, though Oliver wasn't about to take his eyes off Noah. "Give him a good thumping?"

For a moment, Noah looked as though he were considering it, and Oliver could hardly blame him, as he could see the outrage in Noah's expression, even through his own red fog. Because now Noah had muscle to back him up and could have ordered that Oliver be torn asunder with the leftover parts tossed in the Thames, where nobody, not even Jack, could ever find him.

"Jack wouldn't like it if we did that, lads," said Noah, though his eyes stayed on Oliver. "He was right as rain when he left here, even though this one's goin' on like the body'll be found in a ditch or worse." Noah leaned forward, wiping the blood from his dripping nose with the back of one hand. "He washed an' dressed an' all, an' then he went off to hole up, 'cause he ain't like you, ain't no delicate flower, even if he has had some man's pole shoved up his arse."

There was a moment of silence. It filled the room with a terse shock that vibrated the air.

There was nothing Oliver could do to take the words back from Noah's mouth, nor to tend to the men and make them forget what they'd heard. But now everybody would know what had happened to Jack, in spite of Jack's own lack of concern about it, though Oliver could only presume that he would not want it known. Jack had only told Noah because Noah had been staring at him in the small confines of their room at the top of the stairs.

Oliver shook himself out of Nick's grasp, and glared at Noah, and pretended Nick and Len and the rest of them weren't even there.

"Get him out of here," said Noah, jerking his thumb at the door to the kitchen.

Nick obliged Noah. He dragged Oliver off by the scruff of his ruined collar, whereupon some of the buttons snapped off and clattered to the floor.

In the kitchen, Nick let go of Oliver, and he stood, his half-bare chest heaving as he looked at the table in the middle of the room, upon which sat a pile of folded garments and a pair of working man's boots. A cloth cap. Leather-pointed suspenders.

"Get dressed," said Nick, pointing at the clothes. "I don't care where you go, but make yourself scarce from here, you got it?"

It was not really a question; there was a clear threat in Nick's eyes. He was not one of those who relished the glamor of Jack's history with Fagin, so, as it was clear to see, he would not demonstrate Noah's restraint.

Thus warned, Oliver nodded and sidled up to the table, and watched Nick stomp out of the kitchen to slam the kitchen door hard behind him. This left Oliver with only the empty air and no idea where Jack had gone. He only knew he needed to find Jack, if Jack could be found, and beg him to at least rest while his body healed, for Chalenheim had abused Jack with such *force*—

Taking a breath, Oliver lamented the lack of hot water and soap as he stripped out of his once-fine boots and trousers and stockings. He peeled off the remains of the river-stained shirt and let the entire of his outfit drop in a pile on the floorboards.

Then he turned to get dressed, noting with a snarl that Noah had picked out the most base of items for Oliver to wear. Besides the rough, thick boots, there were canvas trousers, a dusty muslin shirt, such as a bricklayer might wear, and a twill waistcoat.

Whether it was by intent or not, as Oliver dressed in the sturdy clothes, he knew he would look like a common laborer. That in the street, when he tipped his cap, the more finely attired ladies and gentlemen would simply ignore him, and the true laboring man would eye him askance as to whether or not he might try for their jobs.

But he tucked in his shirt neatly anyway, and took care to snag the leather-points of the suspender's ends over the appropriate metal buttons, and to pull at the hem of the waistcoat so it hung properly. There was even a dark belcher handkerchief with a lopsided crisscross pattern that seemed as though it wanted to echo a finer cloth and had failed miserably.

The brown cloth cap waited on the table for the last and, as Oliver laced up the sturdy boots, his ankles felt the compression of the leather and his calves felt the weight.

He could easily stomp Noah's face with boots such as these but, for now, as he donned the cap, setting the bill of the cap at an appropriate angle, all he wanted to do was to find Jack. The sturdy clothes of a working man, in spite of Noah's obvious attempt to bring Oliver down a peg or two, would allow him to find Jack, though he had to tear down the whole of London to do it.

13

THE ANGEL AT ISLINGTON

A s Jack went up a rise at the top of Saffron Hill, he didn't stop to look behind him to see if Nolly was following. But he listened, even as he pretended to himself he wasn't. Listened for footsteps hurrying, a shout, his own name said out loud.

But he didn't hear anything, so there was no Nolly following him, which was the way it was supposed to be. Just as it was supposed to be that he was retracing his footsteps, echoing in reverse the path upon which he had led Nolly five years ago when they'd come into London from Barnet.

He'd not thought he'd memorized the route they'd taken so late at night, all those years ago. But his heart remembered, as did his feet, because he did not stray from that path. Such as now as he skirted the tall outside walls of Clerkenwell Workhouse, following squatty Baker's Row, which would take him to Coppice Row, and onward past Sadler's Wells, and along St. John's Street.

It was as though the route had been etched into him somehow, for as the row flattened out, there before him at the far corner of an intersection busy with carriages, and carts, and people on the pavement, clicks of boot heels, and rattles of iron wheels, the snap of a parasol being brought out on such a fair day, was the Angel at Islington.

The air rang with the cry of a bootblack, there was one on every corner, it seemed, and the not-quite melodic clang as all the church bells within earshot announced the hour. It was eight o'clock in the morning with the sun shining in a fair blue sky, white clouds whipping over the rooflines. Far too early for Jack, but not for Nolly, who would be up soon, no doubt, and would discover that Jack had gone. But with Noah to tell Nolly why Jack had gone, it would be all right that way.

The thing of it was, Jack needed to find a place to hole up in, to lick his wounds in private, to sleep until he could sleep no longer. To keep his head down until the white fog that battered at the edges of his vision was shredded away. And till his body no longer hurt, the blood no longer thumped beneath his skin, as though it were a scream clawing to get out.

Before him lay New Road, a wide thoroughfare. Beyond it was the Angel at Islington, the coaching inn where so many northern-bound coaches started or southern-bound ones ended.

Even from where Jack stood, from inside the coaching yard came such a clamor, the sharp snap of whips rising above the din of the street, the horn announcing departures. Clouds of dust speckled with mud rose up as a coach and four horses bounded out of the archway and up the high street, headed at a quick pace with passengers swaying on the roof, and the flutter of a handkerchief from the open window of the coach.

Jack watched the coach until it disappeared. He focused on that above all else, even to the detriment of his own toes, which somebody was stepping on, elbowing Jack out of the way, as if the pavement were not his to walk upon.

Instead of giving the fellow a piece of his mind, as there were too many other folks about to make it a private affair, Jack merely stepped back and tucked his cloth cap back on his head, as if he'd meant to do that all along, and stepped into traffic. Dodging the high, fast-spinning wheels of various conveyances, he nearly got his head taken off by the whip of an omnibus driver, and had to scurry to make it to the other side of the street.

He'd had the vague notion that he might have taken this very same path, all the way up to Barnet where he'd gone, more than once, to search for the fountain his mother had left him on. Which had been his principal occupation on the day he'd met Nolly, though that meeting had seemed an unremarkable event at the time.

But in addition to Barnet being another ten miles, on his past trips there he'd been unsuccessful in locating the fountain, let alone any sign of mother or family. He could not see that far. Not with the fog about him, not with his eyes unable to properly focus.

His legs would hardly be able to carry him that distance and, anyway, the point wasn't to run. The point was to hunker down and weather the storm, to brave it out alone so none of all that had touched Jack would be able to touch Nolly.

A fast-stepping, high-flying phaeton drawn by two milk-white horses dashed into the archway of the Angel, and Jack hurried to follow. With such a robust attraction to gaze at, none of the patrons or staff would be giving Jack much heed; he need not go far to find a bolt-hole, just one that Nolly would not think to examine.

The Angel, he was glad to see, was the perfect, busy place, the yard full of activity: the comings and goings of stable boys; a woman and her dog, which yapped incessantly; a group of young men who, by the looks of their loosened cravats and dusty jackets, had not actually gone to bed, but were standing in the open doorway that led to the taproom with pints of beers in their hands and laughter in their faces as they greeted the dawn by saluting the phaeton driver and his lady friend.

The ostler ran up the phaeton quickly and, after an exchanged word or two, turned his attention to the leather harness, and began mucking with the buckles that tethered the harness to the phaeton.

This was Jack's chance, when all eyes were on the spectacle of the well-do-to gentleman and his lady. It was a fine conveyance they drove, and it was inexplicably early for such as them to be out and about. Usually the rich folk were still abed at this hour, or were lollygagging in dressing gowns and suchlike, while their servants rushed to and fro, bringing hot chocolate, hot water, warm towels, and the rest of it.

That these two were in the yard of a common coaching inn at this hour meant something naughty had been gotten up to the night before. For which effort, Jack mentally wished them all the best as he skirted the crowd that had gathered, and made his way to the right of the archway, where through an open doorway the hotel's clerk was to be found.

In the shadowed room not lit at this hour by candles, Jack could barely see the clerk's expression, but he took off his cloth cap and held it in front of him, as though he were begging for forgiveness in church.

"What do you want?" asked the clerk, his round face and wild hair becoming more visible as Jack stood there. "You want a room? Speak up, I'm a bit deaf."

"I'm waitin' for me mam," said Jack, making his voice a little on the meek side, and reedy, as though he were a stripling. "She said to meet here in a few days, so c'n I get a room?"

"Don't know if we have any," said the clerk, though the registry book was right in front of him; it would have taken him only a moment to check, if he really cared.

"Don't need much," said Jack, trying to sound pathetic and earnest all at once, but it came out more like his voice was breaking, which might work just as well. "Don't mind the stairs; give me the smallest room you got."

Finally, the clerk, who could now be seen plainly and evidenced a round, bald pate upon which dark, stringy hairs

ON THE ISLE OF DOGS

flopped, looked at his registry book. He turned the page and ran his finger down the edge of it, leaving a dark streak.

"Got a room. It sits over the barn. How many nights."

"Three?" said Jack. The question was in his own mind, for he could not fully remember after Kayema had been killed how many days he'd slept curled up in a circle in the hay before somebody had dragged him out. He didn't know how many days he needed, so he would take as many as were on offer and feel his way forward from there.

"Got three," said the clerk. "Half a shilling per night; it's on the top floor, all the way along the balustrade, right over the stables."

Which was why it was so cheap, as those with luggage wouldn't want to climb all those stairs, and those with sensitive noses wouldn't want the stable smell oozing up through the floorboards. But what did that matter; Jack didn't plan on being sensitive to anything in a little while.

"I'll take it," said Jack.

He handed over two shillings from the change purse and got half a shilling's change. Putting that in his pocket, he rolled the coin over and over in his fingers as he took the skeleton key, which was so large it looked like a gate key. It felt as heavy as one, as well; Jack hefted it in his hand.

"Got an apothecary near?" he asked.

"Up the street to the right. Sign here."

The clerk handed Jack a pen already daubed with ink and spun the book around for Jack to sign. With careful letters, round and looped, Jack wrote *Tom White*, which had been Nolly's name in one of the stories he'd told about going to court when his Uncle Brownlow had rescued him. But that was long ago, and Jack had need of the name now. Dotting and crossing, he handed the pen back to the clerk.

"Thank you," said Jack, being on his best politeness, for it was only rude folk who got noticed and remembered.

Jack left the office and, with the entertainment still going on in the yard, he slipped out of the archway and headed up High Street, which divided into two branches almost at once. Jack took the left street, which narrowed, various shops lining each side. The morning's shutters were still being taken off, the front steps being swept and cleaned, doors still being opened.

From somewhere along the street, Jack could smell coffee from a stall, but he didn't need that now. He needed an apothecary, which was just up ahead on his right. It had a gilt-edged sign with a mortar and pestle on it that jutted out from the building and over the street. The door was open, so Jack went in, as if he had every right to be there and had only pleasant and industrious things on his mind.

The shop, with its shelves full of glass bottles of powdered herbs and murky vials of dark liquid, was occupied by a woman and her small child. They purchased something that was briskly wrapped in brown paper.

Jack took off his cap again and held it in one hand, gracefully as he might, as he'd seen Nolly do, and waited while money exchanged hands.

Finally, the clerk behind the counter turned around to look at Jack. He was dressed in a snowy white apron with a high, stiff collar around his neck that already, even at this early hour, looked as though it pained him where it bit into his skin.

"Yes, young man?" asked the clerk, looking at Jack through his half-spectacles.

"Could I get some laudanum?" asked Jack. "It's for me mam. She's feelin' poorly today, an' asked me to fetch some."

Without even questioning Jack's reason why it was wanted, the clerk bent below the wooden counter and brought up an empty brown bottle and a small cork. Tipping a small wax paper funnel into the mouth of the bottle, the clerk filled it with reddish brown liquid from a jug.

Jack could almost smell the bitterness of the liquid, and half-tasted remembrances from when he'd been dosed with the stuff back in Lyme. It was the only thing he knew, other than drinking an entire bottle of brandy in one go, that would let him sleep and keep sleeping, with dreams unfettered by image or sound.

The clerk finished pouring the laudanum into the brown bottle, corked it, and then wrapped it up in brown paper and tied it with a bit of string. This arrangement would be noisy to unwrap, but it was too late to ask the clerk to unwrap it, as that would attract more attention than Jack currently needed.

"Six shillings," said the clerk as he held the small parcel and then held out his other hand, palm up, for the money.

Jack knew that by the clothes he wore, it was not immediately obvious that he could afford the cost of the laudanum. To be seen to be too free with his money, on the other hand, would make him remarkable and thus memorable. So, to be more like the stripling lad he appeared to be, on an errand for his mother, he pulled out the half shilling from one pocket.

As the clerk picked up the coin, Jack dug his fingers into his other pocket, cursing himself for not getting more loose change out before he'd come in the shop. He had to open the clasp on the change purse with two fingers and his thumb, without looking.

Pretending as though he were digging deep for the money his mam had given him, he managed to scoop up some additional coin, and these he counted out, with much labor, into the palm of one hand.

"Here's six full shillings," said Jack. "Could I have my half shilling back, please?" Not that he would need it; there were pockets to pick aplenty in such an active area as Islington.

The clerk dutifully handed over the wrapped bottle of laudanum, and the half shilling as well and, as briskly as he was able, turned to the well-dressed elderly gentleman who had just entered the shop, and who would, no doubt, be spending more coin than Jack just had. Which let Jack slip out of the shop, unnoticed. He stuffed the laudanum in his pocket and stood on the pavement for a moment, letting the sun warm him, smelling rain in the air.

He looked both ways, searching for a tavern where he might purchase a bottle of brandy. When he saw a hanging sign with a goat on it, he knew he'd found such a place.

The White Goat had a bottle of brandy to sell him, even at this early hour, though Jack had to pay out more than it was worth, due to his looks, no doubt. But he put the bottle inside the waist of his trousers, and draped his waistcoat over that, holding onto it as though he had a stitch in his side. Then, much ladened, both pockets jammed full, he walked back down to the Angel.

After strolling through the archway, he went up the stairs to the first gallery, rising above the hubbub in the courtyard, and then up the second set of stairs, much steeper, to the top gallery. There he made his way along the balustrade, around to the end of the gallery, above the stables, where his key fit in the very last door.

As he unlocked the door and went in, the smell of the stable was strong as it came through the floorboards. There was the tang of horse manure, and a strong dusty odor of dry hay, and bags of corn, and the slick-sweet smell of leather oil liberally applied. All of this was preferable to the smell of sewage and rot that made itself familiar around Saffron Hill, of cisterns not emptied, and the clogged gutters that ran down the center of every cobbled street.

Even better was the fact that the window in the narrow room opened out over the alley toward the sun. With that sun, Jack could keep track of how long it took him to get better so he would know how long it took for next time, as there was sure to be a next time.

The room was as wide as the widow, and had a floor that slanted a bit, and had not been rented in recent days. Which was of no matter. Nobody would be wanting it, except for Jack, so he would be left unbothered for as long as he needed it.

When he sat on the bed, the rope mattress sagged and the

bedclothes coughed up dust. Doffing his cloth cap, he let it drop to the floor.

He might need it later, but he did not need it now. Nor did he need his boots, which he unlaced and threw at the wall, along with the sensible stockings that were overly warm on his feet and had itched. And the waistcoat, which ripped along the seam as he took it off.

This left him in his shirt and trousers, and the belcher around his neck. Then there was the change purse, which he pulled out of his pocket and tucked beneath the single thin pillow.

Taking the bottle of laudanum out of his pocket, he unwrapped the brown paper, which crackled noisily and made his brain throb. This he put on the floor. The bottle of brandy was soon standing beside it and, with his hands on his knees, his fingers knuckled white, Jack looked at the two bottles.

With his heart pounding beneath his breastbone, Jack eased himself down to the floor to sit hunkered on his heels, stirring up more dust from the floor, making the smell of hay and horse sweat more powerful in his nostrils.

He uncorked both bottles and, taking a hefty swig of the brandy, poured the entire of the laudanum into the brandy. The sweet, smoky taste of the brandy would mask the bitterness of the laudanum. He would drink a little bit and sleep, drink a little bit more and sleep, and on he would go.

It smelled like a barn in the room, like hay and dust and horses, just as it had in Port Jackson, though he'd not had anything such as he had now to send him to sleep. In that way, it was different. In the way he'd left Nolly behind, it was different.

His head pounded even as he drank, and his eyes were dry as he swallowed, and his heart ached. Each breath a misery. In that way, it was the same.

Taking another swallow, he corked the brandy bottle and licked his lips, tasting the sweet with the bitter, and laid himself down on the bed on top of the bedclothes.

He was in the middle of the bed, where it sagged and seemed to enfold him. From somewhere distant, perhaps behind the plaster walls, he imagined he could hear the scrabble of insects awakened by an occupant in the room.

With each surge of blood, bitter beneath the surface of his skin, he sensed the laudanum taking hold in a slow, vaporous spread through his veins that felt as though it were dragging him below the surface of an ice-dark lake. This was fine by him, for it could not be any more dark than it already was. Any more coated with a white shroud, like a fog above the surface of some body of water.

Thus bound by the images in his mind and dosed beyond his body's capacity to resist, Jack felt his head sink into the pillow, which was so thin he could feel the change purse poking up through it. His fingers were going numb, the rest of him fading into a state where he couldn't feel anything below his waist and, with a last glance at the rust-spotted ceiling, his eyes fluttered closed and he was shunted into pure darkness.

WITH THE TASTE OF DIRT ON HIS TONGUE, JACK LICKED HIS lips, where traces of laudanum and brandy clung, and squinted his eyes open. From where he was lying, curled on his side, his arms wrapped around his middle, he could see that the light beyond the narrow window had darkened, making the edges of the window frame sharper by contrast.

Earlier, Jack remembered that the whole room had seemed faded, with stained walls and the brown floor, the sagging bed. His cloth cap and boots and stockings were in a barely visible pile on the floor, and next to them was the bottle of brandy, still uncorked. The key, as well, was sitting on the windowsill, though Jack could not recall putting it there.

His whole body jerked on the bed. He would have to get up and lock the door, as he'd not done before. The carelessness of it should have shocked him more than it did, and would have, had not his head been so muffled by the concoction he'd drunk.

Pushing himself up on one elbow, he teetered on his hip, gritted his teeth, and pulled himself up the rest of the way by clutching at the narrow windowsill. Once on his feet, he ignored the deep, red throbbing between his legs, ignored the ache in his shoulders, the dryness of his throat, ignored everything but the need to get the key, put it in the keyhole, and lock the door from within.

Not that a good sturdy kick couldn't take the entire of the door out, only that with the door locked and the key in place, should anyone try to get in, he'd hear it before they'd crossed the threshold.

With his fingers he traced the edge of the brass plate over the keyhole, the metal cold against his skin, the sensation of the tiny brass nails like a prickling burr that wanted to imbed itself inside of him. Drawing his hand away, he stood back; beyond the door was the balustrade of the upper gallery, that much he remembered.

The smell of stable and horse and hay had faded and, in its place, was the stink of his own sweat, tainted with laudanum, sweet with brandy. Well, it would be fine enough with only himself to notice it; before he went back to Nolly, he'd bathe. He'd take a real bath in a tub with soap and hot water. Nolly would never know, would not have to know, how Jack smelled now.

Turning back to the bed, Jack scooped up the open bottle of the laced brandy from the floor and took a good, long swallow of it. The taste was as before, the sweet and the bitter rushing over his tongue, his belly, empty of food, cringing as the liquid sloshed about. He did not know when he'd last eaten, but what did that matter? He had what he needed.

Corking the bottle, he placed it next to the wall at the head of the bed, out of the way of his feet, should he need to get up in the dark. Then, kneeling, he reached beneath the bed and pulled out the tin chamber pot. The handle was torn off at the bottom where it should have attached to the body of the pot.

Jack shoved the whole of it in the corner, sucking on his stinging fingers. If he needed to piss, he wouldn't have to go down to the yard to do it, so that was something. Looking out the window at the night grown darker, Jack couldn't see anything save his own outline, faintly drawn in the dust-spotted glass, and the large looming darkness beyond.

Quite slowly, parts of him began to numb, as though falling asleep all on their own, though he stood awake and quite conscious, staring out the window at the darkness, which was the exact blue of a deep, churning sea. A slow sea, as it might look on a ship, cutting through endless high, rolling waves, far, far from shore, with no lights to be seen, save the blinking stars in the dark blue bowl overhead.

He knew he was not at sea, could not be, not when everything smelled as it did of sweet brandy, of the dusty coarseness of the laudanum. Of London, beyond the window glass, the stink of it, of cesspits and filth, of open gutters and cracked brick dust, the acid of coal smoke, the putrid leavings in the alleyways—the whole of it was one stinking cloud in Jack's nostrils, so he knew himself to be on solid ground.

Yet the floor rocked beneath his feet, a gentle sway that had him reaching to press his flat palm on the gritty plaster wall. The movement he felt within him was like a yearning call, as though beckoning him to lift his head to the salt-drenched breeze, as he'd done once long ago when he'd stood on the deck of the convict ship that had first taken him away from his beloved City.

The floor rolled, shifting up and down like an endless wave, and Jack found himself tumbling to the bed. He hit the edge of it with his hip, and though it should have hurt, he barely felt it. Only tasted the salt on his lips, and the chill of damp air moving across the back of his neck as he moved his hands beneath the mattress and used the ropes to pull himself all the way into the bed.

Which left the bedclothes rucked beneath him, stabbing points into his skin, his palms raspy and tender as he tried to get the pillow beneath his head as he curled on his side and pulled his knees up to his chest. This way, if the waves got terribly high, he could merely let them tumble about him rather than trying to fight it.

For the sea would always win. That's what the sailors had told him. They'd called the sea their mistress, their mother, their whore, and not a one of them professed that they could swim. When the ship went down, they'd go down with her, embraced in the arms of the dark, salty water as peaceful as if they'd died in the arms of a lover.

This sentiment Jack had never been able to understand. Could not understand it now, how they would subscribe to the kind of love they would rather die for than resist. The love those sailors had for their mistress, wholly embracing the finality of it when at last they were dragged into the depths. Surely fealty to a king had never required such a sacrifice?

Jack felt cold, his skin prickling, as though touched with ice. He jolted awake, pulled up to clarity, but only in his mind, as he sensed his body was still on the bed.

How could he see himself so clearly when the room was almost pitch dark, with his face half-buried in the thin pillow? But he *could* see himself, curled up in a ball, knees tucked up, arms around himself, shaking as though the wind had pitched the sharp, salty waves over the spindled rails and onto the main deck.

There was no water, though. He was on dry land, at least two stair flights up from the ground. And still the bed rocked him, shifting side to side, pulling him back into his body, where the only thing he could see was the gray-speckled darkness in front of his open eyes. He was awake. Had he even slept?

Wind fluttered against the outside of the window glass, bringing the scent of dawn with it, and the faint sounds of bird-song, a dash of rain. Dust from the street rose high in the air, a faint circle of glittering brown, brushed by some street sweeper's broom. The light through the frame of window glass was dull purple and blue, pinked around the edges, becoming brighter as Jack drew in a breath.

Uncurling, he got up, his limbs as stiff as if he'd been beaten, and walked over to the chamber pot in the corner. Undoing his trousers and undergarment, he drew his cock out and pissed into the pot. The piss splashed up against the rim and along the wall, leaving the air smelling salty-sweet. Then, putting himself away, he did up his clothes and wiped his hands on his trouser legs.

The brandy was corked and on the floor against the wall, right where he'd left it. The key was still in the lock. Jack could see this with his own eyes as he took up the brandy, uncorked it, and drank a huge swallow.

Then, taking a breath, and bracing his mouth against his teeth, he made himself take another huge swallow. He didn't want to wake up while the day was young, startled by stable boys shouting, or the brassy sound of the coach's horn announcing to the world that it had arrived or was just leaving.

Putting the cork in the bottle, Jack set it back on the floor at the head of the bed and, before the unsteady sensation of the floor moving as though it were a ship's deck upon the waves unbalanced him, he climbed back into the bed. Lying on his right side, with his back to the door, the simmer of ache along his limbs and the thudding between his legs rose up until he could not ignore it, though the numb feeling was climbing as well.

Neck and neck, the two sensations struggled while his own ability to ignore either of them fluttered in between like a loose sail in a high wind. He felt his throat make a sound, his tongue pressed against the back of his teeth, and he was ashamed of himself for making it. The sound was a name, the name of the one person Jack could not have around him now, did not want in the room to witness this, Jack's weakness.

The bruises from the workmaster's hands pushed up

beneath the surface of his skin like a stain made indelible, inked into him like one of those tattoos he'd told Nolly time and again that he'd gotten, but never had. Now he had tattoos, and they were written all over him. These darkest marks imbued him as much as the stench of the Thames imbued London, part and parcel of the same thing, one never existing without the other.

If he could bury them, these marks, swallow them deep, as he'd taken the brandy, absorb them fully, as the sailors would a death at sea, then Nolly would never be tainted by them. Nolly could go on as he was meant to, pure as a new flame, flickered with blue as rich as an ocean's night, speckled with silver like stars in velvet.

That was what Nolly was deserving of, and Jack would fall into the water without a struggle if it meant Nolly would be saved from the depths. For this darkness was now Jack's mistress, and even if she wasn't worthy of such fealty from Jack, then surely Nolly was.

THE SUN ABOVE THE ROOFLINES WAS AT SUCH A HIGH ANGLE that Oliver felt the panic rise in his chest before he'd taken even three steps away from the Three Cripples. Jack had gotten such a head start, rising early, taking off, that Oliver felt left behind by miles.

He strode down the little side alley toward Smithfield Market, avoiding the slant of High Holborn, and moved between the buildings and along the slanted stone passage till he reached the top of the slope that led down into the market where, even on a Monday morning, the market was as busy as it ever was.

As Oliver walked along the edges of the paddock where the animals, listless in the heat, were waiting to be slaughtered, his boots soon became slathered with mud, the foul filth of animal leavings, and streaked with blood. But being shod in workingman's boots, he wasn't slipping about, nor feeling the warmth of the slop, but instead was able to march steadily.

With his head held high, and with the force of his moment, he found that the butchers and the drovers and the merchants in their aprons streaked with bloodstains got out of his way. He didn't know why, but found he didn't care, as long as it allowed him to make good time to wherever he was going.

Which was where? If Jack were seeking a hole or a ditch or a cranny to crawl into and die in, then where would that be? The whole of London, a rough map in Oliver's head, suddenly bloomed before his eyes, and he had to stop. The stench of the market rose in his nostrils and, trembling, he covered his mouth with the back of his hand.

There was a loud roar nearby as a bullock was thrown to the ground in preparation for castration, by the looks of it. Oliver moved away as quickly as he could, pushing through the crowds. When he was on the other side of Smithfield, the streets, much becalmed in sight and sound from the market but still busy and thick with traffic, spread out before him.

If he went straight on, he would arrive at Charterhouse Square, where the wagon had dropped them off the day before. But Jack was hardly likely to go to a place he would only barely remember, so then where?

Oliver kept walking. His sturdy boots seemed to hold him up, though the old-fashioned muslin shirt was too thick for this weather, this type of effort. So he rolled up the sleeves, tugged at the belcher handkerchief around his neck, and kept going, past the Barbican and along the edge of the green-swathed Artillery Grounds, until he realized he did not have a destination in mind, not one that made sense.

When he stopped at the edge of the Artillery Grounds, in that moment of inactivity ice crystals began to form in every part of him, edging his limbs with silvery coldness, rushing up to encase his heart, leaving him on the verge of panic. Beneath that, as he stood there, pretending to be calm in front of the passersby, in front of women with baskets on their arms doing errands, in front of the soldiers, red-garbed, lining up on the green, his tears loomed with hideous vulnerability.

He made himself be still and to remain that way until the sense of sorrow passed, and he began to feel warm in his belly.

Though Oliver was not Jack and never would be, he *would* find Jack. Besides, he had a familiarity borne of time and events that could give insight into the warren of Jack's mind. So, if he *were* Jack and in some turmoil, where might he go? The first place, the most obvious place, was back to the *Scylla*. Thusly armed with an idea, specific and clear, Oliver made haste in that direction.

He went down to the river and followed the Thames, sometimes going along the streets that ran parallel to it, sometimes running through grime-blackened alleyways. But the fastest, most direct route was offered by staying near the foreshore, where the dirt path above the wooden pylons that kept the river at bay, although crowded, allowed him quick passage.

Soon the Isle of Dogs was beneath his feet. The skyline was spiked with wooden masts and half-folded sails, and the tiled roofs of warehouses, both sturdy and new, as well as decrepit and sagging. Everywhere was the half-burnt scent of coal tar, the sprightly smell of fresh-cut wood, and beneath that, the dank, muddy smell of the riverbank at low tide.

Oliver scrambled between the disused warehouses, going down the stairs he and Jack had come up just the day before. Below lay the bare bank of the Thames, which, scarred by stones and debris sticking up from the mud, looked like an old battlefield.

Just along was the *Scylla*. She lay on her side. The hulk's ribs sagged inward over her middle, and the heavy beams of her masts lay broken in the mud. With no water to hold her up, her own lack of integrity of structure and the pull of the earth beneath her threatened to cave her in at any moment.

Slogging through the mud, the workingman's boots once

again showed their mettle, for though Oliver was ankle-deep in the filth and mire, the mud never soaked through to his stockings, nor oozed over the tops of the boots, though, in truth, his trouser hems were black with mud inside of a moment.

Once at the *Scylla's* side, Oliver laid his hands upon her. He squinted through the gaps that showed how the sun pierced through to her middle and glinted off dark pools of still water left behind by the tide. The dampness ramped up as though he stood in a dank mist.

"Jack?" Oliver asked this in a normal way, as one would when calling for a companion within easy distance, though hope and panic warred beneath his breastbone. But as there came no answer, he tried again in a louder voice, putting all of his effort into it. "*Jack.*"

Again there was no answer, so Oliver followed the length of the hull until he came to a gap in the shadow of the vessel where the dark beams had split apart under the strain of water that had pulled and pushed until she'd broken. It was not too difficult to slip through the gap and wade through the dark water until he came to where the rag-paper bale, bound in the middle and sagging at its edges, waited.

Oliver found himself staring at the bale, looking for anything that would remark upon the horror of what had happened to Jack, or Oliver's own helplessness to save him. Oddly, there was nothing, no sign of anything that had occurred the day before, save the silent, dark cave of a ship, her own decrepitude a sad reflection of her being of no use to anybody, despite her years of service.

This thought made Oliver's breath feel thin in his throat, a tightness there, though he could not have said why, except it made him think of Jack, traveling to antipodean climes on a ship filled with convicts, bound for a life under a hot sun. All the while Jack had been away, he had longed for home with such passion, which Oliver could not quite understand, as he'd always been in England and never anywhere else.

But the City had always been the center of Jack's world, and he'd wanted to be there so badly that Oliver had agreed to return to it, in spite of his own fears. Never would he regret that fact, nor had he wanted to complain, except that now the City was its own sort of monster, large and untrammeled. If Jack was not at the *Scylla*, then where was he to be found, and how was Oliver to find him?

For a moment, he could only stand there, finally, at last, feeling the coldness of the damp wood rising through the soles of his boots, thinking he only had to determine what he should do next so he could find Jack. Something sensible, something straightforward that would steady the rabbit-like pounding of his heart, and align the tumble of his mind—

His thoughts stopped all on their own, for there, floating in a shallow pool almost at Oliver's feet, was a long red swath, a ribbon of silk, adrift in the water like a slow, scarlet snake.

Oliver picked up the object just as he realized what it was: Jack's red cravat that Oliver had selected for him in the used clothing shop in Winterbourne. Had tied around Jack's neck many a time, had oft reached over to straighten or align in a pleasing way, so Jack, his bright bird, would look his best. That Jack was without it now—

Oliver closed his eyes and gripped the cravat in his fist. Sprinkling down, the water seeped out of it, a gentle rain that dappled his trousers and soaked his arm up to his rolled-up shirt sleeve. And once more, now that he was again standing still, the sense of cold embraced him, twining about his limbs and locking him down.

If he did not think this through, if he did not apply sense to the predicament of how to find Jack, Oliver would be made immobile with fear, and Jack would never be found. Oliver needed to begin again, so he took a breath and opened his eyes and forced himself to concentrate.

Noah had said that Jack meant to hole up somewhere, that Jack had seemed steady when he'd left the Three Cripples that morning. But if Jack was more hurt than he'd let on, if he was more hurt than he *knew*, then Oliver needed to find him. Needed to gather his wits, and steady himself, and find Jack before more harm could come to him. For what if Jack stumbled in the street and local thugs, sensing an easy mark, fell upon him and—

No. That would not happen, for Jack was canny enough to find a safe hole to hide in. The only trouble was whether or not Oliver could find Jack, not just in time, but before something happened to him. And to do that, Oliver needed to be sensible. Needed to put away his childish anxiety. Needed to think as though he knew the whole of London, was the cartographer of Jack's haunts and special places.

Of course, Oliver would check the *Scylla* each day, and then after that, there was Newgate, and St. Paul's, the Post Office, and Blackfriars Bridge, and other places that Jack was familiar with, liked to tarry in, that they had visited together, and where they had left behind them the echoes of good memories. Which would increase the list to the various taverns that were not the Three Cripples, as well as the pie houses they'd frequented.

But to start with, as it suddenly occurred to him, Oliver would seek out the old den in Whitechapel. Jack had taken Oliver there when London had been encased with the last efforts of winter. On that day, ice had been dripping off the eaves of the low roof, the building half-gutted, the slate and brick crashing down to the cobblestone street, the beams cracked, the whole of it an empty shell, not only of its own shape, but also of its own former glory.

To Jack, London was a remarkable place that contained memories and a time long gone past, when Jack had been a member of Fagin's gang, good and proper. Jack had taken Oliver to the old den, and there was a good chance he might have gone back to it. So to there, Oliver knew he must go.

And from thence, if he didn't find Jack, well, there were

dozens of places he might look. And he would look, each day, until he found Jack. For without Jack—

Taking a deep breath, Oliver opened his eyes and looked about him.

The *Scylla* was not intact, but without the water tugging at her, she was motionless and aloft. Above Oliver's head, the wood creaked as it dried in the bright sunlight, the only evidence of which, so deep within her innards, were spikes and streams of yellow light on the dark water.

Oliver unclenched his fist and slowly, carefully, folded the red cravat and stuck it in his pocket. He would return the red cravat to Jack when he found him. Which he would, he most certainly would.

❦ 14 ❦

WHITECHAPEL AND OTHER
LOCALES BUT NO JACK

Oliver followed the path as best he could remember that Jack had taken him on to Fagin's old den in Whitechapel. They'd traveled down Cheapside, followed Aldgate and Cornell, and gone past a church of some sort, whereupon Jack had turned onto a long, narrow lane.

Without Jack to guide him, and coming from the other direction, it took Oliver a good two hours to track the location down. But finally, there, along the narrow lane that was somewhat unremarkable from any other lane, was the once-sagging building that had been filled with broken beams and shattered slate.

Now a new structure was arising in the midst of the previous ruin. A carpenter, in his dusty brown apron, was just coming out of the building, shooing away children who were in the street searching for nails that had fallen in the cobblestone street.

The carpenter had an apprentice, following close behind, whom he tasked with getting those nails, while in the space for a window, a glazer was putting the last touches on the crown glass, using his knife to scrape the leading into place. The window, new, shone and glinted in the sun, and Oliver stood there for a moment as he took it in.

Even this part of London, subject to time and wear and fire, was being built anew. Not that it would last, nothing ever did, but if Jack were to find out Fagin's old den was being remade into a dwelling for common folk? It would break his heart. Thus, Oliver determined not to tell him and would dissuade him from ever returning to this spot. Besides, there were plenty of other grotty places Jack had attached his devotion to; he was not likely to miss this one.

As it was clear Jack was not in residence, not in the face of the cart that had just pulled up, out of which spilled a happy family, all bustle and baskets and a scamper of feet as they threw themselves across the newly hewn threshold, Oliver turned homeward. He determined that along the way he would stop at each place he could think of, places where Jack might go. That he was familiar with. That he loved. That they had been to together.

This meant climbing the slope of the road to arrive at St. Paul's, where the church bells were clanging the hour, and the well-dressed and well-to-do hovered on the narrow steps to shake hands, show off a bit, and chatter about nothing, creating a din in Oliver's ears as he scanned the crowd, looking for Jack.

Oliver even took the time to walk around St. Paul's and to tromp up and down Paternoster Row, where stalls were being set up and attended to. Plenty of folk, as they milled about, getting in his way, looked askance at him in his workaday clothes. They sneered at the mud on his boots, at the soaked hem of his trouser leg, at how the belcher handkerchief about his neck did not quite match any cloth known to be worn by sensible, well-dressed people.

Oliver did not let this stop him, but plowed through the crowds, not calling out for Jack, as that would attract too much attention, but instead peering in every cranny, behind the white columns, amongst the small garden, in the ancient graveyard. He went around the church more than once, his heart thudding, for this was where Jack had last worked and had brought in so much cash.

Surely, Jack would think of returning to the site of his last conquest? But Jack was nowhere to be found, so Oliver tromped up to the Post Office, and went to the restaurant on Butcher Street, where the proprietor grudgingly answered Oliver's questions, but shook his head no, that he'd not seen any such lad recently.

So it was off to Newgate, where the coal-streaked building hove to. It loomed above the road as Oliver approached it, steaming with damp and reeking of sewage and rot, the stones of the building along the street dark gray as if soaked with rain and sweat that would never disburse.

Along Old Bailey Lane, across from the Magpie and Stump pub, the remains of a scaffold were scattered among the cobbled street, as though once the hanging had been done, the bones of the event were allowed to lie where they might. This, at the same time, gave the street scavengers something to go after, as they were now. Never mind that it was ghoulish, they were hard at work, collecting wood and straw and nails and shavings, thrusting bits into worn baskets or folds of tattered cloth.

Oliver looked away. Jack wasn't among them, nor would he ever be likely to be, for scavenging was beneath Jack, as it was beneath Oliver.

Back Oliver went to Smithfield Market, where he intended to circle around the paddocks and stalls and shops as many times as need be. For it could not be that Jack would go to any place not known to himself and to Oliver.

But it was with a heavy heart that Oliver climbed Newgate Street to head back to the Three Cripples, for he knew it was possible that Jack would go to a place only he knew of, or to a new place altogether. The only fact that gave Oliver any peace was that Jack would not leave London, not when he'd waited so long to come back to the City he loved.

∿

THE BELLS OF ST. ANDREW'S CHURCH WERE TOLLING OUT THE hour, six o'clock it was, with the heat of the day finally winding down as the smoke of chimneys sooted to the street, tapping the air with black spots as the twilight streaked purple and gold across the rooflines.

Oliver scooted up Field Lane, barely seeing the grotty handkerchiefs fluttering in the low breeze, or the two slatternly, workworn women who stared at him as he went past. He crossed onto Saffron Hill, going up to the Three Cripples, his feet taking him there with nary a thought, except, at the last, when he had his hand on the handle of the front door, for there he paused.

It wasn't so long ago that he'd been packed full of anxiety at the mere thought of coming here. To meet Jack, to have given in to Jack's insistence that if Oliver were to visit him, and that only once, then Jack would stop bothering him at the haberdashery.

But whether Jack had kept his end of the bargain was not as important as the fact that, of his own accord, Oliver had returned to the Three Cripples to see Jack, and that *more* than once. Of his *own* volition. And this, in spite of everything Jack represented, that the Three Cripples represented.

And here he was again. Yet. Still. Here, even when there was no Jack in residence, he'd come back to the tavern all on his own because, as he knew, as he must admit, even if only to himself, he simply had nowhere else to go.

Before he could open the door, two men pushed out and walked quickly down the street. By their steady, purposeful gaits, Oliver knew they were not drunk, but instead were intent on some errand that, given the fact it originated at the Three Cripples, would be far from legal.

This did not stop Oliver from entering. He stepped into the cool darkness of the tavern, and eyed the scramble at the counter, where customers demanded drink and slapped their pennies down and imbibed without thought to flavor or manners. But that was the way the Three Cripples was, in spite of Oliver's attempts at civilizing it. That effort, without Jack, seemed tame and unaccountably meager in the face of what was, what would always be, because that was the way the lower orders lived.

"*Work'us.*"

The shout came from across the tavern where Noah stood with his hands on his hips. He was wearing his usual bright garb, which, with its checkered trousers and fancy patterned waistcoat, made up the sort of outfit that Noah seemingly considered the height of fashion, and that contrasted sharply with the dull, workaday brown and black his customers wore.

Still, this meant nothing to Noah as he stood there, his eyes narrowing as Oliver came close, for Oliver didn't dare turn and walk away.

It was not that he thought Noah would send Len or Nick after him, in spite of the bruises blossoming in colorful greens and yellows on Noah's face. More, it was that if Oliver did not face up to this moment, confronting Noah and claiming his room, his and Jack's room, then Oliver knew he would not be fit to continue looking for Jack. Though at the same time, he had no idea what Noah truly wanted. Oliver was exhausted at the thought of the effort to find out before he'd even begun the conversation.

"Work'us," said Noah again as Oliver came close. He clamped a hand on Oliver's shoulder and squeezed, just shy of being painfully tight. "Y'need to eat," said Noah now. "Come an' eat."

"I'm not hungry," said Oliver, though this was blatantly untrue. His belly was pressing against his spine, as he'd not eaten since Saturday. But he knew if he did not eat, he would not be able to fall asleep and rest, nor to get up and take to the streets of London once more, looking for his dearest companion, who seemed not to want to be found.

"Don't matter," said Noah. "You're goin' to eat, on account o' I told Jack I'd look after you."

"What?" asked Oliver, his temper starting to rise, for he

could not believe Jack would have left him in Noah's care, *Noah*, of all people.

"Mind me, now," said Noah, in a way that suggested Noah found all of this quite amusing.

Yet there was a strange light in Noah's gaze, as well, as he dragged Oliver by the scruff of his collar to the office, and it was a light Oliver could not define. Especially not when Noah practically threw Oliver into a chair and snapped his fingers at one of his men.

A plate of ham steak and mash and greens appeared in front of Oliver, slapped down on the table, accompanied by a knife and fork and a pot pint of beer. The same was served to Noah, though with somewhat more grace and care.

"You'll eat that," said Noah. "So's I can report to Jack when he comes back, an' he *will*, that I'd done right by you. 'Cause I *am* doin' right by you, givin' you somethin' to eat and not turnin' you out in the streets like the bastard orphan that you are."

Noah began eating with some relish, given that his split lip and bruised cheek, courtesy of Oliver only that morning, must have been giving him some pain.

Oliver sat with his hands in his lap and stared at the food in front of him. It looked newly made, however, rather than being leftovers from the whorehouse and hotel next door, so when Noah pointed at Oliver with his knife, from which dangled some greens, Oliver picked up his knife and fork and made himself eat.

He drank most of the beer. When he finished off the ham steak, he wished for something sweet, half turning in his seat to ask Jack for it—and stopped, his heart in his chest, his eyes hot because Jack was not there, and Noah wouldn't given a tinker's plug for tending to Oliver's sweet tooth. Only Jack knew, only Jack cared, about that.

"Goin' to start blubberin' now, Work'us?" Noah asked this through a mouthful of food, drawing his pint pot to his mouth to wash it down. Shiny beer leaked down his chin, and Oliver looked away.

"No," he said.

"Could be he's found some trouble," said Noah in a conversational tone, belying the fact that he had mash on his cheek. "Or mayhap he's thinkin' he likes takin' it up the arse by force more than he reckoned—"

"Don't talk about Jack to *me*," said Oliver, his voice low. He drew his hands away from the table in spite of the fact there was still food left on his plate. "You don't know the first thing about him, so don't you *ever* talk about Jack to me."

Noah's men loomed in the doorway, and must have heard what Noah had said, but Oliver's heart hammered in his chest, blood pulsing just beneath his skin, and he did not care. Then, when Noah opened his mouth, a smirk breaking through, the mocking, careless words just on his tongue, Oliver lunged, grabbing Noah by the throat, and sent plate and food and drink, and him and Noah, flying.

They landed against the shelf along the far wall with a satisfying thud, with Noah beneath Oliver, which was as it should be. But before Oliver could land a single blow, rough hands pulled him up and flung him against the wall. Noah's men stood there guarding Oliver, while other, more courteous hands, helped Noah to his feet.

For a moment, all was still. Oliver kept his back to the wall, knowing well and good that all Noah had to do was snap his fingers and Oliver would be at the mercy of men who had no connection to Jack, and no love lost for the mongrel who dared lay hands upon their beloved and frightening boss.

Oliver stuck out his chin and gritted his teeth, ready to receive what was coming, and to fight them to the last, taking as many as he could with him.

Someone, Len perhaps, was picking up broken crockery and dented pint pots, but Oliver only had eyes for Noah. Who, at that moment, was rubbing his neck and glaring right back at Oliver.

Noah's mouth was down-turned in a sneer Oliver had seen so

often he could trace the lines that sneer left on Noah's face, and could recite from memory the chain of events that would follow their appearance.

"Everybody out," said Noah, making a motion toward the doorway. "Everybody, an' leave me with this runt for a moment. I'll set him straight, don't you worry."

With round, surprised eyes, the group of men, Len and Nick among them, stumbled over themselves and each other to do as Noah had bid them. The door was shut quietly behind them, which left Noah against the half-filled bookcase, and Oliver against the wall, catty-corner from him.

They stared at each other in silence. Oliver's chest heaved, for he did not know what Noah was about to do. This behavior, the one where Noah retained no witnesses for his bravado, was quite unlike Noah at all.

Noah pushed himself off of the bookcase and came close till the tips of his boots almost touched the tips of Oliver's boots, and his breath, newly christened by ham and beer, spilled over Oliver in salty waves.

"Now you listen 'ere, Work'us. I don't give a rat's ass for you nor you for me, I'll be bound. But I made a promise to Jack an' I aims to keep it, so you don't got no call to be lungin' at me when I ain't raised nary a hand to you, an' gave you food an' drink an' all—"

"I don't care about any of that—" began Oliver, but Noah stopped him by grabbing the back of Oliver's neck, as if he thought that could stop Oliver from doing exactly what he wanted, *when* he wanted.

"Listen," said Noah, leaning close, as if unafraid, or totally unaware, of the state of Oliver, how the blood boiled behind his eyes, how his hands were in fists, ready to do as much damage as they were able. "Listen to me. Your Jack, he's got more sense than most, an' when he walked out of here, it was on his own two feet. He weren't bleedin', he weren't dazed, but he needed to get out, to be on his own."

"But he might be *hurt*—"

Noah shook Oliver, his eyes hard.

"Shut up an' listen to me or I'll chain you up an' whip you like the *dog* that you are."

Oliver froze, shutting his mouth tightly, both not to breathe Noah's salty breath, and also to hold back the rage that wanted to be let loose.

Even if Noah was speaking nothing but nonsense, Oliver realized that lashing out in a temper was going to get him nowhere at all, for though Noah might hold back, one of his men might not, and if Oliver was struck down, then how could he find Jack?

"We ain't friends," began Noah. "But we need to call truce whilst he's away so he won't find us havin' killed each other upon his return. Besides—" Noah drew his hand away, and scrubbed at the back of his head, almost laughing, as if at himself. "Besides, you can't go on makin' me look bad in front of my men. I gots a reputation, don't you see? An' if I let a little runt like you take advantage of me? Well, I'd hate what I'd need to do to you to get that advantage back. Right?"

Oliver felt his eyebrows draw together, felt the confusion in his mind as it struggled to find the way around this remark of Noah's.

"You want me to be—you want me to act chastened when I go out of here." Oliver almost spat the words, but saw by the brightness spreading across Noah's features declaring that this was so. "You must be *joking*. You must have gone quite *mad* if you think—"

"Would it cost you nothin'?" asked Noah, spreading his arms wide. "While I have it in me, Work'us, an' you know I do, to grind you right into the dust, for Jack's sake, an' his sake alone, I don't want to. So, for Jack's sake, could you just do as I say?"

"That's a cruel card to play," said Oliver, but though his face felt tight, something inside of him loosened. Noah, while he would always carry that chip on his shoulder in the shape of the charity boy he used to be, was true to Jack. And, on Jack's behalf, Noah would treat Oliver kindly, or at least as kindly as he might, considering the wall of grievances, both petty and large, that loomed between the two of them.

"But it's a true card," said Noah, and then, quite calmly, he slapped Oliver, hard, across the face.

Oliver gasped, his mouth falling open, his hands clenching into fists once more, but Noah chuffed him upside the head and pushed him toward the doorway.

"There it is," said Noah as he opened the door. "Almost to tears, just as you should be after going toe-to-toe with the likes of me. Get some rest, an' I'll bet you a gold guinea Jack'll be back before the sun comes up in the mornin'."

Noah pushed Oliver out into the melee of men. Oliver stumbled, and hard hands set him to rights.

He was allowed to pass, and this he did, scowling, not liking the feeling of being beholden to Noah. Not liking the sensation of climbing the stairs in the Three Cripples, rising above the Monday evening crowd without Jack beside him. Without Jack to open the door to their tiny room with a bow graceful in its mock courtesy. Without Jack's hand in the small of Oliver's back, warm and gentle, pushing him toward the bed, where they might close the door behind them, and undress each other with slow and careful motions, sharing the night's darkness and trading small kisses before the passion built up between them.

As Oliver turned to close the door behind him, the small, square darkness of the room seemed to break into smaller squares of white and gray. He realized, only then, how tired he was. Too tired to mind that he carried half the dirt of London's streets on his skin. Too tired to care about the bed bugs scrabbling along the seams of the mattress, just out of sight beneath the bed-linen.

But he was not too tired to miss Jack with all of his soul, ragged as it was. He tried to squeeze this back and managed it, but barely, with tight fists and his mouth set to a hard line.

Going up to the drawer in the small table beneath the window, he opened it to find that, while his the letter from Jack and his writing supplies were there, and Jack's pipe and tobacco, the red change purse was gone.

While honor among thieves was a slippery hill to navigate, two of their pillows had been taken after all, Jack had been quite sure, and had assured Oliver of the same, that no true thief would steal anything of value from a fellow thief.

That the red change purse was missing might mean Jack had taken it with him, which would give him money to pay his way wherever he went. Making it likely that he'd gone very far from home indeed, so, all of a sudden, the missing red change purse was a dodgy omen at best, and one not at all reassuring.

Quickly, Oliver made himself prop open the casement window and snagged the blanket from the floor to toss it on the bed in the near dark. Then he sat down on the bed, his shoulders sagging as he untied the thick laces of his boots, slipped the suspenders from his shoulders, tugged off his trousers, and undid the rough knot of the belcher about his neck. The clothes he let tumble to the floor, and he sat there for a moment in only his shirt and undergarment.

The cord in the undergarment that looped about his bare waist had not loosened throughout the day and, in the dark, his hands couldn't figure out the knot. So he left his undergarment on and, instead, doffed the shirt, and let it fall where it might, as well, and it felt as though all of his gentlemanly habits had been completely abandoned in the face of no purpose, of no Jack.

As he sat there and stared out the open window, he could feel the still-hot air wafting in as it carried soot from chimneys and the stench, heated by the day, that smelled sour and sickly all at once. And wished with everything he had that he'd been a stronger friend, that he'd been on the lookout as they'd walked to London Bridge. That he'd been able to save Jack the very moment the threat of Chalenheim had appeared in their midst.

The thoughts scattered in his head weren't making much

sense. He knew he needed to sleep so he could get up and try again, because Jack was worth the hard-won effort it would take to put away all of the strings and threads that made up his fears and worries. He needed to lay his head down on the pillow, the scratchy blanket trailing across his feet, the air a ribbon of warmth in the room that had only barely begun to cool down.

There were places in London, he knew, where the windows were angled just right to catch whatever breezes happened to be going past, to cut out the heat of sun, or to shield from the cold of a winter storm. There were places like that, only Jack—

Oliver stopped himself. He'd had his turn, dictating where they might go and where they might linger. It was Jack's turn now, and he'd selected London, and so London, beneath the high-sloped roofline of the Three Cripples, was where they would stay.

Oliver leaned forward to pull open the drawer in the table and took out Jack's letter to read it once over to himself. As he read the words, they throbbed on the page, as if in time with his heartbeat. The sound seemed so loud that Oliver could just about hear Jack's voice in his ears, as though Jack were reciting the letter to him.

The dark feeling of loss loomed, a yawing void where Jack should have been, at his side, asking why Oliver was mooning over a simple letter. But there was only the room to keep him company, and the space within it that echoed only emptiness.

Oliver made himself put the letter away, which he did, folding it and placing it in the drawer with slow and reverent hands. He closed his eyes and took a deep breath.

If Jack had been there—Oliver stopped for a moment, thinking he shouldn't be having these thoughts—but then he realized Jack would say, in that calm way of his, that it was perfectly fine to be having them, on account of the fact that they demonstrated, even if only to Oliver himself, in that moment, how much he missed Jack and wanted him close again.

Oliver would not cry, and he would not lash out in a temper, or at least not in Noah's direction. He would be calm and sensible, and he would find Jack. He would, because there wasn't anything else he wanted to do, there was nothing as important that needed doing.

He'd look all of the rest of his days, if need be. And if he couldn't find Jack, well, he would enter the nearest workhouse, for at least there, death would come quickly.

15

IN WHICH OLIVER
DEMONSTRATES HIS LACK OF
DIRECTIONAL SENSE

Oliver spent the whole of an entire day on Tuesday looking for Jack. He searched all of the same places, the *Scylla*, Newgate Prison, the Post Office, and the pie shops they liked to frequent. He even went back to Fagin's old den twice, in the desperate hope that Jack would show up there. But this plan resulted in no Jack, only sore feet and an aching heart as he put himself to bed, alone, not caring to wash or even to eat.

On Wednesday, Oliver meant to start earlier in his search for Jack, and had managed to get up and get dressed in good time. But Noah stopped him and made him eat a bowl of porridge, which, again, had been made to order, it seemed, rather than being left over from somewhere else.

There was even sugar and milk to put on top, and this Oliver did. He ate an entire bowl beneath Noah's watchful eyes, as well as beneath the craned and sideways looks from Noah's men, as they lingered in the hall outside of Noah's office.

Oliver ignored them, however, and, wiping his mouth with the back of his sleeve, stood up and pushed his chair back without offering to help with the cleanup.

"Might I go now," he said. He did not ask it, but made his

tone as surly as he could, for Jack's sake, and for the benefit of the audience of Noah's men.

"You may," said Noah, smiling, as if amused at his own pompous tone. "Be back for supper, mind, for I shouldn't like to send my search party out after you."

Without an answer, Oliver grabbed his dark cloth cap and slammed it on his head. With his shoulders stiff and broad, he pushed his way through Noah's men, his sturdy boots clomping on the floorboards as he marched to the front door of the Three Cripples and slammed it behind him.

With his hand curled around Jack's red cravat in his trouser pocket, Oliver made his way along the now-familiar route, down Cheapside and Aldgate, past the Tower, and down to the Thames. There, he wove his way through dank back streets, and followed the foreshore of the Thames until he arrived at the *Scylla*.

Now that it was high tide, she floated like a corpse, adrift like a bundle of brown bones. River silt coated her beams, and the water had soaked into her so heavily that she barely broke the surface of the shining water.

Knowing Jack was not inside of her, Oliver rubbed Jack's cravat between his fingers, then turned away and headed back to the center of London.

He walked with his hands in his trouser pockets, the top buttons of his collarless shirt undone. The morning was already hot, and his shirt was soon clinging to him with sweat. The smells from the gutters thickened in the air, and the sift of dust from cart wheels and horses' hooves stuck fast to everything it landed upon.

He hustled along the pavement and ignored the stares he received on account of him pushing through the crowd in a hurry, and wondered whether the stares were because he was being rude or that his face did not seem to match his clothes. He cared little for the true reason why, though, for what if Jack had returned to the Three Cripples and Oliver weren't there?

Wanting a shortcut, he turned north at the docks, skirted the Tower, and found himself in the warrens of Whitechapel, though he knew it would do him no good at all to check out Fagin's den, for it was an ordinary dwelling now, and would be of no use to Jack, even if he did go there.

Instead, Oliver headed toward home and followed the twisty lanes, whose narrowness allowed the roofs across from each other to all but touch. He passed houses of brick, and shops that sold tin, and little narrow cottages with weaver flags out front until, somewhat footsore, he stepped out into a large market square.

While it lacked paddocks packed with animals bound for the butcher, such as Smithfield Market had, the market square still abounded with sound. Beneath bright awnings and broad, furled umbrellas, fresh vegetables and jars of honey were being sold from stalls. Women with wicker baskets and beribboned straw bonnets held onto the hands of lively children as they talked in high voices while they tried to barter the cost of a cabbage down to a penny.

All around Oliver rose the din and shouts of voices in that square space, which was surrounded on all sides by two-story red brick market buildings that seemed to lean into the square, as if enjoying the display before them.

The day was growing windy, though this failed to cool the air, and in the market square, the wind stirred the dust around, clogging Oliver's throat until it begged for water. He took off his cap and ran the back of his arm across his forehead, then tugged the cap into place.

If he could figure out where he was, then he might try St. Paul's again, or Newgate, or return to the Three Cripples to make sure Jack had not yet returned. After which, he would head out once more, barring Noah's solicitude to get in his way.

As Oliver turned, he stumbled over a loose cobble in the street and, shoving at the nearest thing to keep himself upright, found himself staring at the broad chest of an angry fellow in a much-stained velveteen coat. The gentleman's matching velveteen hat was in the dust at his feet, the dark, shiny purple of it spattered with mud from the puddle it had fallen in.

"Why don't you watch where you're going, *you*," said the man, shoving his fist in Oliver's face.

Two other men, dressed in the same overly fancy way Noah did when wanting to ape his betters, crowded behind the angry gentlemen. One of the men leaned over and picked up the angry man's hat, though the dust had left a terrible stain that would never come out, and scowled at Oliver.

"This arsehole botherin' you, mate?" one of them asked the angry gentleman, his sympathy all for the man in velveteen.

"Fucking shite just barreled into me, like I was of no account," said the man, all bluster and fury. "Look what he's done to my hat!"

"I'm terribly sorry, I only mean to be on my way," said Oliver, though his fists curled at his sides in readiness for battle.

In the confusion and press of bodies, Oliver found himself with his back to a brick wall, surrounded on three sides, outnumbered. By the size of the men's fists, he was in for the drubbing of his life, and what was he doing getting mixed up with some local toughs when he needed to find Jack?

Any moment spent on this was wasted, but a quick glance over the velveteen-clad shoulder told Oliver that although several of the folk in the market were giving their angry group a wide berth, nobody was paying them much mind, and the market activities continued on, unabated.

Oliver ducked the first punch thrown by the man in purple velveteen and curled his fists to give back as good as he got. His cloth cap fell off in the dance that ensued, but after taking a blow to the side of his head, and then to his nose, enough to bleed, Oliver realized, in short order, that he was out of his depth.

He needed to get away, and never mind it was the coward's way out, for as brave as he might prove himself to be to stay and fight, his own honor would never be as important as finding Jack. So, ducking, wincing against a near blow, his breath hitching in his throat, he dodged out, bending down to grab his cloth cap, then sprinted for the edge of the market square.

The clomping sounds of booted feet chased him as he raced up a street lined with brick townhouses and shops. Then he went along a wider avenue, running full out, hearing the sounds of pursuit behind him.

Having no idea where he was, he dashed down an alleyway between high brick walls capped with stone that protected the back gardens of a length of townhouses. The alley narrowed and then widened again, curving a bit in the middle, and seemed to go on forever.

When he got to the far end of the alley, the man in the velveteen coat was already there, a snarl on his lips and dust on his hat that he now wore on his head. Body straining, bewildered beyond all compensation on the street thugs' insistence on continuing a battle over a harmless misstep, Oliver stopped running and whirled around to escape the other way, back up the alley. His lungs gasped for air as he ran, and he hoped the man's bully friends weren't waiting for him at the other end of the alley.

Oliver raced, footsteps pounding behind him, and just as he got to the bend in the alley where it headed up a slight slope, a narrow, green-painted wooden door opened right in front of him. He was skidding to a stop, hoping not to barrel into it, when a skinny black-clad arm reached out and beckoned Oliver inside.

Hot and panting and completely confused, Oliver ducked around the door, which was closed behind him with a click as the iron latch slid shut. There, much to Oliver's amazement, stood a slender gentleman, grey and white haired and of some advanced years, dressed all in black, and wearing spectacles. Dark eyes blinked at him as the gentleman lifted his polished wooden cane, and raised it to his lips, gesturing with it for Oliver to be silent.

In the alley beyond the closed gate, the man in the velveteen coat stormed past, shouting to his friends as to whether or not they'd caught the fucking shite at their end. The answer came as more shouting, that no, they had not, and finally the sound of stomping and racing feet faded in the alley. Which left Oliver standing behind a closed gate, at the bottom of a slope of a very green and verdant garden, looking at the elderly gentleman who had saved him.

"I should go," said Oliver in a half-whisper, clutching his cloth cap in his hand.

"No, no," said the gentleman in black, his dark eyes sparkling behind his thin metal spectacles. "Such excitement you are involved in today, young man. You must join me in a cup of tea and tell me why those bullies were chasing you."

"No, truly—" began Oliver.

The old gentleman raised his hand again to stop him, and for a moment Oliver could only stare. Unbelievably, the two of them were still waiting to make sure the man in the velveteen coat and his loutish friends were long gone. Then, when that happened, Oliver had been invited to tea, which made his head swim a bit.

The gentleman lowered his hand and nodded, having determined, it seemed, that the danger had passed. In that quiet moment, Oliver could see the man was truly a gentleman, that his frock coat, a dark, sensible black, was of a fine-quality wool that had been tailored to fit his slender frame. That his boots were thin and polished, and that everything about him was groomed.

And, lastly, that the man had small tendrils of whitish-gray hair trailing in front of each ear, and that he wore a small, circular skullcap on the crown of his white head.

It became quite clear to Oliver, at that moment, that he had been rescued by a Jewish gentleman, and that he was standing in a Jewish garden, neither of which had ever happened to him before.

"Join me for tea," said the gentleman now. "I've not had an

interesting visitor since—well, in a good while, and you would do me the great favor of distracting me from my own troubles. I'm Myron Yeslevitz, by the way, and you are very welcome in my home."

Mr. Yeslevitz tucked his cane against his breast and held out his other hand for Oliver to shake.

"P-pleasure to meet you, sir," said Oliver, somewhat undone by the courtesy, as it had come amidst the chaos that had been his continued existence. "My name is Oliver Twist."

"That's done, then," said Mr. Yeslevitz. "Now, come along and we shall have some tea."

Without waiting for a reply, Mr. Yeslevitz turned on his heel and walked up a flagstone path that led through a lush garden, which was framed by high brick walls on both sides, and which had a gate at the far end, where Oliver was.

The garden continued up a slope, and contained an expansive array of yellow marigolds and daffodils and pale purple crocuses, and many other flowers that spread out in an array in tidy, dark-earthed beds. Slender trees grew high along the brick walls, intermixed with low shrubs with glossy green leaves. Even the flagstone path was lined with greenery and flowered bushes, and all of it was so thick that, for a moment, Oliver lost sight of the slender line of Mr. Yeslevitz's shoulders.

"Mr. Ye—"

Oliver stopped, as his tongue was unable to make a proper sound for the name. Standing where he was for a moment, he wondered if he should just go and forget he'd ever been there, when he heard the small tinkle of a silver bell and a set of low voices.

He walked along the path where the green-growth was so lush his arms brushed low branches and scattered flower petals behind him like brightly colored snowflakes. At one point, he had to lift away a branch of a carefully trimmed Hawthorn tree, and then another branch of a lilac bush, thick with purple petals, which bespoke much of a gentleman who would allow such a common bush in such an elegant garden.

Everything, from the smallest green thing to the lazy, thick petals of the flowers, smelled as though a great whirl of sweetness had been brought to life. Oliver wanted to tip his head back and simply soak it in, but first he had to excuse himself, for he had an important task to complete.

Oliver stepped out from beneath the verdant branches and into a small clearing. Beyond the clearing rose an elegant townhouse with the kind of old-fashioned brickwork that presented whimsical and eye-catching patterns. Close to the house, a circular patio had been constructed of gray flagstones, upon which was a small, round table that was covered by a fine white cloth.

There were two wrought-iron chairs at the table. The old gentleman was being helped to sit in one of the chairs by a large, dark-haired male servant, who said nothing, but carefully took the gentleman's cane and propped it against the low beam of the overhead trellis. The trellis, the crowning glory of the clearing, was made of white-painted and curved wood, and was thick with vines of pale pink and white roses that soaked the air with a low, dusky perfume.

"Come now, my young friend, Mrs. Becca is just bringing out the tea. Sit here beside me and tell me of your world. Thank you, Asher, that'll be all. I'll be fine."

In spite of being a servant, Asher was dressed almost as well as Mr. Yeslevitz. He gave Oliver a hard look before dipping his head beneath the lintel of the open doorway and disappeared inside the house.

"Come now," the old gentleman said again as he gestured to the other chair at the table.

It was an ordinary chair made of curved wrought iron and was suitable for gardens. But upon its surface and back were tied cushions of richly striped cloth that Oliver knew, without a doubt, would become irreparably stained were he to sit upon it in his current state.

"No, thank you," said Oliver with a nod of thanks. "I would not want to ruin your cushions."

"Rubbish," said Mr. Yeslevitz, waving his hand as if to dismiss this and every other objection that Oliver might make. "What is a bit of cloth between friends newly met?"

Mr. Yeslevitz did not respond to the question, but instead rang the silver bell on the table. Out rushed a comely maidservant who was dressed in somber dark blue from her neck to her toes, with a wide white apron over her skirts and a crisp cap over her dark curls.

"Yes, sir," she said with a quick curtsy.

"Lavena, dear," said Mr. Yeslevitz. "Would you fetch a bit of muslin to protect my oh-so-precious garden cushions from this young man's trousers?"

Without saying anything, though Oliver could see the puzzlement in her eyes, Lavena dashed off on her errand, leaving Oliver alone with the old gentleman once more.

Oliver could feel the coarseness of his canvas trousers and the sweat-stained muslin shirt on his skin. Both were made even more uncouth in the face of such a gracious garden and well-dressed host. It had been forever since Oliver had been asked to partake in something so civilized, especially out of doors, which both he and Jack quite adored—Jack who was still waiting to be found.

But before Oliver could say anything, to blurt out an apology for his untidy state and to excuse himself from the garden to be on his way, a woman came out of the house.

She was dressed in much the same way as the maidservant and she carried a large, round tray, upon which was heaped items for a garden tea: an oval-shaped china plate of cakes, a plate of sandwiches, a small basket with sugar-speckled tarts that looked to have sweet fruit filling, and a large cream-colored pot of tea. A bowl of sugar. A small pitcher of cream.

The woman balanced the tray on the table and transferred all of these items to the table with a complete lack of haste, as though she were performing a small, but much-beloved ceremony.

"Thank you, Mrs. Becca. That looks splendid," said Mr. Yeslevitz as he flipped a snowy white napkin into his lap. "You will join me, young man?"

"I could not, sir," said Oliver. He watched with wide eyes as Lavena came out of the house. She, with as much care as had Mrs. Becca, divested her tray of its contents and covered the cushions of the empty garden chair with two squares of white muslin.

"Is there a problem, Mr. Twist?" asked Mr. Yeslevitz, looking up at Oliver with very still, dark eyes.

Oliver realized, in that moment and all at once, that Mrs. Becca had not left, but was standing by, holding the round tray in her hands, as if she might use it as a shield in her master's defense. As well, Lavena stood near the wrought-iron chair, and Asher's frame filled the open doorway to the house.

"No, sir," said Oliver.

He had never before conversed with nor sat down at a table with anybody of the Jewish faith, unless Fagin counted in that regard. Fagin, who, in spite of his supposed faith and heritage, had been despicable, and this might have colored Oliver's attitude toward any other Jew who he might have met on the street.

There had been very few occasions for that type of encounter, however, so he'd not contemplated the issue at all. Jews and Christians did not mix socially, and that was that.

However, Mr. Yeslevitz was far and away a gentleman and, indeed, was as much of one as Fagin had not been, irrespective of their common religion, and he had saved Oliver, besides. So, instead of refusing, Oliver explained the reason for his hesitation.

"Only that I'm too filthy to join you at such a respectable table."

"Mrs. Becca, Lavena, fetch a washbasin and a pitcher of warm water. And you, young man, will sit down and spare me some of your time before I grow too old to enjoy it." This was said with some asperity, though the old gentleman cocked a white, shaggy eyebrow, which rose above his spectacles like a feather. "I'm about to get a crick in my neck, and if you keep standing there with your tongue in your mouth like that, I *will* get a crick. So sit down."

Amidst the tirade, Mr. Yeslevitz's tone rose sharply, making his accent more pronounced, as though he'd lived somewhere on the Continent, long before he came to abide in London. It would be bad manners to inquire about it, so there was nothing Oliver could do at that point but be obedient and do as he was asked. Still, he took a moment to adjust the muslin cloth squares to protect the cushions before he sat down.

He was about to pick up the napkin that lay on the table beside the white china plate when he hesitated. His hands, dark with grit, the knuckles lined with it, made such a contrast to the white napkin and the white cloth on the table that he did not want to smudge them, even a little.

He looked up to see Mr. Yeslevitz watching him from behind his thin spectacles, a little smile playing about his mouth.

Just then, though, Mrs. Becca and Lavena came out of the house. Mrs. Becca carried a pitcher, with a towel slung over her arm, and Lavena carried a red and white checked china basin.

Both of the women stopped in front of Oliver. Mrs. Becca balanced the pitcher on the table long enough to reach into her apron pocket to hand Oliver a bar of soap, then she picked up the pitcher again and held it poised over the basin that Lavena had placed upon the table.

It was easy to see Oliver was meant to use the basin this way, rather than having it be put on a stand. He did not have it in him to argue with so kind a host, so he watered his hands and laved them with the soap. As he reached for the pitcher, Mrs. Becca lifted it up and poured it over his hands to rinse them.

The water turned a dark gray in short order, and he was ashamed of it.

In spite of this, Mrs. Becca handed him a thin white towel to dry off with. Oliver made himself do it, for to refuse would be bad manners.

Mrs. Becca then handed him a dampened cloth, gesturing at Oliver's face. Oliver used the cloth to wipe away the blood beneath his nose. Handing the cloth back to her, he felt badly at having given her additional laundry to attend to, but it felt nice to be clean in this lovely place, and something inside of him started to uncurl in the face of such civility.

"Very good, Mrs. Becca, Lavena, you may go. We'll ring if we need you."

Only then, in the stillness that fell at the servants' departure, did Oliver deem himself clean enough to pick up the white cloth napkin and spread it in his lap, feeling as though he'd entered a dream from long ago.

"Will you pour?" asked Mr. Yeslevitz.

Oliver did as he was asked, standing up to pour the tea from the china pot into the flowered cups, which were fitted with old-fashioned tea leaf strainers. The tea streamed clear brown into the cups and smelled wonderful.

After pouring out two cups, Oliver handed the old gentleman a cup and a saucer before pulling a cup and saucer toward himself as he settled as much as he dared in his chair.

"I don't know how to pronounce your name, sir," said Oliver, looking at the sugar bowl and wondering if he might proceed. For if he was indeed in a dream, then he might take as much sugar as he liked.

"It's Mr. Yeslevitz, but you may call me Mr. Yes, if that's easier."

"Mr. Yeslevitz," said Oliver, refusing to shorten the name, as that would be rude. "I'm Oliver Twist."

"Yes, I know. You already told me. Is that an English name? Never mind, it probably is. Now, help yourself to some sugar and whatever else tempts you. Those over there are raspberry tarts, which I find quite delightful, though I'm not allowed to have very many."

Feeling slightly gentled by the stream of words, Oliver doctored his tea with cream and sugar, and dished himself out a bit of a slice of cake, two raspberry tarts, and one small, triangle-shaped sandwich. After which, he pushed the plates toward Mr. Yeslevitz.

Oliver waited till the old gentleman had served himself and had taken a sip of his tea before he allowed himself to partake.

A little silence fell between them as they ate and drank in the lovely garden with green things growing all around them. A sense of stillness overtook Oliver and, as he sat at the table, his heart was able to slow and his thoughts to drowse, though he knew he should not be dallying so long, that he should be up from his chair and looking for Jack.

That is until Mr. Yeslevitz straightened up and wiped his mouth with his napkin. His sharp, dark eyes focused on Oliver from behind their spectacles.

"I believe I am owed a story. Why were those brutes chasing you and what are you doing in this part of Spitalfields, a gentile such as yourself?"

"A gentile—oh, I see," said Oliver, determining at that moment to be as honest as he could. "I didn't realize Spitalfields was where I was, but I'd gotten turned around in the market square and bumped into one of them. An apology wasn't enough, so it went to fists quite quickly."

"I see. And why didn't you know where you were, for surely you'd walked to get here, and would be able to remember a simple map of London in your head?"

"I took a shortcut."

"From whence and why-for?"

The question was accompanied by a quiet gaze from Mr. Yeslevitz, who seemed more interested in Oliver than in his own tea.

"I should go," said Oliver. He folded his napkin and made to stand up.

"Thus, we arrive at it, don't we," said Mr. Yeslevitz, waving his hand over the table as if quite irritated with this turn in the conversation. "I serve you tea and cake on my finest china, and yet here you are, ready to dash off simply because we've come to the heart of your story. Getting lost in Spitalfields Market was just the tail end of some chain of events far more complex than an altercation with some street toughs, wasn't it, my young friend."

Oliver sat back down in the chair, feeling the softness of the cushions between them as he studied his knuckles. They were red-raw from the fight in the street, and his hands were trembling.

"I needn't—shouldn't trouble you with my small tale of woe," Oliver managed at last. He worked his jaw to loosen the sudden tension that had built within him.

"Great or small," said Mr. Yeslevitz with a snap. "I am quite sure your story is a good deal more exciting than anything else that has happened to me today."

"It's hardly happened to *you*," said Oliver before he could stop himself.

Horrified at his own rudeness, he looked up, expecting to see Mr. Yeslevitz's reaction as he called for his servant to throw Oliver out of his garden.

But the response Oliver received instead of dismissal surprised him.

"There's the spirit," said Mr. Yeslevitz with a broad smile that took up half of his narrow face. "Though you look gently born, there's a fire in your eyes that has yet to be doused and I, for one, should like to hear the tale that led you to face off with such street thugs as were chasing you." The old gentleman took a sip of his tea, and the cup paused at his mouth before he replaced it in the saucer with a clink. "Go on, Oliver Twist. I'm owed a story, and you might find relief in the telling of it."

"Very well," said Oliver, hesitating. He knew he could leave, but was loath to do so. This was the first bit of comfort he'd known since Jack's birthday, which now seemed so long ago. And besides, who was he to turn away from a debt owed, even if it meant baring his soul to a near-perfect stranger?

"My dearest companion, Jack, was taken and abused by a man of our short acquaintance—" Oliver paused as he watched Mr. Yeslevitz's white eyebrows fly up, as he wanted to be sure of the old gentleman's comprehension before continuing. "—and while I was not able to save Jack from this, I was able to take him home, where I might tend to him. This care he refused."

"However—" said Mr. Yeslevitz with some calm as though he were already familiar with the facts he was hearing, circling his hand in the air, as if bidding Oliver continue.

"However," said Oliver. He swallowed as his body remembered the shock of that moment, the emptiness of the room without Jack in it. "However, in the morning he was gone, for he had taken himself up to hole up on his own, far from me being his plan, as I was told. I worried terribly that he might be hurt and unable to come home, and I determined to find him."

"How long have you been looking?" asked Mr. Yeslevitz, poking at the slice of cake on the white china plate in front of him in far too casual a manner to fool Oliver, for Mr. Yeslevitz seemed extremely attentive to every word Oliver was saying.

"Two days," said Oliver. "Today is the third day, and I know it's not a long time, but I've not been without him for even a short while since the late winter and I find that I cannot—"

"Now, who exactly is Jack?" asked Mr. Yeslevitz, as he leaned forward in his seat. "Who is he to you that you would chase after him hither and yon, getting yourself mucked up along the way?"

Oliver laughed beneath his breath, almost without realizing it. Nobody had ever asked him that question, nor had ever wanted to know about how he felt about Jack, or even to hear about Jack himself. That Mr. Yeslevitz was asking it now was as though a door had been opened into some place gentle and accepting and even, it seemed, interested. Mr. Yeslevitz smiled in response to Oliver's amused sound, and Oliver smiled in return.

"Jack's a dark-haired rascal if ever there was one," said Oliver. The words instantly felt as though he were saying something that somebody else had once said to describe Jack, so he stopped that train of thought and, determining to pull words from his own head, his own heart, continued on in a different way.

"Jack is very dear to me, and he's very patient with me and kind to me. And he's handsome to look at, as well. He's got very green eyes, like the green in this garden—he's quite beautiful, and he has strong shoulders, and such graceful hands, and a wide smile, and such dark, silky hair—and he's very smart. Street smart, more than book smart, you know, but I've never met a more sensible person."

"And how did you two meet?"

"Through a common acquaintance," said Oliver, being as honest as he might be. "We work in a tavern together, and share a room to keep down expenses, though it'd be nice if we had someplace better, or at least a bit bigger so I don't always wake Jack up, as I rise in the morning far earlier than he does. He likes to sleep in, you see, and I like to let him."

"I do see," said Mr. Yeslevitz. "He does sound quite lovely, your Jack."

"He *is* lovely," said Oliver. He smiled, truly smiled, and felt the sweetness of it, the idea of Jack, who was indeed lovely and deserved to be called so. "More than lovely."

"He is your paramour, then?" asked Mr. Yeslevitz, his eyes narrowing slightly behind his glass spectacles. "Well, he *must* be. Otherwise you might not be so concerned about him, I'd say. Nor describe him in such loving terms with that beatific expression on your face."

Oliver barely knew he'd stood up, had thrown the cloth napkin down at the table. That in his haste, he'd bumped the table and spilled his cup of tea.

The brown circle spread on the tablecloth like an incoming

tide. Oliver knew he should not have gotten lost, should not have bumped into those street thugs, should not have come into this garden, and should not have opened his mouth—

"I will be out that gate before you can call the constable," Oliver said, announcing this with his chin held high as he struggled to unwind his thighs from the trailing tablecloth, to find his cloth cap, to be on his way.

"I'm not going to call the constable," Mr. Yeslevitz said as he also stood up, reaching for his cane. "In my day, a gentleman was not a gentleman unless he could hold his own at the card table, shoot a man dead at dawn, and attend gatherings of the bon ton where connubial relations were handed out like party favors. Do you understand? I'm not going to *judge.*"

"But that was a different time!" Finally able to free himself from the tablecloth, Oliver stepped back, away from the gracious table and his overly curious host.

"It might have been," said Mr. Yeslevitz. He moved to block Oliver's way to the path leading to the back gate. "But I am from *that* time and do not share the same sensibilities as can be found in *these* blighted and narrow-minded modern times."

Oliver stood there, gawping, his mouth open, mind racing to determine how he might get past the old gentleman before the constables were called. At the same time, he couldn't very well run roughshod over a host who had been so kind to him, which left him unable to do anything other than freeze where he stood.

"In my day," said Mr. Yeslevitz. He held up his cane and used the curved handle to point at Oliver. "In *my* day, women showed their entire bosoms and wet the front of their dresses to display their legs to anybody who cared to look. People behaved in a way so intimate at any hour that it would make today's crowd faint and swoon at the mere thought of it. A young man such as yourself could not hold his head up unless he'd taken to his bed a countless number of lovers, and it was all to the better if it was more than one at a time. That was the world I came from, so I'm hardly going to judge anybody for loving who he loves."

Mr. Yeslevitz's acerbic nature gentled as he spoke. His eyes softened and became kind, the words coming quickly, as if he feared he would not get them delivered with enough haste to stop Oliver from going.

Oliver looked at Mr. Yeslevitz, his black-garbed form an outline against the lush greenery behind him, feeling as though he were an animal looking for a trap. But perhaps there was no trap, for no servants came out of the house in haste and excitement to banish Oliver from the garden, nor were any constables called for.

All that remained of Mr. Yeslevitz's story was the echo of the words hanging in the perfumed air, and the expectant look on an old gentleman's face that he would be believed, that he'd managed to convince his young visitor of his earnestness, that his only desire was to provide a safe haven, however momentary, from the trials and dangers to be found in the dusty streets of the City.

"I should still go," said Oliver. "For I must find Jack."

"Will you—will you return and tell me that you've found him?"

Mr. Yeslevitz's eyebrows rose, a quite hopeful expression on his face, as if Oliver's search for his lost love, for his beloved Jack, was not just an enticing story told at tea time, but more, that it might return to the old gentleman a sense and semblance of former, more exciting times, now long gone.

With a quick nod, his heart in his throat, Oliver raced down the flagstone path to the high garden door, which opened silently beneath his hands and closed easily behind him. With a sharp breath, he was off, going down the alley, away from the lovely garden and the illicit conversation.

Taking a right at the first wide lane, he raced on, dodging carts and cabs and ladies' skirts until he found himself on a proper avenue, where over the rooflines he could see the dome of St. Paul's.

That was the way home, then, and whether Jack had shown

up there or not, Oliver would be far better off at the Three Cripples than waiting about the edges of Spitalfields for Mr. Yeslevitz to change his mind and call the constables on Oliver, anyway.

∾

JACK DOSED HIMSELF WHILE THE SUN WAS UP, AND AGAIN when it went down, swallowing almost half the bottle at sunset and pissing in the chamber pot before he crawled back into bed. The room smelled like salt and dust, and the wind swirled outside the window, which was still unopened by Jack's hands.

When the darkness came, it took him with a blow to the head, as if a wave had swamped over the bed where he lay, curled up, holding in a tight fist the red leather change purse. The pillow was as hard as stone beneath his cheek, the edges of the pillowslip frayed, just like the bale of rag paper had been in the *Scylla*.

He took with him into the deepest sleep the look in Nolly's eyes as he'd watched Jack and the workmaster together. With Jack bent over. With Chalenheim fucking him from behind, bold and hard. With Nolly witness to Jack's submission, his weakness, not fighting it, not trying to get away.

But Chalenheim might as well not have tied Jack up to keep him from escaping. For just as Allingham had bound Jack to him for protection, Chalenheim could have used the means he'd used before, that of threatening Nolly if Jack had not willingly bent himself over the bale of rag paper.

Jack would have done it, even if he'd not had his arms tied behind his back, the smell of sweet, rotted plums in his lungs, swirling around his head, that old, old smell echoing what the gypsies had used in the rag they'd clamped around Jack's mouth when they'd stolen him from the fountain where his mother had left him.

Nolly might know what Jack was willing to do for him, though he'd been angry in Axminster Workhouse when he'd found out what Jack *had* done, the deal he'd made with Chalen-heim. Nolly had threatened to take a strap to Jack should he ever do the same, should Jack ever exchange his skin for Nolly's. But this time, since Jack had not made any deal, would Nolly forgive him?

The question died on his lips, the sugar of the brandy sticky on his tongue as he fell asleep.

~

THE DIFFERENCE BETWEEN THE GARDEN AND HOME WAS SO great that Oliver ran the entire way to the Three Cripples, fearing he might change his mind and go back to the garden, for the garden was easier than life in the tavern.

Once arrived, the contrast between the garden in Spitalfields and the slope of Saffron Hill was an onslaught to Oliver's nostrils, his eyes, the skin along the back of his neck. For here, the common folk had no access to water to wash with, nor would think to do it, even if they had.

There was rubbish in the street, filth in the gutter, and that certain odor that floated just beyond the Three Cripples, as though not only was the cesspit in someone's cellar overflowing with night soil, the carcass of a pig had recently fallen in and was rotting to a sickly sweet pulp.

But instead of thinking about the tantalizing taste of civi-lized life he had just left behind, he needed to focus on being where he was, focus on the soreness beneath his breastbone where his heart had been beating and had yet to slow down. On his thighs that shook beneath him as he stumbled the last yards to the door of the Three Cripples.

As he swung the door open, he ducked, making himself half a head lower than anybody else in the crowd. And though the customers at the tables along the windows looked at him as though viewing some strangely behaved creature, Oliver kept at it until he got to the bottom of the stairs.

Thinking he was safe, he straightened up and put his hand on the thin, wobbly railing, meaning to go up to the room to see if Jack was there.

"Work'us, did y'find him?"

That was Noah's voice, clear as a bell, even through the din of the tavern, and though Oliver did not turn to look, he managed to answer over his shoulder.

"No," he said.

But Noah had come up, reached out, and grabbed Oliver to turn him around.

"You look like hell," said Noah, shaking his head. "Why're you doin' this to yourself? He said he'd be back, an' he will."

"You don't know that," said Oliver, gritting his teeth. "He could be dead, and there you'd still stand, insisting he was all right."

"An' he is," said Noah. "So come an' eat. Give your feet a rest. Take a moment."

Oliver felt his hands curling into fists and felt the tightness in his stomach blossom into fury. But as Noah flinched, Oliver felt an echoing response in his own body, all over, as though someone had slapped him.

While he had no loyalty to Noah, there'd been a kind of agreement between them, which, though thin, meant that clocking Noah's face with a good hard punch in front of everybody was not exactly the appropriate response for such a banal statement.

Letting his hands drop at his sides, Oliver looked at the crowd of customers that had gathered on a Wednesday evening, with the sky outside the bull's-eye windows pushing with wind, as though promising a bit of rain. At Noah's men, spread out amongst the crowd to keep the rowdiness at bay. At the girls behind the bar, with Len helping them, serving pints of beer and tots of gin as fast as they might. Just another ordinary evening at the Three Cripples with business continuing on, in spite of Jack being nowhere to be found.

"I ate in the street," said Oliver, ducking his head to look at Noah. "I'm not hungry."

"Well, you look like you've been rolled about the inside of a tumbril," said Noah, going on as though they were, if not true companions, then good acquaintances.

"I—" Oliver licked his lips, feeling the soreness in his jaw from earlier blows. He looked down at Noah, standing below the bottom step, and wondered how his life had come to this, that he was actually taking time to explain himself to Noah Claypole, of all people. "I managed to get lost near Spitalfields Market, and got turned around on my way back from the *Scylla* on the Isle of Dogs."

"Then you're knackered," said Noah, deciding. "For Spitalfields is as bad as a rabbit warren. Come an' get a pint of beer, at least, at *least*, so I might tell Jack when he gets back that I didn't let you go up alone without somethin' to warm your belly."

There could have been mockery in Noah's voice, some sly innuendo about what, exactly, might warm what, but on the opposite side of that, exhaustion flooded through Oliver. It was as if the moment he'd arrived home, his body knew this, his mind knew it, and while he longed to be alone, and quiet, there was a look in Noah's eye, somehow earnest and kind. The look might last only the time it took Oliver to drink that beer, but drink it he would.

So he went back down the two steps that he had taken and nodded at Noah. The crowd of regular drinkers moved aside to let Oliver through to the bar. As he went, they all looked at him as if they'd been waiting for him the entire day. He barely heard Noah whistle, but a pint pot of beer was placed on the long counter just as Oliver arrived at it.

Standing with one foot on the brass foot rail and, with his elbow on the counter in the common workingman's fashion, Oliver slowly drank the pint of cool beer. He ignored the fact that the pint pot was dented and not quite clean, but then he'd been gone from the inner workings of the tavern for days now. It wasn't exactly a surprise that, without his supervision, his hard efforts to get the rest of the staff to follow his example had collapsed into ruin.

"Better?" asked Noah as Oliver finished the beer and slid the now-empty pint pot over to Len.

"Yes," said Oliver quietly. "Thank you."

"Get some rest now," said Noah. "An' in the mornin', maybe I'll have some of the lads out lookin' with you."

Oliver slunk back to avoid the hearty slap that Noah meant to land on his shoulder. And thought about how he'd rather Noah be insisting that Jack would come back on his own than to have such an offer made to him.

"No, thank you," Oliver managed to say with some politeness. "I hardly know where I should look next, let alone direct anybody else."

"I see," said Noah.

He backed up a few steps to let Oliver go by him, and this Oliver did as quickly as he could, his hand in his trouser pocket, curled into a fist around the silky folds of Jack's red cravat. Not looking right or left, he hurried up the stairs and into their room. He locked the door behind him and, leaning against the panels, allowed himself to draw his first deep breath of the day. And did not let himself think about Mr. Yeslevitz's garden.

Clouds were boiling into a gray froth outside the open window, sending a freshet of cool air into the room, and this Oliver breathed in as he drew out the red cravat. The silk of it was crushed in his palm, and even when he opened his fist, the silk stayed crimped and was splotched with damp. The whole of it could be fixed for a shilling by a clerk at a used-clothing shop, as he well knew, but it would never be the same without Jack to wear it.

Oliver sank to the bed and drew the red cravat up to his eyes. He hooked his boot heels on the bed rail, and stayed that way for many moments, leaning forward, as if he could reach the tomorrow where Jack might be found. But his eyes grew hot and his chest tight, locking him into a curl, where the mistakes, all his own, piled up inside of him.

For while Jack had gone everywhere that Oliver had asked him, and had risked his entire skin protecting Oliver in Axminster Workhouse, Oliver had returned Jack's gestures with neglect. He had gotten Jack out of Axminster, but then he'd forced Jack into awkward acquaintances with people, some of them his own relations, who did not think much of Jack, and who had taken no pains to hide this.

Oliver had then followed Jack back to London, not hiding his reluctance, not even a little. And when Chalenheim had shown up, Oliver had not saved Jack, had not kept him from harm, and had only been able to remove Jack from the *Scylla* when Chalenheim had determined to leave them for dead. Now, Jack was out in the streets of London, somewhere, and Oliver was unable to find him and bring him home.

If Oliver continued to fail at the task of taking care of Jack, then Jack would find himself adrift and alone, and would think himself unloved. Would believe that his Nolly did not care enough to look for him, to *find* him. Jack would imagine that Oliver was spending his time in a vain and idle manner, caring for his own wants, tending to his own needs. Leaving Jack alone on the streets—

Low, low sounds broke their way free from Oliver's throat, and though he tried to stop them, they continued. They pushed out of him with the evenness of his own heartbeat, sounding ragged and wet as he cried, even as he clenched the cravat to his eyes and willed himself to stop.

He was pathetic to be taking on this way, *pathetic* to be mourning his own loss when he'd not searched every corner, every cellar and alleyway, had not turned over every stone that made up London to find Jack—

If he cried now, as he was, it was as if he had admitted he'd failed. Failed the search, failed Jack—failed at everything. After which, he would never again see that slow smile and the glints in those green eyes, more precious to him than any jewel.

Never feel Jack's skin, silky and warm, beneath his hands, nor shiver at the touch of Jack's fingers along the back of his neck.

Never again know that sweetness, the intimate air between their bodies when, naked beneath the sheets, they came together in the dark.

Never know the sated, drowsy feeling that always came after, when Jack reached for Oliver, and then pulled himself close to tuck himself in the curve of Oliver's arms.

The sounds coming from within Oliver grew louder, and he lurched to his feet, wanting to cast the red cravat away and instead find something he might smash to pieces. Only the cravat had become tangled in his fingers, as if refusing to be cast in such a manner, for such a reason.

Oliver opened his eyes, squinting through damp lashes to see where the red silk had woven between his fingers and looped itself around his wrist, like a friendly thing that wanted only to belong to him. Which made it even worse. Gritting his teeth, Oliver used his other hand to pull the cravat free, whereupon he let it fall to the table beneath the window.

A small breeze stirred the ends of the cravat for a moment before letting it be still. Rain began spattering in through the open window and, with a low sigh, Oliver picked up the cravat and folded it carefully and slid open the drawer in the table to put it away. He wiped his eyes with the back of one hand, and stared out of the window at the rain for a long time, until it grew too dark to see.

16

ONCE MORE TO THE RIVERBANK

At the *HMS Scylla* once more, Oliver stood on the muddy bank, quite close to the hulk now that the tide was fully out. He felt the heels of his boots sink into the marled mud, and tilted his head back.

Even with the trails of fog that drifted around the edges of the horizon of rooflines, the sky was as blue as a robin's egg, washed clean by the rain of the night before, clouds white and puffy, as if they'd never before been touched by coal soot and chimney smoke.

Still, even given the fresh wind that abounded above the rooftops, the smell along the edges of the Thames was soaked with the odor of damp mud and dead fish, and the various sewage of pumps from factories and tanning efforts that poured into the river all up and down its banks.

Up ahead, and coming in Oliver's direction, was a trio of mudlarks. They wore broad-brimmed hats, folded back in the front, and had burlap sacks tied about their necks, with their trousers rolled up to the knees to reveal bare and reddened skin. Who knew what sharp edges, worms, and disease their naked feet were made vulnerable to, but the mudlarks walked along, seeming happy in the bright morning; one of them was even whistling.

Seeing Oliver there, all of them waved to him.

"Anythin' to be found?" one of the mudlarks called.

As the mudlark motioned to the *Scylla,* the three of them came even closer. They stopped when they were close enough to where Oliver could discern their features, but they remained at a distance, as if wary of potential capture.

"There might be," said Oliver.

He wondered if they considered him, in his current, grubby state, a fellow mudlark. And realized that they must think this, otherwise, they would not have spoken to him to ask, let alone to acknowledge him standing there. To be considered such a one did not sit altogether comfortably within him. Still, there was no reason to be rude.

"There's chain and a rag-paper bale," he said, telling them what he knew. "And perhaps there are some iron hooks and eyes, if they've not rusted away by now."

Coming out of his own mouth, the information surprised him, for when he'd been in the *Scylla,* he'd only been focused on Jack, or so he'd thought. Now it was clear he'd seen what value a hulk might have, even when it was not so easily evident.

"If you go in," Oliver said, "be wary of the beams overhead. She's been in the tide like this for a few days, and without the water to buoy her up."

"Thanks, mister," said the one mudlark who had been whistling. "But have you not marked it for yourself, then?"

Oliver shook his head. "No," he said. "You can have it."

There was nothing in the *Scylla* of any value to him. The quicker she was cleaned out and scuttled at last, the better he would feel about it, for when she was put out of her misery, then he could be put out of his. But none of that would do him any good if couldn't find Jack.

Standing there on the bank, the only certainty was that he had no idea where to look next. To be sure, he could retrace his steps of the last three days, over and over, until forever ended. But unless he had some indication of where Jack might have gone, then all of his efforts would be for naught.

He watched the mudlarks scurry about the bent and broken wooden hull of the *Scylla*. He kept himself from pointing out that there was an easier entrance on the far side of her, for it would most certainly be that the mudlarks would not trust him, and would continue on their own way. At the same time, he hoped they found articles and objects worthy of selling, for someone should get something out of the sad, blighted vessel.

He tipped his cloth cap to the back of his head, stared out over the slow river, brown and almost smooth at low tide, and thought about a map that he might get, and though he'd have to borrow more money from Noah, it could be the right idea. He'd create a grid and a sensible sequence, one that moved from the center of the map, which would be the Three Cripples, and go outward, square by square.

At the very least, this would keep his mind from rabbiting in many more directions than he could actually follow, and maybe he'd find Jack that way. Or maybe he'd never find him, and Jack was truly lost to him. And if that were so—

Oliver took a deep breath and attempted to settle his lungs, to settle the unsteady pain behind his heart. To blink away the heat in his eyes that still felt scratchy and sore from the night before.

He could be sensible when talking to Noah and keep his expression plain while walking the streets of London. But here on the bank of the Thames, with the low murmur of the water against the slippery mud, with no one near—he had to tighten his jaw, and felt the ugly emptiness of the attempt, which, without an audience to be brave in front of, was bound to fail. Would fail. Was *failing*—

From inside the *Scylla*, he heard an excited shout, as the mudlarks must have stumbled upon bits of precious iron, and maybe even Jack's newly bought birthday jacket, for who knew where Chalenheim had tossed it when he'd stripped it from Jack's body.

Oliver closed his eyes, clenched his hands into fists, and reached into his left pocket to circle his fingers around the silky ribbon of Jack's cravat. At least Chalenheim hadn't been able to get rid of that. At least Oliver had found it and had taken it back. He would keep it safe and then, after he had it pressed and cleaned, he would return it to its owner.

As he opened his eyes, he nodded to himself and scanned the foreshore of the bank to where it pushed out into the river, where the Isle of Dogs flattened out, and about which the river must curve to continue flowing until it came to Greenwich. Where the fish fry was to have been.

From behind Oliver, there came the sound of footsteps on stone, but he ignored it. If the mudlarks thought he belonged on the banks of the river, then nobody else would think to trouble him there, either to ask him his business or to bid him to go. But then the sound came again, a short, high scraping sound, and, as Oliver turned around, there was Jack—

—Jack, on his knees in the mud, as if he'd taken that last step off the stone stairs leading down to the bank, and it had unsteadied him. Even as Oliver watched, Jack tried to push himself to standing, but his boots were hooked in the mud, and if Jack took another step—

"Jack."

Oliver ran, grabbed his cloth cap from his head, and *ran*. His heart was full, a joyous lightness rushing through him as he came up to Jack and circled his arm around Jack's shoulder to keep him from falling, and settled Jack on a piece of driftwood.

"*Jack.*"

Too quickly, Oliver's joy turned dark, for the acrid, sour smell of Jack, with his head resting on Oliver's shoulder, was laced through with the sharp scent of something bitter that Oliver could not identify.

Jack was filthy, besides. His shirt was sweat-streaked, and

grime circled his neck, as though he'd been sleeping rough in the streets, which made Oliver's heart all but break. He drew Jack close to him, kissing his temple softly, not liking the feel of Jack being so thin, trembling in his arms, as though Jack feared he would yet come to more harm.

Oliver's mind raced ahead to the details as to how he would get Jack back to the Three Cripples safely, how he would convince Jack to rest until he was well.

All of this was overturned when Jack lifted his head to look up at Oliver, safe in the circle of Oliver's arms, and smiled his warm, slow smile.

"Did y'miss me, Nolly?" asked Jack.

"Yes," said Oliver, low, his mouth half kissing Jack's ear as he spoke. "Oh, yes."

WHEN JACK AWOKE, IT WAS RAINING, THOUGH ONLY SLIGHTLY. Beyond the clouds, the sun was battering its way through, making the rain yellow like piss, which the room stank of now. As he sat up on his elbows, the bedclothes, which he'd tugged around him in his sleep, fell away from him like an inattentive lover. The smell from the stable two floors below swam up through the floorboards, thick and sluggish with mud and wet hay.

His mouth felt stiff and dry, and he would have taken any drink that anybody cared to hand to him, only there was nobody at hand. With the door locked, and the window latched shut as tightly as it might be, Jack was alone, though not at home, not even close.

The dream of waves and the salt smell of the sea, the dark, ombre-tinged sky overhead, the flickers of silver stars—all of it faded into the stain-patched gray and yellow ceiling, the rough, dun-colored plaster walls, the floor that slanted away. The dull brass eye of the skeleton key, which was still in the keyhole, stared at Jack as he stared back at it.

Jack sat up, turning his weight on one hip as he leaned down to pick up the bottle of brandy. The cork was on the floor; the bottle was nearly empty. He could go home now.

Standing up, rocking slightly on the floorboards in his bare feet, he opened the window and threw the brandy bottle out. It landed with a crash on the wet stones of the alley.

No shouts rose to tell him anybody had been nearby, so he picked up the small brown bottle that had once held the laudanum and threw it out the window as well. Without waiting to hear it break apart, he grabbed the two corks and threw them out, and felt the sprinkle of rain on his arm, so slight he knew the rain would be ending soon.

He leaned at the waist, his stomach protesting its emptiness, his thighs protesting any movement at all, and picked up the tin chamber pot. It was half full of dark yellow piss, the stink of which rose up at him as he carried the pot over to the window. The piss sloshed about, coming almost up to the brim as Jack hefted the chamber pot and threw the entire of it out the window, and he ended up getting piss on his hands just the same.

Wiping his hands on his trousers, he struggled into his stockings and boots, fastened the thick belt, and slid on his waistcoat, which, without buttons, sagged open. Grabbing the empty red leather change purse, he stuffed it in his pocket. Then, putting on his cloth cap, he turned the key in the lock.

Sparing one last glance at the room, the haggard bedclothes, the spotted glass of the narrow window, he opened the door and walked out, leaving it that way with the key in the lock.

He would not do the polite thing, as Nolly would have, and return the key to the clerk at the desk, no. He would walk out, unnoticed, leaving the Angel and the room at the top of the stairs behind him, as he didn't need it anymore.

Walking home through the slightly slick streets, the rain spattering down uncertain and faint, Jack kept his head held high, belying the common nature of his clothes, the rough state of his person. He did not walk in a steady fashion, as a working man might, but this did not garner him any attention, as everybody in the streets was intent on their own business.

The carts and carriages on New Road clattered around him as he skirted wheels and whips. Once he gained the pavement, he had to hustle to get around the slow sashay of women's skirts, their baskets carried on their elbows, their high voices, all in a group, going on about the changeable weather and the chance for more rain.

Soon, though, Jack was able to get around all of this early morning traffic and head downhill, down Coppice Row, and on from there. He took the same route as he'd taken to lead Nolly into the City five years ago, the same route he'd taken from the Three Cripples only days before. He felt it in his bones that he had to go the same way or risk the ruin of repair that the laudanum and brandy had done.

By the time he arrived at the top of Saffron Hill, he was almost running as he hurried. He slipped on the paving stones and jumped into the street to avoid the sandwich man and his brightly painted signs. He went no faster than he should to avoid drawing attention to himself, but fast enough, and slid to a stop in front of the door of the Three Cripples, just as someone was going in, the door swinging shut in Jack's face.

Staggering back, Jack pulled the door open and stepped inside, where the air was cool and dark, swirling with a taste of rain as a bit of wind came down the chimney into the unlit fireplace. Two men stood at the bar with one booted foot each up on the brass foot rail, their elbows on the counter as they were served a pint pot of beer by the serving girl.

Nolly was not to be seen, though Noah was. He stood at the end of the bar, brightly dressed, as if to draw attention to himself and away from the dark doings at the Three Cripples, and he was talking to one of his men.

Jack took a breath and strode across the room, which grew

brighter as his eyes adjusted to the gloom.

"*There* you are," said Noah, clapping the man he'd been talking to on the back. "Come here, Jack, Jesus *Christ*, come here."

But instead of making Jack walk all that way on his own, Noah came forward and clasped his hand around the back of Jack's neck. He drew Jack out of the taproom and into the kitchen, where the morning sun shone through the window-panes, beaded by the bit of rain that had woken Jack that very morning.

"Where the bloody *fuck* have you been, Jack?" asked Noah. He gave Jack a shake, and Jack tried to steady himself, his knees wobbling, for he did not understand what Noah was upset about.

"D'you see this, eh?" Noah pointed to himself.

As bright as new coins, a black eye painted one side of his face, and a swollen chin painted the other. His lip was cut as well, and purple and blue dappled the line of his jaw. And still Noah pointed, as if Jack were blind, but that the bruising was quite, *quite* important, and Noah needed Jack to know this.

"D'you see what he *did* to me, Jack? An' in front of my men, no less, d' you see?"

"What *who* did to you?" Wrangling himself out of Noah's grasp, Jack took a step back, blinking, pretending his belly wasn't twisting, rolling his insides about, as though the whole of the floor wasn't rocking beneath his feet. "Who?"

"Fuckin' Work'us, that's *who*."

"Nolly?" None of this made sense. Jack stemmed the urge to race upstairs and get Nolly out of bed, where he surely was still asleep, to explain to Jack what had happened. "But why?"

"On account that he didn't believe me when I gave him your message, Jack," said Noah, with a bellow loud enough to be heard in the taproom.

"But you gave him the message, didn't you, Noah?"

"I *did*," said Noah, his hands in fists in the air between them, his teeth gritted. "But 'e said I lied, an' then he laid into me—

you better keep your dog on a leash, Jack, or I'll—do you see what he did to me?"

"He thought you lied?" asked Jack. "He didn't believe you?"

"No!" Noah raised his voice so that it echoed in the kitchen and slammed against the windowpanes. "He thought you were hurt or lyin' in a ditch somewheres, an' he couldn't get to you. He were certain of it, been out lookin' for you, roamin' the streets, pokin' his nose in where he oughtn't to. Said he got lost as well, came back yesterday, all scraped up, like he'd been dragged through the mill backwards."

"Is he upstairs?" Jack asked, feeling his breath grow short. "Asleep?" It was too much to hope for.

"No, he ain't!" Noah spread his hands wide. "Out lookin' for you, that's where he is, like 'e's been every day, trampin' out first thing in the mornin' to somethin' called the *Scylla*, on the Isle of Dogs."

Jack's whole body seemed to dip down, as though his knees had been knocked sideways. Noah reached out a hand to steady him, but Jack smacked the hand away, and stood there for a moment, blinking. He tugged on his unkempt waistcoat, tasting brandy and laudanum, the bitter and the sweet together, in the back of his throat.

"Don't go out, Jack," said Noah, his voice coming from far away. "You've gone over all gray, it ain't right. I'll send one of the lads to fetch him, an' you 'n I c'n wait in my office whilst you catch your breath."

"No," said Jack. The word seemed a whisper in his ears, barely audible in the large room, the sun glinting through the window panes, and Noah standing there, battered by Nolly's fists and unhappy about it.

At least Noah had not denied Nolly a place to lay his head. But it seemed Nolly had gone out each morning and come back at night, as though he'd stayed out the entire day while looking for Jack. And while it would have been more sensible of Nolly to have believed Noah and gone about his own business, working at the counter, serving beer, polishing the brass foot rails, Nolly had not. Instead, he'd—

"I'm goin' out," said Jack. "Goin' out, now."

With acid battering in his throat, Jack shook off Noah's attention and skittered away, going into the taproom and crossing the floor to the front door as fast as he might before Noah could order any of his lads to stop Jack. But then, none of them had stopped Nolly from wearing himself to tatters looking for Jack who had never been lost.

Jack made it to the door and flung it wide on the bright glare of sunshine and the rain-spattered dust in the street. He raced down the hill, plunging into ladies walking on the street, and startling a blind man at the corner. Panting, Jack realized he'd lost his cap, but the din of the day rose up as he crossed the planks over a ditch, and he kept running.

The streets, as Jack went around the important buildings near St. Paul's, became level, and he ran. Ran between the ratty, leaning houses with their stinking gutters and moss-speckled stones, where the damp never dried. Ran where the road rose again around Tower Hill, and the gray, grim pilots that edged the foreshore as they lumbered in the river.

On he raced, his breath growing thin, his vision only focused on what was in front of him: the road, the way to the *Scylla* and the Isle of Dogs, and Nolly.

Around the curve of the river, he staggered along the path that went by the warehouses and docks, spying, as he went, the low line of brown water that told him the tide was out and that the *Scylla* would be lodged in the dirt. Though why Nolly had felt the need to check out the derelict ship every single day— Jack *had* to get to Nolly before Nolly gave up looking for him, which he surely would do before too much longer.

Soon Jack was walking along the bank that was opposite the docks of Rotherhithe, where Bill had once lived amidst the grotty canals and decrepit dens. That far shore was just a smudge from where Jack was on this side of the river, where the wharves that stuck out into the water were lodged in the mud and gravel, as they were meant to float upon the river at high tide. The warehouses were all empty shells, most having been burned out in a fire, the streaks of black and gray leaking up from the glassless windows like ribbons of farewell at a funeral that nobody had attended.

Jack skirted between two warehouses, his boots splashing in the dripping alleyway, until he came to the steep, sharp stone steps that led down to the shoreline. Where, amidst the circles of pooling water that had been left behind as the tide went out, was the leaning hulk of the *Scylla*, her ribs spread and weak, sun-streaked and stained with mud from her heaving in and out of the water. Now stranded, beached forever.

Standing on the near side of her, facing the river, was Nolly. Blessedly there and whole and, it seemed, looking for Jack.

Only now, just as he was about to shout and draw Nolly's attention, Jack could not speak.

Nolly wore the type of clothes Jack was wearing. They looked as though they had been given to him by Noah who, perhaps as an amusing stunt, had chosen to dress Nolly in the clothes of a common laborer, with dark, thick trousers, a shirt with no collar, a waistcoat that sagged with no buttons to fasten it, and a belcher around his neck such as Bill used to wear.

Now, so roughly garbed and, but for the breadth of his shoulders, and the serious expression that narrowed his eyes, Nolly might have been the dusty, footsore lad Jack had taken beneath his wings all those years ago.

Jack should have known Nolly would have heard anything coming from Noah's mouth as a lie. That Nolly had given Noah a good solid thumping, so fast with his fists that not even Noah's lads had been able to pull Nolly off, did not surprise Jack overly much.

The worst of it was that Jack had gone and left Nolly on his own. Jack had gone off, as he always had done, every time he needed to, not looking right nor left, nor considering anybody he'd left behind because, at least before, there never had been anybody to leave behind. His old habits had carried him well back in the day, but now?

Nolly was never going to forgive him.

Jack could not speak or call out, but he stumbled down the stairs just the same. His legs were unsteady beneath him, and the moment his boots came off the last stone step, he landed in the tidal mud on his knees, and the whole world shifted sideways.

Unable to right himself in the marled mud, his hands splayed, bits of gravel digging into the seam of his boots, the palms of his hands, and the squelching sound assaulted in his ears.

Nolly turned and saw Jack there. Jack flinched, as if from a blow, from the blows that would surely land once Nolly got his hands on Jack. And Jack deserved it, he did—

"Jack."

With his cap in his hand, Nolly was running toward Jack, slipping in the tidal mud, but running, propelled forward, his hair flying back from his bare head, his mouth open as though he were preparing to shout to the high heavens that Jack had done the most grievous thing, the *worst* thing—

"*Jack.*"

Now Nolly was close, the cloth cap tossed to the ground as Nolly's hands gripped Jack's shoulders. So close up to those blue eyes, Jack's head rolled back, waiting for Nolly's fists, the sky spinning overhead, the bank of the Thames heaving up toward him. Jack was falling, but Nolly's hands caught him, and settled him on a bit of driftwood.

"Did y'miss me, Nolly?" Jack asked, his own voice coming to him as if from far away.

"Yes," said Nolly, passionate and close all at once. "Oh, yes."

Nolly knelt in the mud next to Jack, his arms around Jack, and he was saying something. Not shouting it, but saying it, clear and low and urgent, in Jack's ears.

"You came back to me, Jack, you came—you came back."

In those words, Jack heard a sigh, like an angel weeping, its wings sweeping down, blocking off the smell of the river, the thick mud all around, the burned edges of the empty warehouses—

All of this was taken away. And was replaced by the undone collar of Nolly's shirt, the line of Nolly's neck, the sweat of his anxious searching all around London. The press of his lips on Jack's temple, soft and sweet. Nolly's arms around him, and the way Nolly's palm guided Jack's head to lie against his shoulder.

Jack could let himself breathe now. His chest was loosening somewhat, but his head was still unbalanced, and the world tilted back and forth as he opened his eyes, squinting into the sunshine sparking off the low brown water.

Jack soaked up the warmth of Nolly's skin, the scent of him, the contrast he made to the damp bank of the river, and tried to make sense of what Nolly was saying.

"I thought you were dead, Jack," said Nolly, his hands tightening on Jack's arms. "That you'd gone off because you didn't want me to see you—die."

"Ain't goin' to die, Nolly," said Jack, his mind not quite to rights as he struggled to find the thing to say that would get Nolly petting him again, rather than clutching at him. "Not on account of havin' some man shove his pole up my arse. It'll take more than that, I reckon."

He felt Nolly's whole body shudder, and Jack tried to sit up so he could look at Nolly's face and see what was going on behind those eyes he held so dear. Nolly startled him, his body jerking beneath Jack's cheek, becoming tense, trembling as Nolly seemed to quiet himself.

Jack wanted to tend to his beloved boy, to get Nolly to express those deep and serious thoughts that were surely rattling about in his head. But Jack's own head ached, and his throat was parched and dry, and the smell of the rotting wood of the wharves was stirring something in his belly as though he were about to be sick. Only he'd eaten nothing for days, so the feeling churned around inside of him with nowhere to go.

"C'n we go home now, Nolly?" Jack asked.

"Yes, of course," said Nolly.

Nolly had taken up his cloth cap and put it on his head, and seemed to be attempting to gather up all the pieces of Jack in order to take Jack home. But Nolly seemed too serious and grim, as though he were deeply afraid Jack would take off again. This Jack needed to repair, and he would, so he licked his lips, dry as paper, and tried once more.

"Came home," said Jack, the words coming out scratchy. "Came home 'cause it weren't the same w'out you."

"Nor without you," said Nolly, whispering, the softness back in his voice, in the press of his lips along the top of Jack's bare head.

Jack's mind was filling with the same white fog that had followed him since that terrible day, and any words he might want to say had scattered themselves into the looming darkness beyond. He clutched at Nolly's shirtfront, the cheap fabric easily turning to wrinkles beneath his clawed fingers.

From above the bank came a loud, sharp whistle. Jack shook his head, barely feeling the side of his face or the scratchiness of Nolly's shirt.

"That's Noah," said Jack, his lips going numb, but the whistle Noah had sent out sparked a memory of a different time, when Fagin's street wolves roamed the City and called to one another in a sounded code no constable could ever break.

"What?"

"The whistle, that's him."

Nolly shifted, and Jack went with him. He sensed Nolly was looking up to the top of the bank, at the top of the stairs from whence had come the whistle.

Then came a shout, and words Jack couldn't quite discern, but to which Nolly responded, his voice rumbling in his chest beneath Jack's ear. Then there was movement and the earth fell away as Nolly stood up, his arms about Jack's waist.

Jack thought he might want to walk now, only his legs

seemed to be moving in an unwanted direction without giving him much notice, so he stumbled and fell, and Nolly caught him with warm hands and a gasp.

Then Noah was there, cursing beneath his breath as he and Nolly talked, words going back and forth, the heated steam of them sailing right over Jack's head.

"We'll both do it," said Nolly, clear as a bell, and when Jack next opened his eyes, he was floating above the river and was being hauled up the stairs, the smoke from the burned out warehouses tasting like ash, the rotten filth from the river on his boots, which Noah held in both his hands. So where was Nolly?

At the other end of the narrow lane between two warehouses, Jack was laid in a bright yellow dog-cart with two high yellow-spoked wheels. Noah climbed up front, and Nolly sat in the back, and Jack sighed and put his head in Nolly's lap and closed his eyes.

The cart lurched into motion, the clatter of the wheels loud in Jack's ears, the motion of the bed of the cart, between the inward-facing black leather seats, feeling as though someone were jerking him back and forth. But Nolly's hands were upon Jack, soothing strands of hair back from his cold forehead, leaning over him to shade him from the sun.

"Got your hat, Nolly?" asked Jack, and when Nolly didn't answer, Jack licked his lips, thinking he'd not made himself as clear as he'd wanted, so he tried again.

Only Nolly's fingers were on Jack's cheek, petting him. Jack became distracted, eyes sliding closed, the jerking of the cart turning into a rolling motion, fluid and smooth.

Any waves lapping at the sides of the cart, struggling to get in and swamp Jack into the water, well, Nolly was there, his bent knees a pillow for Jack's head, his strong arms as good as any railing.

Jack was certain the ocean could not reach him, at least not for now.

✖ 17 ✖

THE WHORE FROM NEXT DOOR

The yellow dog-cart that Noah drove through the rutted streets back into the City was no doubt stolen, as the cart was too new and the horse too carefully groomed and cared for to be something belonging to Noah. And, as well, Noah, obviously inexperienced in such tasks, did not drive with the steadiest of hands, and so the dog-cart, with its high wheels, was in danger of tipping at almost every corner.

With Jack curled in Oliver's arms in the back of the cart, Noah was too far away for Oliver to give him a good punch, so he had to rely on a muted shout when Noah clicked at the horse to go even faster when they managed to get from the foreshore of the river to turn into a broader avenue.

"Watch the corners, Noah," said Oliver, gritting his teeth as he used one hand to hang on to the back seat rail.

Noah only snapped the reins to get the horse to speed up, and Oliver watched the traffic go past them, shying away at the horrid closeness of the tail end of an omnibus, hissing in irritation at the slow sway of a rackety beer wagon, flinching at the click of a drover's whip over the backs of bullocks being driven to market. Till finally all Oliver could do was tighten his arms around Jack's unconscious form, tucked between his thighs, and make his focus be Jack and only Jack.

By the time the yellow wheels of the dog-cart finally came to a halt in the back alley of the Three Cripples, Oliver was all over sweat and regretting he'd ever thought Noah's rescue with the dog-cart was a heaven-sent and timely event.

"Len," said Noah, calling out, and to this he added a high whistle. "*Len.*"

When Len came out, he looked somewhat startled to see such a fancy cart in the dank, dripping alley, but he came up to his boss.

"Take this back to the Strand where Nick found it," said Noah. "An' make it quick. I don't want no coppers nosin' about when I only meant to borrow it."

As Noah climbed down from the cart, he reached toward Oliver.

"Hand 'im over, an' I'll carry him upstairs."

As much as Oliver wanted to deny Noah any part of this, he knew he could not get Jack upstairs on his own, so he would have to accept Noah's help.

"We'll do it together," said Oliver. "You take his feet."

It was cumbersome to lower Jack's body over the side of the cart, but Oliver let Noah hold the entire of Jack's weight while he himself clambered out. Once upon the ground, Oliver instantly took hold of Jack's shoulders and hefted the weight against his own chest.

As he was looping his arms beneath Jack's arms, Noah shifted Jack's boots in his hands.

"What're you laughing at?" asked Oliver with a snap as they slogged across the filth in the yard, the bricks and slats of wood teetering beneath their feet and threatening to topple them into the muck.

"Just what we'd do together to save our Jack, eh?" said Noah.

"He's not *our* Jack, he's *mine*," said Oliver.

He clamped his jaw hard so as not to lash out with something more scathing and cruel that might start a fight between them, as Noah already had bruises from their altercation on Monday. Oliver kicked open the kitchen door and walked backwards through the kitchen and into the passage to the bottom of the stairs.

"Don't you dare drop him," said Oliver. Heart pounding, he made himself ignore the stares of customers who, one and all, had paused in their morning drink to gawp at Jack's limp body as it was being carried.

"I won't," said Noah with some fierceness, so perhaps it was that the stares were getting to him as well.

Still going backwards, Oliver walked up the stairs, his back aching as it curved over Jack, trying to keep him aloft, trying not to fall over at the same time. The steep stairs seemed to impede them at every step, but soon they were at the landing, Noah's boots clomping, the dust swirling in the air from beneath the door to their room. Oliver had left the window open that morning, and so the wind was getting in.

With some effort, Oliver balanced Jack's shoulders on his knee, quickly turned the knob, and opened the door. For once, Noah was acting in concert with him, and together they laid Jack's body on the bed.

Jack's head flopped on the single pillow, as though the effort to go wherever he had been had taken all of his control over his own limbs, his own faculties. Then, just when Oliver bent forward to begin untying the belcher around Jack's neck, he was astounded to see Noah at Jack's feet, undoing the laces from the boots that had already left black streaks on the counterpane.

Yet Oliver found himself, instead of snapping at Noah to go away, oddly grateful, even for only this moment, that Noah would help him. So he let Noah tend to Jack's boots, while Oliver undid the belcher, unbuttoned Jack's top shirt buttons, and slid off the cotton waistcoat.

"He supposed to look that yellow?" asked Noah with a

tremor in his voice, as though he were afraid Jack had the cholera. "All yellow an' gray like he is?"

Oliver straightened up to look at Noah, who clutched Jack's muddy, stained boots to his bosom as though they were long-lost children.

"I thought I smelt laudanum on 'is breath," said Noah, by way of explanation. "But I can't be sure. I should go get a doctor, shouldn't I."

If Oliver had imagined there was any tenderness to be found anywhere in Noah, he hadn't quite imagined he'd see it now, over the care of Jack, who lay ghost-faced and still, unmoving, on the bed.

"No doctors," said Oliver, though he hated to say it. "I promised Jack."

"So did I," said Noah in return. "But what about a nurse? That ain't a doctor, is it?"

"That's a rather fine line to be drawing, Noah," said Oliver, glad for the taste of anger that had risen within him, for it felt better, more bolstering, to be arguing with Noah, as they usually did.

"Not the sort of nurse I mean," said Noah with some vagueness as he placed the boots on the floor at the foot of the bed. They'd get knocked over and spread mud everywhere, but Oliver didn't have the energy just then to make Noah move them.

"You stay here with 'im an' I'll go fetch somebody," said Noah. "Not a doctor, an' not really a nurse, neither, but somebody."

With that, Noah was gone, leaving Oliver on his own in the small room, where the stench of the river, once again, permitted the air.

He reached out his hands in a vague motion, as though they on their own hadn't the slightest idea of what to do next. So he focused on what he could do. He took off Jack's stockings, and then he loosened Jack's belt and took that off as well.

With each garment removed, he paused to determine how

much to the skin he should strip Jack. Enough to make him comfortable, but not too much so as to bare his wounds to the world. For it seemed Jack had been sensitive to that before, enough to make him jumpy and angry all at once.

Oliver knew he would rather cut off his own arm than to place Jack where he felt so vulnerable. So even as the task needed doing, his hands hesitated as he undid the buttons on Jack's trousers, sliding them out of the tabs, and moved Jack's whole body to the side so he might take the trousers off Jack's legs.

The room was warm enough so it made sense, although Oliver found his whole body stiffening when he saw the bruises on Jack's belly where his shirt had ridden up. Long, dark marks continued on down Jack's side, going beneath the hem of his undergarment.

If Oliver were to strip Jack further than his shirt and smalls, he would no doubt find more bruising than his mind, his soul, would know what to do with. As it was, he was able to see what Jack did not want him to see, as the cotton was thin enough to show the shadow of additional bruises on the inside of one thigh beneath Jack's underdrawers, as well as something darker, spatters of deep brown that Oliver knew to be dried blood.

But there wasn't a lot of it, and so Jack had been right, he'd not been bleeding very badly at the time. And besides, Oliver had been warned away, and hadn't yet been given permission to look, let alone to touch, so he eased Jack's inert body to the side and pulled the sheet over him, as though Jack were only sleeping, and not lying there like a gray-skinned corpse.

If Oliver had some water, cool water, he could wash Jack's face and hands, take away the grime from the back of his neck, and make him comfortable that way. But he dared not leave Jack alone, not now. Besides, he couldn't bear the thought of it, so he propped himself on the edge of the bed, and arranged the sheet across Jack's chest, and took Jack's hand in his.

With slumped shoulders, Oliver waited for Noah's return.

And watched Jack's chest rise and fall with each breath, steady though shallow, and wished with all his heart that he knew what else to do.

Presently, he made himself get up to straighten the room, to pick the clothes up off the floor so whoever Noah brought wouldn't trip over them. Folding Jack's shirt and waistcoat, Oliver placed them beneath the table, along with the boots and stockings, and everything Jack had been wearing.

When he got to Jack's trousers, he felt a weight in one of Jack's pockets. This turned out to be the red change purse, which Jack had taken with him. Now it was deflated, empty of money, but that didn't matter, as all of that money had been Jack's anyway.

Oliver put the change purse in the drawer and, after a moment, he took the red cravat out of his own trouser pocket, folded it, and placed it beneath the change purse, shutting the drawer after. Thus, he and the room were as ready as they ever would be, with Jack, still and motionless, upon the bed.

Waiting for Noah did not take long, though as the door opened without Noah having taken the time to knock, Oliver stood up from the bed, his heart racing. There in the doorway was Noah, looking somewhat haggard and pale, and with him was a woman. Not a woman with a sensible bonnet, a white apron, and a nursing bundle under her arm, as Oliver had been expecting. Instead, there stood a fallen woman, though given her age and staunch girth, she was the matroness of fallen women.

She indeed had a nursing basket, but she had no apron and no bonnet. Her hair fell in a mid-morning tumble from the back of her head, which was a sight that although Oliver had heretofore imagined in passing, he had never before seen, and which was certainly of a heightened color known naturally to no proper woman.

Her silk wrapper, as well, was of the sort not meant to be seen outside the bedroom, as it was low across the neck with bits of jet sewn into the wrists of her high sleeves. The hem of the wrapper, shiny with gold ribbon trim amidst the more somber brown silk, swept the dusty floor all about. The smell of her dusky perfume filled the room.

"A whore, Noah?" asked Oliver, his voice loud in his startlement. "A *whore*?"

"The whore from next door," said Noah, half on the way to being amused by himself.

But Oliver was not humored.

"Get her out," he said, pointing, standing between the bed and the door. "Just get her out of here."

The whore advanced into the room, the round circle of the hem of her wrapper kicking up dust and taking up a great deal of floor.

"Noah tells me your friend smells like laudanum on his breath, an' he's been away for a few days. I reckon I c'n help with that."

The whore said this with her gaze steady on Oliver, speaking as though he'd given her leave to do so. But there was no haughtiness to be found on her anywhere at all, just a sure presence that she knew what to do.

"I've brung somethin' to help him come out of it, an' for the pain, as well," said the whore now. "I've had girls whats been abused like 'e has, so you might put your own pride aside an' let me help. You won't get a doctor in here to do the same as what I can."

Behind Oliver on the bed, Jack stirred, as though the strong scent of the whore's perfume had unsettled him. But as Oliver turned to tend to him, Jack sank back into stillness, looking even more ghostly pale than he had when Oliver and Noah had carried him up the stairs.

"What do you have for him?" asked Oliver, making up his mind in that instant as he turned back around to direct his attention to the whore. It wasn't quite like walking across broken glass to admit her into Jack's presence, to allow her to do for Jack what she might for one of her girls, but it was close. "What can you do for him?"

The whore reached into her basket and pulled out a crystal pitcher. It was etched along the sides with designs far too fancy to be seen outside of a high-class dining room, but she handed it over to Noah without hesitation.

"Go an' fetch some water, an' I'll show your friend here how much to give 'im."

"But why do I have to be the one to go?" asked Noah, his mouth falling open in some astonishment.

"'Cause he's *his* lad an' not yours, now get movin' before I plant my delicate an' slippered foot up your arse."

Noah scrambled to do her bidding, which left Oliver ostensibly alone with a fallen woman. The sort he'd been taught never to acknowledge, not even if one were to fall dead at his feet.

As the whore came closer, the cloth of her wrapper swished aside, showing some length of stockinged leg, and Oliver didn't know whether to jump out of the way or to order her out of the room. But she ignored him, though she didn't come between Oliver and the bed where Jack lay so still. Instead, she went on the other side of Oliver, along the wall, and balanced her basket at the edge of the small table beneath the window.

"This 'ere is valerian; it's got red wax about the rim," she began, placing a small brown glass bottle on the table, going about her lesson as if she were quite sure Oliver would be attentive to it. "Give 'im two drops in water every hour, that'll help him not miss the laudanum so much. Here's the glass. You might as well go fancy, eh?"

The glass that she placed on the table was a cut-glass tumbler of the type to serve fine whiskey to gentlemen after a supper party. Along with a silver spoon, she placed two other brown glass bottles on the table and pointed to each one in turn.

"This is the poppy seed one. It's to help him sleep when he's got troubles what keep him awake; the wax about it is pale, d'you see? This other is a tonic what's got milk thistle an' ginseng an' passion flower to help him heal all over; that's the one with the pink wax. Two drops an hour of each, in water, same as the valerian, an' don't forget to put the corks back in. An' here's some raspberry tea leaves, to help in his mind with them troubles that took him to laudanum in the first place. Can you remember that?"

She turned and, in spite of the stench of her perfume and the fact that up close the unsuitable silk wrapper was worn along the edges, the turn of the edge of the lace along her collar frayed with wear, she looked at Oliver as steadily as a governess might, with her charge in her sights and a lesson to be learned.

"Two drops each hour, in water," said Oliver. "But for how many days, and when do I give him the tea? And how should I dose him if he's asleep? Won't he choke?"

"You wake 'im," said the whore.

This time, when she moved past Oliver to get to Jack in the bed, Oliver let her, though his nostrils flared as he took in her cheap scent, and he knew that he would not like to see her hands upon Jack. Oliver liked it even less when she bent over the bed and patted Jack's cheek with three sharp taps that made Jack's eyelids flutter.

"Jack," she said to him, quite stern. "You must wake up now an' take this. D'you hear? Wake up, sit up, an' take this."

Just then, Noah arrived with the crystal pitcher, carrying it in both hands. Some of the water slopped down his shirt front, and the colors of his waistcoat had apparently not been made fast, for they had melted into each other into long ribbons of color.

"You, lad," said the whore to Oliver. She used all of her strength to pull Jack to a sitting position against the iron bed frame, though, afterwards, her hands were quite gentle as she arranged Jack's shirt to keep his modesty. "Make the valerian like I told you, so I can watch an' make sure of you."

Oliver made his mind stop thinking any thoughts at all as he took the pitcher from Noah and poured some of the water into the cut-glass tumbler. Taking the small bottle of valerian, he took off the cork and tipped it over the spoon until he had two large round drops that floated upon the surface of the spoon like tiny brown bugs.

At her nod, he dipped the spoon into the glass and stirred it around, listening to the sounds of silver on crystal make a distinctive clink-clink sound. After a few stirs, she took the glass from Oliver and, with one half-naked knee on the bed, brought it to Jack.

As Jack's mouth was still closed, and he seemingly unaware of her presence, she pulled at his lower lip to open it, and tipped the contents of the tumbler in. Then she clamped her fingers on Jack's nose so he was forced to swallow to breathe, though he seemed to choke on the draught, and coughed and sputtered. But he never even opened his eyes.

"Now, do another with the tonic, an' save the poppy seed for nighttime. It'll give you a rest as well as it will him, so you c'n take that yourself when you need a bit of sleep."

She half turned her head, still kneeling on the bed, to see Oliver standing there with his hands at his sides, though he would not admit to her how overcome he was, helpless, thinking her cruel, wanting to curl up into a small ball until everything was all over.

"Make it up, then, lad," she said, "or you can watch him fade away to nothin', an' that right quick. I ain't about to nurse him, but I'm here to show you how. Got it?"

There was no lie in her eyes; she was as steady as before, and it suddenly occurred to Oliver, though without any charity whatsoever, that to run a whorehouse must take some brains and not a little bravado. So he nodded and made up the second tonic in the tumbler, and was a bit surprised to see her give up her place at Jack's side and gesture that he might assume it.

"You're only tippin' in a bit," she said. "It might look like he can't breathe, but he can when he swallows. D'you see? Now you try."

Oliver gripped the tumbler in one hand and leaned on one

knee on the bed. But instead of patting Jack's cheek sharply, he petted it, and said, low, "Jack, can you wake up for me now and take this? It'll make you feel better."

To his surprise, and to Noah's and the whore's, to hear the indrawn breaths of shock behind him, Jack opened his eyes. They were only open to very narrow slits, and seemed cloudy and muddled, but Jack turned his face up to Oliver's, and squinted, as though he wanted to focus.

"Nolly?" Jack asked, his voice flinted and uneven. "What d'you what?"

"Drink this," said Oliver, barely able to get the words out, so grateful to see Jack awake, at least somewhat. "You'll feel better when you do, I promise."

Dutifully, Jack drank the contents of the tumbler and pulled his chin away, licking his lips when he was finished.

"M'head hurts, Nolly, it hurts." Jack's head tipped forward toward his chest, and Oliver reached out to soothe the lank hair away from Jack's pale forehead.

"You rest now," said Oliver. "And when you wake up, it won't hurt. Or if it does, I'll get you something to make it feel better. Can you rest now, Jack?"

Jack nodded, and though his lips seemed to be moving to say something in response to Oliver's request, no sound came out.

Blindly, Oliver held the tumbler behind him for somebody to take and, without an ounce of propriety, he clambered on the bed to get a better angle. He curled his arms around Jack's shoulders and shifted Jack's body down on the bed, until his head was on the pillow, with his body curled toward Oliver.

"Sleep now," said Oliver as he tucked the sheet around Jack's shoulders. It was too warm for the blanket, but the sheet, at least, would cover Jack from the world.

When Oliver stood up from the bed, he turned to find both Noah and the whore simply standing there, staring at him, somewhat open-mouthed.

The whore, in addition, had pulled her wrapper close. The

expression on her face, the fine lines of her skin showing beneath the unnatural powder she had applied, seemed to indicate she'd seen more than she'd wanted to, and would soon be telling everybody about it. For though she was a whore, even such a one might draw the line at the illicit relationship she'd just seen the evidence of right before her very own eyes.

"How did this happen to 'im?" she asked, after a pause.

Oliver realized she was truly concerned about what had happened to Jack, and probably would not gossip. But Oliver looked to Noah, hoping to be spared the telling of this particular tale, which somehow was the focus of every conversation he'd been having lately. It would not have been any easier to tell it had he been the victim of it, but that would have been preferable than to expose Jack in any way.

"Not that it's any of your business," said Oliver, not caring if he was being rude. "But the workmaster at a particular workhouse has a fondness for boys, and, especially, boys like Jack, who weren't raised to be young gentlemen. Who are a bit rough about the edges, who—"

"You mean he buggers wee lads, the little ones?"

"I don't know, maybe," said Oliver, shaking his head, confused by her frown, the scowl between her smoky brows. "I just know he's had it in for Jack almost from the moment he laid eyes on him, and I couldn't—couldn't protect him."

"I'll get you another pillow for his head," said the whore with a small nod of her head. "An' a little stool so you can sit on it, low like, or rest your feet on it when you need a change in attitude while nursin' him. You keep dosin' him, an' when he wakes up, he'll want somethin' sweet, so's you come by the kitchen next door an' tell them to get you somethin'. Tell them I says so, an' if they give you any trouble, you tell 'em to come to me, Mrs. Louise. I'm at the top of the main stairs, most days."

"Thank you, Mrs. Louise," said Oliver as politely as he could. And though he thought about shaking her hand, he couldn't quite bring himself to do it. "My name's Oliver Twist, and you have been most kind to me on Jack's behalf."

Mrs. Louise smiled at him, showing two slightly brown lower teeth and a crooked front tooth that stuck out a bit. Oliver couldn't imagine any man wanting to kiss her, or lay with her, or any of it—but she was showing him a kindness that only moments before Oliver would have thought beyond the pale. But then, he'd never had the acquaintance of any whore, and didn't know, in general, whether they were kind or cruel.

"Anythin' you need," she said, quite somber and steady as she looked at him, "you just let me know, right?"

"If you'll come down," said Noah, with a cough he did not bother to hide, "then I can pay you for your trouble."

"Oh no," said Mrs. Louise with a wry smile. "For this'n—" She paused to nod in Jack's direction. "There's no charge, but just remember, turn about's fair play an' all that."

"I'll remember," said Oliver as solemnly as he might.

Noah sniggered beneath his breath, obviously on account of the fact that Oliver was now in debt to a whore, of all people. But Oliver ignored Noah because Jack needed the medicine and the care, and Oliver would have peeled his own skin and tanned it into a coat for the highest bidder if he had to, to provide that care.

With a nod at Oliver, her hands pulling the wrapper close, Mrs. Louise went out the door with Noah at her heels.

When Noah failed to close the door behind him, Oliver marched up to it. He was only a moment away from slamming the door shut when he thought better of it and closed it quietly, for he had Jack as his patient, and Jack needed rest, and should not be forced to witness Oliver's temper.

Oliver went to the bed and sat down on the mattress, which, in spite of the fact that it was the new one he'd gotten Jack upon their arrival in London, now felt too thin to be the sick bed for Jack. As well, he noted the telltale scurryings of tiny brown insects along the wall just above the bed, but it would have to do for now.

Oliver took Jack's hand for a while and watched Jack sleep. Jack's color was no better than before, but his breathing seemed easier, which was something.

All too quickly, Oliver heard pounding steps and a knock at the door, and when Oliver went to it to open it up, there was another whore standing there. This one was a bit younger, though her hair was just as untidy as she handed over a low foot-stool, which had a worn cushion with a faded green and white pattern. When she handed over the fluffy pillow, she tried to see around Oliver to where Jack was.

Oliver shouldered his way into the frame of the door, taking the footstool by one leg and the round, soft pillow by the lace-edged hem.

"I'll thank you for these items," said Oliver, making himself remember Mrs. Louise's generosity. "And for you to give us our privacy and not gad about." He added this last because while Mrs. Louise probably wouldn't talk about Jack, who knew that this rumpled miss might do when out of earshot from her mistress.

The young whore stood there, as if expecting a tip, but she'd been impertinent, and he didn't want to give her one.

"Surely your mistress has work for you to do," he said, beginning to close the door, blushing in spite of himself, for he only just remembered what that work might entail.

But the young whore only giggled, as though every day were a lark and this encounter a sweet addition to that.

"I'll be off," she said, and trotted down the stairs, her chin high as whistles and catcalls floated up.

Oliver shut the door fully, feeling grim and tight and angry. But then there was Jack to tend to, and this Oliver did not mind in the least because Jack had come home to him.

Oliver put the low stool next to the small table, and held the pillow beneath one elbow while he chivvied Jack's head on the old pillow on the bed, and stuck the nicer one directly beneath Jack's head. This arrangement was at too sharp an angle, so Oliver pressed down on the pillow to flatten it until Jack's head looked more comfortable.

"I'll look after you, Jack," said Oliver to the sleeping form. "As long as you need me to. Only do wake up and be cross with me for letting a whore into our room, won't you? Then you and Noah can have a jolly laugh over me being polite to a woman such as that, but only—Jack, she was kind, as kind as she knew how to be, given who she is in this world."

From Jack, there was no response, so Oliver sat on the bed and took Jack's hand once more. Oliver leaned over to open the window a little wider so that he could better hear the bells of the nearby church sound the hour.

When he heard those bells, he planned to dose Jack again, and would use the bells to time when he would give Jack more medicine. He would wait, and be patient, and give Jack the care he needed. Besides, Oliver had medicine and had not let a doctor in the room, so what else should happen but that Jack should get better?

THERE WAS A STEADY COOL BREEZE ACROSS JACK'S FACE, making him wonder when he'd left the window open while he slept, and whether or not he should take some more brandy and laudanum. Except, this breeze smelled like an open ditch rather than a stable, and the sour stench covered the faint stirring of rain somewhere close, a rain that would have been sweet to taste, if Jack could but get to it. He opened his eyes.

He felt stiff beneath the sheets, but realized he was wearing only his shirt and underdrawers, and he could feel that his feet and legs were bare. But at least the bed wasn't threatening to swallow him up, nor did the bed ropes creak as he shifted to look about him. And he realized, quite slowly, that the walls were of plaster, the ceiling slanted toward the door, and that there was no hay and horse-shit smell. He was no longer in the room at the Angel.

And there, standing against the wall, his arms crossed over his chest, his gaze focused somewhere beyond the windowpanes, and looking like hell, was Nolly. With the mud stains on the knees of his trousers, his shirtsleeves rolled up, the belcher handkerchief loose about the neck of his unbuttoned shirt, he looked as though he'd just come off a stint of pounding dusty streets before the laying of cobbles.

Along with all of that, and with the marks of the rope still red around his wrists, he presented as rough and uncivilized as any customer at the Three Cripples, especially with the expression on his face as he turned his head to look at Jack, eyes drawn down at the corners, mouth a thin line, and all of him wound up as tightly as a trip string. It must have been that although he might see Jack was awake, he had not schooled his features. Was Nolly angry with him? Of course he was.

"Why am I always the one in bed, w'you nursin' me?" Jack tried for levity, anything to soften the look on Nolly's face, the lack of shine in his eyes.

Nolly had no answer for him, though his mouth trembled, as if he were attempting to keep a shout at bay.

"That's on account 'o me bein' as delicate as a dragonfly's wing, eh?" asked Jack, trying once more.

But again, this seemed the wrong thing to say. Nolly scrubbed his mouth with the back of his hand, and even as he did this, his hand shook. Jack could see the streak of dirt along Nolly's forearm, the rip in his shirt along the seam, the long scrape on the side of his face, the bruise on his temple. None of which had been there when Jack had come down to the bank of the Thames where the *Scylla* had lain. Or had they been there, and Jack had not noticed?

"What is today, Nolly?" asked Jack, hopeful now that he

might get a true response, rather than a reaction as he had, as though Nolly's whole body refused to let him speak.

"Same as it was this morning," said Nolly. His voice swooped down, dangerously unsteady for reasons Jack could not get his mind to focus on. "It's afternoon now, so perhaps you take some of this. I have tinctures to help you heal. I have valerian, to ease your mind, and poppy, if you are in pain, and a tonic."

Nolly pushed himself up from the wall and uncrossed his arms as he came closer to Jack, hands shaking as he moved something on the table.

Turning on his elbow, Jack looked at where Nolly's hand was reaching. There on the table beneath the window was a crystal glass pitcher full of water and a cut-glass tumbler, with a silver spoon leaning inside of it.

Beside the pitcher and the tumbler were three brown-glass vials with cork stoppers and bits of wax around the necks, which had been torn away when the vials had been opened. As to where he'd gotten these articles, Nolly didn't say, but only waited for Jack to sit up.

Jack would have, as he sensed that was what Nolly wanted him to do. Only his arms trembled beneath him, and the insides of his legs quivered. Blood thumped along his arse, inside of it, shrieking for him to be still, and his bare feet could not get traction on the sheets.

A cold sweat broke out on his forehead, on the back of his neck, as Nolly looked at him, standing there at the edge of the bed, a twisted pull to his mouth, an unsettling bright dampness in his eyes, fists trembling against his thighs.

"Will you take something, Jack?" asked Nolly. His mouth barely moved as he spoke, as if his lips were numb. "Will you at least have some water?"

Jack opened his mouth at this, for water would soothe his throat and take away the sticky, thick feeling that the tincture of his own devising had brought. So he nodded and struggled to sit up all the way so he could rest his back on the bed frame.

Once more, as with the last time, his arms shook beneath him, and something in his hips grew sharp as the pillows slipped about. He was unable to manage and, looking at Nolly, was unable to ask for help. For he shouldn't *need* help. After all, nothing had happened to him that had not happened before, and would probably happen again, as that was just how the world was.

But Nolly was who he was and, with careful hands, too careful in Jack's mind, he helped Jack sit up, cupping Jack beneath his arms, and hefted him to sitting. Not wanting to draw attention to himself, Jack shifted on one hip, but of course Nolly noticed, and that made his eyes narrow, his whole body taut as he turned to the table once more.

"Will you take something now?" asked Nolly as he took out the silver spoon and poured the water into the tumbler.

The water made that sound that it did when it ran clean and clear, as if tumbled over wet, smooth rocks in a country stream. Jack's mouth felt as though it were coated with dry, gritty sand, and he wanted that water so badly he reached for it before Nolly was finished pouring.

Water slopped over the table, on the floor, half of it gone from the tumbler by the time Jack raised it to his mouth. His hand quivered; the tumbler clinked against his teeth as he tried to drink from it.

Without saying a word, Nolly took the tumbler from Jack's hand and refilled it from the pitcher. Then Nolly sat on the bed. He tucked himself into the curve of Jack's hip where it was beneath the bedclothes, and faced the same way as Jack as he slid his arm around Jack's shoulders. Holding the tumbler in his other hand, Nolly raised it to Jack's mouth.

There was no anger in the gesture, no recrimination, and it unsettled Jack, sent a ripple of unease up from his middle, a stiffness to his neck. He jerked his hand up and smacked the tumbler out of Nolly's grasp, sending it crashing to the floor, the water spraying Nolly's shirtfront as Nolly stood up, mouth open, shock making his face white.

"Did you let a doctor in here?" asked Jack, his voice hard, even as his jaw trembled. "Did you?"

"N-no, Jack, I didn't," said Nolly. He bit his lip and stepped back, his boot heels crunching bits of broken glass on the floor. "You said not to before, so I only took off some of your clothing in order to make you more comfortable, and then—"

"An' then what? For fuck's sake, Nolly, where'd you get them vials? The pitcher, so fancy, that don't belong to nobody from these parts. So where?"

Nolly backed up, still crunching broken glass with his boots, until his body was pressed against the plaster wall. His eyes were terribly bright, and his chin was lifted, as if he was preparing himself for a blow. But he looked at Jack, right at him; he was that brave, as if from somewhere he'd learned how to stare down the worst horrors, which was what Jack had now become, a tainted, dark-stained horror.

"*Nolly.*"

"You were—Jack, you were insensible and fainted on the bank, and so terribly weak you could barely speak. We got you here, in bed, and your whole body—you were in pain, Jack, but you said no doctors, so Noah, well, he called in a whore, and she—"

Here Nolly stopped, his teeth gritted, his nostrils flaring as though he could still smell the whore's perfume, which all whores applied with abundance, and which, to Nolly, would be a stench as impure as sin.

"A whore." Jack said this without the least humor in his voice. "You let a whore into our room."

The cruel part of him wanted to laugh out loud at the vision of Nolly having to admit a whore to their room, to be as polite to her as he might be to a lady in her own parlor. And, all the while, Nolly would have been seething beneath his skin, for there would be no soap strong enough, nor hot water hot enough to scrub such an encounter from his memory.

"She knew something of medicine, how to treat someone who had been—more than one of her girls, she said, had been, you know, with the work that they do, ab-abused, and so Noah thought—"

"You told Noah?" Jack bit off the tumble of anger in his throat, swallowing the clawed feeling of it. "Fuckin' *shite*, Nolly, why'd you do a thing like that for?"

"*You* told Noah, Jack," said Nolly with a small roar. "And then he came down to the bank, where the *Scylla* was, so it's not like he didn't already know."

Nolly held both of his hands out; one of his shirtsleeves unrolled from where he'd pushed it up on his arms, flopping along his wrist, though Nolly didn't seem to notice his untidy state as he usually would have done.

"He brought that cart. Do you remember the cart, Jack? He knew you weren't well when you left the Three Cripples that day and, as you were insensible and we such a long way from home, I needed his help."

Without thought, but with strength drawn from a sudden fury, Jack wrenched himself up, grabbed the glass pitcher of water, and threw it at Nolly. Except, as weak as Jack was, his aim was off, and the pitcher landed on the wall right beside Nolly's head, sending glass shards into the air, the water spraying over Nolly's face and the side of his neck.

Nolly's whole body stiffened against the wall, his palms flat, his eyes shut tight. He didn't move away, nor did he attempt to wipe the water dripping from his chin, the glass shards scattering like stars on his shirt front. But his breathing was ragged, his chest rising and falling in sharp stops and starts, throat working over nothing, over air. When he opened his eyes, they were glassy and seemed unable to focus, though he was looking at Jack and his mouth moved over words Jack could not hear.

Jack wanted to tell Nolly to get out, to stop treating him as though he were a wee lad who had been roughly used. He was *Jack Dawkins*, by God, and had survived the streets of London for as long as he could remember. A bit of rough handling was not enough to bring him to his knees, not after everything else, not after Kayema, not after Lt. Allingham, and not especially after a no-account workmaster who was only fierce when some small boy was in his sights.

After a small moment, as Nolly's eyes tried to look at anything in the room, anything but Jack, Nolly dipped his head and mumbled something. Jack took it to be an announcement that Nolly intended to get something to clean away the mess because, oh, yes, that was what was important, and not the fact that Nolly had brought a glass of water to Jack's mouth as though he was unable to tend to his own needs.

The door quietly shut behind Nolly's departure. Jack sank back on the bed frame, then slid down until his head rested on the pillows, which were sprawling all anyhow, damp with the spray of water. His bare heels churned the sheets into a rucked tumble, and the movement left him almost gasping as his thighs protested. His backside ached anyway, so he rolled on his side, facing away from the door, and curled his arms around his middle, as he had at the Angel.

Jack closed his eyes, listening for the step on the stair that would announce that Nolly had returned, having revised whatever strategy he had in mind, with more water, more forceful attention. More kindness.

Would it be better to go back to the Angel? Jack had one more night he'd already paid for, so nobody would begrudge him that. Deep within this thought, however, was the knowledge that it wouldn't make any difference, if it hadn't already.

And some part of him, buried even deeper than that, cried for Nolly to come back, to tend to Jack's ills. To bring him a cold cloth for his forehead, some tea, tender words, a kiss on his temple, soft hands in his hair.

But to accept all of that was to admit he'd been wounded.

Abused, as Nolly was calling it now. Abused like one of those working girls who, for letting a stranger fuck them, received a handful of change. Which they would hand over to the madam, who kept them as safe as she might and, when she could not, had vials and tinctures to aid them to a speedy recovery. Only to open the doors to more strangers who would, again, fuck her girls for money.

Jack's stomach churned, his throat closed up, and he thought about the room at the Angel, and pretended he was there. With the stains on the plaster walls and the dust on the windows, the smell of brandy in the air, the stable muck coming up through the floorboards. All very simple and quiet—

But there was no Nolly at the Angel, not like there was here, Nolly with a tumbler of water held to Jack's mouth, supporting Jack's body against his own, his arm warm and gentle around Jack's shoulders. Doing all of this with no words, no shrill nagging, only the sweet scent of him, sweaty and unwashed, the sense of him all around, the lean of his head against the top of Jack's head, steady and true. Being there, close to Jack, wanting only a gesture to direct him as to what Jack needed.

Jack had known all of this from before, in Lyme, in the sick-room of that great house overlooking the sea. He could see, in his mind's eye, the crystal blue shimmer of the whitewashed walls, and smell the sea, clean on the breeze, coming in through the opened window with a bit of rain, keeping the room cool, the only warmth that of Nolly's touch.

Except this time, he'd thrown a glass pitcher at Nolly's head, as if he'd meant to strike him dead, as such a blow could have done, had Jack's aim been better. Why had he done that? Why had he flung that glass pitcher with such fury and intent, on the verge of yelling at Nolly, who had only done his best, his very best, to tend to Jack as he wanted?

There had been no doctors, no prodding, no blood-letting. None of it. Nolly had done what he could, wanted to do more. Would do anything for Jack.

Except turn away, except not watch.

Because Nolly *had* watched, had seen everything. Been witness to Jack being fucked like a girl, with Chalenheim's hands leaving a dark taint of green and black tattoo marks all over Jack's skin that no soap would ever wash away. It would have been easier to bear, had Nolly not been there, witness to everything, even as Jack had endured it, as he'd endured it before, a hot, hard cock being shoved up his arse, not for his pleasure, but for Chalenheim's.

Boys got buggered every day. Jack had known that long ago, and though he would once have wanted Nolly to have this knowledge, he now regretted that it was so. For Nolly should never be exposed to something so cruel, so treacherous and inhumane but, because of Jack, he had been.

If Nolly could not scrub the scent of a whore from his skin, there'd be no way he could ever unsee the evidence that had been put before him when they'd been inside the *Scylla*. He would never be able to see Jack the way he'd seen him before, never look at him the way he had before, his blue eyes full of admiration and sometimes, yes, a little bit of awe, and, as always, with a gaze rounded by the slow, rich glimmer of affection, of love.

That would be gone forever now. All of it. Leaving Jack as alone as he'd been on the edge of that fountain, his backside wet, his legs clenched together, hoping he wouldn't fall off before somebody caught him. Only nobody had, and he was falling still.

❧ 18 ❧

IN WHICH OLIVER DETERMINES
TO PICK UP THE BROKEN PIECES

Oliver closed the door to their room and stood at the top of the stairs, his breath thin in his throat, each moment reminding him that he had slivers of glass all up and down his side.

Jack hadn't meant to lash out, for if he'd truly wanted to hurt Oliver, the pitcher would have been better aimed. Besides, if Jack was demonstrating such a temper, then surely that was an indication he was feeling, if not completely better, then at least a little better. Well enough to know his surroundings and to make demands—wasn't that a sign of health?

But Oliver's lips were numb, his heart sick and sore at the memory of Jack's face, the fury there, the rage of his gritted teeth, his insistence that he was all right. For though Oliver had been able to make Jack take the tinctures before, now that Jack was awake and aware, he might not agree to that. Might not want anybody near him to tend to him. Might actually determine he'd be better suited elsewhere, somewhere where Oliver wasn't. This Oliver could not let happen, though the only way to prevent it was never to sleep, never to close his eyes, for when he opened them, Jack might be gone.

Descending the stairs, Oliver tried to sneak past anybody

who might care to stop him, though, as before, Noah had made himself eagle-eyed, and snapped his fingers to get one of his lads to capture Oliver and bring him to the doorway of the office.

"What the bloody fuck is all over you now, Work'us?" Noah jabbed a finger into Oliver's shoulder, which was his mistake as the finger came away with a glass sliver embedded into it. "Jesus Christ, what the hell is this?"

"'Tis glass," said Oliver shortly, jerking back. "It's all over me so don't touch me."

"You can't come in here, then," said Noah. "Go outside an' take off that shirt an' wash up. I'll get you another'n."

For a moment, Oliver stood his ground, for he was not one of Noah's lads to be ordered about. But then, to do as Noah ordered made sense, as his shirt was full of glass. At least Noah did not press further, and let Oliver go, to go outside and cross the filth-lugged yard to the pump in the alley.

There, Oliver bent over and, pulling off his suspenders, shed the shirt, leaving it on the ground for whomever to take. Then he thought better of this casual cruelty and shook the shirt out and rinsed it beneath several pumps of water. He rinsed his hair as well, and sluiced water over his chest and arms, feeling along his skin with both hands for any leftover glass.

When Noah himself came out with a clean, folded shirt, Oliver was still crouched on his heels and half-naked amidst the foulness of the yard, somehow unable to move forward from either the moment or that spot.

"What happened, then?" asked Noah as he held out the shirt.

Oliver stood up and took the shirt and put it on. As he pulled the suspenders over his shoulders and tucked in the tails of the shirt, he shook his head, as he did not want to share this information with Noah any more than he would have explained what had happened in Spitalfields. Yet, there they were. Noah had helped him with Jack, and so perhaps deserved to know.

"He threw the pitcher at the wall beside where I was standing," said Oliver, looking directly at Noah to hide the lie that the pitcher had actually been aimed at his head. "He doesn't fancy being made an invalid, you see. Thinks he can put it behind him, just shrug it off, and while Jack is tough, certainly tougher than I—"

"Mrs. Louise said," said Noah, interrupting him. "She said it'll go up an' down like the swells of the sea. You can't hardly make him keep to his bed or take any tonics, she said, but you can coax him, an' be sweet to him."

"I don't need *you* telling me how to treat Jack." Oliver's hands clenched into fists and, once again, he found himself fighting his own nature and his abhorrence of Noah, who was beneath him in all things. Besides, it was none of Noah's business.

"I only meant," said Noah, his shoulders going stiff, "that what she meant was it ain't goin' to go smooth, after somethin' like this."

Oliver was about to state, quite clearly and fiercely, that Jack had been through this before, and come out all right on the other side. Only now, that might not be strictly true, for all was not right with Jack.

"Very well," Oliver said at last. "I can account for that, but—"

"But what?"

Shaking his head, Oliver looked at his feet, at the mud-spattered boots that, while so ugly, had taken the wear and tear of his tramping all across London without showing any effects at all. They seemed to be the only thing in his life impervious to ill usage or neglect.

"I need to clean up the glass before he wakes up, and get some cool water to wash his face and hands with."

"Well, you know where the tools are," said Noah. "An' I won't charge you hardly nothin'."

Noah went back inside, and Oliver, utterly still, watched him go.

He was almost sure Noah was joking about charging Oliver anything, but it was clear the debt between them was climbing at an alarming speed, like a runaway horse, even if the tools Oliver might use would be for Jack's benefit. Well, if Noah meant to charge Oliver a ha'penny for every little bit of this and that, then on his own head it would be for the time it took to tally the amount.

Shaking his head at Noah's avaricious nature, Oliver went through the doorway to the kitchen, where he gathered what he needed: a small box of used tea leaves, a hand-broom and dust-pan, a soft cloth, and assembled it all in a bucket. Then he took one of the dented tin pitchers and a pint pot that sat high on one shelf in the kitchen and went back outside to fill the pitcher at the pump.

Thus armed, he made his way through the crowd at the bar and, ignoring the quizzical looks being sent his way, marched up the stairs.

Pausing before the door and expecting another battle, he steeled himself and settled his shoulders. But as he opened the door, to his surprise, Jack was asleep once more, curled up beneath the bedclothes, his head burrowed in the fancy pillow, as if he'd always slept on one.

Thus, Oliver was able to quietly put the bucket down and use the short-handled broom to sweep up the glass and dump it out the window. Then he added water from the pitcher to the small box of used tea leaves to moisten them, and spread them out along the floor near the wall.

When he hunkered down to sweep up the damp tea leaves, there was a satisfying silver glitter of glass shards among the brown. The work steadied him, and his breath slowed, the sweat cooled along the back of his neck.

If they could get this far, he and Jack, then they could get further. It wouldn't matter how great or small the distance, as long as they were together.

～

When Jack opened his eyes again, the room was thick with gloom, and the windows showed a drawing of gray clouds that were bringing the smell of rain. There was an unlit candle on the table and, as well, a tin pitcher and a pint pot resting next to dark brown vials. Beside these articles lay the silver spoon, the only remnant of the fine things a whore had brought to Nolly to let him nurse Jack.

On the far wall was the ragged outline of the water from the pitcher that Jack had thrown. It would take days for the plaster to properly dry and there would always be a stain to indicate something had happened, but nobody would know what that had been. Nobody save for Nolly and Jack.

As for Nolly, he sat on a low stool with his back to the window. He was wearing a new and mostly clean shirt, and was bent over, causing his suspenders to pull across the sharpness of his shoulder blades.

It took Jack a moment to realize Nolly was fussing with the boot in his lap, and that he was using his fingers to draw out tiny shards of glass. Each shard he extracted went into a dustpan at his feet, making a faint plink sound as it landed.

Jack noted the floor was swept and streaked with dark lines, as though Nolly had used water to gather up the dust and the broken glass. Nolly's feet were bare in front of the stool, perhaps to test for slivers, with both of his stockings rolled together and tucked in the opening of the other boot.

The boots, Jack saw with some clarity, were workingman's boots, rather than the more sculpted and fine-leathered gentleman's boots Nolly had acquired in Winterbourne. Which was, again, another way Noah had probably thought to cut Nolly down to size, to dress him in rough clothes, to make him common right down to the skin. But didn't Noah know that was impossible?

Jack sighed and licked his lips, and Nolly lifted his head, but only slightly. His focus remained on his own hands and the upside-down boot between his knees.

"C'n I get some water, Nolly?"

Jack's voice felt thin, the words awkward in his mouth, not just because he was so thirsty, but because he was so terribly afraid there would be no water on offer. That Nolly would shrug and remind Jack that the pitcher of water was right there, within hand's reach, if Jack wanted it, but that Nolly was quite busy now, picking glass out of his boot from the pitcher Jack had thrown at his head while trying to kill him.

But that wasn't what happened at all.

"Yes, Jack," said Nolly.

Nolly put the boot down and stood up, moving the stool back with the heel of his bare food. With careful hands, he poured water from the pitcher into the pint pot, both of which would be indestructible, a choice not made by accident, Jack was sure.

The sound of pouring water made Jack's tongue want to hang out of his mouth, like a dog panting in the heat, and he tried to move into a sitting position, but it was the same as it had been before. His arms didn't want to cooperate, and his legs flat-out refused to aid him.

Nolly, again, and without any hesitation whatsoever, gently pulled Jack to sitting, and looked away as Jack tilted on one hip. Then Nolly held out the pint pot of water; Jack curled his fingers around it.

It was obvious that Jack's hand shook, and that if he took the pint pot, he'd only spill it all over himself, which might lead to him, all over again, attempting to throw the nearest thing to hand at Nolly's head. But Nolly only waited because he'd obviously learned from Jack's earlier temper tantrum that some types of assistance made Jack angry, though more with himself than with Nolly.

Nolly continued to stand there with seemingly no resentment whatsoever, his hand still supporting the entire weight of the pint pot. Jack watched as a drop of water curled over the brim and slid down over Nolly's fingers.

"All right," said Jack, swallowing. "All right."

He jerked his chin up at Nolly, unable to say the words to give permission that Nolly should sit down and help him drink, but wanting to give it just the same.

With a small nod, Nolly sat down on the bed as he had before, his hip tucked against Jack's hip, facing the way Jack was facing. With boldness Jack would not have expected, Nolly slid his arm around Jack's shoulders, supporting him upright while he guided the pint pot to Jack's lips and tilted it so Jack could drink without effort. Jack drank.

The water was as cool and delicious as if it had been drawn from a secret well in a deep, dark wood. That it was probably only water from the pump in the alley behind the Three Cripples didn't change anything. Jack's whole body sighed as he drank, water rushing into his belly in a cool curl, his shoulders relaxing.

He drew his head back to take a breath. Nolly held the pint pot in front of Jack's mouth for a moment and then, when Jack dropped his chin, Nolly lifted the pint pot once more. Jack took several large gulps and held them in his mouth before swallowing them with a gasp. When he was able, Jack lifted his hand and pushed the pint pot away, watching with careful eyes as Nolly turned to place it on the table.

Nolly never let go of Jack, never moved away, as he was surely tempted to do. But he didn't. Rather, he remained close, holding Jack as Jack wanted to be held, but did not, currently, have the temerity to request.

This tender moment, perhaps, was all Jack was going to receive once Nolly pulled his wits about him and determined Jack did not deserve to be held so, to be cosseted, to be cared for. Caught when he fell.

When Nolly did move away after a moment, it was only as far as to sit on the stool next to the bed. The stool was a short-legged thing, not even high enough to be a milking stool.

Nolly's head and shoulders came up just above the surface of

the mattress, or would have had Nolly been sitting up straight, as
was his wont. Only now, he was curled over his own lap, as if he
still had the boot between his knees and was tending to it,
picking slivers of glass out of the sole with his thumb and
forefinger.

As Jack sank against the pillows, he could look down at the
top of Nolly's head, where his golden hair was, truth be told,
tousled and not quite clean, as if days had gone by since Nolly
had tended to it. That might be, though it was worrisome to
consider the notion that Nolly hadn't taken the time for his
very-held-dear ablutions.

"Light the candle, Nolly, would you?" Jack asked, rubbing his
palms across his face in the dark. He had to fix this and
wondered whether he could.

As Nolly hurried to do as he was bid, Jack gritted his teeth
and drew himself upright against the bed frame, blinking as the
match clicked into brightness. The candlewick hissed as Nolly lit
it, and the smell of warm beeswax filled the air, making Jack
wonder if the whore had brought the fancy candle along with the
brown vials.

Jack had taken the change purse and all of their money with
him, so where had Nolly gotten the money for the items? Was he
again borrowing against his wages? But Jack was too tired to
think about it overly much and, besides, he was distracted by
Nolly, who was now bathed in golden light as he sat back down
on the stool, curled forward as before, his face white, his eyes
not meeting Jack's.

"I should never have left you on your own," said Jack, letting
the words slip out of him, an apology and explanation all at once.
"I should have stayed an' let you—only—"

Jack stopped talking, his breath panting out of his mouth, as
though Nolly had not just given him a long, cool drink of water.
He could barely manage it, but the words needed to be said. Jack
was brave about most things, couldn't care less about the others,

and nothing ever mattered, as everything could be got around, or glossed over, ignored, even. But not this.

"Didn't want you there, Nolly," Jack said, licking his lips, feeling parched and undone. "Didn't want you watchin' that, havin' to see it, but you did, an' you never looked away. Just stared, like I was somethin' not fit to be human, like you didn't care at all—like you didn't *care*—"

Jack stopped as Nolly raised his head and lifted himself on the stool, his head high as he looked straight at Jack, brave as a lion. The light of the candle cut gold into those blue eyes, right there in front of Jack.

"He *made* me, Jack. He said—" Nolly's jaw worked as Jack watched, as if Nolly were putting the words together on his tongue before uttering them.

"He told me how he'd found us and then, when I offered myself in your place, he just laughed. Then he told me if I didn't watch, he would take the first bit of sharp wood that he could lay his hands on and shove it in you, in your—where his cock was going to go, and that you would bleed to death even before the tide came in to drown us. So I had to watch every a-awful moment of it. C-couldn't turn away, had to trust that he wouldn't —wouldn't do that to you when he was done a-abusing you."

After the words were spoken, Nolly closed his mouth tight, pulling his lips against his teeth, as if to keep from saying anything else. And that was because, in Nolly's mind, what he'd already said was shameful enough. His inability to save Jack or look away, even, all of it would be hard-packed and heavy, a weight to carry around forever, with everything being his fault, the blame his to own, as if Nolly had done any of it on *purpose*—

All of this, the realization of it, swirled in front of Jack's eyes like a gray fog over icy waters. The curve of Nolly's head, the golden mess of his hair, became obscured by the pall of a pale shroud coming down upon Jack, and he felt sick, deep down in his belly.

There had always been an in-born tenderness in Nolly's

person, a certain dignity. But that sweet lad, who had made his way seventy miles to London all on his own, had encountered Jack. Who, with his tricks and sleight-of-hand, slight-of-voice, had managed to embroil Nolly with a gang of thieves. Had introduced him to Fagin who, far better than anyone else, could turn an innocent into a pickpocket in nothing flat. Nolly, however, had retained the grace of his breeding longer than Fagin had imagined he could, driving Fagin quite mad with his lack of success, a disaster which had made Jack laugh, but secretly.

Only now, the workmaster, with a word to Nolly, and with his hands upon Jack, had managed to trample all of what Nolly was and had held onto so dearly. Turning him inside out, and saddling him forever with the memory of what had happened in the *Scylla*, in the curved hull of a water-logged hulk, good for nothing but scrap and firewood.

Jack felt as though someone had punched him and, drawing his arms over his belly, curled low on the bed, made a sound that he did not want to admit to, his mouth open, a groan, some wordless plea. His eyes closed against the fog that swirled around him, obscuring everything from his sight, save for the memory of the look on Nolly's face that day when he'd watched Jack. Watched with unblinking eyes, and it was only now Jack knew the threat that had been behind it.

"Jack."

Jack heard the rustle of bedclothes before he felt the warmth of Nolly as he sat on the bed, tucking himself into the curl of Jack's body, but gently, placing his hands on Jack. On Jack's shoulder, on Jack's forehead, waiting lightly there, as if for permission, but bending close so when permission was given, Nolly would be ready for whatever Jack needed.

"Jack, please—"

"Yes," said Jack, in a hissed whisper. "Yes, yes, please, Nolly. Don't mind me, don't ever mind me, only could you—could you—"

Could you hold me, Jack wanted to say, only he couldn't find the breath to say it. *Hold me, and hold me, and hold me. Never let go. Never let up, never stop fussin' over me, no matter what.*

But he *was* saying the words, because his mouth tasted them. He felt the soft weight of Nolly's body pressing on his as Nolly wrapped his arms firmly around Jack and bent down, leaving small kisses on Jack's temple he'd so longed for but had turned away from. Now Nolly was giving them, as he always had, as if Jack's foul treatment of him had never been.

The words that tumbled from Nolly's mouth now, those soft, soft whispers, were not of recrimination or to scold, but instead were spoken to spread something tender all over Jack, in and around him, in a way that made Jack sigh. He kept his eyes closed, and let the words soak into him, as though they were a gentle and forgiving rain.

"I'm here, Jack, my bright bird, I'm here. Here and here and here," said Nolly, each word accompanied by a kiss, a touch, a gentle pet. "I won't leave you alone. I will hold you. I will catch you."

Jack's body jerked, though he took a deep breath and reached up to keep Nolly's hands moving on him, for Nolly's hands had stopped.

It was only when Nolly continued touching him, slowly, carefully, that Jack thought about the moment on the bank near the *Scylla*, when he'd stumbled to his knees, his head spinning as though he were falling from a very great height. And how, without a word, Nolly had caught him. Safe and sound he'd been in Nolly's arms. Safe and sound as he'd never before been, not that he could remember.

Now, on the bed, with Nolly all around him, Jack felt again the surety of a safety that embraced him just as Nolly did. For Nolly never said what he didn't mean, at least not to Jack.

He had witnessed Jack at the most merciless place, naked and struggling, right there in front of him, and considered the fault his own. That was the kind of love meant for kings in stories, the kind of fealty and devotion Jack surely didn't deserve, though that was what Nolly was doing, was offering up, as he always had done.

"Ain't nobody's fault, Nolly," said Jack, his throat thick, his tongue numb, leaving him almost choking as he spoke. "You know that, right?"

Nolly stopped, though after a pause and an indrawn breath, he continued, more slowly now, one hand on Jack's head, fingers stirring through his hair, the other hand resting on Jack's waist, a warm, comfortable weight.

"Maybe," said Nolly finally. "Maybe."

Jack opened his eyes, thinking to argue this point. But when he did, with the outline of Nolly's body above him traced in candle flame, and the gleam of the tin pitcher on the table, there out of the corner of his eyes, he knew he didn't have it in him to go after Nolly's reluctance to admit he was not to blame, at least not just now. Not with his head aching as it was, and the throbbing bruises Chalenheim's hands had left behind, seemingly all over his body and inside of him, no, he didn't have it in him.

"Could I have some more water, Nolly?" asked Jack. His mouth was so dry so quickly after his last drink that his lips felt cracked from it.

"Yes, yes," said Nolly. He leaned away and, reaching for the pitcher, poured Jack some more water. His body was limned in the candlelight, golden hair falling against his forehead as he took up the pint pot and relaxed once more at Jack's side, holding Jack, helping him to drink.

Jack drank, then pushed the pint pot away from him and toward Nolly, nodding.

"Now you. You must be thirsty after tendin' to such a troublesome one as me."

This actually got a small smile curling at the edge of Nolly's mouth as he obediently took several swallows of water, drawing the back of his hand across his mouth afterwards.

"Will you take something else, Jack?" asked Nolly, with one arm around Jack, the other balancing the pint pot on his bent knee. "The whore, she said she could smell laudanum on your breath. Did you take laudanum, Jack? She said you would need to sleep and sweat it out of your body. That's what the valerian is for, and the poppy, if you are in pain. Do you want it, Jack? I could mix it for you, I know how, now."

Nolly didn't move as he said this, but his blue eyes were round as he looked down at Jack in the curve of his arms. Round and open and oh, so very dear, so willing to do as Jack wanted, brave enough to suggest something Jack might not want, simply because it would make Jack feel better.

But the look Nolly gave him was so hopeful, wanting to do something to make it better for Jack, and told Jack that Nolly also needed something to make it better. So, it seemed, in this way, in letting Nolly help him, Jack might be helping Nolly to repair his sense of ownership of the disaster that had been made out of their wholly innocent excursion to a fish fry in Greenwich.

"Yes," said Jack, with a small nod. "Yes, all right."

Instantly, Nolly stood up again. He took the silver spoon and opened the dark brown vials, the narrow corks popping off beneath his quick hands. He tipped out a few drops from each vial and poured more water in the pint pot, then stirred the contents with the silver spoon.

Tapping the spoon on the edge of the pot, he laid it on the table and held out the pint pot to Jack. Then, as before, Nolly sat down next to Jack, not even waiting for permission, and held the pint pot to Jack's mouth.

Jack drank the contents in two quick swallows, wincing at the slightly bitter, smoky taste. Then he pushed the pot away, and settled against Nolly's shoulder, sighing.

"You'll sleep now," said Nolly. "Rest a while, Jack, will you?"

"I will," said Jack, blinking slowly, thinking he must be imagining how fast the tonic was working. "But will you stay with me, even if I don't know you're there? Come into the bed with me, an' let us sleep that way, with your arms around me, an' don't let go."

Jack's voice cracked as he said the words, feeling as though his whole being was wide open. He trembled to hear Nolly say no, that he had things he needed to tend to, that it was too early for him to go to bed.

But as before, Nolly said nothing of the sort. He only got up to check the lock on the door, and to use the slat to prop the window open, to move the dustpan out of the way from being stepped upon, and finally, to bend and blow out the candle, cupping the flame with the curve of his palm, his face alight in a gold glow for one brief moment.

The wax hissed as it cooled as Nolly used his hands to push Jack gently toward the wall. Then Nolly climbed in, fully dressed as he was, bare feet mingling with Jack's, his face on the pillow. Jack sensed Nolly's eyes were open in the dark.

"I'll watch over you," said Nolly, his breath gentle on Jack's face.

"Glad to hear it," said Jack. "Wouldn't be able to sleep, else." Only he said it not as he'd meant to, with a joke in his tone, but instead with a quaver, a little high pitched, as if he were a much younger boy, afraid of the dark, afraid of the memories in his head.

"Me as well, Jack," said Nolly. He moved closer so their chests were touching, so Jack could dip his head and tuck it beneath Nolly's chin. "I was afraid you'd send me away. That I'd have to sleep somewhere far from you. That I wouldn't be here when you needed me, or—" Nolly swallowed, his cheek moving on the pillowslip. "Or when I needed you."

Only Nolly, as brave as a lion as he always was, could have admitted something that bared his soul down to the bone. It answered Jack's fear of being so exposed, gentling it, tamping it down, for it was between them as it always had been, in this moment, in the dark. Where they could share their fears, and comfort each other with soft words, with closeness.

Jack felt Nolly's heart beating, the warmth of that body close to his own, and sighed, hunkering down so he could be small, and Nolly could curl around him. Nolly was sleeping on the outside of the bed because Jack needed it that way. Even though Jack had never asked for it, Nolly still knew. Nolly always did.

The rain finally came and, for a moment, Jack thought Nolly would get up, concerned about the state of the table or the floor, if the rain were to come in through the open window. But Nolly did not, and the rain, it seemed, was slanted the other direction, as there was only the faint faraway sound of water falling on the cobblestones in the muddy alley, on the rooves across the way.

A shift of cool air filled the room, erasing the smell of beeswax and honey. Turning the night's darkness into something sweet and gentle, muting the growing sounds of the taproom below as customers piled in and ordered their drinks and shouted for more, shouted for something grand to fill their hearts with, to take away their never-ceasing labors and the sewage in the streets, to make them mindless and heedless of the grit and toil that made up their every waking hour.

Jack thought to say something to Nolly about this, but his mind was too lax and his mouth wouldn't respond in any way, and besides, Nolly probably already knew what Jack was thinking. Knew what men drank too much beer over. How it was that way in every taproom and tavern in London. What Nolly was always struggling against and enjoining Jack to understand.

But the bare shimmer of comprehension slipped away from Jack's consciousness as the darkness grew behind his closed eyes. The closeness that Nolly granted him, now, as always, surrounded him. He was safe. He would not fall. Not with Nolly to catch him.

JACK SUFFERS HIMSELF TO EAT MILK TOAST, WHICH HE SHARES WITH OLIVER

The rain seemed to have lasted most of the night, for when Oliver awoke, it was cooler. There was a small, almost timid breeze coming in through the casement window, stirring the charred wick of the burned-down candle. The air tasted, perhaps, of more rain to come, and of more clouds to dim the heat, to scour the sour air that had been London's constant companion for many days.

Oliver eased his arms from around Jack's shoulders and sat up in the bed where they had slept as two small boys might who were afraid of the dark of night, the sounds of a storm, of the nothingness that might swallow them whole had they not each other to cling to. But the darkness was gone, at least for now.

Oliver planted his bare feet on the floorboards and, hunched over, rested his elbows on his thighs. The day lurched ahead of him at a racehorse pace, for while at long last Jack had allowed himself to be tended to, there was more he might need, but yet might not let Oliver know of it, let alone ask for outright. And though normally Oliver's sometimes clumsy attempts could be brushed aside, as Jack often did, this time, Oliver wanted to do better by Jack, to give Jack what he needed, what he wanted, rather than what Oliver had determined what was necessary.

To that end, he stood up. At least he could get another pitcher of water, for Jack's thirst seemed to be ever present, though the whore—Mrs. Louise—had also mentioned that Jack might want something sweet at some point. This was a dubious bit of advice, for ever did Jack prefer the savory to the sweet; he liked a good beefsteak and would choose it over a steamed pudding, even one that had sweet, warm cream to pour over it.

Oliver's belly woke up and yanked at his innards, demanding its own way, and now that Oliver was aware of this, he needed to tend to it. But first, Jack's water, and where were his stockings? His boots?

"Nolly."

Whirling around, Oliver saw Jack trying to sit up, his face pale, silver sweat on his forehead. He managed to rise to his elbows, then his face tensed as he curled forward, fingers curling on the thin sheet like claws.

"What is it, Jack?" asked Oliver, going forward, his hands held out, ready to do whatever Jack required, so glad that Jack was letting him. "What can I do? What do you need?"

"I need the—" Jack stopped and waved toward the floor.

"The what, Jack? Do you want more water? I was just about to fetch you some."

"—the privy."

"There's the chamber pot beneath the bed I can get you," said Oliver, thinking there was more beneath what Jack was saying that he didn't understand.

"No, the *privy*."

"Ah—"

All at once, Jack's countenance, the way he held one hand to his belly, made sense. Oliver looked about the room and finally espied his own boots, though not Jack's. But given Jack's drawn expression, the gleam of his teeth as he held his breath, Oliver knew it didn't matter, that to take the time to dither over such a thing as whose boots were whose would be foolhardy. So he hustled Jack into his trousers, and shoved his own boots on

Jack's feet, sans stockings, and gently levered Jack to his feet. He opened the door, letting in a bit of cool breeze that came up the stairway.

"Can you make it?" asked Oliver, quite low for Jack's sake as well as his own, for it wasn't yet a foregone conclusion that Jack would not shove him off and tell him to mind his own damn business.

"If I keep movin'," said Jack, straightening up and pushing Oliver's hands off him. "Long as I keep movin'."

Oliver had been where Jack was now, though that predicament had been his own fault, on account of his lack of willpower regarding a castor-oil-laced pear tart.

"You go in front," said Jack, shoving Oliver a bit roughly. "An' don't let 'em stop me or I'll have shite runnin' down my legs."

"Yes, Jack," said Oliver, feeling the sweat build along the back of his neck, as if he himself were the one in such a state. Luckily, the privy was in the alley directly behind the Three Cripples. "I'll walk quickly."

And walk quickly Oliver did, down the stairs and along the passage, with Jack behind him. They managed to get into the kitchen before nobody, not even Noah drinking his morning coffee at the near end of the counter, could bid them so much as good day.

The kitchen's back door was stuck with the rain from the night before, but Oliver yanked it open. He hustled across the yard, his bare feet balancing on the morning-cool bricks and stones and the length of wood that had been placed so nobody would have to actually walk in the several inches of filth that seemed a permanent fixture between the tavern and the length of the alley.

He heard Jack behind him, clomping in Oliver's boots, the laces untied, and slipping. Just at the edge of the alley, several feet from the leaning wood hulk of a privy, Jack brushed Oliver aside, flung open the door, and slammed it behind him.

Oliver heard the wooden latch clunk closed, and then Jack as he rustled out of his hastily donned trousers. Then Oliver didn't listen any longer, but stood still a moment, the wretched intimacy of it sweeping over him. He backed up a bit to give Jack his privacy, as anybody would want, feeling as though he had lost something he would not be able to find.

But there was something else gained, if it might be described as such. For Jack had not shoved Oliver aside, nor told him to fuck off. Instead, he had let Oliver help him, and might continue to do so, if Oliver could stay steady and not wring his hands as though Jack were some baby bird that had tumbled out of its nest, but rather, that he was Jack, in all his sensibilities and experiences. For as important as it was that Jack be cared for, with that care at Oliver's hands, it was equally important that Jack be allowed to retain his dignity.

So Oliver backed up all the way until he was standing beneath the small wooden awning that hung over the kitchen door, curling and uncurling his bare feet against the muddy cobblestones, crossing his arms over his chest and then uncrossing them just as quickly.

For a moment, he patted his thighs, and listened to his belly growl and roll about, and thought about the work to be done in the taproom, because it was easier to distract himself with such thoughts, even though any work he might do would never make any difference to anybody, let alone to anybody who might actually *care*—

Then the door to the privy banged open and Jack strode out. He was stuffing his shirt into his trousers and redoing his belt, clomping along in Oliver's boots, and came right up to Oliver as if he meant to push past him to go inside.

"Stench too much for you, eh?" asked Jack, his eyes a bit narrow, dark lines of sweat drying in front of his ears.

"No, Jack," said Oliver, making his tone quite even. "I just wanted to give you your privacy, as you would have given me mine."

Oliver waited a moment while Jack looked at him, his

features settling a little, the curve to his eyes becoming more familiar, the corner of his wide mouth pulling up.

"Did you—did we make it in time?" asked Oliver, not sure how else to put it.

"That *we* did," said Jack, taking it in stride as he usually did, jovial and candid, though Oliver saw some lingering tenseness along Jack's jaw. "Might even want a bath later, only now—" Jack patted his belly with a small laugh. "Only now I'm terrible hungry, ain't that queer?"

"Not really," said Oliver. Relief moved through him like a small, steady tide. He put his hand on Jack's forearm and pushed the unbuttoned cuff up so he might stroke Jack's skin, to feel its silky texture, but also to see whether Jack was overly warm or overly cool. "When did you last eat, anyway?"

Oliver attempted to think it through, for food had not been on his mind of late, as any meal he might have eaten had been forced upon him by Noah, or gently given by Mr. Yeslevitz. But as for Jack—

"Well," said Jack. He scratched the length of his dark eyebrow with one thumb, using, as Oliver noted pleasantly, the hand Oliver wasn't grasping so Oliver could keep grasping it. "Seems to me it was Saturday night, though I cannot recall what."

Oliver opened his mouth, gathering enough breath to land the point home, that it was almost a week later, and how could Jack *possibly* have not eaten whilst he was away? But then he saw Jack cringe, the small drawing in of his shoulders, the preparatory wince.

"Could you eat now?" asked Oliver, quite gently, in spite of the alarm in his mind. "The whore, that is, Mrs. Louise indicated to me that after your imbibing such a great deal of laudanum, that you might want something sweet? But do you, Jack? You usually would prefer a bit of roast, or perhaps fried potato with butter."

"No, somethin' sweet," said Jack, squinting, as if he couldn't quite believe what he'd just said.

"Can I take you back upstairs and then fetch it for you?" asked Oliver, hope in his voice. It was easy to see by Jack's pale color and the exhaustion in his eyes that he needed more rest. Though, as Oliver had already determined, Jack deserved to decide. "Or mayhap we could spruce up and go out."

"You'd fetch me somethin'?" Jack moved in close, clasping Oliver's forearm to link them together. The smell of the sour sweat on Jack's skin was stronger now, though Oliver did not back away.

"What would you like?" Oliver asked. He gave Jack a small kiss on the cheek and tasted the salt and the metallic trace of something that seemed to permeate Jack's skin. "What can I bring you, Jack? A slice of chocolate gateau? Apple Charlotte? Or perhaps you might enjoy orange custard pudding, though I might not be able to get that in this hot weather."

"Anythin' sweet," said Jack. "Mayhap somethin' with honey in it?"

"Yes, Jack," said Oliver, pleased to be given such a specific task.

He slid his hand from Jack's arm, and looped it about Jack's waist, glad to note that Jack was neither too warm nor too cool, though he seemed a good deal too thin for Oliver's sense of peace. Jack wanted feeding up, and Oliver meant to do it.

"Let's get you upstairs, for you look as though you could use more rest, rather than being up and about, and if—" Oliver paused in speaking as he urged Jack to go through the open doorway into the kitchen. "—and if you'd like food more than water, or water more than food, just tell me, Jack, and I shall fetch it directly."

"Food," said Jack, somewhat unsteady on his feet, but perhaps that was on account of Oliver's boots slipping about and the untied laces almost tripping him.

"Are my feet bigger than yours, Jack?" asked Oliver. "Surely that cannot be."

"Mayhap a bit," said Jack with a little smile, thumping the boots for effect.

"Here, wait a moment," said Oliver, letting go of Jack's waist to reach for a half-full bucket of water. "This won't be enough to make much of a difference, but our feet are mucked with filth and sewage."

Quickly, he took one of the aprons and, soaking it with water, wiped his feet down, and then the soles and the laces of the boots still on Jack's feet. The apron would need to be washed, so Oliver put it in the basket with the rest of the growing pile of laundry to be done. Then he looped his arm about Jack's waist again, and together they proceeded into the passage, him padding barefooted, and Jack still clumping his boots for effect.

Which, of course, drew Noah's attention, causing him to stride toward them with some purpose. Then, standing at the end of the passageway with his hands on his hips, he did not let them pass.

"You up, then?" asked Noah to Jack, though he was not as much asking as he was announcing.

"He's headed right back to rest," said Oliver, butting in as rudely as he might. "Aren't you, Jack."

"Yes," said Jack. "Nolly means to fetch me a bite to eat just now."

"D'you need any money?" Noah reached into his pocket to jingle the coin there and, as before, directed the question at Jack.

"Might do," said Jack, as if he thought that the fact no money had been coming in the past week was something he needed to rectify.

"Yes," said Oliver, holding out his hand, for although his debt to Noah was piling up, Jack should not be the one to worry. So, very casually, he said, "Jack and I shall be back to work soon, but for the present, I'm not too proud."

"Well, then, here you go."

Noah pulled his hand out of his trouser pocket and counted coin into Oliver's palm with his thumb. He gave Oliver a great deal of coin this time, since Jack was watching, so Oliver didn't pull his hand away until Noah did.

"I'll mark it in the books," said Noah with a laugh, gritty and low.

Oliver ignored him. Then he put half of the coins in his own pocket, and gave the other half directly to Jack, who stuffed the coins away very casually, as reflected his opinion of their worth, but at least now they both had money to spend.

"Shall we go up, Jack?"

Oliver tugged, tightening his grasp on Jack's waist, and allowed Jack to determine when they would push Noah aside and slowly climb the stairs to their little room. This they did, with Jack in front, setting the pace.

Oliver did not stare, but noticed Jack's stride had a small hitch in it, as if he were favoring the sore spots on his body that he wouldn't let Oliver see. Oliver knew he could not make Jack show him; Jack would share or not, in his own time.

When they got up to their little room, Oliver opened the door and closed it behind him, watching as Jack sagged down on the bed and plied the boots off his heels with his bare toes.

The line of grit and pushed-in dirt along Jack's ankles was so obvious to Oliver's eyes that he wanted to insist they embark on Jack's prior suggestion of a bath. But then, as Jack lay on the bed, his head hitting the pillows with a small thump as he swung his legs up on top of the counterpane, it was easy to see it would be too much. Besides, the first order of the day was food, something sweet for Jack, but not overly heavy. And then water, and medicine if Jack wanted it, and peace and quiet to follow.

"Nolly," said Jack. He lay quite still on the bed, his hands at his sides and his eyes fully closed, as though he were a corpse. "Why're you starin'?"

"I'm not," said Oliver stoutly. "I'm merely considering. Here, I shall put the money in the drawer in case we have need to purchase anything." With quick hands, Oliver put the coins from his pocket into the red change purse, and used his fingers to tuck a fold in the red cravat that, perhaps, Jack might want to know had been recovered, only not just yet. "Meanwhile, I will make myself presentable, and hie myself thither into the streets."

Oliver paused as he saw Jack smile at this old-fashioned turn of phrase and sat down beside Jack on the bed. He pushed at Jack a bit, until Jack curled onto his side, his legs curved around Oliver's hips.

Oliver stayed motionless for a moment, his head bowed, his eyes half-closed, thinking that if there were an angel close by he might thank for this moment, aloud or silently, whatever was required. For now he had Jack home, safe and sound, and whatever troubles they might face, they would do it together.

Then he opened his eyes and busied himself with his stockings and boots, standing up, pulling up his suspenders and tucking his shirt in his trousers, finding his waistcoat, his belcher, the cloth cap, and looked down to see that Jack had dozed off. So he pulled the thin curtain closed, but left the window open, and silently left the room.

The direction Oliver was headed was obvious to him, and so gave him some pause. He had no wish to be very far from Jack at present, and should be close by if Jack called for him, if there was aught that he needed. But Mrs. Louise had promised Oliver that he could come by the hotel and get something sweet for Jack, and Oliver had the idea, somehow, that in spite of his rude garb and unwashed state, he would not be turned away.

He went out through the kitchen and into the alley to turn up the path that led to the back door of the hotel next door. He knocked and waited and then thought that perhaps he was meant to go in, but the door was opened within moments, and a stout white-aproned cook stood there with flour on his round, red cheeks, and his hair in spirals on his sweaty forehead.

"What is it then?" said the cook with some briskness. "Come

on, come on, the pastry is just ready to come out, and the missus don't like to be kept waiting."

The cook opened the door and turned to go back to his task of rescuing fresh pastry so, taking this as a sort of invitation, Oliver followed on in. He closed the door behind him, and was suddenly surrounded by warm smells of bread cooking, and ham frying, and the deep, ochre-toned smell of coffee that had just been brewed.

The kitchen was painted with whitewash, as was typical in many households, with racks of pots and pans hung on the walls. There was a large table in the middle, close to where the nickel-plated cast iron range was putting out a great deal of heat. That the kitchen was as clean and as organized as any Oliver had been in was a surprise to him, especially regarding the neighborhood in which it was situated.

"What do you want?" asked the cook as he pulled a metal baking sheet out of the oven, a heavy folded cloth wrapped around his palm. He placed the sheet on the wooden table, and Oliver watched as a deep red sauce, glittering with sugar, oozed quite slowly out of the corner of one of the pastries.

"Matilda," shouted the cook to the ceiling. "*Matilda!*"

Jumping back at the shout, Oliver bumped into the door, but stayed in the kitchen; he was on an errand for Jack and would not be kept from it.

"Mrs. Louise said I might come by," said Oliver, trying to stave off any attempt at dismissal. "That I might come by and get something made for my friend who's been ill. Something sweet. She'd told me he'd need that now in his recovery. I'm Oliver, from next door."

"*Matilda*, get in here," shouted the cook at the ceiling again, as if he'd not heard Oliver. "The tray is just about ready for the mistress!"

Then the cook wiped his sweaty forehead with the folded cloth and turned to look at Oliver.

"Yes," said the cook a bit more calmly now, as if the shouting had gotten his frustration out of his system. "She did let us know. Sweet, did you say? Would milk toast do, d'you think? 'Tis easy to make, and I'm in a bit of a rush, being all by myself this morning."

Oliver smiled, but could not help it, for milk toast had been the special treat Mrs. Bedwin would make for him when he was ill. It was one of the first meals she'd fed him after Uncle Brownlow had brought him home from the magistrate's court, and again when he'd come home to the townhouse for good. It was a dish for fussy children to get them to eat, and the memory of it was accompanied by other ones, in quick succession, pleasant and soft, and he was about to delve into them, quite happily, when he realized the cook was waiting for his answer.

"Yes, please," said Oliver in a polite voice. "That would do quite nicely, only would it be quite unusual to ask for honey to be included somehow?"

"I can put that on the toast," said the cook, readily enough. "Would you care for some coffee whilst you wait—*Matilda*, at last."

The door to the kitchen opened and in stepped not the slatternly whorish girl who had delivered the stool and the pillow to Oliver's door the night before, but instead a housemaid. A well groomed, tidily attired housemaid, who ignored the cook's scoldings and sweaty face, picked up the already-arranged tray and, without a word, sashayed out of the kitchen, closing the door behind her with one well-shod heel.

The cook began to stomp around a bit, but not in an unfriendly way, which gave Oliver the courage to speak up.

"Coffee, you say?" asked Oliver. "I'd love some; it smells quite lovely."

The cook, without slamming anything, poured Oliver some coffee into a sturdy white kitchen mug, then pushed a china bowl of crumbled sugar and a small dented tin pitcher of cream at him.

Oliver's mouth was already watering as he added chunks of

sweet sugar and the white cream, and he took the proffered spoon and stirred the contents of the mug. Even before it touched his lips, he knew it would be good coffee, smooth and warm to the belly.

He blew on it and took a swallow and sighed. And found that the cook was casting a glance his way as he stirred something in a black-bottom saucepan.

"You ain't coming to work for the missus, are you?" asked the cook as he turned back to the stove. He was arranging slices of bread over an open grill on a clever tin-wire frame that held the slices aloft so he could attend to other things.

"No," said Oliver quite gently, surprising even himself, for before all of this, he would have railed at the cook and stormed out in a fit that anybody might make even the mere suggestion of such a thing. "I work in the taproom at the tavern next door."

"Seems like you're the sort what could do more, what with the looks you've got, and the breeding."

The cook stopped, his back still to Oliver, shaking his head, as if he'd reconsidered that line of conversation, given how he and Oliver were only just met.

"It's good enough to be going on with, for the present," said Oliver, acknowledging without saying directly that, of course, he had more ambition than he was currently displaying.

And for the moment, well, it was astonishing all over again to find another small kindness in the cook's acceptance, his deft hands as he prepared the milk toast for Jack, kindness amidst the disaster that London kept proving itself to be. But where there was darkness, there would also be light, and so Oliver took another sip of his coffee, enjoying the feel of the thick handle in the curve of his palm, the warmth that moved slowly through the crockery.

He watched with approval as the cook took the toasted slices, slathered them with butter and drizzled honey from a china pot, then cut the toast into pieces and placed them carefully in a white bowl before pouring the warm milk over everything.

"Shall I add more honey or sugar? What do you think?" asked the cook. "The crystals'll make it look nice."

Though the cook seemed willing to do either, he gestured toward the bowl of cut-up sugar, and it was obvious to see that this was what Oliver should agree to. He nodded and finished up the last of his coffee, and left the mug on the table, near the center so it would not get knocked over. He was ready to take the bowl, and wondered where he might find a spoon, when the cook held out his hand.

"See here," the cook said, assembling the crockery as he was speaking. "The plate goes on top, so it don't spill whilst you're carrying it. And the spoon goes on the plate, and here's a napkin, so your hands don't get overly warm on the journey."

This was so thoughtful that Oliver didn't quite know what to say. The cook worked for a whore, and Oliver had been taught to consider those sorts of people to be beneath him, in all the ways that mattered. And yet, the cook had been kind, so Oliver picked up the assembled meal for Jack, and gave the cook a bow of his head.

"Thank you," he said, for even a whore's cook deserved his best manners. "It smells delicious, and I appreciate the speed with which you made it."

"'Twas on the missus's orders," said the cook, as if this was the entire of it, that his own attention to detail had nothing to do with it. He mopped his neck with his apron, which seemed to help not at all. "And if your prayers for more rain are answered, then I'm well satisfied. Bring those back later, when you're done with them." The cook nodded at the bowl in Oliver's hands.

"I will, sir," said Oliver, and stepped aside as the cook opened the door to the alley, where the air, though less warm, was a great deal less sweet smelling. But what did that matter when he had such a treat for Jack?

Walking as quickly as he might, Oliver balanced the covered

bowl in his hands, carrying it on one palm while he slid the spoon into his trouser pocket, which was a clever thought, for soon he had to open the door to the kitchen, and then to the passage, and then, at the top of the stairs, to their room. Where he found Jack in the position Oliver had left him in, dozing in the warmth of the morning, which made Oliver smile all over again.

He put the bowl on the table beneath the window, kicking the low stool out of the way, and left the plate on top of the bowl to keep in the heat. Then he sat very gently on the bed and put his hand on Jack's shoulder. If Jack woke up, then Oliver would offer him the milk toast, but if he did not, well, the milk toast would keep.

Low in his throat, Jack made a sound and turned his head toward Oliver's hand. Oliver allowed himself to trail his fingers up Jack's neck, but carefully, in case Jack didn't like it.

"Jack," Oliver whispered. "Are you still hungry, Jack?"

Jack opened his eyes, frowning for a moment before he was fully awake, as if he weren't quite sure who was there, who was touching him. He seemed almost on the verge of sitting up in a hasty manner as he reached up his hand, tightening his fingers on Oliver's.

"Nolly?"

"Yes, Jack, yes, it's me. I'm sorry, I didn't mean to startle you."

"Did y'bring me somethin'?" asked Jack.

This was said in a way that Oliver could tell was meant to be cheerful so Oliver wouldn't worry. But it was too late for that, for he'd seen Jack's reaction, felt the tenseness of Jack's body on the bed. And would happily have been hanged at Newgate Gaol for the outright slaughter of Workmaster Chalenheim. For doing this to Jack, for touching Jack, for *hurting* him—

"Yes, I did," said Oliver. He had to stop that train of thought, lest he alarm Jack. He did his best to keep his voice steady. "If you'll sit up, I might assist you. Here."

As soon as Jack was halfway to a sitting-up position, Oliver pulled the pillows up and leaned them against the iron bed frame so Jack might relax upon them. He made himself ignore the small, dark squall of brown bed bugs scattering along the wrinkles beneath the pillows because there was nothing he could do about that now.

As for Jack, Oliver was at the ready to assist if needed, but he kept his hands to himself, standing up to pull the napkin out from beneath the bowl, fluttering it in the air. He let Jack shift himself, but watched out of the corner of his eyes, just in case Jack needed his help.

"Now, then," said Oliver. He bent to lay the napkin on Jack's lap, as though he were a black-garbed, white-aproned waiter in a fancy restaurant. He saw Jack's gentle smile and knew Jack understood what he was doing. "We have for you a delicious bowl of milk toast, courtesy of the hotel next door."

Oliver placed the spoon in Jack's hand and, holding the bowl in one hand, lifted the plate with a flourish and put it beneath the bowl so it might be easier for Jack to balance in his lap.

"Would sir care to taste to see if the dish is pleasing to the palate?"

"Pleasin' to the what, now?" asked Jack, though Oliver was quite certain Jack knew what the word meant. But as Jack poked at the slices of toast glistening with butter and honey as they slumped in the milk, it seemed the confusion was real. "What is this? Somethin' I'm meant to eat? Looks like old glue."

"'Tis milk toast," said Oliver. He sat down on the edge of the bed, and felt the weight of some disappointment that not only did Jack truly not know the dish but also that he might not be inclined to like it. "It's made of bits of toasted bread, buttered, with honey on top, in warm milk. It's quite lovely, I assure you."

"If you say," said Jack. He held the spoon in his hand, in his fist, as he normally did, as though it were a ladle of some sort. But he dutifully brought a bit of toast soaked in milk to his mouth and pushed it in, slightly dubious for a moment. And then his eyebrows flew up.

"Oh," he said, around a mouthful. "That's not so bad, is it."

This was not a question, for in short order, Jack managed to polish off half of the bowl, paying more attention to the bits of toast that were more butter than honey, and licked his lips after each bite. But then his eating slowed, and he nodded as he slid the spoon back in the bowl, as if quite contented with his portion.

"D'you want the rest, Nolly?" said Jack. "There's plenty here."

At that moment, Oliver's belly took the opportunity to growl with rage that nothing had yet been given to it, so there was no way he could state to Jack that no, indeed, Jack should finish it because Oliver was not the least bit hungry. Because he *was* hungry, for though he had eaten while Jack had been away, it had been food almost forced upon him, and except for what he'd partaken of in Mr. Yeslevitz's garden, he could remember nothing of the taste, or of the enjoyment of the food.

"G'on, Nolly, just take it. Just do."

Jack held out the bowl, and Oliver took it with both hands. Without a word, he tipped the bowl to his mouth and drank the warm, sweet milk. Then, without any manners at all, he shoveled in the pieces of honey-drenched toast, scraping the bottom of the bowl for all of the last bits. He was tempted, even, to lick the entire surface of it, had it not been apparently clear there was nothing left to lick.

"You ain't been eatin' neither," said Jack as Oliver lowered the bowl from his face.

"Not really," said Oliver. He set the bowl and the spoon on the plate on the table with a little clink, then drew the napkin from Jack's lap and used it to wipe his own mouth before folding it and putting it in the bowl.

"I was taking laudanum those days," said Jack with some sternness, even to the point of shaking his finger at Oliver. "An' so didn't know my own mind, an' didn't eat, but you—"

"Don't scold me, Jack," said Oliver. "Please. None of that mattered when you were missing."

"Weren't *missin'*," said Jack, scowling now. "Was just gone for a little while, is all."

In another moment, they would be quarreling again. It would be over nothing Oliver could define, except that the cross words they were exchanging had to do with whether or not either of them had eaten, and were not actually about what had happened to Jack, which they seemed to keep burying beneath everything else between them.

But perhaps that was how it would go, that ever between them would be this underlying anger and discontent. And even while Oliver longed for it not to be so, he had no idea how to change it so they might share their pain between them and start on a journey with a much more pleasant prospect. Rather than this, this moment between them, with Jack scowling, and Oliver's mouth open, unable to determine an appropriate reply. It was indeed as though they were walking on eggshells, though he'd never thought that the old adage would apply to him.

"I thought you were gone for good, or that you were—" began Oliver, hoping to start somewhere.

But before he could say the word *dead*, Jack leaned back and shoved at Oliver's leg with his bare feet.

"I left you a message w'Noah," said Jack, snarling.

"And I'm to believe a thing he says?" asked Oliver with some fury. The heat rose in his face. He felt it at the back of his eyes. He stood up and took several steps away from the bed.

"Why would you even imagine my response to *any* message from him would be anything but disbelief?" Oliver spread his hands wide as his discontent took hold of him, unable to stem the flight of his temper. "Well, Jack? Did you think of that? Noah and I have never been, and never will be, even the *remotest* of acquaintances, let alone bosom *companions*. And yet you were asking me to take the word of a man I consider to be a *scoundrel*."

Oliver closed his eyes. He regretted the taste of the words, the flash of anger, for Jack didn't deserve his ire, and it was not Jack's fault that Noah and Oliver never got along. Oliver had to make this right, he had to tend to this directly, before the stew they were in became foul with bitterness and hidden misunderstandings. So he opened his eyes and firmed his jaw, thinking of what to say.

And there Jack sat, his bare feet rucked in the bed-linen, leaving dark streaks behind, his collar undone, the shoulders of his shirt slipping off him as he balanced on the flat of his hands. It seemed as though Jack meant to determine whether or not he would go or stay, and hadn't quite decided yet. If it came to that, if Jack made for the door, Oliver was going to have to *let* him—

"Jack, please," said Oliver, moving closer, right up to the edge of the bed so Jack might strike him if he wished. "I didn't believe Noah. Perhaps I should have, for though he doesn't care much for me, he does for you. But I was half mad with worry, even before you left that morning."

"Nolly."

That stopped Oliver, just the one word, the name only Jack called him by.

Jack was looking up at him. His mouth was pulled against his teeth, as though he were struggling with some harsh inner thoughts he did not want revealed.

"Sometimes," said Jack, slowly now, looking down at the rumpled sheet between his thighs. "Sometimes, I just has to go, d'you see? An' you has to let me. You *has* to, only—"

Oliver held his breath, feeling the pulse of blood beneath his skin slow, as his heartbeat slowed, though he still felt warm all over.

"—only as jolly as you an' Noah can be together—" continued Jack.

"Jolly?" asked Oliver, his voice rising. "What do you mean, *jolly?*"

"—I shouldn't never forget that you despise him so. Next time, if there's a bit of paper about, I c'n leave a note."

"A *note?*"

Jack laughed beneath his breath as he looked up. This did not surprise Oliver as much as it might have, for Jack was prone to be amused at what the world around him considered to be serious or sacred.

Oliver was on the verge of getting worked up again when Jack, still huffing with laughter, patted the bed beside him. With much gratitude, Oliver sat down near Jack and waited for him to speak. Which he did, his mouth smiling as well as his eyes, his fingers gesturing to his face.

"You both carted me home to the Three Cripples, right?" said Jack. "But when I'd first come back that mornin', Noah was whinin' about how I needed to get my dog on a leash, an' *oh, look what he's done to me.* As if he weren't fully capable of defendin' his own self. No, he was like a large child, runnin' to carry tales an' snifflin' to his playmates. Gives me a laugh every time I think on it."

Jack was smiling at Oliver, but with some caution, as if he was only now thinking that perhaps Oliver wouldn't find it as amusing as Jack hoped it would be, a diversion and commiseration with Oliver all at once.

"He does make such an inviting target," said Oliver, relenting on his anger. He was grateful to Jack for giving him a way to do it, and so he gave his response the mock seriousness he knew Jack would enjoy. "The temptation is ever there to strike him, though you would think that by this time, he would not be so surprised by it."

"There's my lad, now," said Jack, and though he seemed on the verge of inviting Oliver to move closer, he did not, so Oliver remained where he was. "Bit of a rest might do me," said Jack now. "That ought to satisfy you, at least."

"You're not bedridden forever, Jack," said Oliver, pleased that Jack was behaving sensibly. "Just until you're not so pale and drawn."

"Well, I've got—" Jack stopped to yawn, his red mouth wide. "—a full belly, an' now the rest of me wants to sleep again."

"Do you want me to go?" Oliver made himself ask this, though nothing could be further from his desire at that moment.

"Stay or go as it pleases you," said Jack with the utmost casualness. Then he dipped his head, his demeanor easing into something more gentle and vulnerable. "Stay."

Jack slipped down on the bed and pulled the pillows with him. His legs brushed Oliver's for a moment, then he stretched out along the length of the bed.

With Jack's eyes closing, and given the warmth of the morning, Oliver refrained from pulling the sheet up around Jack to keep him safe from the world. Instead, Oliver moved to the short stool and scooted it to where he might sit upon it with his back to the wall to watch and wait until Jack woke up.

Soon, Jack would be objecting to such oversight, but for the moment, Oliver was glad to be where he was, in the room, watching while Jack fell asleep, safe, where Oliver could see him.

❧ 20 ❧

CONFESSES THE STAIN ON
HIS SOUL

There was a bit of rain in the air that Jack sensed, just before there came a knock at the door. With half-opened eyes, he struggled to sit up, watching as Nolly leaped from the low stool where he'd obviously been dozing, as unsettled by the knock as much as Jack had been awakened by it. Thinking it was probably Noah, Jack rested back on his elbows and yawned and scratched between his legs, and casually realized he was actually hungry again.

But it was not Noah, for as Nolly opened the door, Jack could see that a woman stood there, her long flounced skirts already forcing their way through the half-opened door. While part of him was wondering why Nolly's Aunt Rose would have made the journey on account of him, Nolly stepped back and, with a short bow, bid the lady entry.

At which point Jack saw that the flounced skirts were silk and that the woman's hair was done up as though she might be about to set out for a fancy cotillion, even though it was only the afternoon. It was obvious to even the most casual observer, or himself, scrubbing at his eyes with the heel of his hand as he properly came to wakefulness, that this was no lady.

She was a whore, plain and simple, and this was made evident

349

by her too-fancy dress, by the powder on her skin, the paint on her cheek and lips, and the rich perfume that preceded her as she entered. As Nolly *allowed* her to enter.

"What the hell, Nolly?" Jack asked, not at her entry, for he himself had known a whore or two back in the day, but at Nolly, for such an action had never been imagined in his mind nor in anybody else's.

That *Oliver Twist* would bid entry to a *whore*. It was one thing to know Nolly had encountered her previously. It was entirely another to actually see it happen in front of his very own eyes.

But, straight away, Jack could see it wasn't as simple as all that because when the whore acknowledged Nolly with a slight nod, Nolly's nostrils flared, and his mouth remained a thin line. He did, however, take the trouble to close the door behind her gently and with the utmost decorum.

"'Tis pleasant to see you awake an' so cheerful," said the whore, directly to Jack.

"This is Mrs. Louise, from next door," said Nolly, with a gesture that told Jack quite plainly that Nolly would have preferred to *not* remember his manners. "Mrs. Louise, may I introduce Jack Dawkins."

"A pleasure to meet you properly at last, Jack," said Mrs. Louise. "An' to find you rested an' lookin' so well."

"Only on account of Nolly lookin' after me, though them medicines are from you, I take it."

Nolly had not said as much, only no doctor had been in to see Jack, so the connections were settling in Jack's mind. However, Jack couldn't fault Nolly for this evasion, for he must have been desperate to get Jack some help, and had done whatever he could, including admitting a whore into his presence.

"An' how did you enjoy the milk toast? Cook said he made you some."

Which thusly answered a question Jack had not even thought to wonder about, for it was quite apparent that the source of all of Nolly's assistance, the medicine, the stool—which in and of itself might prove to be an amusing subject, as there was only one thing that a whore would need a stool as short as that for— and the food. All of it had come from next door where resided the bastion of whoredom, and if Nolly weren't looking quite so serious and stern about the current situation, Jack would have burst out laughing.

"It was quite good. Nolly an' I shared it between us. He's got quite the sweet tooth, you see."

"I see," said Mrs. Louise, looking at Nolly, her graceful eyebrows rising slightly. "You had only to say, you know, an' Cook would have made extra."

"It was well enough, the amount I had," said Nolly, barely moving his mouth.

It did seem as though Nolly was trying to get past her circle of skirts by pressing himself to the wall so he might be nearer to Jack than the whore was. Mrs. Louise must have seen this, for she moved quite close to the bed, and was completely in the way, though she did not sit down. Which Jack would not have allowed her to do anyway, not with Nolly having that frown on his face, holding himself so politely and drawn up, quite put out at her presence, in spite of having admitted her into the room with his own hands.

"Well then," said Mrs. Louise now, casting a look about her. "I see the pitcher an' glass I brought over has quite disappeared, though that can be put on Noah's tab. As well, I can bring the crockery an' spoon back with me, but I've brought you something, Jack, some sweet oil that might soothe your battered skin a bit."

Now it was Jack's turn to frown because he'd been doing his best to convince Nolly, silently and otherwise, that there was barely any part of him that felt sore or banged up. And while it might have been he'd been close to success, he was successful no longer.

The whore already knew the truth of it, and the fact that

Jack, stupidly, had not instantly denied it was also making Nolly quite attentive to what the whore was doing with her reticule. It jingled at her waist as she opened it to pull another brown vial. This one was the same as the others, except it was a bit larger, and the cork stuck out and so was tied about the mouth of the vial with a bit of brown string.

"Remember the string, Oliver," she said, handing the vial to Nolly.

To Jack's amazement, not only did Nolly take the vial from her without wincing, but he was looking at her with some attentiveness, as if what she was saying was essential knowledge he was truly and actually interested in.

"This is not for ingesting," said Mrs. Louise, continuing on. "It has lavender, which actually wouldn't harm you if you took it by itself, but the frankincense would, and the arnica oil, so when you're done applying it, tie the string firmly on."

"Yes, thank you, Mrs. Louise," said Nolly.

Nolly stood there, looking at the bottle in his hands, hefting it in his palm as if considering all of the good he could do with it. Then he looked up at the whore once more, his features composed and polite, but at the same time as though he were conversing with someone of distant acquaintance that he had no true feelings about, either good or ill.

"I do appreciate your assistance in this," said Nolly, now. "And if ever you are in need likewise, do let me know."

Which, as even Jack knew, meant entirely the opposite; the favor that had been done must be acknowledged, but in no way would it ever be returned. As to where Jack had learned that, well, sometimes walking down the street was enough to pick up tidbits of this or that as might later prove useful.

"Apply it as often as you'd like, though it does soak through cloth if you are overly liberal with it, d' you see?"

"Yes, Mrs. Louise," said Nolly.

Mrs. Louise snapped her reticule shut, leaving Jack to wonder what other wonders might be tucked inside. Then she bent forward to pick up the bowl, the napkin, and the spoon, giving Jack a nice, wide view of her broad bosom, right down to her smoky pink nipples.

As Jack watched Nolly jerk his head to one side, he could only grin, for he knew Nolly had seen them as well. It was quite possible Mrs. Louise had *meant* them to see her charms, for never had there been a whore who did not enjoy tempting men to sample her wares.

"I bid you good day, gentlemen, an' do come by if there is aught else that you need."

Nolly jumped to open the door for her, wide, so her skirts could get through and, with his knuckles white against the dark brown panels of the door, he shut it softly and quietly behind her. Locked it. And then turned to Jack, the vial held tight in his hand.

"Might I—" Nolly stopped, brow furrowing as a faint wind came in through the open casement window, making the thin square of cotton dance over the table. "Might we put this to good use?" He lifted the vial in Jack's direction. "I could assist you with the places that are difficult for you to reach on your own."

There was a fancy word that Jack did not know to describe these words coming from Nolly, this hesitation and guarded air, as if he knew Jack would refuse him and was doing everything in his power to overcome that, even before it happened. And though Jack knew full and well Nolly's offer was not some sly attempt to see what Jack did not want him to see, the result would mean Nolly would see it just the same. And that, Jack could not allow.

"We should put it on you an' them wrists of yours," said Jack, turning the attention back to Nolly. "An' your belly, though it must be somewhat settled after all this time."

Jack sat up on his backside, as though nothing ailed him, that no part of him twinged in protest, or hummed, or felt overly warm or stiff. As if, in fact, he was as hale as he'd ever been and had no need of sweet oil.

"No," said Nolly, jerking away as he held the vial to his belly. "I don't need any of it, but you do."

This astonished Jack more than Nolly's admittance of the whore, for there was evidence abounding that Nolly did indeed need some tender care for his own sake, not least of which were his red-raw wrists, and the gentleness of his soul, which had been battered and bruised, perhaps beyond all causal repair.

Jack pushed himself to standing, wincing in spite of himself. But he needed to get out of bed to see to his beautiful boy, his beloved boy. Who, as Jack knew and could plainly see, had run himself ragged since that awful day on the Isle of Dogs. Looking out for Jack, looking *for* Jack, without tending to himself even once, for his shirt hung from his shoulders as rumpled as though he were a bricklayer, his trousers mud-stained, and in fact everything that he wore, had been worn since that day, looked as though it'd be better off in a dustbin than on Nolly's body.

Nolly had tramped through London looking for a Jack who had not been lost, fought with Noah, waded up to his knees in the river muck of the Thames's shoreline, consorted with whores and cooks of whores, and hauled Jack out to the privy posthaste, and all of this without a word of complaint. Not to mention the marks that had been left behind by the grotty, rude streets of London and its inhabitants, by the workmaster's hand. Nolly had borne the entire of it without any consideration whatsoever to his own person.

Walking quite slowly across the short distance of the room, Jack soon was toe-to-toe with Nolly who, even when backed up to the wall, held the vial in both of his hands, as though it contained magical properties of healing that could be put to good use, if only Jack would let him. Which Jack would not.

This might soon become apparent to Nolly as Jack took the vial from his hands, feeling the warmth Nolly's skin had left on the glass, smelling the faint scent of lavender that had infused the brown string coiled around the cork and the lip of the vial.

"We're puttin' this on you, now," said Jack, quite low. "An' it might be that once it gets dark, I'll let you—"

Bending his head, Jack stopped speaking, not quite wanting to promise something to which he could not commit, and began untying and unwinding the string. The string left slender lines that spiraled around the cork, as though a dark brown vine had grown and been cut away, only to be let to grow again.

Once Jack had the cork out, the sweet oil's scent rose thick in the air, settling on Jack's skin, wafting in the faint breeze. Only Nolly pulled away, acting as if he thought it might burn his skin were he to allow Jack to apply it.

"No, Jack."

Nolly put up both of his hands, a plea, a barrier. Except now Jack could more plainly see the marks the rope had left on Nolly's wrists, the grit beneath Nolly's fingernails. The streak of dirt along his neck. Bruises from somewhere Jack could not trace.

"Why-ever not, Nolly?" asked Jack.

Depositing the cork and the string on the table beneath the open window, Jack tipped the vial and poured some of the oil into his palm. The smell was stronger now, with the low warmth of lavender and the bright, sharp scent of something else. And when Jack put the vial down to reach for Nolly's wrist, Nolly knocked his hand away, sending the oil from Jack's palm to spatter on the surface of the table, the thin curtain, the panes of glass.

"What the *fuck*, Nolly," said Jack, not holding back on his frustration. "You only want to help me, an' I mean to do the same."

"No."

"*Nolly*."

"I said *no*." Nolly gritted his teeth when he said this, and there was such darkness in his eyes, a hardness to his flushed cheeks, that Jack stepped back, the skin along his jaw tight. The smell of lavender was so thick now it was hard to swallow.

"Just tell me why, then." Jack breathed hard through his nose, feeling frustration rising up in him again, a bitter coil that threatened to spring within him and take away every ounce of everything tame.

"Because I don't deserve it," said Nolly, sternly.

"What?" Jack almost laughed then, his mouth open, blinking through his astonishment. "Whatever the fuck d'you mean by that? You've made yourself my servant, my slave, even, so how do you not bloody deserve a little bit o' kindness? From me, your very own?"

This stayed Nolly from saying no outright, but it did nothing to quell Jack's growing panic, for in all of this they should not be silent with each other, should not keep secrets. Should not let anything be buried so deep that it might fester, left alone in the dark.

"Tell me, Nolly," said Jack as he reached out to tuck a strand of dark, golden hair behind Nolly's ear. "Just tell me true so that it may be as it always is between you an' I."

There was a long pause as the perfumed air rose and fell with the slight breeze and whispered along the inside of Jack's mouth, tasting bitter and gracious all at once.

"Jack," said Nolly, in a voice so low that Jack had to dip his head down to hear it.

"What, Nolly?" asked Jack.

He braced himself for the words to come, that Nolly had had enough, was going to leave him, was going to take his few belongings, which Jack couldn't even list in his mind, and head out for a fairer location.

Perhaps Nolly would not even stop in London, but would go elsewhere, out in the country, where the air was always sweet, and the sky always blue. And this on account of Jack, who had the manners of a wild dog, who did not believe in banks, and who only wanted to drink and smoke, play cards and, at the end of the day, willingly slept in his own grit and sweat.

"I need to tell you something, a c-confession."

Nolly was stumbling over his words, which he'd done more than once since Jack had come back, since, in fact, that day on the Isle of Dogs. Something fluttered uncomfortably in Jack's belly, for that wasn't like Nolly, except when he was worked up, upset about something.

"Better out than in, Nolly," said Jack, knowing it was true, that no matter how bad Nolly might think it was, surely it wasn't as bad as all that.

"The letter, how he found us, I mean. Workmaster Chalenheim." Nolly's head remained bowed, his neck bared to Jack's gaze; he was so curled over that he might tumble forward before he could get the words out.

"Hey?" asked Jack, reaching to where he could just lay his hand on Nolly's shoulder, leaving a perfumed stain of lavender and frankincense. "Tell me?"

Nolly's slow breath stopped Jack from saying anything more; the set of Nolly's shoulders told him that whatever Nolly had to say, it was not going to be long in coming.

"The letter," said Nolly, again.

"What letter?" Though as Jack asked this, he did recall, with some clarity, even, the handful of letters Nolly had insisted on writing. That Jack himself had aided in posting. "Which one?"

"The one to Dr. McMurtry. That was how the workmaster knew where we were."

Jack saw Nolly draw in a breath, saw the faint shudder that went through Nolly's whole body, and narrowed his eyes, determined to unravel what had happened before Nolly collapsed in on himself.

"How's that, then?" asked Jack, his voice gentle.

"I'm unsure, exactly," said Nolly, teeth gritted, as if to steady himself to tell the whole of it. "But the letter alerted the doctor, it seems, to the fact we were not still in the workhouse, where he'd thought we were. I'm unsure whether the doctor went on purpose, but when he was at Axminster workhouse, he talked to Master Pickering. The workmaster must have gotten wind of the letter somehow and seen the return address and then—so it's *my* fault that he knew where to find us. I'm to blame for what happened to you."

Jack's eyes fluttered closed, and he drew a breath, wishing he knew how to turn the tide of this, the raw, endless circle of it, that he knew what to say to get Nolly to raise his head, to not be so willing to bare his neck on some chopping block for Jack to take his head off.

Had it been months ago, or even weeks, Jack was sure Nolly would have folded onto his knees and cried into his hands like a small, wee boy whose sensitive heart was not created for hard choices and difficult days, but rather for a mother's soft hand, outstretched, and summer ponies in a wide, grassy field.

Only none of that was to be found, merely this room. The mark on the old plaster of a glass pitcher thrown. The sweet oil staining the table top to dark. The rucked bedclothes, the sour smell of them. Nolly, disheveled and waiting. Not crying. Not saying anything.

As Jack waited it out, Nolly's eyes focused on the edge of the bed, his shoulder tense beneath Jack's hand, as if he was only a moment away from twitching Jack's touch away from him.

"D'you want me to punish you for it, Nolly?" asked Jack. "Punish you for somethin' so out of your reach?"

Nolly's face crumpled for a fraction of a heartbeat before he raised himself and drew back, but it was enough to tell Jack the answer. That there was no need for Jack to punish Nolly, if indeed he could be enjoined to do so harsh a thing to the best lad he knew, for Nolly was doing it to himself. Had been doing it, from the moment he'd awoken on the *Scylla*, his hands tied.

Nolly had been running and tending to Jack, not eating, not sleeping, not bathing, not doing anything, any of those many things that made him the Nolly that Jack knew. Knew and loved. Adored. And, secretly, admired, for being who he was, for standing up to Noah, for fighting against the low station his life had brought him to, holding his ground against the onslaught of daily indignities, so far from his home and everything he knew—

And all this to be with Jack. To take care of Jack and, in doing this, in loving Jack so completely—and now Jack was undone.

Scrubbing at his face, Jack turned away, alerted an instant too late that he'd spread the sweet oil into his eyes, and stumbled even as he tried to blink away the film, the sting. Nolly was right there, his hands gentle on Jack's shoulders, easing him to sit on the bed, then sitting next to him. Not saying anything, but pulling on Jack's sleeve so Jack might use it to wipe his eyes.

Had there been cool water and a clean cloth, Nolly would have used it, but the pitcher sat empty with no opportunity to refresh it. It was senseless to yearn for fresh water to wash with when he'd only recently been grousing about it, but there it was. Nolly had the right of it, as he did, as he often did, though Jack knew he was sometimes slow to see it.

"I give in," said Jack. Not mumbling it, for he was not ashamed to admit it, except that he did not yet know what he was willing to give in to.

Nolly's arm came around his shoulders, gently, almost carefully, in a way that made Jack's heart clench.

"And I, as well," said Nolly.

Jack felt the press of Nolly's lips on his shoulder, so lightly, as if he did not want Jack to know.

"But what're we giving in to, exactly?" asked Nolly, soft and sweet.

Squinting, Jack made himself look at Nolly, who was becoming more clear as the oil slipped from Jack's eyes. Nolly looked dour and serious, as if counting his sins, exacting retribution for them, and demanding payment in a pound or two of his own flesh, while counting none of Jack's sins.

"Bath," said Jack. He spread his fingers to count upon because there were a very great many things that needed doing. That he knew Nolly wanted to do, or have done. That having been done would turn out to be the very exact thing that was needed. "Clean clothes. Clean sheets, as well, to get rid of the bugs." Jack dropped his hand to brush against Nolly's leg and sighed. "Then the sweet oil. But only—" He raised a finger and pointed at Nolly. "After it gets dark."

"Why?"

"Because." Jack considered this. He knew it was important which direction his answer took, for only moments ago he had enjoined Nolly to be honest with him, and so he should be with Nolly. "'Tis only that I have so very many bruised places on me now. If it's dark, I could bear it better if you couldn't see them so very well."

Nolly huffed beneath his breath, as if he were holding back a burst of temper, while at the same time contemplating where to get the coin to pay for all of this.

Jack held back a long-suffering sigh. When would Nolly understand, utterly and completely, that London was full of money for Jack to take, and there was no need for anybody, least of all Nolly, to concern themselves with something so dull as wages?

"We'll go to Smithfield," said Nolly, leaning to bump his shoulder with Jack's, which Jack took as a signal he was to disagree with Nolly at any point in the conversation, should the direction of it not suit him. "We can have our trousers and shirts brushed, and have both our boots cleaned whilst we're in the bath, for I do like these boots." He held out a foot to show Jack the rough-scraped leather, the thick soles. "And then—"

"Food after?" suggested Jack, knowing full and well that if he ate, Nolly would also eat. As he should do, for he was thin to Jack's eyes. This, in turn, became a slightly worrisome idea, given Nolly's normally healthy appetite, for he had never been one who needed such encouragement. "An' then bedclothes? There's a laundry on Field Lane where we can drop 'em off, as they does a good job washin' the lice an' bugs out of traded goods."

The look of dismay on Nolly's face at the mention of sleeping in bedclothes that had been washed alongside ones where might have resided somebody *else's* lice was enough so that a smile was building on Jack's face, feeling warm and good, as though they were doing those things, those sorts of things that proper folk did when their lives were in a disarray.

Had Jack been alone, he might have found and taken more laudanum, but with Nolly here, it was a different day. A different life. A better life. Certainly one more focused on being clean. Which, given how much of Jack's life had been spent not being clean, made him feel rueful.

"Yes, Jack," said Nolly, and even before Jack lifted his head to look, he could feel Nolly's smile. And upon seeing it, answered it with one of his own.

"Should we leave the oil here, or—?" asked Nolly.

"Leave it," said Jack. "I don't think it would carry well, and I've no desire—"

Jack stopped, his words faltering in his mouth. He didn't want to suffer Nolly to worry about yet another thing that might be wrong with his Jack, which was, of course, the idea of standing naked in a bathhouse, waiting for dark, waiting to permit Nolly to touch him in all the ways that, while having been so tender and gentle before, now only filled Jack with a dull dread.

✣ 21 ✣

HOT WATER, CLEAN SHEETS,
AND SWEET OIL

When Jack stripped the bed of bed-linen, a handful of bed bugs plinked to the floor and scurried away. Jack deliberately did not look at Nolly as he used his hand to sweep away the remainder that were crawling across the bare, flocked mattress, as if looking for a place to hide. That bugs were always present was not news, even though Nolly preferred not to think about it, but that didn't mean Jack had to go and shove the idea of it into Nolly's face.

Jack rolled up the sheets and pillowslips into a bundle, and slipped on his cap as Nolly slipped on his. Together, they made their way downstairs and out the front door of the Three Cripples.

The smell of rain was still about, making the air somewhat dank and fulsome as they headed down the hill to Smithfield Market. Skirting by foot traffic, they made it to Peter Street in good order. There, they found a laundry that would take the bed-linen and wash it in boiling water, hopefully with enough soap to take the small little frown from Nolly's face, which he made as yet another bed bug fell on the counter in front of them where Jack had placed the bundle of linen.

"Never mind that, sir," said the laundress from behind the

rough counter; she was a blowsy woman who had quite soaked through her cotton dress, which stuck to her in places. "Happens all the time."

"Very good," said Nolly. "We pay when we pick up?"

"Yes, sir," said the woman. "About an hour, if you please."

"Yes, thank you."

Nolly gave the woman a nod and, having given the place a good going over with critical eyes, turned to Jack and shrugged. Of late, Nolly was more resignation than acceptance, but Jack didn't know what to do about it. The bed-linen would be clean, and they themselves would be clean.

Perhaps they could hire a charwoman to come up and tidy the room, though this would only have a temporary effect, on account of them clomping in with their boots caked with dirt and other detritus that they might drag in upon their persons. Not to mention the amount of bugs crawling behind and sometimes along the plaster walls.

But Jack didn't say anything, and he and Nolly kept going until they reached the bathhouse, which was located down a side lane, in a low, two-story dwelling in a small, damp-stoned court. Jack had passed the bathhouse upon occasion whilst doing jobs back in the day for Fagin, but had never stopped in for a bath. Nolly had been the one to visit the bathhouse, back in the winter days, with tuppence in his pocket and a load of grief in his heart.

The air in the street in front of the bathhouse smelled like smoke and ash and soapsuds, of water left too long before being dumped in the street, of old sweat. The building, which leaned slightly over the cobbled street, had a sense of desperation about it. For who, if they were starving, would spend their last pennies on a bath? And this while they had no idea where their next meal was coming from? Well, Nolly did, and liked baths, and so here they were.

"Same as you remember it?" asked Jack.

Nolly opened the door and nodded his head, as if he were

having a conversation with himself about how much he did or did not remember. His eyebrows went up a fraction, and he gave Jack a bit of a smile to share the humor of it.

"Yes, of course," said Nolly. "There's the same mold on the glass, and the same smoky, damp air coming out of the upper-story windows."

As they went in, Jack could smell the mold Nolly spoke of, which, in such wet conditions, seemed to coat every level surface, and even grew along the slender lines of the leading in the windowpanes. How Nolly had managed to come here on his own for a bath and not run away just as quickly as he'd arrived would forever be a mystery to Jack; however, it might be that Nolly had been just that desperate.

Behind the sagging counter was another woman, this one more tidy than the one at the laundry had been, but only in the merest way. She was writing something on a square of slate. Jack could see that the slate pencil was damp, as was the slate, for the writing was smearing even as she wrote. Then she put the slate and pencil away, wiped her hands on her pale gray apron, and looked at them.

"Can I get you some baths, gentlemen?" she asked, professionally enough, given her surroundings.

"What you got?" asked Jack.

"We have first water for tuppence, soap for ha'penny, and for an extra penny more we can brush and set your clothes to rights."

"Do you polish boots?" asked Nolly with a sliver of hope in his voice.

"No, sir, but there's a boot-black at the corner, right enough, an' he does a tolerable good job."

Out of the corner of his eyes, Jack saw Nolly shake his head. Something was amiss about the idea of going to see a boot-black on the street, though it couldn't be the bare penny it would cost to get their boots cleaned. But Jack had barely enough energy to be doing what they were doing, and never mind ferreting out Nolly's concerns about something seemingly so small.

"We'll have two baths," said Nolly with some decisiveness. "And our clothes, could you give them to be brushed, and the stains got out as best as possible?"

The woman frowned as she looked at the state of them.

"That'll be a penny each," she said. "More if they proves too difficult whilst the lad is working on them."

"Yes, indeed," said Jack in a rush, for he did not want Nolly to object to the cost, nor even to query what else might be on order. Jack was willing to take a bath, and then he wanted to go home. There, Nolly would want to use the sweet oil, and though Jack might balk at the idea, he had made a promise.

A lad came by just as Jack was doling out the pennies to the woman and, without a word the lad gestured that they should follow him. This they did, going down the steamy, damp passage, past the gray lengths of canvas that flapped at their passing of each door. The air was hot with the fug of steam, making the skin along the back of Jack's neck itch. But a promise was a promise.

"One of you is in here, sir," said the boy. He pointed at the canvas door. "There's a bucket of cold at the ready. The rest of the baths are full, so the other of you'll be upstairs."

There was a quick moment when both Jack and Nolly hesitated, though it didn't matter to Jack which room he took, only that he would be parted from Nolly for longer than was comfortable.

"Nothin' else down here?" asked Jack, but he took no further pains to explain himself.

"No, sir," said the boy. "The bathhouse is right busy today, so there's a limited selection."

"I see. Well, Nolly, you take this one, an' I'll go upstairs." And this on account of the second story might be even less salubrious than the ground floor. Nolly had been so patient with Jack, with everything, that he shouldn't be made to suffer for it.

"Yes, Jack," said Nolly. "You won't leave without me, will you? You'll stop back when you're done?"

Nolly's question was timid, his eyes round, as if he feared Jack would take off without a word, but Jack would rather cut out his own heart than do that again.

"Nothin' to write a note on, y'see," said Jack, reminding Nolly of their earlier conversation. "So I won't be goin' anywheres without you."

That was all Jack could say in front of a stranger who might run to gab to everybody he knew. But Nolly seemed satisfied with this for, with a quick nod, he ducked behind the canvas curtain that flapped against his straight back as he went into the room.

"This way, mister," said the boy to Jack.

Jack followed the boy as the passage led past other canvas-draped doors, past splotched and faded yellow plaster walls that bowed outward in the middle to a set of rickety stairs that got narrower from the halfway landing, and creaked desperately beneath Jack's footsteps.

The boy didn't seem to notice any of this, but led Jack to the first canvas doorway, which, from the layout of the place, would face over the back alley. That was fine with Jack; there'd be less noise from the street, and he could use the bath as Nolly might, as a respite from the heat and noise of the City.

"Leave your clothes what wants brushin' outside the door, mister," said the boy. "We'll bring 'em back quick as we can."

Then the boy waited, holding out his hand for a penny, which Jack gave to him, even if only to make him go away.

"Here's one for my friend, so see that he's well looked after."

Jack handed the boy another penny and, as the canvas flap settled into stillness after the boy's departure, Jack turned to face the room.

A long tin tub took up most of the floor, and was filled to three-quarters with water that was hot enough to steam a bit, even in the heat. A tin bucket of cold water stood at one end, and while Jack dreaded using it without Nolly's steady hand to guide him, he was on his own.

He took everything off and, bending naked, put his clothes outside the door, wondering how nobody had ever gotten their clothes stolen. Drawing the canvas closed, he put his boots and stockings near the door and, with a sharp breath, got in the water as quick as he might. Best to get it over all at once, after all.

The sting of the hot water in such places, intimate and private, that had been abused and ill-used, made him want to jump out again, to fling cold water upon himself, and to tell Nolly a lie about it. But a bath, the few he'd had, had never made him feel as bad as a lie, especially one to Nolly.

What's more, he usually felt better after a bath than before one, in spite of still not being used to the feeling of water all over his body, splashing against his skin as though he were a rock being pounded by sea waves. Well, perhaps not sea waves, but close enough to, so that he sat very still and let the water settle about him.

When the water was calm upon its surface, like a lake of glass, Jack reached for the soap on the little curved-out bit of tub edge. The soap had been there a while, so was slimy, but he rinsed it off, took the flannel cloth, and washed himself from his face to his toes, being gentle with those parts of himself that needed him to be gentle. Then he bent forward, dipped his head in the water, and lathered it up with the soap.

This was, as usual, the part where the soap got into his eyes, as he'd not Nolly's knack for avoiding such a woe, but a bit of water with not so much soap in it took care of that right quick. Bending forward again, he closed his eyes and rinsed off as much soap as he could, enjoying the feel of wet strands of hair, like seaweed, where his fingers ran through them beneath the surface of the water.

Finally, he stood up and reached for the bucket. As the warm water from the tub streamed down his body, he took no time to think about it before he poured cold water all over himself and his hair to rinse off the soap. Of course, it would have been a much neater result had Nolly been the one to do the pouring, but there it was. He'd gotten water on the floor. In spite of that, he was clean as he'd ever been, and while parts of him still ached, felt tender, his skin seemed to sigh with relief. It would get better by-and-bye, as he was always telling Nolly.

Looking down, Jack saw, perhaps for the first time in clear light, the marks from the workmaster's hands. The once-black bruises were starting to fade, though they now made powerful green-and-yellow patterns that ran in the shape of fingers around Jack's hips and between his thighs. Across his belly were streaks of bruises, thin lines of blue black, made, most likely, from the rag-paper bale that he'd been bent over.

Standing there, he clenched his jaw and let the sheer terror of that memory flow through him, the degradation of it, his anger, the helpless shock of his worst fear coming to life—he let all of that run through him. As it swept up and down and twisted in his belly, he bade himself to get used to it, for it was not going away.

Though, with time, as he knew, the power of any memory would fade, particularly if he refused to let it hold any sway over him. The workmaster had been—*was*—a cruel, despicable man, and did not deserve any part of Jack, or any more of his time.

That last tenet would be hard to conquer; the after-effects, as they tended to, would filter in and out of his mind at odd moments, at inauspicious moments. However, he was getting used to the fact that Nolly had been there this time, and that he insisted on being near Jack, and on having Jack near him. This had never before happened, as Jack, weathering whatever storm, had always been on his own. But such was no longer.

Perhaps it was better this way, to be connected to Nolly, where Nolly could see all those parts of him, the raggedy, unkempt, bruise-stained parts. For even as Jack had let Nolly close, closer than he'd expected, Nolly had never, not once, turned away.

Oh, to be sure, he might have had some qualms about what he'd learned about Jack, and was forever fussing at Jack to be *clean*, but never had he made Jack feel less in any regard. And so, maybe, Jack's highly polished ability to distract and dissemble was no longer needed.

It was then, and only then, that he realized he had been doing that very duplicitous thing with Nolly, perhaps all along. And this in spite of Nolly having seen Jack at his worst, while being sick on a moving coach, slick with fever, shaken and unsteady on his feet—being raped—and lastly, having undergone the ignominy of having to clear the way for Jack's hasty need for the privy.

Nolly had moved back to give Jack his privacy, while Jack, in the darkness of the stinking privy, had sweated it out, his face tucked in the crook of his arm while he emptied his bowels with the speed that defied memory. Such a reaction of his body had been, he supposed, the combination of not eating, of taking so much laudanum and brandy, and then, at the end, of downing a pint pot of beer in almost a single swallow.

The moment in the privy had left him streaked with sweat that cooled not at all as he'd come out to find Nolly standing by the door, barefooted in the muck and filth of the yard, as if waiting on Jack to attend this thing, this raw, earthy thing, was as simple as waiting for Jack to bring him a nice little tot of gin, with sugar besides. And that, perhaps, was the purest kind of love, not turning away when something was ugly or difficult.

"Jack?"

Startled, Jack turned toward the canvas that, while it had Nolly standing on the other side of it, had not yet been pulled aside.

"Don't come in, Nolly," said Jack, his voice squeaking a bit. "Not just yet."

"Very well," said Nolly, with a little cough. "I'm all done and dressed. Your clothes are here for when you want them. I'll be downstairs, but you needn't hurry."

With that, Nolly's footsteps faded down the passage; Jack stood so still that he could even hear the squeak of the narrow staircase as Nolly went down it with some purpose, tread by tread.

Jack decided, then and there, that though he still might be shy come darkness, Nolly's love was a love so deep and calm that Jack simply could not get his clothes on fast enough.

ON THEIR WAY BACK TO THE THREE CRIPPLES, JACK MADE Nolly stop at a pie shop to get them a pair of pies to eat, as it was a wonder that Nolly had not complained about his belly heretofore now. At the Three Cripples, which was filling up with the usual loud and terribly thirsty customers, Jack had gotten them beers, while Nolly had rushed up the stairs to make up the bed with the clean bed-linen that they'd collected on their way home. Then, when Nolly had come back down to the taproom, they sat at the round table beneath the window and downed the pies and drank some cool beer while the wind kicked up and the clouds roiled into long, gray shapes outside the windowpanes.

"Will it rain, d'you think?" asked Jack, around a mouthful of pie.

"I reckon it will," said Nolly, attending to the crumbs on his fingers with studious grace, licking each finger separately.

"What're you doin' that for?" asked Jack, shaking his head, as if he'd caught Nolly performing the crudest of acts. "Use your sleeve, for Christ's sake, like any other fellow would."

Nolly made a scoffing sound and attempted to look irritated, which was the best result that Jack could have wanted. Especially when the expression was exchanged for a small smile as Nolly finished off the last of his beer. Just as Nolly placed the pint pot on the table, and ran his shirtsleeve across his mouth, the skies darkened and, after a stiff gust of wind that shook the door in its frame, the rain began to pour.

"It's dark now," said Nolly, with some seriousness.

"Did you bring on the rain?" asked Jack, in a tone he hoped would amuse and distract, though he knew it was a lost cause. For not only had he promised Nolly about the sweet oil, he'd made a promise to himself about not keeping Nolly from any more truths, horrible or otherwise. So Jack amended with, "Well, that'll cool it down a bit, y'think?"

"Yes, it should," said Nolly, still serious. "So, are you going to let me take you upstairs and tend to you with the sweet oil, or aren't you?"

Jack nodded yes, because of course he was, and got up directly, pushing the pint pots toward the middle of the table, where someone would collect them or not, and left the crumbs from their meat pies where they'd been flecked. In echo, Nolly stood up and began to walk toward the stairs, and there was nothing Jack could do but follow on close behind, almost on Nolly's heels.

When they got to their room and shut the door behind them, the rain was rushing outside the casement window that they'd left open, though the rain was at such an angle as to be no danger to the thin cotton curtain, nor the scarred wooden table. The clouds thickened, black and purple, and far away there was the pounding of thunder that seemed to fill Jack's ears and mimicked the thumping of his heart.

In the space between the rain and the thunder, there came a waft of cooled air that smelled sweet, like green things growing, as though they were in the country somewhere. The light coming in through the window was a faint gray, and anything brighter was obscured by the clouds and the rain.

It was better that way, for though Jack could see perfectly well, as Nolly must also be able to do, everything was drift-edged, as though it had been tinged with soft smoke. Which meant that when Nolly reached out his hands to Jack, Jack was startled, but not so much that he moved away.

"Show me where, Jack," said Nolly, his voice soft, his nearness a warmth, a presence that helped to steady Jack, in this moment, when he was about to bare his darkest marks to his beautiful boy.

Jack took Nolly's hands in his and placed them on his belly, then on his hips, circling Nolly's fingers back and forth to copy the lines the workmaster hand's had left, then drew Nolly's hands down between his thighs, where the worst of the soreness still lingered. After that, he coiled Nolly's fingers about his wrists, and then, almost as an afterthought, about his elbows, which had been twisted behind him for a very long time.

"That's about it," said Jack. "Do what you will." He spread out his arms, which Nolly would be able to see, even in the near gloom.

"You're not about to be sacrificed, Jack," said Nolly with a snap that somehow lightened the heaviness in Jack's heart, for Nolly seemed to be going at this in exactly the way Jack would have wanted him to, that is, with his usual sharp temper and at the edge of his patience from the first moment—all of which made it feel that much more like the goodness, the solidness, of everything that they had shared.

Jack snorted, for it was better thus than what might have been if Nolly had been exceedingly tender with him; Jack was gratified that Nolly had heard him when he'd begged for Nolly not to be always so gentle with him.

"You would want to do the same for me, as you well know," said Nolly now, as his hands went to Jack's neck.

Jack lifted his chin so Nolly could start undressing him, which would be all the way to the skin, as Nolly must have wanted to do since that dreadful day.

Very slowly and with much care, Nolly undid all the buttons on Jack's shirt, slid off his waistcoat, and the shirt, and moved on to Jack's belt and trousers, graceful and silent in the near-dark until he knelt down to take off Jack's boots.

"Would you rather stand or lie down, Jack?" asked Nolly.

Jack could sense Nolly was looking up at him, his hands on Jack's bootlaces, simply waiting for Jack to tell him what was wanted.

"Stand," said Jack, and the answer came straight from his belly, as he did not want to feel like an invalid, any time soon or ever.

"Very well," said Nolly.

Helping Jack to balance, Nolly quickly divested Jack of his stockings and boots, and these he placed somewhere along the wall, from the sound of it. Then Nolly, shadowed gray in the near-darkness, stood up and stepped to the table to take up the vial of sweet oil. He unstoppered it, soaking the air with the scent of lavender flowers and other spicy smells that Jack could not identify, though it was soothing to inhale them.

"I'll start slowly," said Nolly.

The scent of flowers became even stronger, for Nolly had poured a measure of oil into his hands and was rubbing his palms together. And when those hands touched Jack's skin, they were warm, and the oil soaked into Jack's belly, into the muscles, into the tenseness there.

True to his word, Nolly went slowly, moving his fingers together over Jack's belly, back and forth, with firmness, because Nolly seemed to know that anything else might make Jack feel tickled. This went on for a moment or two, and then Nolly bent close and ran his hand along Jack's hips, both at once, then down both of Jack's thighs and up again. He performed these motions quite slowly and with some deliberation, as though to get Jack used to where Nolly's hands were, what they were doing, and where those hands would soon go.

Normally, such a gesture, with Jack being in the altogether, as well as their closeness, would have made Jack's cock stand up like a prince. But, as it had been of late, the flesh between his legs stayed silent and still, defeated by the memory of recent cruelty and of cruelty from long ago.

"As you see," said Jack, clearing his throat with a cough. "I can't quite manage."

"Well," said Nolly, as if considering this while his hands moved between Jack's thighs, the edges of his fingers stirring Jack's private hair, leaving traces of sweet oil there. "As it happens, I've not felt anything since that day either; my only passion is to be near you and see you safe. To take care of you, just like this. Now, may I? Will you let me?"

"Yes," said Jack.

Nolly's hands were soft and slow and warm-scented with the oil.

Jack's thighs trembled only the slightest bit as Nolly eased the oil about Jack's bollocks, and behind them, till finally those fingers swept back across Jack's anus, which smarted, enough so that Jack struggled to hide his wince.

The wince had gone through his entire body, so Nolly knew it had hurt, thus Nolly took some more oil in his hands, and went even more slowly, going more gently between Jack's legs. All of this was to the good, for the delicate, bruised skin, after the initial touch of the oil, was being coaxed into a more tender state, in which any stings, any aches, were brought to defeat by the healing grace of Nolly's touch.

The oil made Nolly's hands slide easily, even while Nolly's grip was firm. It was when Nolly straightened up and moved closer, close enough for Jack's skin to feel the roughness of Nolly's canvas trousers, the edge of his worn, muslin shirt, that Jack felt the balance of his head go awry. For while before Nolly had been touching Jack's intimate parts, now Nolly was circling Jack's wrists with his fingers, touching this ordinary place on Jack's body with the *same* tenderness, the *same* love.

As Nolly's fingers slid up Jack's forearm to the crook of his elbows and back down again, it was as if Nolly were caressing him, as he might do for comfort, or just the closeness of being with Jack, for whatever the reason. Because he liked it, because he wanted to. Because he loved every part of Jack equally.

"Nolly?"

Jack trembled. He did not know what he was asking for or even what he needed, but his head was unsteady from the touches on his arms, which were just as tender as when Nolly's hands had been on other parts of him. These less intimate touches spoke of the one thing so dear to Jack's heart: that all of him was beloved by Nolly just the same. *All* of him.

The gentle sweep of Nolly's palms upon him, with Nolly being as careful with his arms as with anywhere else, drove a sense of being unravelled to spike right up inside of Jack, making him jerk, his arms flailing, and he realized, inside of a quick moment, that if he didn't sit down, he was going to fall down.

"Say, say, say," said Nolly, in the way that Jack had often done to soften the moment so that it might be cared for in the way that was needed.

Jack fell into Nolly's arms as a desperate man might leap from the deck of a burning ship and into the wilds of the ocean, where he is sure to drown. But better that fate, for Nolly to know the depths of Jack's weakness, than to ever be without the comfort of those arms ever again.

Through the haze in his head, Jack felt Nolly return the embrace, but gently, and that he was helping Jack to sit on the bed with some great care, but never in that way that Jack had feared, in some timorous, hesitant way. No, Nolly's arm was firm around Jack's shoulders, and his other hand never left Jack's waist. And Nolly was speaking, though the words seemed to come through a white shroud that had lowered itself in the room without Jack noticing.

"Jack," said Nolly, in a way that sounded as though he'd been repeating it. "Come back to me now, come now, sit up with me, or would you rather lie down and put your head on the pillow?"

"I'm all over oil," said Jack, mumbling out the words as best he might. "An' we've just done up the bed."

"Never mind the bed," said Nolly, cross now, which made Jack smile. "Here, I'll push the coverlet back so you'll have nothing but clean sheet beneath you."

Jack did as he was told, for with that arm about him and that sweet, loving voice so near telling him what to do, how could he do otherwise? So he lay back, and when his head hit the pillow, everything seemed to swim about him, and the pillow to move as though surged upward by an errant wave.

But Nolly was there, sitting on the bed, his weight pulling the mattress down near Jack's hip. His hands on Jack's face were steady and cool. Stealthily, the sound of rain outside of the open casement window became stronger in Jack's ears, to the point where he could hear the patter of it on the cobblestones in the alley below.

"Are you all right Jack? Do you want me to stop? Is it your head again? I've got those tinctures still at hand."

"Don't want no fuckin' tinctures, just want you here w'me, doin' what you're doin'."

"Then I shall continue until you bid me to stop."

Nolly continued much in the way he'd been doing before, his hands gentle on Jack's skin regardless of where they roamed, treating every part of Jack, from the darkest marks between his thighs to the palest, softest skin along his ribs, exactly the same. Slowly, slowly, he went over each part again, stroking the oil into Jack's skin, and Jack began to realize that the sweet oil was a miracle potion because all the aches and the soreness were ebbing away, slinking into corners where, as he knew from previous encounters with likewise hurts, they would soon disappear altogether.

"'M'oiled up now, Nolly, good an' proper."

"That you are," said Nolly, a gentle smile in his voice. His hands rested on Jack's belly, folded over each other, as if Nolly were about to start on his prayers. "When you're up to it."

"If I were up to it," said Jack, chuckling deep in his throat. "I'd be givin' you a good seein' to."

But instead of making Nolly laugh, as it was meant to do, Jack felt the seriousness in those hands, as clearly as if he could see Nolly's face in the rainy gloom.

"Were you—were you able to manage, Jack, after Port Jackson?"

Thus stilled in his attempt at amusement, Jack knew he should be honest. For this was Nolly, after all, and Jack needed to be true.

"I was," said Jack. He cleared his throat and reached down to clasp the back of Nolly's hands, as if he meant to join Nolly in his prayers. "But it was after a while. Comin' home to London on the *Bertha May,* there was a woman—" Jack stopped, for he had never spoken to Nolly of this part of his past. Still, Nolly deserved to know what had happened. "She was some ten years older than I, an' was kind. Her name was Nina, an' she was kind to me."

Jack's throat closed up, remembering that time, the harshness of the marine's touch, and Nina's gentleness after the dry, unthinkable roughness of Port Jackson.

"So you were intimate with her, during your return voyage."

There was no recrimination in Nolly's voice, though there was some surprise, as would happen with anybody, but Jack felt the need to explain just the same.

"She had the brightest blue eyes, Nolly, like lamps in the dark, the sweetest smile, the softest bosom—"

Again Jack stopped, his throat filling up, even as he felt Nolly's hand moving oh-so-slowly up and down Jack's arm.

"I don't have a soft bosom," said Nolly with all of his usual seriousness. Which, given the subject matter, made Jack suddenly want to laugh out loud, though that would have been as unwelcome as it might have been at a funeral. "But I hope I shall do as right by you as your sea-going Nina."

There was not a speck of jealousy in Nolly's voice, just the steadiness that had become more evident every day that Jack knew him. As well, there was only gladness, and a sense of gratitude that Jack had had somebody to care for him during his long voyage home.

"My sea-going Nina," said Jack, repeating the words, rather enjoying the flavor of them.

"And what happened to her? Where did she go?"

"Not sure," said Jack. "We neither of us spoke of our plans, we was just fuckin' an' pettin' on each other wherever we could find a spot, givin' each other comfort in the dark. But I think she said she was goin' home to her family. There might have been a husband a-waitin' for her for all I know, 'cause she said it just like that, *my family,* like it was terrible important to her."

Unasked by Nolly was the question as to how on earth Nina had managed to get the ticket home to England, when only a full pardon would have set her free. But then Nolly, with his usual tact, began instead to curl his fingers behind Jack's neck, to cup him there, to spread more oil, which filled Jack's nose with a pure, flowery scent and quite distracted him.

"We'll do you next," said Jack. His voice rose drowsily in the air, and he knew if they didn't trade places, then, soon enough, Jack would be sound asleep, leaving his beloved Nolly untended to. "In fact, we'll do you now, while it's still rainin'."

"Why while it's still raining?" asked Nolly in a voice that sounded as if Jack had been telling a story, and Nolly wanted him to continue with it.

Jack sat up, pushing up on his hands, feeling only the echo of any aches and pains, as if they'd left him long ago. He turned to look at Nolly, who was a gray outline in the near-dark, and listened for a moment to the high-pitched sound of rain pattering and splintering into shards on the cobblestones in the street.

"On account of I want to remember you an' me, just like this, with that mad, sharp sound outside the window, while we take care of each other like we do." Jack reached out to Nolly's face, cupping it in the palm of his hand. "Although, you should be much more bare to the skin than you are at present, if I'm to do my bit."

"Yes, Jack."

Nolly stood up as promptly, as if he'd been waiting for that very request, and divested himself of all of his clothes more quickly than Jack had ever known him to do. Though, of course, the garments were folded and placed carefully on the floor near the wall, rather than being tossed in the dark, which was what would have happened had Jack been in charge of the disrobing.

"Shall I stand?" asked Nolly, naked in the darkness, the tone of his question gentle and low.

"As it pleases you," said Jack. "But what would you rather?"

"To lie down next to you," said Nolly. "If you would let me."

"'Course I will," said Jack.

He did not even have to consider it, for he knew, deep down inside of him, that Nolly's closeness would put the final touches to his healing, would chase away the last of the bruises, and would even begin to erase the noisome memories in his mind. Besides, them being skin-on-skin together was always a pleasure and, as Nolly slid into the bed next to him, and settled himself on the mattress facing Jack, Jack felt a shudder of something akin to bliss race through him. And he was glad the bed-linen was clean so neither of them would be bothered by bed bugs, at least for a while.

"This is very well," said Jack. "Only I need the sweet oil now. Can you get it?"

Obediently, Nolly leaned back and, reaching out his arm, brought down the vial of sweet oil. This he handed to Jack, cupping his hand around Jack's fingers to show him how to keep it upright. Then Jack smiled, tilted the vial, and drizzled it along the length of Nolly's arm.

"Jack!"

"Now we'll both be all over oil, an' the sheets will be spoiled forever."

Of course, this was meant to amuse, and Jack could see the

curve of Nolly's cheek, the glint in his eyes as he shook his head, doing what he always did in pretending to be severely disappointed in Jack. Which was all to the better, for it meant they could go on a bit less grimly than they might otherwise have done.

"Where shall I start, Nolly?" asked Jack.

"Anywhere you like," said Nolly, nodding his head where it lay on the pillow, making the pillowslip rustle.

Jack remembered Nolly's wrists had been bound with prickly hemp rope, and that for the whole while Jack had been gone, they'd probably gone untended to. Now that the dirt and grit of the river had been washed away by the bath, Nolly's skin would be even more sensitive. So Jack started there. Taking the oil from Nolly's arm, Jack rubbed it between his two palms, shifting his shoulder beneath him to do it. And then, circling his fingers around Nolly's wrists, he rotated slowly back and forth, gently, the oil warm, the low, purple smell of flowers growing between them.

"And here?" asked Jack, as he moved his hands to Nolly's jaw. "I noticed a wee bit of bruisin' here an' below your eyes. When did that happen?"

"I got into an altercation, a fight," said Nolly, with some honesty and no hesitation. "There were three of them and one of me, so I threw down my honor and ran."

There might be more to the story, but Jack was glad Nolly had told him, though it must have stabbed at his fierce heart to have backed down like that. As well, though Jack didn't ask, it must have happened during that time that Jack had been gone, with Nolly frantic in the streets, throwing himself into trouble in an effort to find and rescue Jack, who hadn't needed either.

With some care, Jack traced the sweet oil across Nolly's cheeks and then down his nose, swiping a bit along the angled lines of his jaw.

"Anywheres else?" asked Jack.

He expected to be told that Nolly's belly hurt after the punch the workmaster had given him, or that his feet were sore from all the walking he'd done. Instead, Nolly lifted Jack's hand and placed it on his breast. Jack's palm was right over Nolly's heart, the low thumping feel coming up through the warm skin.

"Hey?" asked Jack now. "What is it?"

"My heart aches, Jack," said Nolly, low. "From not keeping you from hurt, from not being able to stop it."

"No, no," said Jack, with some haste. He clasped Nolly's face in both of his hands, being careful not to get the sweet oil in Nolly's eyes. "'Tis not your fault, not any of it, right? Right, Nolly? You do understand that, don't you?"

"Perhaps," said Nolly, his hands coming up over the back of Jack's. "I know the words, because you told them to me, but I can't seem to believe in them. Not now, at least, maybe not ever."

"Well," said Jack, and now his heart had begun to ache as well. "I'll just have to believe for the both of us till you do, then."

"That'll be forever, it feels like," said Nolly.

Now with Nolly so close, and the rain turning hard and loud outside the window, coming down like silver spikes, hitting every surface as though they were made of ice, Jack was very glad to be where he was. For even naked to the skin, breast-to-breast and hip-to-hip with Nolly, which he'd thought would make him feel edgy and uneasy, he felt better than he had in ages.

The difference was Nolly, of course, because in Port Jackson, after that first time being forced into Lieutenant Allingham's bed, Jack had walked with a limp and had moped about the barn, looking at the mound of feed hay for the cows and horses. There was no climbing into that mound, not with the various marines always milling about the compound, for they would have taken advantage of Jack before he could even blink, had he not been on his guard. That dark time lasted an entire month, and there'd been nobody who cared.

But here he was, so soon after being forced against his will, in bed with Nolly, every part of him vulnerable, and yet he felt no fear. He felt no desire either, alas, but he also felt no trepidation, no concern. There was only a languorous heaviness to his body, and the slight weight as Nolly wrapped his arm about Jack's waist, ever so lightly, as if he meant to pull it away were Jack to object.

And just as it was when Nolly took care when being astride Jack, Jack was moved, deeply so, by being the sole object of Nolly's concern and tender touches. Nolly never made a fuss about it, or waved his arms in a dramatic fashion, he merely held Jack up when he needed it, and lay at his side in the quiet dark, only touching Jack where Jack could bear to be touched and nothing more, nothing Jack didn't want.

"I could do you a favor, you know," said Jack, putting his hand on Nolly's hip, unable any longer to hold back on demonstrating Nolly's careful consideration meant to him. "I gots my hands right *here*—"

"No, Jack," said Nolly. His hand about Jack's waist curved up to pet the length of Jack's ribs, going back around to trace his spine. "It wouldn't be fair, and besides—" Here Nolly stopped to give Jack's nose a quick kiss. "I want for nothing, not when I can have you just as you are, just like this."

"That sounds like a declaration of love," said Jack, and he meant it to be sassy and maybe slightly brash, but he failed utterly and it sounded like a question, as if his heart, his very soul, had risen up in the hope of hearing more of the same.

"Oh, I do love you, Jack, I do, I do—"

But here Nolly stopped again, for between their bodies, Nolly's cock had begun to warm and fill with blood, and that brought a smile to Jack's face, a small laugh building in his throat.

"No," said Nolly, quite firmly, brushing Jack's hand away from his groin. "It's all very well, but we shan't be doing anything until *both* of us can manage."

"But sometimes we do one without the other, eh? Don't we?"

Jack was about to start in with his best coaxing patter, but

Nolly gentled him with both hands on Jack's shoulders, sliding up to Jack's neck, where he clasped Jack close with the utmost tenderness.

"We do, but that's our choice. This is not a choice, not when you can't participate. So, *no*, Jack, and I mean it."

"It might be forever till I can," said Jack, teasing, because at the rate he was going, it wouldn't be very long at all.

"Then I shall wait forever."

Nolly gave a sharp little nod, and Jack knew that any more joking about it might put Nolly in a real temper, so he didn't say anything more to convince Nolly how fun it might be.

Instead, Jack relaxed his neck on the pillow, and breathed a sigh, feeling the length of Nolly's arm still upon him, and the cool breeze that shifted about the room from the open casement window. A distant flicker of lightning lit the room, and there, before him, was Nolly's face on the white pillow, limned in light, his blue eyes looking at Jack, in the way they did, with such seriousness, such devotion, that Jack was warmed all through.

"We'll sleep like this, you an' I," said Jack. He reached up to trace the edge of his palm along Nolly's face, now in darkness.

"Me an' thee," said Nolly, the words half-stumbled behind a yawn. "'Tis blessedly cool, now."

"Want me to close the window?" asked Jack. "Will you get cold?"

"Not with you to warm me," came the low, sleepy answer.

For Jack was Nolly's blanket, just as Nolly's was Jack's, and that was that.

22

WORKING THE STREETS IN
LONDON TOWNE

Sunshine poured in the open casement window and had already dried the thin cotton curtain. Oliver sat up, completely naked, with half the bedclothes twisted about his ankles and the other half on the floor. He felt something cool along his side, and found the vial of oil miraculously mostly corked. There was a small circle of oil stain on the bedclothes, but nothing to worry about, so he placed the vial to stand on the table just as, beside him in the bed facing the wall, Jack also stirred.

"Time is it?" asked Jack with a grunt, rolling over and poking Oliver in the ribs with his elbow as he scrubbed at his eyes. "I mean to go out."

"I beg your pardon?" asked Oliver. He knew he was looking at Jack as though Jack had grown two heads, but it couldn't be helped. "It's not even nine o'clock, and what do you mean you're going out? Out to *work*?"

"Yes, to work." Jack sat up now, too, his hair dark witch-weed about his head, his body silky warm in the early morning's coolness, the gift of a night of rain. "I'm all clean an' oiled now so it should be a right easy thing slippin' my hand into some old duffer's pockets."

This made Oliver laugh out loud, though the prospect of Jack so soon on the streets quite filled him with worry.

"But are you ready to go out?" asked Oliver. "You still need rest."

"An' I tells you I don't need nothin', 'cause I'm ready to go," said Jack quite firmly as he crawled across Oliver's bare legs to get out of bed and stand up. "I'm well enough rested. I needs to be gettin' back to what I knows best, on account of that's the best tonic I know."

Oliver looked at Jack, all up and down as he fumbled for his stockings and trousers and everything else. It was easy to see, after the bath and the soothing of the sweet oil, that Jack did look better. His face had more color, his shoulders moved with more ease and, overall, he was much as he'd been before—before they'd taken the shortcut to get to London Bridge and everything had turned so disastrous. But he was loath to let Jack out of his sight, so perhaps—

"Might I come with you, Jack? Like we did before, you and I?"

The moment he'd asked it, Oliver knew he should not have. For there was a long moment of silence as Jack pulled his muslin shirt over his head and began to tuck it into his trousers, his beautiful mouth turned down in a frown.

"I don't have to, but I would if you wanted me to—"

Oliver's words stumbled to a halt. It was difficult to know where the balance lay, between wanting Jack where Oliver could see him, take care of him, and letting Jack be Jack.

"Some other time, perhaps," said Jack. He shook his head as he tightened his belt and did up the buckle. "When I've proven myself to myself."

As Jack looked at Oliver, his green eyes so dark in the morning light, there was nothing Oliver could do but nod in agreement. Besides, he knew well the power of focusing on something other than a troublesome worry or a memory so bad that it threatened to tear the heart asunder; work was a good cure for all ills.

"You will be careful and not get yourself arrested, right?" asked Oliver. He got up as well, since the day was underway, and reached for his shirt from the pile where he'd put it. "Look, my shirt is cleaner than yours, so will you take it? For my sake?"

Unspoken was the idea that a slightly less bedraggled Jack would attract slightly less attention whilst on the street. It wouldn't be much but it would help, so Oliver stood there in the altogether and continued to hold the shirt out as he shook it at Jack.

"Please, Jack? For me?"

This must have done Jack right in, for he sighed as if put-upon, but seemed very pleased at the same time, if his secret, small smile was anything to go by. He stripped off the shirt and tossed it on the bed. Then he took Oliver's shirt and tugged it on, and tucked it in beneath the waist of his trousers, struggling until Oliver stepped forward to undo the belt whilst Jack put the shirt where it needed to go. When Jack was to rights, Oliver re-fastened the belt and snagged Jack's waistcoat and cap from the floor.

"You'll look like a vagrant without these," said Oliver, trying to be serious, but he enjoyed the sight of Jack fussing with his attire, as if Oliver weren't standing there quite naked. "And I shall miss you while you're out."

Jack said nothing, but arranged his cloth cap on his head in that jaunty way that he liked to do, and gave Oliver a quick kiss on the mouth. It was not a passionate kiss, but it held much affection, a promise for the hope of tomorrow, which, while it hid its own sorrows, also held the promise of something good.

"You'll be here?" asked Jack as he opened the door to go out it and down the stairs. "Waitin' for me?"

"Of course I will, Jack," said Oliver, fighting some unease at the sight of Jack ready to go to work, while he himself would have to remain behind. "I shall probably help out in the taproom, and see if I can set things to rights down there."

"Save them from themselves, you mean," said Jack with a wink, and then he was out the door, eager and bright, leaving a dim shadow of himself behind.

Which left Oliver standing there, blinking at the door.

He wondered how things had come to this, where he was standing stark naked in a room at the Three Cripples, all on his own. But this was Jack's way of keeping busy, just as Oliver would have done and, indeed, had done, in the past.

So Oliver got dressed and finished by putting on his sturdy boots, which had proven their mettle over and over, and slipped the suspenders over his shoulders. He stood up, leaving his cap and waistcoat in the room, and went downstairs.

He planned to grab an apron and get to work, following, of course, Jack's industrious example, the thought of which just made Oliver smile to himself. But nobody noticed, so he didn't have to explain anything to anybody.

HIGH HOLBORN WAS FILLED WITH FOLKS GOING TO SATURDAY markets, and high-stepping horses pulling thin-wheeled gigs, and even a wagon cart of wooden crates filled with fat pigs bound for Smithfield, down the slope of Holborn to where it crossed the newly covered Fleet Ditch.

It was into this sprawl that Jack plunged himself, though normally he had better sense than to hunt so close to home. But there was a shakiness about his limbs that told him he should not be too far from the tavern, that he should stay where he knew every inch of the street, where he knew the dark side alleys he could scurry into when the danger of a constable's blue uniform wandered too near. And close enough to where Nolly was to give him courage.

It was not the thought of picking pockets, nor of his own

hand going into those pockets, that distressed him. Instead, it was the whirl and spill of bodies all around him, all unknown, presenting some danger he could not define that left his mouth dry and curiously sped up his heart in a way that was becoming uncomfortably familiar. So he walked along the pavement, his hands in his pockets, pretending to purse his lips in a soundless whistle. Then, after a bit of that, he pushed his cap aside to scratch the back of his head as he mulled over the window of a print shop.

There, posted on the inside of the fine-sheeted glass, were color pictures with drawings of society folk saying foolish or cruel things. Of the common man in outlandish weather with an amusing expression on his face. And even of the Queen, her round cheeks and wide girth looking pompous instead of digni-fied, all of which was suitably distracting.

As was the milliner's shop after that, and a dainty tea shop that was already thick with customers, wealthy enough to wear their finest to drink tea in dainty china cups. After that was another print shop, a cobbler's, and a shop that sold baskets of every shape, for every purpose, and on it went, until Jack's mind was filled with images he could focus on as he walked along, rather than the shifting crowd about him.

He almost wanted to go home, but he could not, for to do so was to admit to Nolly that he was afraid. Which he wasn't, not exactly. He was not afraid of the people, but rather of the move-ment, of the activity that was unpredictable in its actions. It pushed past him on the pavement and rushed along in the street so hasty and seeming at such speed that it made the skin around his eyes twitch, until he had to draw backwards on the pavement and press his back against the brick wall between two shop windows, a faint sheen of sweat on the skin of his forearms, the back of his neck.

With his palms flat against the brick and taking slow, slow breaths, Jack assayed the crowd. He looked at the shops along each side of the street, at the depth of traffic, at the amazing peculiarities of each figure, their mode of dress, which way they were headed, and contemplated this until his heart slowed, and he didn't feel so cold.

He picked out a mark, a gentleman in a pale top hat on the other side of the street who loitered outside of James Smith & Sons, which sold umbrellas. To buy an umbrella would have been a foolish thing to do on such a day as this, with the bright sun blazing overhead, and the clouds of dust rising high beneath the carriage wheels, the drover's whips, the shoes, and boots, and slippers of everyone passing by, going this way or that.

But in London there was always the chance of rain, so the gentleman was soon joined by another gentleman. Together they assayed the selection of umbrellas and wiped their foreheads with quick dabs of their handkerchiefs, which were snowy white and, even from this distance, as Jack could see, were of good silk.

Slowly, maintaining his guise of a casual laborer who was only out for a stroll on such a fine day as this, Jack crossed the street. He went at an angle so that when he arrived on the pavement on the other side of the street, he was in front of the shop next to the two gentlemen and the umbrella store.

The shop Jack was in front of was an elegant bakery that looked to be selling the fancier sort of bread. The display in the window would have made Nolly's mouth water, for it had iced buns and folded tarts with sugar on top. There was also an arrangement on a raised glass platter of little square cakes covered in chocolate that Jack had never seen before, though these were being sold quite quickly, as the white-aproned clerk was continually taking several from the window and placing them carefully in folds of waxed paper.

Jack turned and, making as though he wasn't certain which way he was headed, stumbled into one of the gentlemen, the first one in the pale top hat, and relieved the gentleman of his slightly sweaty silk handkerchief.

With a puzzled look on his face, Jack paused at the edge of the pavement, as if he wasn't in a hurry, and certainly had not just picked a man's pockets. As he left the two gentlemen behind, they were still talking about umbrellas, how costly they were, and whether the shopkeeper might be inclined to give them a discount if they purchased two at the same time.

Heading up Holborn brought Jack near the vicinity of crowds and shops that were less of the common variety and more of the refined. Gone were the carts carrying cages of pigs, the coster-monger with a wheeled barrow of sweet turnips and fresh chard, and the girl with a tray hung about her neck selling string-tied bunches of faded violets. Instead, were the stately governesses with their finely bedecked charges, portly bankers with their tittering wives on their arms, and a bold trio of young men, dressed in bright trousers and checkered waistcoats, striding down the pavement as if they owned it, making everybody get out of their way as they went.

Including Jack, who was made to jump into the street, but not before he reached into the closest young man's waistcoat pocket to draw out his pocket watch.

Unfortunately, the watch was firmly hooked to the young gentleman's watch fob, which was clipped in an intricate way into his waistcoat buttonhole. The chain jerked and broke at the head, and the watch went clattering to the pavement. And Jack, with the gold woven chain in his hands, knew he had to get away. But not too fast, or he would attract attention.

So instead, he stepped back, as if equally astonished that such travail had happened to the young man, who gaped at the shattered watch and began to shout curses that made a group of nearby ladies blush. Jack added his shocked murmur to the throng and shoved the chain in his pocket.

Now he needed to go back to those places where his common workingman's garb would not stand out so much, so he crossed the street to the other side and headed back down Holborn. When he got to Shoe Lane, figuring he might pass for a cobbler's apprentice, he turned onto it and headed down towards Blackfriars Bridge. The bridge would be busier than anyplace else on a Saturday, so, feeling more contented than when he'd set out, he mingled with the foot traffic, and took his time, as though he were totally at his leisure and did not have a stolen silk handkerchief in his pocket, and a watch fob chain in the other that most definitely did not belong to him.

~

As Jack approached it, Blackfriars Bridge was half-coated in a shifting gray pall that came from the south bank of the Thames, from the tanneries and black-chimnied factories that hugged the water and chuffed out smoke into the air and filth, and oozed fragments into the water to be carried to the sea.

On the north bank it was little better, being upwind. From the spot where Jack stood, he could watch the steam-ferries puff beneath the bridge, their smoke stacks almost scraping the stone arches, for even though the tide was in, commerce and transport could be stopped for no man, nor even the moon.

There was a small dory boat being rowed by two fellows who had obviously had too much beer by mid-morning to be wary of the low height of the bridge's arches, nor of the speed at which the steam-ferries were passing it by. Brown waves crashed up the dory's sides, and the men rowed and laughed loud enough for Jack to hear.

It made him smile to think of being that reckless on the water; he never had been and never would be. He could swim a bit now, thanks to Nolly, who was at the Three Cripples, doing whatever industrious task he might to keep from thinking of Jack out in the streets.

Or at least that's what Jack hoped Nolly was doing, working, rather than worrying. Working, as Nolly liked to do, his hands busy at some soothing task. And this in spite of the fact that Jack could keep them both, and could make enough money so Nolly could have time to read those books he was always on about, and not have to spoil yet another shirt with sweat-stains and beer spills and the shift of damp that made the dust stick to everything in the taproom.

A great deal of the traffic, since there was so much of it on the bridge, both foot and wheel, had to move at a slower pace than it normally might. Those folks who could afford a carriage clucked past Jack with their noses in the air.

Those on foot, wearing thin leather boots and silk slippers, fine cloth rustling, black top hats shimmering in a sideways spiral where the felt had been pressed down, pranced by him, as if deigning to notice him. But Jack noticed them, noticed all of them, those whose pockets bulged with a handkerchief or a wallet, or where the shine of a gold watch peeked out from beneath a jacket lapel, or a reticule twinkled, beaded with jet, was held just a tad too loosely.

If they had it and flaunted it in such a way, then, by rights, they deserved to lose the possession of it, and Jack was there to determine who would be who. That is, based on the marks that Nolly always preferred Jack to steal from: the gentlemen in fine brocade waistcoats with velveteen cuffs on their jackets, and those ladies, whose lace on their bonnets would not let them look to left nor right without them fully turning their heads.

And even the petted and spoiled child in a push-pram that Jack spotted now, who was far too old to be carted about, but whose insistence on distracting its parents made them the perfect mark. The child was ugly besides, with snot running from its nose that its white-capped governess wiped and wiped at, to no avail.

They suited Jack's purposes just fine. Nolly would approve, besides, as spoiled children deserved to have their little straw hats taken from them. Or better yet, the mother or father deserved to be fleeced, for neither of them, though their child was not two feet from them, ever gave it even a glance, leaving its care to a virtual stranger who was paid to do the tending.

Jack narrowed his eyes and tugged at his shabby waistcoat. It had been not so very long ago that he'd had a proper jacket and hat, and had blended in with the crowd; the day he'd spent at St. Paul's in the outfit of a gentleman had been sweet and dreamlike. In contrast, being now so shabbily attired, his skills were even more critical. But he'd honed them for years and, as he clenched and unclenched his hands into fists, tugging at the seams of his trousers to make sure they were straight, it would be like stepping into a picture frame carved especially for him.

He moved away from the edge of the bridge and the narrow stone staircase that led down to the water, and crossed to the other side. He kept close to the gray-stone parapet and walked slowly, as if he was in no hurry to be anywhere and, like many, was enjoying his Saturday at leisure. Carts rolled across the cobblestones with low roaring sounds that echoed off each side of the bridge and added to the din of clattering footsteps.

Jack got about halfway across the bridge and tucked himself into the pedestrian refuge. There, he waited for the little family of three and the governess, who was dutifully garbed in black, her eyes down as she guided the push-pram along the pavement.

She was in front of the well-heeled parents, the couple long enough in wedlock to have a child, though they did not act conscious of it in any meaningful way. The child kept turning about in the push-pram, trying to grab the edges to stand up and gain its parents' attention, but the governess was quick to scold, and the child was forced to sit down.

Just as the push-pram crossed in front of Jack, he jumped into the street between the parents and the governess's round black skirts, and threw up his hands, as if he were startled.

"Oh," Jack said, not pretending to be anything other than what he was, a ragged street lad who had impeded the forward movement of a man and a woman who were, no doubt, his betters, and who were far superior to him in *every* way. Jack whipped off his cloth cap and clutched it in his hands. "I'm awful, terrible sorry, sir."

The man waved his gloved hand between them, dismissing

the incident, Jack, and his apology all at once. Jack hastened out of the way and stumbled, landing full against the gentleman. His hands went quickly inside the silk brocade waistcoat, and then he flung himself back, as if he feared that he might be capable of transmitting the pox or something equally vile.

"Terrible, *terrible* sorry, I am, sir, terrible."

But the man, without a word to Jack, took his wife's arm and, linking it with his, marched away. The governess and the push-pram were barely able to keep up. This left Jack holding the slender wallet, which he slipped into his trouser pocket with one hand, while with the other he replaced his cloth cap on his head, shaking it as if bemused at the incident, over so quickly, with no one harmed by it.

That was a good job well done, but the day was young yet, and the tide of casual strollers and easy-going folk was still thick and deserved more tending. This Jack would do as only *he* could.

He sashayed along, hugging close to the parapet to avoid being shoved off the pavement and into the street proper, for there was not enough leeway to avoid the rolling carriage wheels, the thunder of an over-decorated barouche, and the hasty, side-stepping horse whose owner should have known might be unsettled by all the traffic and noise, but hadn't.

Jack hunched against the stone and waited while the beast's backside skated back and forth in front of him, only mere inches from his face. Finally, the horse pranced on, going at far too great a speed for the thick traffic, but Jack just shrugged his shoulders and walked until he came to the middle of the bridge. There he paused to stand above the keystone arch and leaned over the parapet to look at the rushing water below.

The river at high tide was gray and brown and flecked with a dark-cream foam that spilled and danced about stone the piers where they rose out of the tumbling water. The water rolled like a song, repeating itself over and over, the dank mist rising up at Jack, smelling sour like sewage, and busting through itself in a hurry to roll away, roll away to the sea.

Jack smiled and patted the stone, and thought that if he had a stick to throw in the water to watch it get swallowed by the foam, he would. Still, he'd best be about it while there was daylight and fine weather and all those fancy folk with their silk handkerchiefs just hanging out of their pockets, and reticules barely clung to by the tips of their well-groomed fingers.

Whistling a bit, Jack shoved both of his hands in his pockets. He crossed to the up-river side of the bridge, and leaned back against the parapet where the cool stone leached the heat from his body and made him feel calm and at home. He lingered and watched the people and carriages go by, and he was seemingly witness to the entire of London, as though it had determined, at that very moment, that it needed to pass in front of him.

The smell of the river filled his lungs as he tasted the scent of burnt ash on his tongue and the acrid sting of coal tar in the back of his throat. He could hear the clatter of iron wheels and the murmur and rhythm of voices of the folk as they went about their business. His eyes beheld the refuse being drawn out to sea on the white-rolling brown foam.

And there, above the smells and the din, rose the dome of St. Paul's Cathedral, which, when viewed from a far-enough distance, as he well knew, looked almost exactly like the cap of a tan-brown mushroom.

The whole of London laid itself at Jack's feet, and Jack smiled.

23

IN WHICH THEY EAT LADY APPLES FRESH FROM THE COUNTRY

The smell of rain chased Oliver back up the street, nipping at his heels like a hopeful animal. But the sky was too clear for rain, and blazed yellow and bright overhead, slicing through the crags and valleys of the rooftops, lighting up the puddles along the cobblestones, and got into Oliver's eyes as he turned the corner up Field Lane.

His hands were full of parcels of food, which were done up in brown paper and tied with string. And in his pockets was a special treat he thought Jack might like, if his appetite was up to it when he came back from the streets. As well, it was important that Jack be welcomed home after his first day picking pockets; Oliver had done his best to time his errand correctly.

As Oliver stepped through the doorway of the Three Cripples, which was propped open by an ash barrel somebody had dragged over, the dark coolness of the taproom washed over him. There were only a few customers gathered at the bar, sharing the dimness and stillness with each other while they drank. Oliver knew it would only be a short while before even the taproom was warm enough to make his shirt stick to his skin, but the coolness was a blessing in the meantime.

As was the sight of Jack, sitting beneath the window at the table Noah liked to use to play whist and drink with his lads.

Jack was alone, his back to the window, his jacket laid over the back of his chair. He had tipped in his seat a bit, and his shirt was pulling at his shoulders, the thin waistcoat fluttering about, unbuttoned.

Jack had rolled up his sleeves, showing the bruises from the rope that had been tied around them, which were still bold brands. The bruises looked better than they had the day before, but they were visible enough that Oliver thought to tell Jack that he might roll down his sleeves, for as he'd been particular about Oliver seeing them, Jack would not want the rest of the world to get even the merest eyeful.

But then, in the back of his mind, Oliver could hear Jack's snort of dismissal, the wordless equivalent of Jack stating loudly and clearly that he did not give a rat's arse if anybody saw, so why was Nolly to care. Oliver did, though he did not know if he could come up with a likely way to say it that wouldn't make Jack cross with him.

"I meant to be back before you'd returned," said Oliver, rushing up to the table. Panting, he placed the items down and smiled and wanted to wrap his arms around Jack to hug him, in spite of there being eyes to espy them.

Jack looked up as Oliver pushed the parcels of food to the middle of the table.

"Didn't know where you'd gone, but I figured you'd be back, so beer's comin'," Jack said, his eyes wide and calm and happy as he looked at Oliver. "Thought to order you a tot of gin, but we can get that later, if you've a mind to."

"Perhaps," said Oliver. "But look what I've brought you."

Oliver unwrapped the bread and the cheese, then the entire of a beef and onion pie, the crust of which was still warm and glistening with grease. Lastly, he pulled out of his pockets two new apples, which were so recently picked that the leaves on one had yet to start curling, let alone to brown.

On such a big round table, the gathering seemed quite meager, rather than the grand feast he'd imagined when he'd purchased the items. There was one sixpence left in his pocket from the handful of coin he'd borrowed from Noah, which needed to be put away before they spent it.

With the backs of his fingers, Oliver pushed the pie toward Jack, as it was the hot, savory dish that Jack was most likely to want to eat first.

"I'll get spoons from the kitchen," Oliver said, and he dashed off before Jack could say no, that a knife would do as well.

By the time Oliver came back to the table, two spoons and a knife for the apples clutched in one hand, one of the girls had brought two pint pots of beer so cold that the outside of each pint was clustered with pinpoints of silver.

"This looks to be the very thing I was a-wantin' without even knowin' it," said Jack, smiling and rubbing his hands together. He took a long swallow of his beer first, as if the food wasn't sitting there waiting for him.

Then Oliver realized that while Jack was sitting against the wall, the other seats, any of which Oliver might sit in, were a good deal further than a hand's length away from Jack. Whether this was on purpose, Oliver could not know, but he thought it might be unconsciously done, especially when, as Oliver dragged the chair closer to Jack, Jack looked up at him, eyebrows going up.

"Miss me, eh?" asked Jack in a completely level way that had anybody heard it might be interpreted that they'd been out of each other's company for a good solid year at least, and that Oliver had missed Jack, as anybody might.

But how could Oliver say it out loud, that of course he would miss Jack, even if Jack had only been gone a mere moment? He could not, for Jack would not like him saying it so earnestly where anybody might hear.

Oliver felt the twisting beneath his breastbone to think of it, that he could not have found Jack, had Jack not determined, on his own, to come home again. How could Oliver have weathered that loss? He knew he could not have. And, just as Jack had picked up one of the spoons and was digging into the beef and onion pie, Oliver had to sit down or risk his knees buckling beneath him, his head filling with gray fog, a white shroud coming down, all over him, a wet cape of nothingness.

With the touch of Jack's hand on his arm, Oliver felt the whisper of Jack's kiss on his cheek, and heard the soft flow of words, the closeness that he so feared to lose. And tried to breathe, for to smell the beer and the damp, warm fug of the taproom was to know his surroundings, to know where he was.

"Hey?" asked Jack, closer now, his chair knocking against Oliver's. "You need tendin' to, you do."

"No, I'm the one taking care of you," said Oliver, insisting upon this, his lips numb, blinking, feeling a cold chill sweat on his forehead. "I'm the one—"

"Bollocks to that, Nolly," said Jack. "Here, drink this, an' listen to me. We takes care of each other, right? That's how we are, you 'n I. Me 'n thee."

Oliver felt the cool metallic rim of the pint pot on his lips and tasted the beer on his tongue. The beer was fresh and cold, the swallow of it good, and he felt foolish.

"I'm sorry, Jack," said Oliver. He took the pint pot from Jack's hands and put it on the table. "I did miss you, your first day out, for the thought of losing you again—"

"Delicate as a petal, you are," said Jack, though he did not sound as though he were mocking Oliver. More, that he was resigning himself to having to tend to Oliver, all his hurts and ills, his pedantic ways, fussy as a miss—

Jack stopped. Looked at Oliver through half-lidded eyes.

"Gave you a turn, didn't it, all this." Jack didn't explain what he meant, but then, he didn't need to.

It was on the tip of Oliver's tongue to say, in a scathing way, that it was a miracle Jack had come home at all, when he realized what a truth it might have been. A horrible truth, for what if something had happened to Jack, and Oliver was never to know? So he nodded, and took another mouthful of beer, and held it there while the sharpness of the hops cut into his tongue, which gave him something to think about instead of Jack going missing again.

"You did," said Oliver, after he'd swallowed. "Maybe I should go out with you, next time. Tomorrow even, to make sure you're all right."

"No need," said Jack, scraping his hair out of his eyes with his fingers. He shoveled a large, dripping spoonful of the pie into his mouth, and chewed, his cheeks bulging. And, having swallowed only half of that mouthful, he pointed the spoon at Oliver. "I'll be all right on the streets, as I always have been, never you fear."

"But Jack—"

"Nolly, listen to me now. The sooner we goes back to the way it was, the sooner we can make it like it was."

Oliver knew it could never be as it had been, and Jack was a fool if he thought so. He determined not to keep silent on this opinion, though he tempered his words.

"I don't see how we can do that. How can we do that?"

"'Tis simple, Nolly, m'love, we're going to march on, an' that's that. I've never been one to stay in the mud, not if I c'n crawl out of it."

Jack went back to eating, steadily alternating between huge mouthfuls of beef and onion pie and large swallows of beer. And Oliver let him, for Jack was still too thin in his person and too gray about the eyes, though the bath and the rest the night before had done him good.

It did Oliver good to see Jack eat besides, but he shook his head, wondering how they always came to the crossroads of a quarrel, when everything was all right now, surely everything was all right? Which it was, or would be, if only Oliver could stop picking apart everything Jack did or said.

"I want to crawl out of the mud with you, Jack, only I've never—"

Oliver had to stop again, as though something had slammed into his chest. For he had never had to watch someone he loved as much as he did Jack get hurt before. Not like it had been on the *Scylla*.

"I don't know if I can crawl out as readily as you seem to be able to do," said Oliver.

Shame at his own lack of fortitude itched beneath Oliver's skin. He looked about him at the growing crowd gathering in the taproom as the afternoon wore on. The air was filling with the smell of sweat and the sight of work grime brought in from filthy streets, all of which seemed to be pushing at Oliver and made him want to get up and run until he was very far from where he now was.

"I'll show you," said Jack, wiping his mouth with the back of his bare arm. "You just keeps on, like it's all sweet as sunrise, an' just keeps on till it is. D'you see?"

"Yes," said Oliver, his voice low, for even if he did not believe it, it was easy to see Jack did.

"So what're them?" Jack changed the subject with obvious ease and pointed with the heel of his grease-smeared hand toward the middle of the table where the rest of the food waited.

"Those are Lady apples, fresh from the country, or so the woman selling them from the street barrow told me."

Oliver reached to hand the biggest, rosiest apple to Jack, the one with the leaf still so green and fresh there might even have been traces of dew on it.

Jack plunked the spoon into the half-eaten pie and pushed it at Oliver, in so uncouth a way that Oliver was certain, quite certain, in fact, that the gesture was entirely put on. But then he was distracted by Jack as he reached for the apple and held it in the cup of his palms, as though it were a treasure. His eyes closed, and his lashes lay soot-dark against his pale cheeks.

"Been a long time since I 'ad an apple," said Jack as he brought the apple up to his nose to smell it. "Truth, it's been a long time since I been home in the spring in time for Lady apples."

Oliver saw Jack go still, his chin ducked down, the apple in both of his hands, fingers clasped about it as though he were praying. And thinking. And remembering all those winters and all those springs that he'd been kept away from his beloved London.

It moved Oliver, this adoration of a simple apple, so much so that he wanted to do something to add to the contentment that had relaxed Jack's shoulders.

"Shall I slice it for you, Jack? And feed it to you piece by piece?" Oliver reached out his hand, keeping the gesture low and private from the patrons filling the taproom and bustling up to the bar. "Please let me do that for you, Jack."

Jack practically shoved the apple at Oliver.

"Fuckin' apple," Jack said. He scrubbed at his eyes with the back of his hand and scowled at Oliver. "I already told you. Don't you look at me that way, all tender an' everythin'—just *don't*, got it?"

For a moment, Oliver hesitated. They were on the verge of another quarrel, with Oliver trying to help, and Jack refusing him. But when Oliver saw Jack's mouth tremble beneath the cuff of his undone sleeve, Oliver determined otherwise.

"I *will* look at you that way," said Oliver, scooting as close as he might, turning his back on the entire taproom, shielding Jack from staring eyes. "Because I love you and can't bear to see you hurting. I won't fuss, Jack, for I know you despise that, but please, do not ask me not to care."

Jack was stonily silent, and Oliver feared everything would come undone, simply because he could not keep his mouth closed. But in that moment, Jack pushed the knife toward Oliver as he looked the other way and squared his jaw.

"You have to do this in the taproom, don't you," said Jack.

"No," said Oliver. He'd messed up again, done the exact wrongest thing.

But Jack turned to look at Oliver, his eyes bright, a small, almost helpless smile on his mouth.

"You do pick your times, Nolly." Jack shook his head and shoved his unbuttoned sleeves back up his forearms. "Just cut the bloody apple, if you've a mind to."

So Oliver did, cutting the apple in half, and then in half again, trimming out the core of seeds, the stem, and laid each pink and white curve in front of Jack. Jack ate each slice, his eyes half closing, chewing contentedly, and then, using his finger, he plinked one of the slices at Oliver so he would eat as well.

Oliver obliged Jack, and the apple was delicious. As was the rest of the beef and onion pie, and the bread and cheese. And the second round of beers that Jack had waved at one of the girls for. It was like old times, sweet as ever it might be, with them dallying away the drowsy afternoon, the noise level rising in the tap room, and the regulars crowding up to the bar, all elbows and dusty boots.

And Oliver could see, at least a little, what Jack meant. For here they were, as they had been before, as if they had always been that way. Together, enjoying a meal at the Three Cripples. Soaking up their little corner of stillness while the rest of the world boiled and shouted around them.

But of course, just as they were finishing off the second apple, with most of it still going to Jack, as Oliver made sure, Noah came over to them, dragging Len and Nick in his wake like two large, powerful fish on a line. They came to a stop next to the table, and Noah gave Jack a hearty clap on the shoulder.

"How was it, then?" asked Noah. "Did you come back flush?"

"Indeed, I did," said Jack with a broad smile that showed his sharp teeth. "Gold an' coin an' notes. It was as easy as if they was handin' it to me."

Jack's eyes were so bright as he looked up at Noah, and Oliver knew, in that moment, that he'd neglected to ask what Jack's take was, as Jack liked him to do. But it was too *late* to ask because Noah already had.

Jack was already pulling out a gold watch chain, two wallets, three handkerchiefs, and a large handful of coins. He piled all of these on the table, which Noah and his men were standing around so the stolen goods would not be seen by prying eyes.

"You can give me what you like for the chain," said Jack with all casualness and pride. "But it's worth quite a bit, seein' as how it's pounded gold an' of excellent workmanship."

Noah picked up the gold chain and stirred the links in his palm with a finger while Oliver watched, feeling confounded and cross at the way the pleasant meal shared between Jack and himself had gotten waylaid into an exchange between a pick-pocket and his fence.

"We could melt this," said Noah. "An' sell off the bits."

Noah looked up from the chain and smiled at Jack, as if sharing between Jack and himself the satisfaction of a job well done. Then Noah picked up the wallets and handed one of them to Nick while he poked through the other one.

Both of the wallets were sleek with use and fat with bills, leaving Oliver to wonder if somebody's life savings had just been taken from them. But what was there that he could say about it? Picking pockets was what Jack did for a living, and there was nothing Oliver could do about it.

"Maybe you've a mind to pay off Work'us's debt to me," said Noah to Jack. "Seein' as how he's completely given up tendin' to the taproom of late."

This remark of Noah's was followed by a grin, more sneer than pleasant exchange, and Oliver felt his whole body stiffen. The debt was fairly high, as Noah well knew. But what Noah also should have known was that since Jack had gone back to work picking pockets, Oliver could return to working in the taproom, and he soon would have earned back the money he'd been advanced on his wages.

"Easiest thing in the world," said Jack. He took the wallet from Noah's hands and pulled out a five-pound note. "How much is it? You can take it off my percentage." He held out the note to Noah, who took it so quickly that the paper snapped in the air. "I'll keep the rest of these bills, an' the coin in my pocket, an' you c'n have the wallet back." Here Jack paused to hand over the now-empty leather folder. "An' whatever you make from the chain, an' you an' Nolly are squared up, eh?"

"That sounds about right. It was only about three guineas anyhow, but that interest was sure addin' up."

Noah's mockery stung as it always had. Luckily, Noah didn't stick around for any reaction, but instead nodded to his men, and off they went toward the office, stopping at the bar to get several pint pots of beer to drink while they discussed the disbursement of their ill-gotten gains.

Blood pounded behind Oliver's eyes as he sat there and tried to think of a way to stem the flood of fury now racing through him, and not just at Noah, for that feeling was always a matter of course, but at *Jack*. Jack, who had, simply and without any apparent effort whatsoever, swept any dignity Oliver had hoped to cling to in paying back a debt to a person he'd never wanted to borrow from in the first place.

It didn't matter that Jack had not even felt the loss of the repayment for, of course, there was more where that came from, as Jack was always fond of saying. More where that came from, and none of it earned by Oliver himself.

All of this was a permanent black score against his person, one he would not be able to erase, even if Noah were to never bring it up to torment Oliver with. Stolen money had been used to pay back an honest debt, one Oliver would have willingly borne for forever and a day, since the cost of it had tempered Jack's suffering and brought him ease.

But now Oliver could not even shoulder that burden, and never mind having utterly failed at every other attempt to take care of Jack, to take care of Jack and himself together.

"If you'll excuse me," said Oliver, taking great pains not to raise his voice, nor to shove the chair back with overly great force. "I must take a moment."

With that, he began to walk off, determined to head some-where where he might have a bit of privacy to rage what was in his heart. As he reached the center of the taproom, he couldn't decide whether to head out through the kitchen to the back alley or to go up to their room and slam and bar the door behind him.

He was stymied in either of these choices, however, for, with some scuffling motions and hasty strides, Jack was at Oliver's side, his fingers curling around Oliver's elbow.

"Where you goin', Nolly? We ain't done eatin' yet, an' I've a mind to take us out on the streets to get you somethin' for them sweet teeth of yours."

Oliver clenched his fists and jerked his elbow back, striking Jack in the chest. Jack, who must have gone from blithely unaware to stunned for air in a single heartbeat.

Whereupon, Oliver strode away, for now he'd added injury to Jack to the ever-growing pile of his own faults, and thought maybe it would be enough if he could reach the room, slam the door behind him, and shove the bed against it.

Thus, he raced up the stairs, but Jack was close behind him, too close to be shut out by the door, for he slipped in, stronger than Oliver in this, and slammed the door himself, locking them both in the small space of their room, with the air hot and damp and no room to run.

With Jack blocking the door, a confused frown pulling at his features, Oliver backed up until he knocked into the table, which caused it to rock against the plaster wall beneath the windowsill.

"Nolly, whatever is the matter?" asked Jack as if he had merely wandered in on Oliver in a temper rather than having trapped him with nowhere to go. "Why're you lookin' at me like that?"

Just as Jack reached out to him, Oliver could see the tail end of a wad of folded notes jutting out of Jack's pocket, and that the line of his trousers was pulled down by the weight of loose coin.

There was no end to the amount of money Jack could simply take as he saw fit, objects and articles, precious and necessary or merely adjuncts to the average person's day, all of which they would find having vanished at the first indication they were needed.

But there was no earthly way Oliver could object to this. He'd come back to London with Jack, *for* Jack, knowing full and well what the result would be. This, Jack with money flying out of every pocket, and he, Oliver, with anything he might contribute shaded quite pale in comparison.

"Nolly," said Jack. He stepped closer now, his hand coming to circle the back of Oliver's neck, so gently it made Oliver want to cry. "Sweetheart, whatever is the matter? Tell me now, just tell me."

With a roar from the center of his chest, Oliver shoved Jack on the bed, wincing as the coins jingled in Jack's pocket and several of the notes came loose and fluttered upon the bedclothes.

Oliver went to the door and kicked it hard enough to rattle it on its hinges, and punched the wall beside it, feeling the satisfying smacking crunch as the old plaster crumbled away in several crescent-shaped dents. But instead of waiting on the bed, as any sensible person might have done, Jack came up behind Oliver, grabbed his shoulders, and pulled Oliver back to press him against the wall.

"Nolly," said Jack, his hands firm on Oliver's shoulders, his voice firm beyond the din in Oliver's head. "What is this, what's got you so riled, just tell me. Nolly, c'mon now, *c'mon.*"

"Get your hands off me, Jack, or I *swear*—"

"You'll swear what?" asked Jack. His eyes sought Oliver's, and he did not look away, did not hide. "I ain't afraid of you nor your temper, so just tell me what's wrong, an' we'll talk it out, me an' thee, like we always do."

With a sudden movement, Jack clasped Oliver's face in his warm hands, his green-eyed gaze calm and certain. Oliver found himself blinking quite fast and, unsteady on his feet, reached up to cover Jack's hands with his own. Not to push them away, but to hold them while his heart pounded, and the pounding slowed, and the flush on his cheeks cooled.

Jack tipped his head to one side, not asking anything, not saying anything, just waiting, watching Oliver, as he did sometimes. Except his expression now was one of confusion tempered with concern, and it was this, and the sweet brush of Jack's thumb across Oliver's cheek, that undid him.

He stepped away from the wall and moved into Jack's arms, which immediately circled around him, tightly, just as tightly as ever Oliver needed them to be, and Oliver returned the embrace, just as fiercely, his throat thick with the effort not to cry.

"Say, say, say," said Jack as he patted Oliver's back and petted him, which only undid Oliver even further, to the point where he could not catch his breath. He could not let go of Jack, either, to push the tears back, so he shut his eyes tightly and hung on as best he could.

"C'n you tell me now that there's nobody to hear?" asked Jack. "Your lips are at my ear, w'out another soul to hear you, so c'n you tell me now?"

Oliver knew he had to, for ever had it been between him and Jack the agreement to be true. And Oliver would be, though when he swallowed to take a breath, it felt like glass shards going down.

"I don't—" Oliver began, and then he had to take another breath to get all the words out. "I no longer have any dignity."

Jack tried to pull back a bit, as if to look upon Oliver's face and divine some meaning from it. But Oliver held Jack too tightly to let him go, so Jack stayed close, petting Oliver's back, and reached up to clasp the back of his neck.

"Why is that, my love?" asked Jack. "Why is that, now?"

Then Jack did pull back and, sitting on the bed, pulled Oliver down to sit next to him. With his arm ever about Oliver's shoulders, the warmth of his body came through Oliver's shirt, and Jack's hand was on Oliver's where they were clasped trembling in his lap.

"Wherever has your dignity gone, then, Nolly? Did I take it somehow?"

Oliver felt double the shame of it, once that he'd not been able to pay back his own debts, and twice that he'd allowed his temper full rein without having attempted to stop Jack or to explain it to him, though how could he have done in front of *Noah*—

"You did," said Oliver, quite low, so low that Jack had to bend close to hear. "I wanted to pay my debt back on my own terms, with honest money, money that I'd *earned*—and then you went and paid it with *your* money—"

"No, no, Nolly," said Jack, with some earnestness. "That's not how it is, don't you see? The debt is ours just as the money is ours, whatever the source. Like it was when we was on the road, doin' all that travelin'."

Jack leaned forward to tuck himself into the curve of Oliver's shoulder, as if he meant for Oliver to embrace him in return. And this Oliver did, one arm slipping about Jack's waist, for he could not help it, not with Jack so near, and so warm and calm.

"But it's different in London," said Oliver, trying to swallow away the stiffness in his throat. "I ran up the debt to take care of you, and for your birthday, and if I don't pay it back, it's as though I'd not taken c-care of you at all."

Instead of replying, Jack leaned in and kissed Oliver's cheek, and swept his lips across Oliver's temple, all the while staying close and still, so present and steady, and it was all Oliver could do to choke back a sob. He had to scrub at his eyes with the heel of his hand because he could not make Jack understand and, in the face of this tenderness, the fierceness of his rage had almost no place to go.

"We're together now, ain't we, you an' me?" asked Jack, quite softly, his lips brushing Oliver's cheek. "But I see now what it is that's got you so unhappy, with me, an' with us."

"I'm not angry with *you*, Jack."

"Yes, you are," said Jack, nodding, so close his lashes brushed Oliver's skin. "An' you have a right to be, for I didn't understand an' marched all over everythin' you'd been doin' an' plannin'. Ain't that it?"

That was exactly it, though it took Oliver a moment of gathering his courage to be able to say it out loud.

"Yes," he said, admitting it at last. "And in front of Noah."

"*An'* in front of Noah, which was probably the worst part of it, eh?"

Oliver nodded and looked at his hand, still clasped in Jack's on his lap, and squeezed Jack's fingers with his own. He felt unable to say anything, even to agree. The dregs of his temper tasted bitter and made him feel foolish for having gotten so angry. But he had good reason to be, he *did*, only—

"The worst part," said Oliver, as he licked his dry lips and wished for a good swallow of beer to help his fury-parched throat. "The worst was having it done so quickly, as if I'd had no part to play, even though the debt was mine. Do you see that, Jack? Can you understand it?"

Making himself look Jack in the eyes, Oliver raised his head. He found Jack looking back at him, in that way that he did, with neither anger nor amusement at Oliver's admission, but rather with a sweetness in his eyes as he nodded his understanding.

"Went about it a bit blithely, I did," said Jack with a thoughtful frown. "Mayhap I was shown' off, seein' as how successful I'd been my first day back on the job." Jack said this now, a satisfied smile curling his mouth. "Like a celebration, I was seein' it, out with old debts, in with new income. But I stomped on you whilst goin' about it, an' for that, I'm sorry, truly I am."

"You needn't apologize to me Jack, for my temper. I ruined it for you, your successful first day back, when I only meant to help you celebrate it, by getting you something nice to eat. I *ruined* it."

"You couldn't have," said Jack. "An' you didn't, for that was a lovely beef an' onion pie, the best I've ever had, an' to come back to that, an' to your sweet face? Never mind it now, Nolly, but you should listen to me. Are you listenin'?"

"Yes, Jack," said Oliver as quickly as he might, grateful to push his temper away, grateful to listen to Jack's voice telling him something that he needed to hear.

"You an' I," said Jack, saying the words carefully, watching Oliver to make sure that he was attentive. "We're together, right? Right?"

"Yes, Jack."

"An' that means that it's not my money, nor is it yours, but it's *ours*, an' sometimes I'll bring in more, an' sometimes you will. It all goes in the red change purse, see, an' we each takes from it what we need, an' puts in what we can. Think of it—" Here Jack paused, squinting his eyes as he thought of what to say, and Oliver watched him, rapt with absorption. "Think of it as our own Bank of England."

There was such a satisfied smile on Jack's face as he came up with this that Oliver had to smile in return, and the feeling of it, of Jack waiting for Oliver's smile, as he was doing now, helped to push back the discontent in Oliver's breast.

"It'll be the Bank of the Red Change Purse," said Jack. "An' we the only two members. Here—"

Jack stood up and grabbed the bank notes that had fluttered out of his trouser pocket earlier, as well as the coins, and, with his other hand, pulled open the drawer to take out the red change purse. At the same time, released from the drawer, the red cravat slithered almost on to the floor, though Jack was quick enough to catch it in his fist.

Turning to look at Oliver, he put the red change purse on the table, and held out the red cravat, which was now threaded between his fingers.

"Where did this come from?" Jack didn't ask it as though he were accusing Oliver, but instead with some puzzlement, as though he couldn't imagine how the item had found its way back to him.

Oliver hung his head, for the cravat might have retained the poison of that day, and here he'd brought it back with him.

"Nolly."

Jack's voice was quite soft, so Oliver looked up to see Jack folding and unfolding the cravat between his hands, tenderly and with some care.

"This is all that's left of my lovely outfit," Jack said.

He looked at Oliver and shook his head, as if in despair over Oliver's nature that he should collect such things. Yet, at the same time, Jack bent down and kissed Oliver's forehead, and then sat down next to him, bumping Oliver's shoulder with his own.

"I found it floating in the water of the *Scylla*, and carried it around in my pocket," said Oliver. "When I was looking for you, it was like a talisman, reminding me never to give up hoping."

"An' this in spite of the fact that I was never lost, nor was I goin' to die in a ditch."

But Jack did not say this with recrimination. Instead, his eyebrows went up as if he were, at last, putting all the pieces of what had happened to Oliver while he'd been away. Jack clutched the red cravat in his hands, even as he sat there, quiet and still, putting everything together.

"Put those notes an' the coin in the purse," said Jack now. "This is what we're goin' to do."

Oliver did as he was asked. Taking up the red change purse, he grabbed each fallen note and carefully folded each into thirds to stuff it in with the other notes, and then slid the coins in alongside the notes until the purse was quite stuffed and bulging.

Before Oliver could object, Jack took one end of the red cravat between his teeth and ripped it down the middle. He ripped each half into half again until he had four slender ribbons of red. Then, taking the change purse away from Oliver, Jack put it on the table and placed the four ends of ribbon in Oliver's hands.

"Hold those tight," Jack said, and when Oliver did this, Jack began to braid the lengths of silk into a four-part braid that was slender but strong, the silk strands folding over easily into each other, until at last, Jack held the end of one long, red braid.

"Hold out your hand," said Jack. "Your left one."

As Oliver did so, Jack pushed up Oliver's sleeve and began winding the braid about Oliver's wrist, circling it three times, twisting the end of the braid each time through one of the spaces between the braids, until the whole of the braid made a sturdy, thrice-circled bracelet.

"Hold that," said Jack.

He guided Oliver's free hand to grasp the ends of the braid, and then tied the ends of it into a small, hard knot. Jack stood up and took the matches from the drawer, lit the candle, and made Oliver stand next to him. Taking Oliver's wrist in one hand and the knot of silk in the other, Jack held the knot over the flame, and kept Oliver's hand firmly still while the knot of silk burned into a hard red-and-black square.

"There," said Jack, finally letting go of Oliver's hand. He pinched the candle flame out between his fingers. "That should last you until it unravels."

"And when it does?" asked Oliver, somewhat stunned that he'd let Jack do all of this without objecting, not even when the heat of the candle had seemed quite close.

"Then we'll braid it anew, an' go on, like we do, you an' I."

Oliver felt such a rush of love, of tenderness, that he wanted to fling his arms about Jack and hold him and pet him and let him know how much, just how *much*—

But that would startle Jack, and perhaps be more than might be comfortable for him, so instead Oliver moved close, ducked his head beneath Jack's chin and slowly and carefully pulled Jack into an embrace. This Jack returned with some steadiness and, for a moment, they stood there while the warmth of Jack's skin soaked into Oliver. So close, he could smell the sweetness of Jack, the essence of him, so familiar, so well-loved, and it almost took the breath from Oliver's body to discover how passionately and completely he loved him.

"I love you Jack, for you are kindness and patience itself."

"You say that like it's some sacrifice I'm makin'," said Jack, with a little laugh. "It ain't, you know, it ain't no sacrifice lovin' you."

"Sometimes," said Oliver, wanting to insist upon this. "Sometimes it must take you a great deal of effort, being with someone like me."

"Bollocks to that, Nolly, m'love," said Jack. He pulled out of Oliver's arms and stepped back, though he still clasped his forearms. "When will you ever learn, eh? You're the sweetest thing ever to happen to me, an' the bravest lad I've ever known. 'Tis no effort to love you, no effort atall. An' one day, maybe sooner than you think—" Here, Jack paused to give Oliver a saucy wink. "One day I'll be able to show you just how well I love you."

"I don't need proof such as that, Jack," said Oliver, somewhat overwhelmed and flustered by such bold declarations that nevertheless, and in equal measure, heartened him in a way he'd not thought possible when their quarrel had started.

"An' what if I wants to give you a good seein' to, eh? What about that, then?" With mock fierceness and a wide smile, Jack slipped his hands about Oliver's waist and pulled him close. "You'll never know when, you'll never know where, but at any moment, my cock'll determine to wake up, an' then, well, *then* you'll see."

Jack meant this as a threat, but with the laughter in his eyes, and a quick kiss on Oliver's mouth, so bold and swift it quite took Oliver's breath away all over again, there was no threat, nor anything like it. Just the sweet moment as they stood with their hips together, warmth transferring between the canvas of their trousers, a gentle stillness overtaking them.

Feeling of the weight of the red braid upon his wrist, Oliver looked down at it, and twisted his wrist about to test that weight, and to feel the feel of silk against his skin.

"D'you like it?" asked Jack.

"Yes, I do," said Oliver with utter honesty. "But wherever did you learn to braid or to make something like this? Was it in Port Jackson?"

"It weren't the marines," said Jack. "It were them convicts on the ship headed out, when they'd take a woman convict an' wanted to keep her as their own, but they ain't got no rings or nothin'. They'd make a braid like this. Nina taught me how to do the braid, an' how to burn the silk."

"So I'm the *woman?*" asked Oliver, a bit startled. "Am I?"

"Shite, no," said Jack with the utmost derision in his tone. "I'm just tryin' to explain to you. The braid is like a ring, committin' us together. It don't matter whoever you are, just as long as you an' the other person are together."

"So, you should have one as well, Jack," said Oliver, quite liking the idea in his head.

"An' so I shall," said Jack, nodding. "When we find the right bit of silk, the right color to match your eyes."

"Your eyes, you mean," said Oliver.

"I'd rather look down an' see the color of yours, if you don't mind," said Jack with some dignity. "Or maybe we'll trim this one back an' make a red one for me out of it, eh? You like that idea better?"

Feeling shy, Oliver ducked his chin and nodded.

"Yes," he said.

Jack put his fingers beneath Oliver's chin and made him look up.

"Then that's what we'll do, but we'll let you wear it for a bit, so when I take a strand an' put it on me, it'll still carry traces of you."

Oliver turned his head to kiss the middle of Jack's palm, and Jack smiled and let him do it.

"Shall we get you somethin' for those sweet teeth of yours, now?" asked Jack. "An' maybe somethin' more to eat as well, for you didn't have hardly none of the apple nor the pie, an' as we left it behind, the scavengers have probably got it by now."

"Your forgiveness is enough of a meal for me, Jack," said Oliver, doing his best to put some earnestness into it, as if he'd meant it just the way he'd said it.

"Oh, for pity's sake, Nolly, will you *just—*" Then Jack stopped, having obviously glimpsed the smile Oliver had been unable to hide, and ruffled Oliver's hair. "You're havin' me on, ain't you, you rascal."

This small joke on Oliver's part seemed to have eased the last of the tension between them, and relaxed Jack's shoulders, and brightened Oliver's heart, for as long as they could talk it over as they had, to listen and reply as they had, then nothing bad could ever last between them.

"All right, then, get your cap. Wait, we left them downstairs, didn't we? An' now they're probably stolen!" Jack raised both of his hands, as if in dismay over this event. "Now we'll never have caps again!"

This last was said in mockery of Oliver's earlier drama, but was met and matched with a quick kiss from Jack to take away the sting. Then Jack took some money from the red leather change purse, and tucked it back in the drawer. He stuffed the coins with the others already in his pocket and jingled the whole pile of them just for effect.

"So," he said, looking at Oliver. "Sit down or stand up?"

"Sit," said Oliver, at once. "Could we go to that place on Butcher Street, the one with the garden?"

"Hell, yes," said Jack. "It'll be much cooler there than standin' in the street, an' we can linger over our beers. Hopefully they won't have run out of sweet things for after. Then we can wander back when it gets dark, an' maybe hold hands when we think nobody's lookin'."

Oliver smiled at the idea of this, and at the sight of Jack as he tugged Oliver's sleeve over the red bracelet. For while they both might proclaim their feelings for each other, it was nobody's business but their own.

But so Jack would know, truly know, how Oliver felt, Oliver lifted his hand, the one with the bracelet on it, and let the sleeve fall back to expose it. And then, with some care, he pushed away strands of dark hair from Jack's forehead, and leaned up on tiptoe to kiss him there. And then on his nose. And then he finished up with a quick, almost chaste kiss on Jack's mouth.

All of which made Jack smile quite broadly, which was to the better, and made Oliver feel quite happy with them both.

☙ 24 ❧

A RETURN TO THE GARDEN

When Jack awoke, the window was lit by a vast amount of sunlight, which made him squint. He was about to pull the sheet over his head when he realized Nolly was very carefully and quietly getting out of bed.

That was what had awoken Jack, though the tremor to the mattress caused by Nolly's movements would not have jarred a mouse. But Jack was not a mouse, though he watched as quietly as one while Nolly hunted for his clothes and then leaned against the wall to put on his stockings.

Jack wondered where Nolly was aiming to be going, for Jack could not let him go alone, though if Nolly only meant to tend bar in the taproom, then Jack would take the opportunity to go back to sleep.

As Nolly was pulling on his waistcoat and tying his faded belcher handkerchief about his neck, he looked up, as if somehow alerted to the fact that he was the focus of all of Jack's attention.

"I didn't mean to wake you," said Nolly, and while there was some curious shyness in his voice, he smiled at Jack, which made waking up on so bright a morning worth it.

"Where're you bound, Nolly, eh?" asked Jack. He thought

about sitting up, but only stretched his arms and folded them behind his head. "Goin' to work?"

"Work can wait," said Nolly. Which, of course, it could, since Nolly's debt to Noah was fully paid up. "I thought to go and visit a friend, a new acquaintance I made."

"A new acquaintance?" asked Jack, and he wondered when it had been that Nolly had had the opportunity. A stab of regret laced through him that he'd not been available on that day so Nolly could have shared the visit with him.

There was a single pause, a single silent moment before Nolly spoke again with a hesitation that Jack marked and determined to ease.

"You should make all the friends you like, Nolly," said Jack. He struggled to sit up, all tumbled in the bedclothes, and scratched his head as he yawned.

"Yes, but this particular acquaintance—" Nolly grabbed his cap and ran his fingers through his hair. "Well, he bade me let him know when you were found again, you see, and since you are found, I would like to keep my promise to him."

"You told somebody about me? Somebody I don't even know?" This struck Jack as the oddest thing, the queerest thing, since he'd never considered that Nolly would speak about him to anybody, let alone a stranger.

"Well." Nolly hesitated and wiped his hands on the front of his canvas trousers, as though girding his loins for some difficult task. "I had gotten lost, you see, in Spitalfields, and this kindly old gentleman gave me aid. In return, he wanted to know what I was doing and why I was lost."

"You got lost lookin' for me." Jack well and truly got up now, and shoved the bedclothes back as he swung his legs over the edge of the bed. "Noah told me."

"I did, a bit," said Nolly. "Mostly I was merely turned around, as the streets are a rabbit warren down that way."

Nolly waited a moment, watching Jack as he stood up and stretched and scratched his belly; it was nice to have Nolly looking at him like he was doing, quiet and thoughtful behind those serious blue eyes.

"Would you come with me, Jack?" asked Nolly as he reached for the pile of Jack's clothes on the floor.

It was interesting to note the difference that, instead of offering that Jack *might* come along, which is what Nolly would have said if he didn't really want Jack's company and was only being polite, Nolly was requesting that Jack *did* come along, and this, of course, he could not refuse.

"Yes, yes, of course," said Jack. He got dressed as fast as he could, pulling on his stockings and trousers and the rest of his garments, which, as always, were rumpled from their nighttime abandonment. Raking his hands through his hair, he finished up by tying his belcher, batting Nolly's hands away, as Jack was a damn expert at tying knots, and Nolly would only slow him down. "Spitalfields, you say?"

Once Jack put on his cap, they were properly ready, but just before he opened the door, he snuck his finger along Nolly's wrist, where the red silk cravat, made into braided circles, looked so fine against Nolly's skin. He was rewarded by Nolly's smile and the pet of Nolly's hand as he traced the silk right over the top of Jack's hand.

"Off we go, then," said Jack. He was glad to have a reason to be jolly, for he felt better than he had in days, since before—well, in days. It wouldn't do to dwell on what had been, any more than it would to worry about tomorrow's troubles.

They went out of the bedsit. Jack closed the door behind them and, like schoolboys being truant from school, they fairly tiptoed down the stairs, crossed the taproom, almost empty at this hour and smelling like stale beer, and slid out the front door and into the sunshine.

"We can cut around Smithfield Market," said Jack.

He led the way down Saffron Hill and along Field Lane to High Holborn. The traffic there was as fierce and thick as it ever was, and Jack did his very best to be alert without looking as though he were about to piss down his own leg with nerves. But London was his home, by God, and nobody, not even a cruel, vindictive workmaster, was going to keep him from enjoying his life, and, even more importantly, from loving the boy that he loved.

"And then the Artillery Ground, I think," said Nolly, his brows drawn together. "I've only been to the gentleman's garden, and that only the once. But it's off of Spitalfields Market, that I do know."

This being said, Jack set their path so they would miss most of Smithfield Market, with the lowing of cattle, and the squawking of geese, and the sounds of animals being slaughtered. Going upwind of the market, they avoided most of the smells, as well. Which, on such a warm day, with the sun bright against a blue sky, was only to the better.

They did not talk, but with Nolly staying close at his side, eagle-eyed and on the lookout, Jack was content to lead the way. They went past the Artillery Ground, and the very posh area around Finsbury Square, which, at one point, he and Charlie Bates had staked out for an entire week, just to see how long it was before the constabulary in the area told them to go back to where they came from.

They scooted along Union Street to the lower end of Spital-fields Market, which, on a Monday, was jammed to the gills with stalls selling all things green and sweet-smelling, from onions to flowers and everything in between. The awnings, unlike those around Saffron Hill, were striped and bright and were tightly tied against the blazing sun, protecting those who sold as well as those who bought.

Jack took in the scene, resisting the impulse to empty those unaware folks of the contents of their pockets. That was a task, as well as a pleasure, for another day, for they were bound for the residence of the kindly old gentleman whom Nolly had made the acquaintance of.

"Fancy a pie?" asked Jack. "Or a bit of sausage? There's a stall right over there." Jack pointed, and watched Nolly shake his head as he took off his cap, only to rearrange it once more, demonstrating a bit of nerves that Jack found endearing.

"Perhaps afterwards," said Nolly. "We'll only stop a little while, I promise."

The notion of Nolly not wanting to eat until later was quite curious, for never had Jack known such a thing to happen. But as Nolly looked about him, eager and content, it must be that the thought of a visit with the new acquaintance was so pleasant as to overcome all else, so Jack didn't press the issue.

"Which way, then?" asked Jack as they stood at the edge of the market square. "This or that?"

"This way, towards—" Nolly made a motion with his hand, pointing it like a blade to indicate the way. "We have to go to the top of the market and go over, and then go down an alley, as that's the only way I know how to get to there from here."

"Fair enough," said Jack, smiling a bit at Nolly and himself on an adventure that not only did it court no danger, and involved no crime, neither one of them had any idea how to get to where they were going. "Is it up or down from the market?"

Nolly led them both along the edge of the market, skirting the festively covered stalls and the content and smiling folk who were selling vegetables and small sachets of spices until they reached the upper border of the market. Then they made good strides as they headed up a nice, clean lane lined with brick houses and shops, their front steps swept and washed, and which had very little horse shit in the streets, which was something.

They went until they reached an intersection, which the cornerstone sign marked as Crispin Street. There, Nolly took them left until they finally turned into a narrow alley that bent at the middle so Jack couldn't see all the way down it.

"Is this the alley?" asked Jack, though it was easy to see it was, for Nolly was striding down it with some confidence, looking at each tall brick fence and, in particular, at the doors that led into each garden.

"Yes," said Nolly as he walked down the slope and, just where the alley took a small bend, he stopped and held out his hand. "This is the one. This is the green door that I went through before."

Jack looked up and tried to count the rooflines, but the various chimneys and tall, green trees got in the way and bungled his count.

"Look, Nolly," Jack said, pointing. "This one's got three chimney pots, all painted white, just together there, an' they've all got smoke comin' up. So if we go around front—"

"And look for those particular pots—"

With Nolly smiling so broadly, it was easy as anything to follow him back up the alley, around the corner to the left, and down the street, which, as Jack noted, was called Steward Street. The whole of the street was lined with two-story brick dwellings, with the brickwork done in a curious, old-fashioned way, where the darker bricks were laid out in one pattern, and the lighter, rose-colored bricks were laid out in another, making each house unique. The dwellings were more compact than the ones in Soho, but they were grand in their own way, and posh, as well. Several of the houses had housemaids out front, sweeping and scrubbing the steps, and while there were no trees along the street anywhere, the street was not overly warm in the sun, and there was a sense of dignity about the place.

"This is the one," said Jack as they walked along. He eyed the chimney pots. Many were painted white, as that seemed the local fashion, but only one home had a cluster of three white pots that were spouting smoke. "It's got a four, it's number four. G'ahead, Nolly, you knock."

Together they went up the two white steps to the green door, which was painted the exact color of the garden gate in the alley.

Jack made sure to stay close to Nolly, in case he should need the support. But quite boldly, Nolly lifted the brass knocker, which was polished to gleaming, and knocked on the door three times. The sound echoed inside of the house with a somber quietness. Such a house that Nolly had stumbled upon would be, of course, the finest on the block.

Presently, the door was opened to show a comely housemaid wearing a black dress, a snow-white apron that covered her from throat to feet, a lacy cap on her shining dark hair.

"May I help you?" the housemaid asked, and then her mouth stayed open. "Mister Oliver, is it you, indeed? Have you come to visit the master?"

"Yes, I have," said Nolly in the very way that he would, had he and the housemaid already been acquainted. "Is he at home and taking visitors?"

"Why, yes, Mister Oliver, he'd love to see you. He's in such a state today on account of that letter, you see, so won't you come in?"

Without any ado, the housemaid stepped aside and pulled the green door wide to admit them. Jack followed close on Nolly's heels as they entered.

The maid, instead of bidding them to wait, gestured with her hand that they were to follow her.

Jack tried not to gawp as they went along the cool, dim entryway that led off in three directions. They passed several richly appointed and equally cool and dark rooms on either side of the passage until they came to a long, broad sunroom that looked out over a green, sunlit and shadow-dappled garden.

Just then, an older woman came up to them. She was dressed much as the housemaid was, although her cap was of finer lace, and she had a chatelain of keys that dangled from a narrow leather belt about her waist.

"And what do we have here, Lavena?" asked the woman, as if about to scold the housemaid, but then she stopped.

"It's visitors for the master, Mrs. Becca," said Lavena with a small curtsy.

"Is it you, Mister Oliver?" asked Mrs. Becca. With dark eyes, and seeming pleased with the sight before her, she looked both

Jack and Nolly up and down. "Lavena, run to the kitchen and tell Cook there will be two more for luncheon. Run quickly, now."

As Lavena trotted obediently off and disappeared down the passage toward the interior of the house, Mrs. Becca turned to them. But, instead of scolding them, as Jack quite expected, given their rough state and unannounced visit, she held out her hand to clasp Nolly on the arm.

"It's so good of you to come, as you said you would. Particularly today, for he's gotten a letter from his daughter-in-law, and it's no good, it's no good at all. So won't you come and have a wash, you and your friend? And then I'll send you out."

Lavena came rushing back, a little breathless, carrying a pitcher in her hands. She handed the pitcher to Mrs. Becca, who went over to a washbasin on a stand that stood at the entryway to the sunroom.

Nolly knew what to do, for he went directly over and washed and dried his hands, leaving Jack nothing else to do but exactly the same, though he made a concentrated effort to act as if this was what they did every day, go to a stranger's house and immediately wash their hands. But the soap was soft and smelled sweet, giving Jack a fairly good hint as to why this household held such attractions for Nolly.

When the housemaid had carried the pitcher and slops away, Mrs. Becca reached up and, without asking, took both of their caps and held them against her skirts.

"Do go out and tell him luncheon is coming, and distract him as you might. I'll have Asher bring out a third chair."

Mrs. Becca left to attend to her duties, leaving the two of them in the sunroom, which, it being a warm day, was a bit close, as the sun was shining all gold and yellow through the sparkling glass.

"Do we go in?" asked Jack.

"I think so," said Nolly. But he paused, taking a swipe to push his gold hair from his forehead, and looked at Jack. "It was like this the last time I was here, all welcoming and casual, not like anyplace else, you see."

"I see," said Jack, though he didn't, really. The sort of folk who Nolly would consider an acquaintance, enough to pay them a visit a second time, would normally be the same sort who would throw Jack out on his arse the moment he opened his mouth. And though Nolly was probably not aware of this division, Jack determined it might be best if he said as little as possible. "Well, should we go in?"

"Yes," said Nolly, licking his lips, demonstrating a brisk set of nerves. "We should, before Mrs. Becca comes back and finds us standing here like two fools."

Then, being the brave lad that he was, Nolly turned the knob on the clean, white door, and opened it into the garden. Which burst before Jack's eyes as a green tumble of bushes and branches that stretched off into what must be a very long garden indeed.

Up close were pink roses and red, vibrant and alive against the outline of white-painted wooden beams overhead that carried lush, trailing vines that cast cool shadows across a flagstone patio. Where, next to a round table covered with a white cloth sat an elderly gentleman reading a letter that he held in both hands.

As they stood there, watching, the gentleman put the letter on the table, took off his thin metal spectacles, pulled out a handkerchief, and furiously scrubbed at his eyes with it.

It was a private moment, and Jack considered that they should leave him alone with his grief. Nolly, instead, went right up to the table, making a bit of noise as he went, which alerted the gentleman, who raised his head and wiped at his nose.

"Who is it?" asked the old gentleman in a tone of much irritation. He put his spectacles on, looping the thin wires over his ears, and stared at Nolly. "Oh, it's you! You've come to see me, here—"

The old gentleman pushed the papers away, folding the handkerchief on top of them, and stood. As he held onto the chair with one hand, he reached out to Nolly with the other.

"Come, come, now, come and sit. And your friend," added the old gentleman as he espied Jack standing there. "Come and distract me, only do. Your timing is perfect."

"We don't want to disturb you whilst you were reading your letter," said Nolly.

"Rubbish," said the old gentleman with some vehemence. "I've read it three times already, and it always says the same thing, that my daughter-in-law wants to stay in Brighton, and won't come home because it makes her too sad."

This thought seemed to make the old gentleman quite sad as well, for he sniffed and wiped at his mouth with a shaking hand, leaving Jack quite surprised that he wasn't more circumspect with his feelings, as most proper folk were. For, of course, the gentleman was proper folk, with the house that he lived in on such a tidy street, and his servants being so well dressed and competent. Not to mention the garden, which went on further than Jack could see.

As well, the old gentleman was wearing one of those skull caps Fagin had sometimes sported, when he was in a mood or his head was cold. But whether Nolly was aware that the old gentleman was Jewish was another thought altogether, for Nolly did not pull away from the old man's sputtering words, nor seemed affronted by the display of emotion.

"Won't you sit down?" asked the old gentleman. "Asher, bring another chair. Where is my bell? Here it is." The old gentleman rang a silver bell just as a muscular servant, well-dressed as the other servants were, came out carrying a wrought-iron chair and cushion, as if it weighed nothing, and placed it on the flagstone patio next to the table.

"Will you send word, Asher, that there's to be luncheon for three today?" asked the old gentleman.

"It's already been done, sir," said Asher with a short bow. He cast hard eyes Jack's way, which immediately made Jack feel more comfortable, for at least someone wasn't fooled into thinking he wasn't a renowned and dangerous person of the streets.

As the servant left, the old gentleman took Nolly's hand and shook it, and Nolly shook the gentleman's hand in return.

"How good of you to come see me on this wretched, blasted day. And you brought a friend?"

As those dark eyes turned Jack's way, he knew that it was only moments before he was sent packing, for such a man as this, with a house and servants and obviously plenty to spend on the frivolities of a garden, well.

Such a man would not be interested in Jack, but rather only in Nolly who, with his usual careless poise, seemed able to attract rich and elderly gentlemen. Who, in Jack's experience, took Nolly beneath their wings, and saved Nolly from all future exposure to care and want and dirt and bedbugs, which was exactly the way Nolly liked it.

Thus, Jack expected that soon, quite soon, he was to be traded in, and this in spite of all he and Nolly had been through together. Then Jack was ashamed of himself for thinking of it, as Nolly would never be that cruel. Still, the situation bore waiting and watching so perhaps the old gentleman might not find a reason to send Jack on his way, Nolly-less.

"Mr. Yeslevitz, this is my friend and companion, Jack Dawkins. Jack, this is Mr. Yeslevitz, the gentleman I'd told you about, the one that saved me that day and let me into his garden."

"Oh!" said Mr. Yeslevitz. His delight widened his smile and reached his eyes, brightening his face in a way completely foreign to Jack, having only ever experienced posh folk who frowned or simpered, but never who smiled. "He is found! I'm so glad, so very glad of that. And that you brought him to meet me, for he *is* lovely, just as you described. It's a pleasure to meet you, Jack Dawkins."

Mr. Yeslevitz held out his hand for Jack to shake, and there was nothing for Jack to do but return the gesture.

"Lovely, am I?" asked Jack, completely unable to hide his flustered surprise that someone would call him such a thing.

"Yes, lovely," said Mr. Yeslevitz as he let go of Jack's hand and waved at the two of them that they should sit down. "With beautiful green eyes, and broad shoulders, et cetera, just as Oliver described you to me. You've got quite the eye for detail, Oliver."

"Beautiful?" asked Jack. He could not help but ask the question aloud, even as he sat down and scooted his chair in.

"Yes," said Mr. Yeslevitz as he threw up his hands in irritation. "Beautiful *and* lovely, as well as handsome and kind, with strong shoulders and graceful hands and dark silky hair—have you never viewed yourself in a looking glass?"

"Not recently, no," said Jack. He looked at Nolly who was, suddenly, quite busy fiddling with the tablecloth, making sure it was properly draped across his thighs.

"Don't they have looking glasses in your part of London, Oliver, which is—?"

"Saffron Hill," said Nolly with a little nod. He now looked up, but only at Mr. Yeslevitz.

"That's a very insalubrious neighborhood, to be sure," said Mr. Yeslevitz, taking a moment to ring the silver bell with some ferocity, as if quite put out that none of the servants had attended upon them in the last moment or so. "Whatever are you doing up there? Well, not that it's any of my business, but I'd say, in thinking about it, that it might be easier to hide who you are to each other when everybody else is skulking about with each their own secrets to keep, such as in Saffron Hill."

Jack's mouth fell open, though not a sound came out, for it could not be that the old gentleman, the *kindly* old gentleman, had just said what Jack thought he'd heard.

"Never mind me prattling on," said Mr. Yeslevitz, waving his hands in the air as if dismissing any concerns Jack might have. "I know all about you, Jack, you and Oliver both, so let's none of us stand on ceremony. Not when I've gotten some company to distract me—"

With a sudden starkness, Mr. Yeslevitz's face crumpled up and, blindly, he reached for his folded handkerchief. As he was unable to find it, Nolly reached over the table to hand it to him, brushing it against Mr. Yeslevitz's fingers so he could take it without having to see it.

"Thank you—so very kind—just give me a moment."

They waited as Mr. Yeslevitz took off his spectacles and wiped his eyes, leaving them reddened and sore looking, and put the spectacles on again. Then he scrubbed at his mouth, which trembled a bit.

"I'm very sorry to hear about your daughter-in-law insisting on being so distant from you," said Nolly with some kindness. "But why doesn't your son just bring her home?"

Too late, Jack espied the dark silk armband twined around Mr. Yeslevitz's upper left arm; the cloth of the mourning band was so dark against the black wool suit he wore that it was easily missed. Only now did Mr. Yeslevitz touch it with the tips of the fingers of his right hand, as though it was a touchstone to him.

"Oh," said Nolly, and his cheeks flushed hard red, as if at the oversight. "I'm terribly sorry not to have noticed before, so very sorry."

"You're good to say so, Oliver," said Mr. Yeslevitz in a small, faint voice as he collected himself. "I myself often forget, and will walk to the study and expect to find him there so I might ask him about the latest shipment, and whether it's been ordered for the new bookshop. Though of course it has, and is sitting at the warehouse even now, up in Tottenham Court. Gathering dust, for all I'm able to pay any interest in it."

"How long has it been?" asked Nolly, for which Jack was extremely glad, for it was one thing to know that a fellow should be polite when talking to the bereaved, it was another thing entirely to understand the delicate intricacies that surrounded such a conversation. "If I may ask," added Nolly.

"You may," said Mr. Yeslevitz. "It was this last winter, in January, that my poor Joshua caught the most dreadful cold and slipped into an illness from which he never recovered. My daughter-in-law, Mara, who you might, perhaps, one day meet, was so taken with grief that I sent her to our house in Brighton. But with only sad memories waiting for her here, she's loath to come back—ah, Mrs. Becca, thank you for your most welcome distraction of food. Just bring the tray over, quickly now, for my young friends are quite famished, aren't you, Oliver. And Jack."

There was a moment of silence as Mrs. Becca lowered the tray to the table and began unloading the contents: fresh cut strawberries, a pitcher of cream, a bowl of cut lumps of sugar, as well as a plate of triangle sandwiches, a sort of baked pie that looked to be made mostly of cheese, a pot of tea, and three bowls, already ladled out, of some kind of creamy brown soup, which she placed in front of each of them. As well, she set out two additional sets of silverware and two snowy-white napkins; Jack took one set, and Nolly took the other.

"Can you serve yourselves, gentlemen?" asked Mrs. Becca, as she lifted the tray and held it against her aproned skirts. "Cook is having a terrible quarrel with the stove just now, and I must go and assist her."

"Is it smoking again?" asked Mr. Yeslevitz, evidently well-versed in the problems Cook might be having. "We just had the man in for repairs."

"'Tis the same problem as before, sir," said Mrs. Becca. "I'll tend to it and let you know, so do go on and have something to eat, and let these young men distract you from your troubles."

With that, she was off in a swirl of dark skirts, leaving the table ladened with food. She also left some silence behind, with only a low growl from Nolly's belly to fill it.

"Help yourselves, lads," said Mr. Yeslevitz. "Let us not stand on ceremony. Jack, I hope you will find the food to your taste, but only do let me know if there is aught you desire that you do not see."

Mr. Yeslevitz flipped his napkin onto his lap, and Nolly did likewise, with the napkin flared out so that it snapped a little bit before being laid calmly on his lap. Jack knew better than to try the same gesture, though he did by now know how to use a napkin in the normal way, even if he wasn't very elegant with it.

The moment of silence grew as the plate of sandwiches and the pie were handed around. This gave Jack the pause to think, for there had been so many levels to the words that Mr. Yeslevitz had spoken, not least of which had been the profuse compliments paid to him, by way of Nolly's description of Jack, while he'd been away. Not to mention the odd notion that Nolly had actually bared his soul to a near-perfect stranger, and told that stranger just about everything to be known about Nolly, and about Jack, and about them together. About who they were with each other.

"Nolly," said Jack, quite low, hoping Mr. Yeslevitz was a bit hard of hearing, as many elderly folk were, rich or poor. "Whatever did you mean, tellin' him about us?"

"He hardly had to say anything," said Mr. Yeslevitz from across the table, with hearing that was, evidently, sharp as a hawk's. "Not with the way his face was glowing, the way his eyes lit up with sparks when he talked about you. I just put it together and guessed, and he did not deny it, and so there we are."

"There we are?" asked Jack. He was suddenly too hot beneath the dappled sunlight, and completely unable, at that point, to hide his astonishment and his dismay. "There we *bloody* are?"

"Eat your soup, Jack, and listen to me." Mr. Yeslevitz's expression grew quite stern as he pointed at Jack with his spoon. "This is *my* house, *my* garden, and I will not have—I will *not* have the stodgy, narrow-minded, judgmental attitudes of this City, in this day, with all of its terrible modern opinions, intrude upon it. I have known too much sorrow, too much loss, to send away the compliment of real love, real honesty, when I encounter it. And, as I told your friend only days ago, there will be no constables called, no arrests, so, for pity's sake, can we just enjoy our luncheon as civilized people do?"

Mr. Yeslevitz huffed and went on eating his soup, as if he were quite exasperated with Jack and would consider him not only narrow-minded, but troublesome, if he were to continue on as he'd begun.

Jack looked at Nolly, spread his hands wide, and mouthed the words: *There we are?*

To which Nolly responded in kind, with a little shrug, as if he too were a tad overwhelmed with their welcome: *There we are.*

"There'll be no whispering at my table," said Mr. Yeslevitz. "If you have something to say, then out with it, *out* with it."

"We're—" began Nolly, entering into the conversation with some braveness, because that was the way he was. "It's only that we're not used to such acceptance, having only encountered disgust and rejection. And it's illegal, besides."

"We could hang for it," said Jack, testing the waters. "It's a hangin' offense, you see."

"Not in *my* garden," said Mr. Yeslevitz. "Nor in my house, nor any of the houses I own, nor in any of my shops in Duke Street or those about the market square, not in Brighton, either at my pier or in the house there, nor anywhere that I command. Now, could we please, *please* change the subject? Unless, of course, you'd like to tell me how you met, for that would be an altogether more enjoyable subject than fretting about foolish laws that ought not to have been written in the first place, and anyway needn't apply to us."

There was a story there, long and well-written, about the days when Mr. Yeslevitz was a dashing young man, only Jack did not know the details of. It seemed, however, that Nolly knew some of Mr. Yeslevitz's history, for he was less surprised than he ought to have been by the old gentleman's tirade. Which Jack should take as given, as a rebuttal of pretty much every convention Jack had learned to associate with the higher orders. And, though some posh folk, perhaps more than some, wrote their own laws and ruled the tiny fiefdoms of their households, Jack had never understood it to be quite like this.

"So?" asked Mr. Yeslevitz as he finished up his soup and reached for the pie that might be made of cheese. "How did you meet? Do tell me of it, for I should genuinely like to know."

Nolly opened his mouth, but Jack feared Nolly would recite the simplified version, which, as it was very evident Mr. Yeslevitz liked the small details, would be the wrong version.

"I shall tell it, Nolly, if I may," said Jack as he spooned some of the brown soup into his mouth. "Oh, this is quite good, eh?"

"'Tis mushroom soup," said Mr. Yeslevitz. "It's Cook's special recipe from Germany, where I'm from, but that was years ago. Do go on, once you've determined who is to tell me how you met."

"Jack will tell it," said Nolly. He was attentive to his soup and, almost done, was already reaching for a triangle-shaped sandwich, which suited Jack just fine.

Jack began the story at the beginning, eating his soup as he went. He told the good parts and the bad, as well as his part in the story where Nolly was kidnapped into a thieves' den, and was taken back again after his harrowing rescue by old Mr. Brownlow. And how Jack was arrested soon after Nolly had gotten shot, and how, after Jack's return from being deported, he sought Nolly out, and how their friendship had grown from there.

"Are you still a pickpocket, Jack?" asked Mr. Yeslevitz as he handed out slices of the pie. Which, when Jack took a quick bite, turned out to be a delicious and savory cheese and onion pie baked in a crust.

"I don't take from my close acquaintances, if that's what you mean," said Jack, worried now that he'd said too much, been too honest.

"Well, I did wonder." Here Mr. Yeslevitz paused, a small

blush on his cheeks, as if he were embarrassed by his own temerity at asking such a question.

"Nolly only lets me take from them who wants takin' from, who won't miss the little I take, or from them what deserves it, such as those who are cruel to their servants."

"But isn't that still theft, regardless who the victim is?" asked Mr. Yeslevitz, his thin white eyebrows wrinkling together.

"That's what I told Nolly, but it seems to make a difference to him, so that's how I does it."

With his heart starting to pound a little faster, Jack waited. It was one thing for a fine gentleman to admit such as them into his garden, it was another thing for Mr. Yeslevitz to turn a blind eye to Jack's profession.

"It's what he knows how to do, Mr. Yeslevitz," said Nolly, though it was easy to see the explanation fell on now-deaf ears.

"Well, surely there's something else you could be doing, what with the intelligence you've demonstrated to me. Like Oliver here—Oliver, you said you work in a tavern, so there, you see, Jack? You could work in one of my shops and make an honest living. Why, I've got several shops just empty and waiting for a clever clerk to run them, be it Jew or gentile, I don't care, just as long as they can keep records and make the proper change, and be pleasant without turning into some servile, glad-hander. But, never mind. You'd be too bored in a shop, whether it be a draper's or a bookshop or anything. Oh, dear me, how insistent on being entertained is this younger generation."

Mr. Yeslevitz shook his head and carried on eating his cheese and onion pie, as if it were all that concerned him, that and Jack's overly intelligent nature with nothing to show for it. This took Jack aback, for it was nothing anybody had ever said to him before, not even Nolly, though it might be that Nolly had wanted to say something about Jack's line of profession, only he loved Jack too much to be critical.

"You mustn't be so disparaging of Jack's choices, Mr. Yeslevitz," said Nolly, taking, as Jack could see, great pains to say the old gentleman's name with some care. "For he has done quite well for himself, living on the streets as he has, since the day he was taken by gypsies."

"Oh?" asked Mr. Yeslevitz. His head came up from his plate and he looked at Jack, his dark eyes now bright behind the lenses of his spectacles. "You left that part out, Jack, about the gypsies. You do seem to be doing quite well for yourself, and are well-mannered for having been raised by gypsies."

"No, he wasn't raised by gypsies," Nolly hurried to say. "They sold him to Fagin, who raised him to be a thief." Only too late did Nolly appear to realize how this might be taken, for he actually winced as the echo of his words died in the air. "I'm terribly sorry, I didn't mean for that to come out the way that it sounded."

"*Fagin*," said Mr. Yeslevitz with a scoffing sound. "Jewish, of course, I should have known, for while many of us are quite civilized as we make our way in the world, when we fall, we fall hard."

The conversation had taken so many turns, but Jack found himself thinking of Mr. Yeslevitz's words that he'd spoken only moments ago. And determined it would be a great deal better to talk about shops and commerce rather than Fagin's lapsed faith and his propensity to gather a pack of street wolves about him to do his dirty work. And it would save Nolly, as well, from having to justify his association with Jack.

"Excuse me, Mr. Yesle—" Jack fumbled on the odd combination of sounds, and felt badly about it, for he'd been shown nothing but kindness and should be able, at least, to say the man's name.

"Just call me Mr. Yes," said Mr. Yeslevitz. "I won't take offense, I promise."

"Mr. Yes," said Jack, with a grateful nod. "So you said you had shops standin' empty. Yet all about, I see plenty of folk workin' in the market an' that, so why couldn't you just hire a clerk?"

"That's my sad tale, to be sure," said Mr. Yeslevitz as he

reached for the strawberries and cream, completely forgoing the sandwiches. "Hand me that bowl, Oliver, and the cream and sugar, and don't tell Mrs. Becca how much I've taken, right?"

Nolly nodded his agreement, and when he took the bowl of strawberries back from Mr. Yeslevitz, he emptied half of what was left in the bowl on his plate, and the other half on Jack's, which was fine by Jack. Jack picked up one of the strawberries with his fingers, and ate it as it was, touched by spring and ripe-red.

"You see," said Mr. Yeslevitz. "My son, Joshua, was to have taken over those empty shops, and had gone to the London docks to pick up a shipment. But it being so cold, well, it was a bad cold that took him, that or ship's fever, the doctors would never tell me for certain. It's due to that sad fact, and my inability to put out the word, that I'm in dire need of clerks. I'm made immobile by being overwhelmed. Do you see? There's only so much I could concentrate on since he passed, may God bless him. And, since spring has come, all I want to do is sit in my garden and weep."

Mr. Yeslevitz scrunched his mouth tight, as if he were fighting another bout of such weeping at that very moment. Jack felt poised on the edge of his seat, and would have danced on the tabletop, if need be, to distract the poor fellow from his own sadness, when Mr. Yeslevitz shrugged, and rang his silver bell.

"We shall have some sherry," announced Mr. Yeslevitz with some firmness. "For why should I be sad when I've got such fine and interesting visitors come to see me? And who will come to see me again if I've proven myself to be not too much trouble to be with?"

In light of such honesty and not a little despair, there was nothing Jack could do but slam the table with the flat of his hand.

"You may be all the trouble you like, what with you feedin' my friend such fine food, and bendin' your ear to us, and offerin' up your sympathy."

"And fine food for you as well, young Jack," said Mr. Yeslevitz with a smile, as if glad to be distracted from his own woes. "Though I notice you did not take any sugar with your strawberries."

"That's because Jack doesn't like sweet things overly much," said Nolly with a grave nod. "He'll take a bit of roast and some fried potatoes over a slice of chocolate gateau any day of the week."

"And here we are serving you only sweet things," said Mr. Yeslevitz. He shook his head and made *tsk-tsk* noises as he rang the silver bell again, hard and impatient, as though he'd been ringing it for ages. "There you are, Mrs. Becca, keeping me waiting, as usual."

"What can I get for you, sir," said Mrs. Becca, her smile as serene as if he wasn't ever grouchy and, in fact, was not so now.

"Bring out the sherry and some glasses so we may have a toast, my young friends and I. And bring out the noodles, the ones Cook fries with onions and cheese and that leftover chicken. Don't tell me there aren't any from yesterday, and hurry before Jack starves to death. Why, just look at him with those hollow cheeks; it's quite a shame to see such a thing at my table, quite a shame."

And thus Jack found himself being served the most delectable bowl of fried noodles he'd ever encountered, which he shared with Nolly, because, of course, how could he not? Well, he couldn't not, not with the way Nolly's eyes widened at the bowl that was dripping with cheese and was flecked with bits of sweet, fried onion. As well, Jack found himself growing warm on several small glasses of sherry while Mr. Yeslevitz toasted Jack as being the most delightful pickpocket ever to be seated at his table.

But the best part, the most unexpected part, was the feeling of being included inside of a warm, convivial circle that Jack would have heretofore considered Nolly's territory, and Nolly's alone.

For here, in the garden, all green and lush, with the trees

casting shadows as the afternoon lengthened, Mr. Yeslevitz turned to Jack as often as he turned to Nolly with a question or a request for more about how they'd met. And then Mr. Yeslevitz would laugh when the story was told to him, or his eyebrows would rise with astonishment as he leaned forward to hear more. Then he'd ply them both with yet more sherry, and shake his head, and make them both promise not to tell Mrs. Becca how much he'd had to drink.

All of this filled Jack with a sense of belonging, of ease and acceptance, so different than he'd known before. Certainly Jack had never been within the company of a right proper gentleman who spoke to Jack the exact same way he spoke to Nolly, as if there were no difference between them and never had been.

Whether Nolly was aware of this was yet to be discovered, though it was easy to see, as Nolly leaned back in his chair and smiled over at Jack, that Nolly was happy in a way he'd not been since their return to London.

It wasn't just that Nolly was dissatisfied with their grotty little bedsit over the taproom of such an insalubrious tavern, nor the stench of the overflowing privy, nor the bed bugs, nor even the utter lack of anything clean, and good, and quiet.

It was, as was presently plain to Jack, that Nolly had been missing the sort of company as they were sharing now, at a table covered with a cloth as white as snow, with the kind of conversation they were having between them, of stories of the old days— though Jack could hardly credit the number of duels Mr. Yeslevitz reported that he'd participated in—of those times where folk were less inhibited and more accepting, where the roads were full of dashing highwaymen, and the gardens full of parties attended by ladies in see-through dresses.

In those days, those bad old days, Jack would have been hailed as a hero, and would have been begged to share more of his tales of thieving and stealing, as if it all were a glorious game. Which, of course it was not, but *had* it been, then Nolly would have been at Jack's side in these stories, holding his pistol aloft to fire a shot in the air to startle the ladies into swooning, and to aid Jack in relieving one and all of their valuables.

Such fanciful ideas made Jack smile, and when he felt a touch on his arm, he looked up to see Nolly looking at him, his eyes sleepy and warm.

"Are you happy, Jack?" asked Nolly with a sweet smile. "Are you happy we came?"

"Yes," said Jack. "I'm happy we came, an' I'm happy you're happy."

Jack knew his smile was ridiculous and lopsided, but he wanted to kiss Nolly so very badly and pull Nolly's smile inside of his skin, where he could keep it warm and safe forever.

"If you'll excuse me, I need to go in the house for a moment," said Mr. Yeslevitz, all of a sudden. He scooted out his chair and, grabbing the cane leaning against one of the flower-draped wooden posts, escorted himself into the house.

Which left Jack and Nolly alone in the garden.

"D'you remember the last time we kissed in a garden?" asked Jack before he could fully examine the truth of that particular memory. "I mean, before that—just when we were kissin', not after."

"I remember," said Nolly, ducking his chin a little to look up at Jack through his dark lashes. "Do you want to kiss me now?"

They'd been given a moment, a gold-gilt, green-shadowed moment, and so Jack leaned forward and kissed Nolly on his beautiful, lush, strawberry-stained mouth, savoring the feel of that mouth, and the taste of sugar on them, and the soft way Nolly's mouth parted for him. How Nolly's hand came up and ever so gently cupped Jack's cheek. And how Jack found his blood warmed by this, warmed and racing about inside of him, and how, from far away, like an echo of a memory, it seemed, came a low rush of pleasure that Jack felt in his belly.

He sighed, smiling as he kissed Nolly, and then kissed him again. Would that he provided Nolly with no expectations, Jack could court the new feelings within himself, and let them wax and wane as they would until, when it suited them, they would grow strong enough to remain. Then Jack could take Nolly in his arms, and see to Nolly's pleasure as well as his own.

And while they could never go back to where they'd started, as too much had happened since then, they would be back to where they should be, sharing satisfying talks between them, and good meals, and walks in the country, particularly those next to the water where there might be birds to watch or ponies to ride. And afterwards, they could share the quiet darkness, and make their promises to each other over and over, all anew, each time they made them.

PAYING A CALL AT NUMBER
FOUR STEWARD STREET

I t was several days after their luncheon in the garden with Mr. Yeslevitz, which, due to the amount of sherry they'd all taken, was sheened with the feeling of having been completely and utterly glorious, that Oliver began to understand what it was Jack had been saying to him, and this more than once.

"What do you mean, he wants to offer me a position?" asked Oliver.

Wiping at the back of his neck with his hand, he wished he'd taken a moment to wash up at the pump. To have removed the traces of sweat from the morning's work, where he'd attacked the endless tide of dirt and dust that invaded the Three Cripples on a daily basis. And, as well, to have removed the faint dapples of beer that clung to his skin.

Jack sighed and pushed the cards across the table, away from him, as if completely exasperated that they were playing beggar-my-neighbor, though it had been his idea in the first place.

"Look, he kept on about it, weren't you listenin'?" asked Jack. He held his hands up, as if he meant to box Oliver's ears, though he would never do that. He only wanted Oliver to pay attention to what he was saying. "On an' on he went about it, empty shops a-boundin', an' no clerks to run them. One of them shops was a bookshop—you couldn't have been *that* deaf with drink."

"I did hear him say it, but—" Oliver wrinkled his brow and took a sip of beer, trying to drag up the memory that Jack was presenting so it made the kind of sense that Jack wanted him to see in it. "The whole time I thought he was trying to convince *you* to take on one of the positions."

"No, no, foolish boy." Jack shook his head and gathered up the cards to tap them together; he shuffled them as he talked. "He's got a shipment of books in a warehouse in Tottenham Court somewheres, gatherin' dust. He's just a-waitin' for you to step up an' take care of it for him, on account of he can't make no decisions after poor Joshua passed. Were you even listenin', Nolly?"

"I was listening, truly, but I didn't hear it the way you heard it."

Oliver hung his head and stole one of the cards from Jack's fingers and flicked it against the table-top. They were quite alone in the low of the afternoon, with the early morning drinkers having gone and the evening ones not yet arrived. Still, he kept his voice quiet, for it wasn't anybody's business but their own.

"Do you truly think that he meant for me to ask him?"

"Even if he didn't—an' you know he did—Nolly, this is your heart's desire, an' I won't let you just turn away from it."

"My heart's desire." Oliver tasted the words as he said them. He did not quite want to get his hopes up, but the way Jack put it, he did have a sense that things might be different if he wanted them to be. If he was brave enough to take the chance. "But I would not want to trade on so short an acquaintance."

"Oh, rubbish to that," said Jack, using the word Mr. Yeslevitz had used to express his disdain for this notion. "He'll be pleased to have been asked, an' to have somethin' to think about other than his own grief. Why, you'll get the position, an' a good wage, an' do somethin' decent an' clean that ain't about servin' beer to the down-and-outs."

"I don't mind serving beer to anybody—" began Oliver, and he meant to go on to convince Jack that he wasn't the type to complain, except Jack shook his head.

"It's everythin' else, an' I know it," said Jack, his eyes shining dark green with his conviction. "So why don't you give yourself a chance to be happy, Nolly, eh? Why don't you just go an' do what you've always wanted to do?"

"But I won't leave you behind, Jack," said Oliver, and already his heart began to hurt at the thought of losing Jack all over again.

"You won't," said Jack with some certainty. When Oliver made a face, Jack repeated himself. "You *won't*, I tells you. For wherever you bide, I will bide. I mean, I'll still work here, an' use Noah as my fence—"

"And why is that?" asked Oliver a little sharply, glad to have something besides his own destiny to talk about. "Why do you give him any part of what you take? I mean, besides him fencing the actual bank notes and the odd watch chain, what does he do for you?"

"What? Whatever are you saying, Nolly?" Jack looked at him, eyes wide at this sudden change in the conversation.

"You're not a small boy, Jack, in need of housing and feeding," said Oliver. "You quite earn a full living for yourself now; the red change purse is overflowing, as you well know. But as for anything other than what needs to be fenced, you hand over fifty percent and why? What does he do for you that you can't do for yourself?"

"Should I start my own gang, then?" asked Jack, putting his usual and meant-to-be-amusing spin on the words. He leaned forward, slouching over the table with his elbows upon it, as though he were the worst of reprobates. "Would you be in my gang, were I to start one?"

"I *am* your gang, Jack, and well you know it," said Oliver with more asperity than he meant to, though he liked the idea of it all the same, that they were their own gang, just the two of them. "But you see what I mean, don't you? You know what I'm saying is true. You don't need him. You never did, except that he gave you a sense of the old days, when you were in Fagin's gang—"

Oliver stopped, as he felt perilously close to making critical and disparaging remarks that, besides being unnecessarily cruel, would not help him convince Jack to see the sense of his argument.

"I'll make you a deal, Jack. Are you listening?" asked Oliver.

"I'm listenin'," said Jack, making a little face, as though he was completely overwhelmed by being talked to in such a way.

"I'm sorry Jack, I don't mean to be cross about it, but will you listen? I'll make you a deal in that if I go and ask for this position, and get it, then you'll come with me and pick pockets on your own terms. You'll keep that money for yourself. I mean, for us. It'll be *our* money that I earn, and *our* money that you steal, and not anybody else's."

"Not Noah's, you mean," said Jack dryly, for, as ever, he could not be fooled.

"Yes," said Oliver. "That's what I mean. I don't wish him ill, but—"

"You don't like it here."

"I don't like *us* here."

As this declaration echoed in the near-empty room, it suddenly clarified what exactly the problem was. It wasn't merely their reliance on Noah Claypole's continued affection and reverence for Jack, at least not completely. It also had to do with the sense of not having made their own world for themselves.

At the Three Cripples, Jack was living on his past, and Oliver, in being near him, felt as though he was existing in limbo. They needed to make a change, and to make it together, instead of doing it as they always had, which was to favor one of their desires over the other.

In light of what he had just said, Oliver imagined that surely Jack would want to think it over, to give some consideration about cutting off business ties to someone he associated with happier days. But, as he usually did, Jack surprised him.

"Let's go now, then," said Jack, standing up. He took the single playing card from Oliver's fingers and, putting it with the rest of the cards, slipped the deck into his inside jacket pocket. "We go there now an' ask him, an' when he says yes, then we pick out a new place to live, closer to where you'll be workin'. This very day we shall do it. I'll tell Noah, an' we'll let bygones be bygones, with no harm done between us."

"You'd do that for me?" asked Oliver, looking up at Jack. He doubted it would be that easy or straightforward and, besides, he was beginning to feel slightly dizzy at Jack's sudden agreement.

"For you, Nolly?" said Jack as he tugged on his cotton waistcoat in a way meant to be casual, though his expression was quite stern, as if he were disappointed Oliver did not already know this. "For you, the world. An' you should know that by now."

"I do know it, Jack," said Oliver, getting up. His throat felt thick, and he had to struggle to get the words out. "But it moves me so, each time."

"I'm doin' it for us, as well, so c'mon," said Jack. He slung an arm about Oliver's shoulders in the friendly, warm manner he had that made Oliver feel the love and affection all the way through to his soul. "We'll go now afore your courage runs out, an' you shall see the truth of what I speak."

Briskly, they left the Three Cripples and, beneath a blazing blue sky, they retraced the steps they'd taken several days ago. They skirted the mid-week slaughter and animal dung that was thick in Smithfield Market, and hurried along the lanes and streets that led to Spitalfields. There, they walked right down Steward Street, as they knew the number and didn't need to count chimney pots to find the right residence.

As they mounted the ever-swept and shining steps, this time Jack banged the brass knocker to announce them. And soon, quite too soon for Oliver's nerves, and before he could even draw a breath to calm himself, came Lavena. She opened the door for them as ever she had before. Except this time, after she gave them a small curtsy, she did not bid them entry.

"Is your master at home?" asked Oliver, feeling as though he'd run out of air halfway through the question. "Can we see him? Is he accepting callers?"

For a moment, Lavena looked a bit troubled, as if she'd some terribly bad news to share, such as the fact that they were no longer welcome at the residence on account of them getting so drunk last time, and because they were sodomites and, also, because Jack was a thief.

"I'm so sorry," said Lavena. "But the master has gone to Brighton to see Miss Mara. He was so enlivened by your last visit that he made up his mind to do something about her absence from home and off he went."

Just as Oliver was absorbing this information, from behind Lavena came footsteps clicking on the entryway tile, and there appeared Mrs. Becca, as groomed and as calm as ever.

"Why are you standing with the door open—oh, Mister Oliver and Mister Jack, how good of you to pay a call. But I'm very sorry, Mr. Yeslevitz is not at home. He has gone to Brighton to fetch Miss Mara."

"Oh," said Oliver. He wanted to fidget and scratch his head and distract himself from his own errand, which Jack would no doubt tease him for later. Yet he could not forget the look on Jack's face when he'd encouraged Oliver to follow his heart's desire, and this strengthened him to go on, as nothing else would have done. "Do you know when he'll be back so that we might call at a more auspicious moment?"

"Not for some weeks, I'm afraid," said Mrs. Becca, frowning a bit. "But why don't I give you the address to his house in Brighton. Then you might write and ask him yourself. It'd do him no end of good, besides, to get letters from home. Would you write him if I gave you it?"

"Yes, indeed I would," said Oliver. His chest relaxed with the relief of not having to pursue his heart's desire quite just yet.

Writing letters from a distance was much easier than having to beg for employment in person. "I'll write him this very day."

"Good, and thank you. Lavena, let these young men in whilst I fetch the address."

Mrs. Becca went off into the dark, cool house, leaving Lavena to open the door so that they might enter. Which they did, though after only a slight moment's hesitation, Lavena left them alone to attend to her tasks.

There they stood amidst the low gloom of the front entry-way, waiting in silence. Though, as Oliver's eyes got used to the house, he could see that the floor gleamed and there was no dust anywhere. As well, the air smelled of cleaning oil, and there was a slight other scent that must have been fresh-cut flowers, for it smelled a little bit like roses.

Oliver didn't dare look at Jack because, of course, Jack was smiling. Oliver could tell that without looking. He could also tell that Jack was on the verge of laughing out loud, most likely due to the fact that Oliver was being asked to write a letter, *yet* another letter, and that as soon as Oliver had written it, they would race to the post office to send it. And that Oliver would have to wait, days and days, for a response. And that his entire future, his heart's desire, awaited the return of the man with whom letters would be exchanged.

As to why this might be amusing to Jack, Oliver did not want to admit to, because if he allowed the irony of it to become more clear, then he too would be dissolving in hysterics, right along with Jack. At which point, Lavena would kick them out, and they would be welcome no more at Number Four Steward Street.

But that, as Jack would say, and as even Oliver knew, was rubbish. The future held good things for them both and, in addition to holding Oliver's heart's desire, would provide for them newer, hopefully more salubrious surroundings, and a total lack of the type of customer who frequented the Three Cripples.

It would be a better life. A Noah-less life. A life meant for him and Jack together. And that was worth waiting for. Worth writing letters for. Worth risking the vulnerability of begging entry into employment at a bookshop that Oliver wasn't even sure was meant for him. But Jack was certain it was, and so Oliver swallowed the sharp feeling in his throat, and tried to remain calm and poised.

"You laughin' Nolly?" asked Jack as they stood in the silent, posh entryway, waiting for Mrs. Becca's return.

"Almost," said Oliver, holding his hysteria at bay. "Almost."

Oliver was able to keep from feeling just about anything as his nerves gathered together while they waited for Mrs. Becca. When she returned to them, coming down the main hallway at a brisk pace, she gave Oliver a slip of paper.

"That's his private residence in Brighton, you see," said Mrs. Becca quite gravely. "And, as you know, I wouldn't give his address to just anybody."

This was said as a slight warning, at which point Oliver nodded to show he understood.

"It won't leave my hands, Mrs. Becca," said Oliver. "Thank you so much."

"Yes, thanks ever so," said Jack. "We need to be goin' now. Won't trouble you any further."

Mrs. Becca opened the door for them and bid them goodbye, and as they both rushed out the door and raced down the steps, it was all they could do not to crumple in a heap on the street. Instead, they waited until they'd rounded the corner and were all the way to Bishopsgate Street and well out of earshot before they made any expression at all or exchanged any words.

"Holy *shite*, Nolly, you an' them fuckin' letters!" said Jack. He was half bent over with laughing, though he reached out to tug Oliver on the sleeve to keep them both walking in the direction of the Three Cripples.

"I'm sure to get a response this time," said Oliver, smiling, for he couldn't help it. Things were going to turn now, they were going to go the right way, and happiness would be theirs. "And get employment in a bookshop, if it's true, if you heard correctly. And you'll go with me when I go, right, Jack?"

"Whither thou goest, m'love," said Jack, smiling at Oliver. "Whither thou goest."

This quote was straight out of the Bible, which Jack evidently knew by heart, though he didn't seem to have much call for religion. But the ancient words sounded lovely coming out of Jack's mouth, with his eyes glinting green the way they did when the sun was bright in the sky.

"Me and thee," said Oliver, in kind. "I'll kiss you when we get back, if you'll let me."

"You'll kiss me now," said Jack.

Then, with some boldness, Jack clasped Oliver by the back of the neck, and drew him beneath a sagging awning that had collapsed beneath the weight of the recent rain. And there, in the shade of the torn canvas, Jack kissed Oliver full on the mouth, and then again, and then once more. Leaving Oliver breathless and staring at Jack's eyes shining in the shadows.

Oliver vowed they would always be together thus. They deserved to live good lives without fear, to live them together, and to be happy, just as they were now.

That such happiness was his and Jack's made Oliver's heart feel full and, dipping his head, he kissed Jack, just once and very softly.

"Take me home," Oliver said. "Will you do that, Jack?"

"Always," said Jack.

And that was all Oliver had ever wanted or needed.

∾

WOULD YOU LIKE TO READ MORE ABOUT THE ROMANCE between Oliver and Jack? Pick up *In London Towne* today! (https://readerlinks.com/l/2237723)

∾

WOULD YOU LIKE TO READ A COWBOY ROMANCE? CHECK OUT *The Foreman and the Drifter*, the first book in my Farthingdale Ranch series. (https://readerlinks.com/l/1703675)

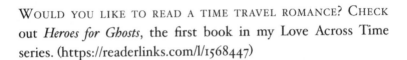

WOULD YOU LIKE TO READ A TIME TRAVEL ROMANCE? CHECK out *Heroes for Ghosts*, the first book in my Love Across Time series. (https://readerlinks.com/l/1568447)

JACKIE'S NEWSLETTER

Would you like to sign up for my newsletter?

Subscribers are alway the first to hear about my new books. You'll get behind the scenes information, sales and cover reveal updates, and giveaways.

As my gift for signing up, you will receive two short stories, one sweet, and one steamy!

It's completely free to sign up and you will never be spammed by me; you can opt out easily at any time.

To sign up, visit the following URL:

https://www.subscribepage.com/JackieNorthNewsletter

facebook.com/jackienorthMM
twitter.com/JackieNorthMM
pinterest.com/jackienorthauthor
bookbub.com/profile/jackie-north
amazon.com/author/jackienorth
goodreads.com/Jackie_North
instagram.com/jackienorth_author

AUTHOR'S NOTES

The first bits of writing that I do on a new book are always colored by my fraught emotions, the self-doubt writers have, and the questions they ask themselves: Is it a good enough idea? Am I a good enough writer? Did I leave the iron on? (That last one is almost not a joke, because when you feel unsure about your writing, the easiest thing to do is to worry about something else.)

The fifth installment in my six-book series about Oliver and Jack is, basically, about how the two young men fall in love and make a life together in London.

As you've just read, book #5 is very dark. Not the darkest dark, but dark enough and, sadly, Jack takes the brunt of this and Oliver has to pick up the prices.

Hopefully I did the subject matter justice; it is my concern about doing it right that initially caused the delay in my progress on this book.

One of my favorite tasks involved in writing a book is doing a read-through. Usually I do this at a point in the story where there might be a handful of scenes missing, just before I hand the manuscript over to my editor and cover designer.

Sadly, this time around, a Bad Cold held me up, but I did a

read-through of On the Isle Of Dogs anyway because I wanted to know what the hell was going on in my story.

You see, a nice chunk of the scenes in the middle of this book had been written while Under the Influence of cold medicine. And this, my friends, will open the avenues of your mind in unexpected ways, but sadly, does not add to the pleasure of writing. Thus, I needed to find out what Oliver and Jack had been up to. Thus the read-through.

Turns out, they both were off on their own doing foolish things, getting into fights (Oliver and Noah), getting lost in London (Oliver), getting into more fights (Oliver), and dosing oneself with laudanum and brandy (Jack).

I also discovered during my read-through that I'd lost track of days, in that in one scene it's both Saturday and Sunday, and in another day, that went on for ages, was nothing but Wednesday, Wednesday, Wednesday. (To be fair, Jack was high on laudanum.)

A special shout out to Darcie and Hannah, two marvelous fans of the Oliver & Jack series who wrote to ask me if everything was okay because they'd not seen me online in a while and wanted to know how the book was coming.

My feeling is that this is the best book in the series due to pacing and the fact that I really had a handle on the characters. Authors should not have favorites, but I do, and it's this one, at least in this series.

A LETTER FROM JACKIE

Hello, Reader!

Thank you for reading *On the Isle of Dogs,* the fifth book in my Oliver & Jack series.

If you enjoyed the book, I would love it if you would let your friends know so they can experience the romance between Oliver and Jack.

If you leave a review, I'd love to read it! You can send the URL to: Jackienorthauthor@gmail.com

Jackie

facebook.com/jackienorthMM
twitter.com/JackieNorthMM
instagram.com/jackienorth_author
pinterest.com/jackienorthauthor
bookbub.com/profile/jackie-north
amazon.com/author/jackienorth
goodreads.com/Jackie_North

ABOUT THE AUTHOR

Jackie North has written since grade school and spent years absorbing mainstream romances. Her dream was to write full time and put her English degree to good use.

As fate would have it, she discovered m/m romance and decided that men falling in love with other men was exactly what she wanted to write about.

Her characters are a bit flawed and broken. Some find themselves on the edge of society, and others are lost. All of them deserve a happily ever after, and she makes sure they get it!

She likes long walks on the beach, the smell of lavender and rainstorms, and enjoys sleeping in on snowy mornings.

In her heart, there is peace to be found everywhere, but since in the real world this isn't always true, Jackie writes for love.

Connect with Jackie:

https://www.jackienorth.com/
jackie@jackienorth.com

facebook.com/jackienorthMM

twitter.com/JackieNorthMM

pinterest.com/jackienorthauthor

bookbub.com/profile/jackie-north

amazon.com/author/jackienorth

goodreads.com/Jackie_North

instagram.com/jackienorth_author

Made in the USA
Monee, IL
09 September 2022

13647143R10277